More praise for THE SECRET LIFE OF EMILY DICKINSON

"Charyn's novel breezingly chronicles [the life] of Emily Dickinson. Unfazed by the challenging lack of event in his subject's biography, Charyn recasts her life . . . as a dream of desire."
—*The New Yorker*

"Audacious. . . . Seductive. . . . Charyn has never written more powerfully. . . . A poignant, delicately rendered vision."
—Joyce Carol Oates, *New York Review of Books*

"Charyn tells the truth but tells it slant. . . . He has re-created [Dickinson's] wild mind in all its erudition, playfulness and nervous energy."
—Ron Charles, *Washington Post*

"A vivid impersonation . . . a stylistic achievement. . . . Emily's growth is brightly drawn."
—*Publishers Weekly*

"Jerome Charyn is merely one of our finest writers, with a polymorphous imagination and crack comic timing. Whatever milieu he chooses to inhabit, his characters sizzle with life and his sentences are pure vernacular music, his voice unmistakable."
—Jonathan Lethem, author of *The Fortress of Solitude*

"*The Secret Life of Emily Dickinson* is astonishing. Charyn gives Emily Dickinson a new life, and one with a rush of energy and power. I shall never see her or her poetry in the same way again."
—Frederic Tuten, author of *Self Portraits: Fictions*

"Wonderful . . . full of touching moments and humor. . . . [Charyn] sketches a delightful portrait of a wonderful poet."
—Jack Edson, BuffaloRising.com

"Charyn masterfully evokes the roiling and attenuated perceptions of a teenage girl with a fevered, breathless, poetic style."
—*Newark Star-Ledger*

"This book is an excellent companion to Dickinson's poetry and biographies. The language is entertaining and convincing; the story, full of humor and wit."
—*Historical Novels Review*

# THE SECRET LIFE OF

*A Novel*

# EMILY DICKINSON

## Jerome Charyn

W. W. Norton & Company
New York · London

Selections from *The Letters of Emily Dickinson*, including Gib's quote on p. 331, which was
taken from L873 to Mrs. J. G. Holland, late 1883, were reprinted by permission of the
publishers from *The Letters of Emily Dickinson*, Thomas H. Johnson, ed., Cambridge, Mass.:
The Belknap Press of Harvard University Press, copyright © 1958, 1986, The President
and Fellows of Harvard College; 1914, 1924, 1932, 1942 by Martha Dickinson Bianchi;
1952 by Alfred Leete Hampson; 1960 by Mary L. Hampson. Selections from *The Poems
of Emily Dickinson* were reprinted by permission of the publishers and the Trustees of
Amherst College from *The Poems of Emily Dickinson*, Thomas H. Johnson, ed., Cambridge,
Mass.: The Belknap Press of Harvard University Press, Copyright © 1951, 1955, 1979,
1983 by the President and Fellows of Harvard College.

For information about permission to reproduce
selections from this book,
write to Permissions, W. W. Norton & Company, Inc.,
500 Fifth Avenue, New York, NY 10110

For information about special discounts for bulk
purchases, please contact W. W. Norton Special Sales
at specialsales@wwnorton.com or 800-233-4830

Manufacturing by Courier Westford
Book design by Charlotte Staub
Production manager: Devon Zahn


Library of Congress Cataloging-in-Publication Data

Charyn, Jerome.
The secret life of Emily Dickinson : a novel /
Jerome Charyn. — 1st ed.
p. cm.
ISBN 978-0-393-06856-6
1. Dickinson, Emily, 1830–1886—Fiction.
2. Women poets—Fiction. I. Title.
PS3553.H33S43 2010
813'.54—dc22

                              2009038977


ISBN 978-0-393-33917-8 pbk.

W. W. Norton & Company, Inc.
500 Fifth Avenue, New York, N.Y. 10110
www.wwnorton.com

W. W. Norton & Company Ltd.
Castle House, 75/76 Wells Street, London W1T 3QT

1 2 3 4 5 6 7 8 9 0

To Georges and Anne Borchardt,
*for their friendship and devotion.*

And to Robert Weil,
*for helping me discover the book
I really wanted to write.*

*To shut our eyes is Travel.*

—EMILY DICKINSON, 1870

# CONTENTS

AUTHOR'S NOTE *11*

*1* HOLYOKE 15

*2* CARLO & CURRER BELL 73

*3* SISTER SUE & THE LOST SOULS 141

*4* THE VAMPYRE OF CAMBRIDGEPORT 193

*5* QUEEN RECLUSE 239

*6* JUMBO 279

*7* THE BOY IN THE BARN 333

ILLUSTRATIONS AND PERMISSIONS 349

# AUTHOR'S NOTE

SHE WAS THE FIRST POET I HAD EVER READ, AND I WAS HOOKED and hypnotized from the start, because in her writing she broke every rule. Words had their own chain reaction, their own fire. She could stun, delight, and kill "with Dirks of Melody." I never quite recovered from reading her. I, too, wanted to create "[a] perfect—paralyzing Bliss," to have my sentences explode "like a Maelstrom, with a notch."

It was the old maid of Amherst who lent me a little of her own courage to risk becoming a writer. "A *Wounded* Deer—leaps highest," she wrote, and I wanted to leap with Emily.

We had so little in common. She was a country girl, and I was a boy from the Bronx. She had a lineage with powerful roots in America, and I was a mongrel whose heritage was like an unsolved riddle out of Eastern Europe. Yet I could hear the tick of her music in my wakefulness and in my sleep. Suddenly that plain little woman with her bolts of red hair was as familiar to me as the little scars on my own face.

But I wasn't interested in writing a novel about a recluse

and a saint. I soon discovered that Dickinson was terrifying in
her variety; she could be bitchy, petulant, and seductive, and
also a mournful, masochistic mouse in love with a mystery man
she called "Master," and to whom she would have sacrificed all.
"I've got a cough as big as a thimble—but I dont care for that—
I've got a Tomahawk in my side but that dont hurt me much.
Her master stabs her more," she writes in a letter that was probably never sent. Whatever her turmoil, she was pleasuring herself with her own words. "Master" could have been any of half
a dozen married men she secretly adored, or no one at all. We
do know that she had some kind of serious flirtation near the
end of her life with a widower, Judge Otis Phillips Lord, that she
even considered marrying him, but was constantly holding him
off. "Dont you know you are happiest while I withhold and not
confer—dont you know that 'No' is the wildest word we consign
to Language?"

Her brother Austin often spoke of Emily as his "wild sister."
And she was wild in her own way. She had a ferocious intelligence that must have frightened her at times, and frightened
those around her, including her own father, Edward Dickinson,
who once served as a congressman from Massachusetts. Thomas
Wentworth Higginson, the editor and writer she clung to as her
"Preceptor," dismissed Edward Dickinson as "thin dry & speechless." Yet this speechless man is at the center of my novel. Their
curious connection served as a kind of courtship. He loved Emily,
feared her, and kept her a child, while she danced around him
like some local Scheherazade. "I do not cross my father's ground
to any House or town," she loved to recite. But she crossed her
father's ground many a time in her poems and in her fiercely
imagined life.

Her real Preceptor, however, wasn't likely Higginson but her
sister-in-law, who remained Emily's surest reader. "Sister Sue" was
also a very complicated creature, who had a whole tribe of Dick-

insons to deal with. Emily likened her to Mount Vesuvius and the Gulf Stream. Susan loved to smolder, and Emily stayed in her spell for thirty years.

She seldom spoke of the eight or nine months she spent at Mount Holyoke Female Seminary in 1847–48, yet this first "break" with Amherst was an important one and helped crystallize some of her longings. It is at Mount Holyoke where the book begins as she becomes embroiled with her Tutors and fellow seminarians, who are trapped in a religious awakening she manages to resist. Though the novel clings to the line of Emily's life, I have also included several fictional characters, such as Miss Rebecca Winslow, the vice principal at Holyoke, who will introduce her to the art of poetry; Zilpah Marsh, a seminarian, who conspires against Emily; Tom, the handyman at Holyoke, who hypnotizes her with the tattoo on his arm; and Brainard Rowe, a Tutor at Amherst College, who courts her when she's nineteen.

The novel will be told entirely in Emily's voice, with all its modulations and tropes—tropes I learned from her letters, wherein she wears a hundred masks, playing wounded lover, penitent, and female devil as she delights and often disturbs us, just as I hope *my* Emily will both delight and disturb the reader and take her roaring music right into the twenty-first century.

⟶

I WOULD LIKE TO THANK THE EMILY DICKINSON MUSEUM FOR its graciousness in allowing me a private tour through the Homestead, and for the privilege of standing quietly in Emily's room and looking out her west window to the Evergreens of Austin and Sister Sue; it was my first long glance from the window that emboldened me to feel her very own "Slant of light."

I have followed the line of Emily's life wherever I could, but I have also taken liberties within that line. There was no Lunatic Asylum in Northampton until 1858, but I have pretended that there was. I "kidnapped" the fire that nearly ravaged Amherst in 1879 and moved it to 1883 for the sake of my story. The Dickinsons lived on North Pleasant Street from 1840 to 1855. But North Pleasant had another name—West Street—while Emily lived there, according to one of her biographers, Alfred Habbeger. And this is the name I have used.

*New York and Paris*
*April 2009*

# PART ONE

## *Holyoke*

*Mount Holyoke Female Seminary*

*South Hadley, 1848*

# 1.

TOM THE HANDYMAN IS WADING IN THE SNOW OUTSIDE MY
window in boots a burglar might wear. I cannot see the Tattoo
on his arm. It is of a red heart pierced by a blue arrow if memory
serves, & if it does not, then I will let Imagination run to folly. But
I dreamt of that arm bared, so help me God, dreamt of it many a
time. We are not permitted to talk to Tom. Mistress Lyon calls him
our own Beast of Burden. She is unkind. Tom the Handyman is no
more a beast than I am.

If he lights our stove or repairs the windowsill or bevels the bottom of our door, our vice principal, Rebecca Winslow, has to be in
the room with him, & we poor girls have to run to Seminary Hall
so that we will be far from Temptation. But I wonder who is the
tempter here, Tom or we? There are close to three hundred of
us—if you count the Misses Lyon and Winslow, & our seven Tutors,
& Tom, the only male at Mt Holyoke. Heavens, I'd as lief call him
Sultan Tom & ourselves his Harem. But Mistress would expel me
in a wink dare I whisper that. And Tom is a sultan who depends on
crumbs. He lives in the shed behind our domicile, a place so dark
& solitary that a cow would die of loneliness were it trapped inside.

He cannot come to the table when we dine, but must feed on whatever scraps are left. My room-mate, Cousin Lavinia, sneers at him, says Tom reeks of sweat. She is a Senior & cannot stop thinking of her suitors. Lavinia has hordes of them, the sons of merchant princes & potentates or boys from Amherst College who would love to sneak onto the grounds & serenade *their* Lavinia, but could not get past Tom & so have sent her half a mountain of Valentines. She is positively engorged with them.

"Cousin," says she, after cursing Tom, "how many notes from Cupid have you received so far?"

"None."

"That's a pity, because I'd opine that a girl hasn't lived at all until she has a hundred beaux."

There never was a show-off like Emily Lavinia Norcross. But I'd start a war between our families if I bludgeoned her.

Mistress Lyon summoned us to the assembly hall. She stared at us all, the perpetrators and the innocent parties. "I forbid you to send off those foolish notes. I will not tolerate such frivolities. We do not celebrate Valentine's Day at Holyoke." And she promised to dispatch Miss Rebecca to the Post Office to discover if anyone dared challenge her decree. But she did not interfere with the Valentines that kept arriving like missiles, as if *any* letter that had already been franked were a sacred thing. She wanted our election, and would suffer nothing less. The girls of Mt Holyoke had to avail themselves to be the little brides of Christ, & said brides did not scribble Valentines harum-scarum to the boys of Amherst. The sign of our election was a dreamy gaze into the atmosphere & strict attention to our calisthenics. But I was consigned to Hell, though I had never received nor sent one paltry Valentine. And Lavinia, with her half mountain, was a member of the elect who had discovered God in Mistress Lyon's sitting room, had prostrated herself & prayed. But my mind would always drift during Devotions, & I'd think of Tom's Tattoo. Tom had become my Calvary.

Lord, I do not know what love is, yet I am in love with Tom, if love be a blue arrow & a heart that can burn through skin and bone. Tom and I have never spoken. How could we? Mistress Lyon would have him hurled across the grounds if ever he dared address a bride of Christ. Still, I watch him in the snow, sinking into perilous terrain, rising in his burglar's boots only to sink again & again, as if in the grip of some bad angel who would not leave Poor Tom alone. I pity him caught in the cold without a cup of beef tea. And how can a sinner such as myself help the Handyman? Soon he will start to sneeze & have a monstrous coughing fit & I will wonder if Tom is weak in the lung.

Holyoke does not believe in hired help. We girls make our own beds & have our individual chores. I am the corporal in charge of knives—no, the animal trainer, since knives are part of my menagerie, like tigers & tigresses, though I never call them such. I distribute the knives during meals & wash them in our sink. Mistress does most of the cooking, & until recently had her own pair of burglar's boots. But she can no longer do the heaviest chores. Her ailing back will not permit her to collect the trash or repair stovepipes & pump handles. So Tom is on the premises by sufferance alone & Mistress pretends not to see him as much as she can. Pointless to send him notes. Tom does not belong to the population of readers. And no one amongst the faculty will deign converse with our Handyman. Miss Rebecca has taught herself to instruct Tom with a form of sign language & a few gruff shouts. If she wants him to repair the water pump, she performs a little pantomime. She gurgles for a moment, weaves around Tom as if she were a well, then stiffens into pipe or pump handle, & before she's done, the Handyman has grabbed his tool box & disappeared into that spidery land below the sink.

But there are no Tutors in the snow to interfere with Tom as he rises and sinks like a burglar. I do not have an inkling of why he is out in that little Siberian winter beside Holyoke Hall. The wind is fierce & there is such a howling that the Lord Himself would take cover, though Mistress Lyon might call me a blasphemer for having said so. She, I'm sure, would declare that God can traverse the snow without tall boots. But that still does not explain Tom's leaping about. Is our Tom constructing his own crooked path for the butcher & grocer? But why would they cross Siberia when there is an open passage to the front gate that Tom shovels every morning at six? Harum-scarum, it is the mystery of Holyoke Hall.

Then I catch the melody of Tom's design. He is not on a meandering march. He is searching in the snow. He sinks again, & I fear that Siberia has swallowed him until he rises up with a creature in his arms, a baby deer frozen with fright, looking like an ornament on some cradle & not a live thing. It must have wandered far from its family & panicked in the snow. Lord, I cannot see its eyes. But Tom the Handyman keeps the stunned little doe above his head & tosses it into the air as you would a sack. And what seems like an act of consummate cruelty isn't cruel at all. The little doe unlocks its legs and starts to leap. What a silent ballet before my eyes! A baby deer gliding above the snow, conquering our little Siberia in half a dozen leaps, & disappearing into the forest, while Tom watches until the doe is safe.

## 2.

THE FEMALE PRAYER CIRCLE MEETS ONCE A MONTH IN LYON'S sitting room. The Circle consists of local duchesses & dowagers who behave like benevolent crones toward our seminary. Holyoke was founded on their largesse & that of their dead husbands. They look sinister *sometimes* in their black vails, yet they have been known to feed chocolate and caramel to Holyoke girls. They arrive in their chaises & Tom has to tether the horses. He stands on guard while Miss Rebecca offers the coachmen hot cider & leads the duchesses in their black capes to Lyon's door. We cannot help but hear the turmoil & the ecstasy as our benefactors labor for the Lord. They shout & thump & sing in raspy voices that sound like the melancholic croaking of frogs. But God has every sort of angel, young & old, sweet or brittle as the duchesses of Monson and Belchertown.

I must confess that I look forward to their croaking—it soothes a homesick girl. But there is a price to pay. Mistress Lyon is filled with impossible fervor. I fear that her meetings with the duchesses will cost me my scalp. She summons to her sitting room all the "unsaved," girls who have not declared themselves as Christians

& hence cannot become worthy wives or teachers & missionaries. There are twenty-five of us. We kneel in front of her desk & are not supposed to glance at Lyon while she herself is caught in rapture of the Lord. But like little burglars we steal looks at her in the bonnet she wears—it billows round her head, white as a mast. Her face has gone to leather, & looks but half alive. Yet her blue eyes are pierced with God, & her long nose quivers as she addresses us in a voice weakened by years of hard work, a web of spit forming upon her mouth.

"My dear little daughters, this house belongs to God. It was built by His direction, and we must be worthy of Him. Can none of you profess your faith?"

When we do not answer, Lyon leans back in her brocaded shawl. "Is this how we thank Our Savior? Clarissa Brown and Maude Munison, will you not rise up out of human depravity and rescue your soul from eternal damnation?"

"Mistress," says Clarissa, who doesn't have the least bit of backbone, "I will, I will."

But when Maude does not rise up and leap into the lap of God, Lyon shakes her head. "Hellfire and no hope for Miss Maude Munison."

And thus she goes down her little list, interrogating us all, as if we were prisoners of war, locked in the dungeon of Mt Holyoke. "Sarah Cowper, I know your father well. Is he squandering his tuition money on a no-hoper?"

And Sarah, the Cicero of our class, says, "I do not yet belong to Christ, but I am trying to *feel* God."

"Then is there hope, Sarah?"

"Yes, Mistress . . . for myself and Father's tuition."

Mistress frowns, her blue eyes very brittle. "Hold thy tongue, young lady! You must not tempt God with talk of tuition. You will write an essay for me, Cowper, on the corrosiveness of humor misspent."

And she continues down the list while she bludgeons us with pictures of our lost souls wading through eternity until we are as stunned & helpless as that little doe in Siberia. Sixteen of us still without hope. Finally she gets to the last name on the list.

"Miss Emily Dickinson, your father might be the earl of Amherst, but Squire Dickinson has no sway here. He has not confessed his faith, but will his daughter reveal her love of God?"

I feel like a winter leaf buffeted about in Lyon's own storm. But I do not tremble in front of her and our little class of sinners. It is only Father who can make me tremble. He has the wrath of God in his wayward eyebrows. But Father suffers a little without me. He swears to Mother that he can only survive on the Indian bread I bake. He loves to have me near, so I can play the piano, or read him passages from Revelation in the library, or tell him for the hundredth time about the particular boot Lord Byron had to wear on his clubfoot, & he complains that he will have to kidnap me from Holyoke one day soon or starve to death. But he's mighty slow for a kidnapper. I keep waiting to hear the sound of his chaise & the bells on the reins of Henry the Horse.

"Mistress, my father is a most religious man," I declare in my mousy voice.

She strains to listen. We must shout in her presence. She has gone deaf in her service to the Lord.

"Daughter, I cannot hear you."

And so I shout like a horn, but my horn is meager and not made of fine metal.

"My father is never without his Bible, Mistress. He wrestles with the Lord's angel day and night."

Mistress dons her thinnest smile that she reserves for backsliders.

"Then Squire Dickinson must be another Jacob who climbed the ladder to God. What did he see in Heaven, child?"

I do not have an answer that would satisfy her. Father never feasted on God's face. He wasn't Jacob who stole the birthright of his twin brother with great guile. He had no twin.

"Has a cat caught Miss Emily's tongue?"

"No, Mistress."

"Then tell us what the earl of Amherst found at the top of the ladder?"

Maude Munison giggles under her breath, but the other brides of Christ do not make the least little sign.

A single tear descends my cheek. I will not wipe it away. Mistress stares at me, her face as red as Esau's. Suddenly she starts to cough & cannot resume her Inquisition. She unfolds a handkerchief & wears it like a mask. I can see the outline of her lips. Miss Rebecca comes running into the room, scrunched up like an elf caught in a moment of panic.

"Vanish," she clucks. "Ungrateful girls, you have provoked Mistress into having a fit of phlegm." Now she glares at us. "Hurry, hurry. To your rooms. And no loitering. Heaven help any girl I catch who is not engaged in silent study."

❧

IT IS THE CURSE OF HOLYOKE. *SILENT STUDY.* WE ARE A LITTLE nation of whisperers on a hill forty rods from the village church where brides of Christ who were already saved sat in pews while rats & mice leapt upon their laps. But Miss Rebecca is always sentencing us to silent study, as if we don't have enough silence at South Hadley. We have to whisper in the library, whisper in the dining room, whisper in the pantry, whisper in the space-ways, whisper on the stairs, but I haven't a soul to whisper at while I pad up to the fourth floor. The other scholars from our little séance shun me now. I have upset Lyon with my prideful talk of Father wrestling with an angel, & sent her spinning into an attack of the ague until she had to hide behind her handkerchief.

Cousin Lavinia wasn't in our room. She must have been reading her Valentines in some secret alcove. And so I have my silent
study without Lavinia. I ask the Lord to forgive me for heaping
distress upon our principal, though she shouldn't have called
Father the earl of Amherst. He's no earl. Our Tutors might suspect that Satan was inside me, that it was Satan who spoke, not
Miss Emily, the scholar & would-be bride of Christ on the fourth
floor. But God & Mistress Lyon live in the land of Prose, while
Satan sings. Foul, with sulfur as his perfume, Satan is still a Poet.
Yet I prefer Father's primitive Prose to Satan's Poetry. Father has
no songs, neither for himself & his family. He moves in silent
sweeps.

Perhaps Father *is* an earl. He rides across town in his chaise,
Horse Henry in the lead. God alone ever saw such a gallop. I fear
for Father's life, & for the lives of those who might step blindly into
his path. I never knew a cautioner man, except when he's in his
carriage.

There's a knock on my door. Miss Rebecca enters pious as a
mouse. She hasn't come to chastise me.

"Mistress would like a word with you."

Her gentleness disarms me, & I start to cry.

"Missy, I did not mean to provoke Miss Lyon into a fit of phlegm.
I am mortally sorry if I have wounded her. Sometimes I have the
Devil inside me."

"Tut," she says. "You're the daughter of an earl, and you think
that gives you privileges. Well, we do not have such a high opinion
of the Amherst aristocracy."

My crying stops in an instant, as if my tear ducts were scorched
with fire. This is the Rebecca I know, with acid in her veins, always
wearing that ruffled ruche round her neck & her yellow gloves;
her eyes are pale, & she has a cruel, tight mouth. She could be one
of the female assassins that Elizabeth of England kept around her.
But assassins are not exemplary at a "dame school" near a moun-

tain, & Miss Rebecca has no cause to cut our throats with razors inside her yellow gloves.

I walk downstairs & knock on Lyon's door.

"Emily Dickinson, Mistress. You asked for me."

She's reclining on her settee, wrapped in a shawl. She wears a handkerchief round her neck, like an invalid with a ruined throat. She clasps my hand & begs me to sit beside her.

"Forgive me. Sometimes I go too far. I should not have mocked Squire Dickinson. It was my own pique. Our critics call us a band of Puritan witches and nuns. A dame school will lead girls to perdition. We should study wifeliness, not the art of Alexander Pope. Do you think I ought to run a cooking school, Miss Emily?"

"No, Mistress."

"We are scholars, not cooks. But when my daughters won't give themselves to Christ, I feel utterly helpless . . . Is there hope for you?"

"Mistress, I'm as hopeful as any daughter of an earl."

I never said another word. *Two* encounters in the same day with Emily of Amherst had exhausted our poor principal. She shuts her eyes & starts to wheeze. I did not think it ladylike to listen.

I tiptoe back upstairs. That night I dream of Esau with his ruddy face & hair. He lived with us at Holyoke as our one & only male scholar. But in my dream Esau had Tom's Tattoo, & I did not need any Daniel & his lions' den to interpret it for me. I wanted Tom the Handyman to be my room-mate. I'd have spent the night beside his Tattoo, & all the mistresses and monitors in the world wouldn't have been able to yoke me from him, not even that assassin with her yellow gloves.

# 3.

THE ONLY TATTOO I EVER GET IS A RAP UPON MY DOOR AT 5 in the morning. It is Missy & her breakfast squad calling me to action. I have to rise quick as a sorceress & rush to the basement without the least tumult on the stairs. Father's angel must have accompanied me, because I glide off each stair like a girl with velvet soles. I bow to Rebecca & the chief of her monitors, Zilpah Marsh, who possesses a faint little mustache & the shoulders of a man. Zilpah's father is a stable hand & her mother a housemaid in one of the secret societies at Amherst College. She herself is the poorest girl at Holyoke & her tuition had to be waived, but Zilpah is part of Mistress Lyon's "experiment" to raise up young women of modest means & have them found their own female seminaries.

Zilpah Marsh is ornery as a snake, but most gentle to me. She's in love with Austin, my older brother, & it's no big secret. He's a Sophomore at Amherst, & Zilpah must have spotted him on the campus or at a secret society. Brother is hard to miss. He's as handsome as the Squire, with a shock of red hair that's visible for a mile. She dreams of marrying Austin one day, though he has never laid eyes on her, & I doubt that Brother would ever marry a girl with a mustache, faint as it is. It would not concern him one jot that she's the daughter of a stable hand. Austin would consider the quality of her mind. We Dickinsons are not horse traders when it comes to matters of the heart. When we marry, we will marry for love.

Zilpah steals up to me in the bake room, while I prepare the morning bread. Aside from collecting & cleaning knives with a soapstone, I am the school baker several times a week. If truth be told, the girls are delirious over my puddings & bread. I never vary the formula, at Holyoke or at home. The magic lies in the measuring cup. A dollop of molasses too little or too late, the wrong pinch of salt, & you will have soapstone in the pan & neither bread nor pudding.

"Miss Em'ly," she says, careful not to soil my baking smock with hands that have been tinkering with whale-oil lamps. "Can I get you some gingerbread from the pantry, or another sort of sweet?"

"Rebecca will punish us for breaking the rules—no eatables before breakfast."

"Don't you bother about Rebecca! I run the school. She's in love with me."

"Zilpah, you must not say that," I say, trembling with the intrigue of it.

"She touches my hair—it's the only time she takes off her glove. She even writ me a poem. Don't you want a sweet?"

Zilpah disappears and returns with a fortune of gingerbread. We nibble while I peruse the oven. I dare not ask Zilpah about Miss Rebecca's love poem, though my mind is like a massive flint-stone of sparks & syllables on fire. And while I imagine Rebecca's words, Zilpah starts to recite—she's memorized the poem.

> *Your smock is stained with wild berries*
> *That bear the color of your lips,*

*And I the huntress with her heart as prey,*
*But when—*

The huntress appears in the bake room with her yellow gloves, drawn to Zilpah's voice, though she could not have heard more than a whisper. But she hasn't lost her cunning.

"Have you both been conspiring against me?"

"Yes," says Zilpah, who sashays past our vice principal as if she were invisible. And I cannot help but stare at Rebecca, who turns suspicious.

"Child, you must not pay attention to Zilpah Marsh. She does not have your breeding."

"No, Missy. Her father is most certainly not an earl."

And I am stunned by my own harshness. I do not hate Rebecca. I watch her in wonder. I have never met a Poet. Her lines are like little panthers poised to strike. She's an assassin who could harm & hurt with one of her panthers, & I a baker of bread, who should worship at her feet.

But it's the scholars who worship me in the middle of breakfast. They have caught a whiff of my bread all the way from their rooms. Their eyes are watering as they sit down. They have to whisper in the dining hall, & whisper they do.

"Cake," cries Lydia Fisk under her breath. "Our Emily can turn the commonest loaf into cake."

I ought to burn with pride, but it's fear I'm filled with. Bread & cake are nothing beside a huntress in a chaotic field of words . . .

There is a crisis afoot when we return to our rooms. The whole fourth floor is suddenly swallowed up in billowing black smoke. A bitter wind has forced the smoke & its deadly sparks back down the pipes of our Franklin stoves & made of each stove a red hot inferno. We all have to retreat to the stairs, while Miss Rebecca wades into the blackness with her yellow gloves & a wet horse blanket covering her like a tent. We hear her howl as she wanders into a room. She returns to us with the horse blanket sizzling.

"Where in thunder is the handyman?" she growls. "The heat is insufferable. I couldn't get near the pipes."

Tom arrives in an old coat, carrying a crowbar & a bucket of snow. He must feel irregular around us, away from the dark comfort of his shed. What could he possibly think of a harem full of girls in the midst of revival meetings? Do we bother the bit of peace he has? He steps timidly but soon regains his poise. He dips the crowbar into the bucket & then charges into our infernal fourth floor. We listen as he bangs away at the pipes. The smoke begins to clear.

Tom emerges, his eyebrows covered with soot. Miss Rebecca does not even offer him a cup of water or a wet rag to wipe the soot from his brows.

# 4.

I WALK ABOUT IN A VAIL. NO ONE QUESTIONS ME BUT
Zilpah Marsh.

"Miss Em'ly, why in tarnation are you wearing black?"

"Someone has to mourn Tom," I say.

"What if Tom don't need mourning?"

"Well, I haven't seen him live or dead in a week."

"That's because he's shut up in his shack."

Zilpah must consider me queer, but I laugh to know that Tom is
still among the living. It is a nervous laugh, the laugh of a seventeen-
year-old maiden who's never been courted & kissed by a man.

"Did he fall off the roof?" I ask, frightening myself with my own
morbid Imagination.

"Silly creature, Tom don't climb roofs. He's shut in, that's all.
He has the grippe, and Mistress won't let him out of the shack. She
fears he might contaminate us all. She'd ship him on the stage to
another town, but Tom has nowhere else to go."

"Where's he from?"

"Lord knows," says Zilpah Marsh, as high and mighty as Solo-
mon's Sheba.

"But Tom isn't a ghost. He must have his own people *somewhere*,"
I say.

"What people? Tom grew up in Northampton, inside the insane
asylum."

"Zilpah Marsh, I don't care a bean if you are our monitor. It is
most wicked of you to imply that Tom is feebleminded."

"I said nothing of the sort. The asylum has an orphan's wing.
That's where Tom was reared. Rebecca told me so. She says Mistress plucked him right out of the orphan's wing."

"And what's his family name if I might be bold enough to ask?"

"Don't you comprehend my meaning, Miss Em'ly? He's Tom-of-
any-town."

"I never heard anything so ridiculous in my life. We do not have
nameless children in Massachusetts."

"We most certainly do. The paupers' association looked after
Tom, but they never got around to giving him a proper name."

I don't believe a word of it. *Northampton Tom.* And then I shiver
at the appalling truth. Tom was tribeless. Perhaps that was why I
seem so soldered to him, as if the two of us wore the same hot bolt.
I have all the fruit a name and family can bear, but I might as well
have been shaken out of some orphan's tree.

I couldn't even tell time until I was fifteen. Father was convinced he had taught me himself, but I just didn't understand the
circling of a clock. I was mortified, like a child caught up in the
great mystery of numbers & dials on a replica of the moon's own
round face. But I solved the riddle, saw the dials as the wings of a
bird hovering over mountains on the moon with numbers rather
than peaks. I could feel in my mind a shadow that the bird left over
every numeral, a shadow that darkened as the numbers grew, &
thus brought us from breakfast to midnight, round & round again.
But it was an orphan's trick.

I couldn't leave poor Tom to rot all alone in his shed like the
drudge that Mistress imagined him to be. I had to plead with Zil-

pah Marsh, who could wander wherever she wanted without drawing any suspicion onto her shoulders.

"Zilpah, I have to see Tom."

"Impossible," she opines. "Tom is sick as a dog. Missy and I have
to wear masks. His bile is all black. I feed him China tea from Missy's own hospital kit and whatever crusts we have left."

"What about winter apples and hot potato pie?"

Zilpah scorns me with one of her highfalutin glances. "You are
doltish, Miss Em'ly. Mistress wouldn't waste that kind of grub on a
handyman. She'd as lief send him back to the insane asylum in a
cart and find another orphan."

"That's heartless."

"Well, child, it's a heartless world."

Clever as she is, Zilpah Marsh is no match for a girl who taught
herself to tell time by looking for shadows on the moon. I'm loathe
to take advantage of her weakness for my brother, the Squire's son.
But Lord, I'll do anything to get near the Handyman.

"Zilpah," says Orphan Emily, "my darling brother might be
visiting next week." It's mostly a lie, but there's a parcel of truth
attached to the word "might." Zilpah's ears prick at the mention of my brother. Her eyes grow alert. Her interest in Austin is
unbounded.

"Will the young squire be sitting in the parlor with you, Miss
Em'ly?"

"Why not? My own brother has to be on the list of male callers.
And who would keep him off the grounds? Tom is much too ill."

"Gracious," she says, just like one of Mistress's dowagers.
"Would it be much of a burden if you introduced me to the young
squire?"

Her face darkens, as if she's having a dialogue with herself. "Not
as the daughter of a chambermaid. I would not want that mentioned. But as your classmate. Will you swear on the Bible not to
say a word about my Ma and Pa?"

I pity her mustache all of a sudden, but I still set the trap, even if I'm hellbound in all my wickedness.

"I swear, but you have to do me a favor first."

Suddenly her eyes are hard as glass.

"I wouldn't be much of a monitor if I started doing favors for every little nun at Holyoke—what is it you want?"

"Take me to Tom's shed."

Lord, punish me for my pride. I have underestimated this stable hand's daughter. She has much poetry in her blood. She pretends to slap me, touches my face with the tips of her fingers.

"I love the young squire, Miss Em'ly, but you ought not have attempted to bribe me. It belittles you in my estimation."

# 5.

WHO CAN FATHOM THE WAYS OR MEANS OF ZILPAH'S HEART?
She rouses me at 5¼ of a cold, cold morning, but it's not to join
the breakfast squad. While we're wrapped in our shawls like woods-
men of the far north, she takes my hand & leads me down to the
kitchen & dining hall, through a rear exit that had escaped my eye
until now, & into our own little Siberia behind Holyoke Hall.

We walk in great drifts of snow, our legs disappearing under
us as if amputated by the frozen weather, & we arrive at Tom's
shack, near the southern wing of the seminary. Zilpah does not
even bother to announce herself with a knock. She gathers her
legs out of the snow & sails nonchalantly into the shed, pulling me
along. My ears were pounding, & I was full of vertigo, but I wasn't
blind. Tom's shack looked as if a hurricane had visited & torn out
whatever it was you might call a home. The shed had nothing but a
dirt floor, no writing table or chair, no Bible or bookcase, no chest
of drawers—nothing but a tool box, a heap of clothes, a whale-oil
lamp, a blanket, & an old crooked cot with the Handyman therein,
feverish & forlorn.

His beautiful blond hair has gone to straw in the agony of his illness, but his blue eyes burn in the weak light of the lamp; he's truly a man on fire, even with his haggard face.

Zilpah masks herself with the shawl, but I do nothing of the kind. She shouts at me through the mask. "Keep away, or you'll catch sick."

"Zilpah Marsh," I shout back, my anger all aboil, "you and Miss Rebecca and the whole establishment are cruel, cruel, cruel."

And she starts to huff under her mask. "Is that the thanks I get for leading you to Tom?"

"Dear, when did you last feed Tom and bring him some water?"

"Don't I have ten thousand chores? And a handyman with the grippe isn't so high on my list." She has a tantrum near poor Tom. "Damn you, Emily Dickinson! You can run back to Amherst in your father's buggy and join a sewing circle. But if I don't succeed at this dame school, I'll be sentenced to a life of cooking and scrubbing floors in some squire's house."

She runs out of the shed, the shawl flying around her like a battle scarf. I'm grateful she is gone, but I do have a dilemma. I have never talked to Tom, & I don't know how to begin. He follows me with his blue eyes, as if he were assaying a foreign animal—from Holyoke Hall rather than the forest—a scholar who treads up & down the stairs, sits at the piano, & prays in the dark.

I gather my courage & break into the singsong that passes for speech whenever I'm excited. "Are you thirsty, Mr. Tom? I'd have brought you some water if Miss Marsh had allowed where we were going."

I hear him sob, & I'm much too ashamed to look! It's all part of his agony. I long to comfort Tom, to rescue him from a snowdrift like that baby deer, but I cannot. The sobbing stops as suddenly as it began, & Tom himself breaks into speech. His voice is softer, gentler than I had imagined, softer than our handyman at home.

"Missy, will ya talk some more?"

"Why, Mr. Tom, I talk all the time. I am the most talkative girl in creation. I'd talk a streak here at Holyoke, except we have that whispering rule."

Lord, if he isn't whimpering again!

"Missy Marsh never talks to me . . . her and that lady with the yellow gloves."

"Do they ever feed you bread and butter and apple cider from Mistress's cellar?"

Tom titters. "Cider's for the gentlefolk and their farmhands, and for the ladies who sit on porches, not for a plain mechanic what learned all his stuff in the asylum. It's lard and grease. No butter for Tom. But tell me a story, *Miss.*"

Tom is so emphatic that I feel a little paralyzed.

"About dragons and kings? I'm not much of a person for tall tales. I am missing in that sort of Imagination. But I could retell the Bible for you, chapter and verse."

"Not the Bible, Miss. *Your* story."

Now I am puzzled *and* paralyzed.

"I have little story to tell. I've been nowhere, Mr. Tom. I haven't traveled much more than the eleven miles between Amherst and Holyoke. I sit with my Bible and my books. I am seventeen, for God's sake, and not one year more."

Tom guffaws, & I can see the little gap in his mouth where a tooth is missing. It's still a pretty sight.

"Why do you laugh?" I ask, timider than ever.

"It wasn't to hurt ya, Miss. I laughed, because you have your dragons and kings, and I have not a-one. I am a child of Massachusetts."

"And so am I, Amherst born and bred."

"But not a nurse and a matron for your Ma-ma. And a deacon with a broomstick for your Pa-pa. Deacon spilled the Bible into my ears whilst he beat my bottom black and blue . . . Does your Pa-pa read the Bible to ya, Miss?"

"Every morning when I'm in Amherst."

"And does he slap your bottom with a broomstick in the middle of the read?"

"Of course not," I say, feeling feverish. "Squire Dickinson would not dream of doing such a thing. No squire would. Fathers do not beat their daughters in the best of families."

"That's where the dragons come in," says Tom, like a deranged philosopher.

"Mr. Tom, I do not see where dragons have anything to do with my Pa-pa."

"That's the whole *pernt*," he says, meaning point, I suppose. "You have a whole line of Pa-pas in arrears. And ain't all the Pa-pas like dragons and ogres and kings in the closet? . . . but tell Tom about your Pa-pa, Miss?"

"Shouldn't I find some eatables for you first?"

"Eatables can wait," he says with a shrug. "Does the squire ever laugh out loud?"

"Mr. Tom, Father forgot how to laugh."

"Didn't I say so? Your Pa-pa's a dragon. All he knows is to suck on fire. And his Missus, is she a lady dragon?"

"Mother's a mouse," I hiss like the dragon's little daughter & frighten myself. Where did that venom come from? We're all fragile around the Squire, as if one harsh word might shatter us. But that talk of dragons must have exhausted Tom. He starts to snore with a rumbling sound in his throat. I cover him with the blanket & touch the side of his face with my hand while he sleeps. I had never before been so daring with a stranger, or any man, including my male cousins.

I'm ashamed to describe the electricity of my contact with his raw, red skin—my cheeks are ablaze with the delight of it. I steal out the shed in search of comestibles & drinking water for Tom.

# 6.

LORD, I FORGOT ABOUT THE BREAD! MISTRESS WILL THROTTLE me for neglecting my chores & allowing three hundred females to starve at the breakfast table. But I can smell the most delicious crust as I lope back into the basement like some wolf cub out of little Siberia. I have maligned Zilpah Marsh, who presided over the ovens while I was secretly with Tom. Zilpah baked the morning bread & put out the knives. And when I arrive with the wind, scholars & Tutors clap their hands. I notice nothing but Miss Rebecca's yellow gloves, how the fingers never bend—there's little suppleness in the leather. And then I look beyond the leather & happen upon her face. Her eyes get narrower with each clap of the gloves. The sound is like a gunshot.

"Bravo to the baker!"

She knows I did not bake the bread. Her subterfuge frightens me.

The clapping & sporadic chatter stop, & we fall back into the world of whispers, eat our mashed potatoes & drink our milk in silence. The milk clings to Zilpah's mustache, & she resembles a sea captain, far beyond her years. The bell rings at 7¾, & we begin

returning to our rooms for silent study. But I have to run counter
to Miss Rebecca's clock, steal bread & butter & sweet apple pudding from the pantry, & sail out the rear of Seminary Hall.

Tom sits in the flickering light of the lamp, captive to the little
curtain of gray that smothers the blue in his eyes. But I don't care
about colors. I feed Tom with my own hands, wash his face with my
handkerchief, & wipe him dry with the edge of my shawl. I'm the
one who shatters the silence, & I shiver at my boldness.

"Mr. Tom, will you show me your Tattoo?"

Tom's suspicious. Proper girls aren't supposed to peek at Tat-
toos. And I have to encourage him a little.

"The arrow of love on your arm—will you reveal it to me and
not another soul?"

Tom doesn't even look into my eyes. "Miss, I wouldn't know an
arrow of love even if I saw it."

"But you have a heart burnt into your right arm, with an arrow
running through it."

"Ain't a love arrow, Miss. It's an orphan's mark. We all carried
that tattoo at the asylum. It was our only heritage."

"What heritage?" I ask, caught in Tom's web.

"The heritage of a broken heart. What else?"

Tom devours the last lick of pudding & rolls up his sleeve.
Lord, I must have been color-blind. The tattooed heart isn't
red at all. It's pale blue; the arrow alone is red, redder than
Amherst's one and only fire wagon, redder than Pa-pa's winter
underwear or Ma-ma's sewing basket, redder even than Austin's
ragged red kite.

Tom wriggles his arm, & the red arrow cuts deeper into the
blue heart. I'm dazzled, held in the sway of that arrow & all its cha-
grin, as if the Commonwealth of Massachusetts had stabbed poor
Tom.

I have a great mind to touch Tom's Tattoo, but both my arms
feel paralyzed. I can sense that something's wrong. Tom's blue

eyes are a-flutter. His face becomes a tight mask. A shadow climbs up the wall of the shed.

"Dickinson, what on earth are you doing here?"

I recognize the somber, scratchy drawl of Miss Rebecca, who must have followed me to the shed. I know she means me harm. She's worried that I might snitch on her & Zilpah, & she'd like to blot me out of Mistress Lyon's books, make it so I'll disappear from South Hadley. And I'm frightened of her legerdemain with leather gloves.

"Missy," I say, without staring her in the face. "I brought some food for the Handyman. I figured he could use a little company."

"Look at me, child, when I talk to you."

I twist about, all a-tremble. But I have my own cavalier in this shed, poor sick Tom. It ain't yellow gloves he's scared of. It's her assassin's stick, that talented tongue of hers. Miss Rebecca can tie him up with words.

"Mum," he says meekly. "The young miss . . ."

Miss Rebecca is beside herself.

"Shut up," she hisses like a deranged cat. "You have no business in this discussion. You'll speak when you're spoken to."

And my trembling stops. What sort of girl would let down her own cavalier?

"Missy, you ought to be politer to Tom."

Her eyes roam in her head like a mad lady. She has a mind to thrash me with her yellow gloves. But there's a witness, mute as Tom might be. Her eyes stop roaming as she starts to calculate. Feeding a handyman is enough of an infraction to have me expelled. But Missy can't talk about my imbroglio without worrying that I might mention hers.

"Miss Dickinson," she says, "you will resign as a scholar and return to Amherst, or I will expose you and Tom."

Yellow gloves don't matter now. I can match her tongue for tongue.

"I'd be glad to oblige, Missy, if you add your name to the resignation roster."

Miss Rebecca trembles with murderous intent. She raises one arm to deliver a slap. But Tom purrs at Missy like a Poet.

"If you tetch her, Mum, I'll have to tetch you back. And it won't be pretty."

Miss Rebecca isn't sure what to do. She hadn't counted on Tom talking back. Her own angry engine has come to a halt.

That's when I have my coughing fit. I cough & cough, & I can't seem to stop.

Missy savors her sudden triumph.

"Dickinson, I believe you are contagious. You'll be quarantined immediately and sent home to your father."

She wraps her cloak around my shoulders and whisks me from the shed without another word to Tom.

# 7.

I LISTEN TO THE SOUND OF HIS BOOTS ON THE STAIRS.
Brother does not have to tread with a seminarian's silent steps.
The staircase shivers as he strides from landing to landing. I greet
him at my door, while the other brides of Christ watch with much
wonderment. He does not have my mousy chin. His hair is much
redder than mine.

"Austin, you cannot kiss me. I have the croup."

But Brother always has his own way. He kisses Emily over each
eye.

"I have missed you beyond credulity," I say, while he gathers me
in his arms, picks me up like a stray bundle, & wraps me in a blanket he has brought from the chaise.

"Brother, you must put me down. *Immediately.* I have been cautioned. I may not leave the premises."

"And I, Sister, have been cautioned to bring you home. The
word came on high from head-quarters."

There is only one head-quarters. *Pa-pa.* Mary Lyon must have
delivered a missile to Amherst, warning Father that I had the croup

& might become a menace to myself & Mt Holyoke. And Father sent his emissary, my darling brother, with horse & carriage.

In spite of our differences, Austin has remained my dear "twin." And it isn't only the divine accident of our red hair. Austin has moved on to the company of his classmates at the College, & he has little time for mortals like me, but our minds seem to travel along a similar route. Austin is always the first to smile whenever I tease Pa-pa. He would not dare tease Father himself, but he is often an accomplice in my little tricks. Brother helped me tie a ribbon around Henry's neck when I wanted to show Pa-pa how he was neglecting his own horse . . .

Zilpah Marsh is waiting in the parlor, like someone in a trance. She trembles at the sight of Austin & his rich red hair. I'd promised to introduce her, & introduce her I will.

"Austin, you must meet our class monitor, Miss Zilpah Marsh. She—"

But Austin glances at Zilpah's manly shoulders & faint mustache, nods once, & sails out the front door & into the March wind with his own sister on his arm. He helps me into the chaise, still bundled up in the blanket, & clucks at Henry the Horse, who would as lief recognize me as he would a burr in Holyoke Hall. Father's horse is not overly fond of females. But I am thinking of Tom & how desperate he must be without a female soul to care for him. I miss the stark boundaries of his shack, the freedom of having no furniture, nothing to enslave the mind.

The horse is as blanketed as I am. The wheels are bound in burlap to protect us from sliding on the ice. Even Henry wears leather mittens over his shoes. Austin wraps his own head in a scarf—my God, we're all mummified!

And slowly, with the horse breathing hot plumes into the air, we plunge toward Amherst in Pa-pa's chaise.

I DO NOT COUNT THE MILES. I LISTEN TO HENRY'S BELLS WHILST I am mummified. I'd swear we were heading north as the crow flies, but Holyoke girls chatter of going *down* to Amherst from Hadley's hills. I lean into Brother as his body rocks against the rhythm of the chaise. And I must have dozed with all that rocking & the music of Henry's bells.

I awake in Father's arms. He carries me from the chaise into our "mansion" on West Street. I do not see Mother or Little Sister, though *little* is the wrong word. Vinnie is near tall as I am & far prettier. She is not cursed with Sister Emily's chin. She will have ten thousand marriage proposals ere she is seventeen. But I cannot locate the least sign of Little Sister. Perhaps she & Mother both suffer from the fear of Father's commandments.

"*Do not excite Emily*," he must have pronounced & held them in hiding. And if truth be known, Emily does not want to share Pa-pa upon her homecoming. He says not a word to me, as if his presence alone were enough of a greeting on a winter night. He is not wearing his greatcoat, & I worry that the wind will eat him alive. Horse Henry is nervous around Pa-pa, who has not rubbed his hide once or deigned to notice him. It is Austin and not Pa-pa who leads Henry to the carriage house.

Father's red hair ruffles out & turns wild in the bite-bite of the wind, & for one brief moment I do not recognize him. He looks to be as much of a burglar as Tom . . . before the Handyman took ill. But Miss Em'ly would rather not think of Tom. The lace of Father's cravat unravels a little & cuts a line into my cheek. The cravat is cold as ice, & I wonder if Pa-pa is wearing a rapier round his neck. The village crones will scream that Squire Dickinson slew his own daughter upon her return from that convent where the chief nun neutered Miss Em'ly & remade her into a witch. But I am not slain at all. And the witch of Holyoke loses all her powers once she's inside the paternal abode.

I am helpless in Father's house. He carries me up the stairs, &
suddenly my wounded cheek is well again, though it throbs from
its nearness to Father's side-whiskers. Said whiskers do not scratch.
They are smooth as silk. We pass the Squire's own bedroom, which
I can only map out in my dreams. Never have Little Sister or I been
inside that chamber. The door is always shut, & even Mother rec-
ognizes its dominion.

Lord, I would not spy, but how many times did I find her sneak-
ing in & out, as if she herself had little right to enter. Such is the
sway that Father has on one & all. Mistress Lyon must have been
right about Pa-pa. He does have the bearing of an earl. It isn't
only that he's Treasurer of the College & that he once served in
the State House. He's the most prominent lawyer in town, & he
loves to take his morning walk. I have seen the citizens of Amherst
cower & cross the street whenever the Squire marches to the Post
Office to collect our mail. And it matters little to him that I had
addressed a letter to Austin or Little Sister. Father rifles the letter while he walks, breaking my own little "wafer" seal, & seems to
dance to the very sound of my words. So Little Sister has said to me
more than once.

Heavens, he has even been known to laugh! And when I told
her in protest that it was beyond my comprehension to imagine
Father on the very same street with laughter, Sister swore that he
danced like an intoxicated bear. Not only perused the letter but
had learned it by heart upon arriving at our doorstep & did take
much pride in key phrases that he would troll across his tongue
like a chocolate truffle. I'd rather believe in the wildest tale of
the *Arabian Nights* than believe Lavinia! But Little Sister has never
been known to lie.

We pass Brother's bedroom, which is often empty now that he is
up on College Hill. Then Pa-pa delivers me to the "Female Dormitory," as he has christened the room I share with Little Sister. And
I must now confess that the room-mates I have at Amherst and at

South Hadley are both called Lavinia. But I prefer Little Sister to Lavinia Norcross and her hundred beaux. Sister would never spy on me or make fun of Tom.

Swirling in Father's arms, I feel like a broken doll. *Pa-pa*, I want to shout, *I am not your favorite feather, but a woman with a ferocious will.* I do not utter a peep, & Father plunks me under the quilt with the same brutal tenderness that has become his signature. Little Sister is not on her side of the bed. Father must have exiled her to Austin's room until I am cured of the croup.

Father is not the kissing kind. And I am startled when he pecks my scalp, his mouth like a toad that rains magic down upon my head.

"Damn that dame school of yours," he says. "I have been lonesome without you, Emily. I like to have both my daughters in the house. We will start our regimen in the morning."

I dare not ask him what regimen he means. Instead, I shake. But still I manage to squeal, "Father, at what hour will you wake me?"

There are furrows in his brow.

"This isn't Holyoke. You're convalescin'. Sleep as long as you like."

"But I have bread to bake."

Dare I dream, or does his daughter see the hint of a smile upon Father's somber face?

"Leave the baking to Mother and Lavinia," he says. "Not one chore while you are ill."

"But it is my recreation," I do my best to insist. And he seems startled that I would defy one of his commandments and cardinal rules.

"Emily, I do not surmise much recreation in having my daughter cough her lungs out in front of a mountain of dough." And then, Lord alive! he does smile. "Even if it is a great sacrifice and does hinder my appetite. I must have lost my reason. I shouldn't have lent you to those fanciful dames at Holyoke."

"But Father, I had the croup long before I set foot in South Hadley."

"Then you did a good job of hiding it from me. Go to sleep. And no more palaver about baking bread."

Father abandons me to the dark. I am always a general *after* our debates, mounting attacks that will never happen, not in Father's lifetime or in mine. I cannot sleep. I feel like a stranger in my own bed. I must be a bride of Christ in spite of my penchant for Satan & his tricks. I start to cough & sob in the same minute. My sobbing must have summoned a figure out of Hell, wrapped up in a fiery color that can shine on a moonless night.

"Emily," whispers the demon, "do not cry," and climbs into bed with me in a cape that feels on fire. But my flesh does not burn or explode.

The demon takes my hand under the covers and has the cheek to kiss me on the lips. I am paralyzed for a moment—until I realize that it is Little Sister who has crawled into our bed, wearing a bright orange coverlet that can glisten in the dark.

"Sister," I purr, "did the Patriarch"—meaning Pa-pa—"hide you and Mother in a box?"

"Practically," she whispers in my ear. "We are not to disturb Princess Emily while she convalesces under his roof."

"But Mother could have protested . . . or found a lawyer to argue her case."

"And risk Father's wrath? Heavens, no! Mother's champion would melt under Father's gaze."

"As would we," I declare.

"As would we."

And both of us laugh that half laugh of co-conspirators caught in a similar maze. Suddenly I am as tired as the Devil & fall asleep in Lavinia's arms.

# 8.

PART OF OUR FAMILY LEGEND IS THAT MOTHER DEFIED FATHER
once and only once in her life—on the day I was born. The Squire
had forbidden her to paper her bedroom walls. He wouldn't even
let the paper hanger, Lafayette Stebbins, into the house. It was
Father's belief that the paper hanger might interfere with Mother's delivery. But Mother did not want to welcome me into the
world with peeling brown paper on her walls. So she intrigued
with the paper hanger, visited him on the sly, & offered to pay him
out of her own pocket.

It was my precarious luck that the paper hanger arrived with his
ladder and materials a few hours before Mother was delivered of
me. And I woke with a shout to the bright yellow weave of tulips
on Mother's wall. Of course, much of this can't be true. Even Mer-
lin himself couldn't have scraped the walls and hung that yellow
paper in a matter of hours. Pa-pa must have given in to Mother
and let her have her way, and I was born in the shadow of Lafayette
Stebbins's stepladder. Perhaps my own stubborn streak grew out of
Mother's single act of defiance. I've always been partial to bright
colors. That's all I care to say.

But why hasn't Mother visited with me?

It's Pa-pa who knocks on my door & enters in his usual armor—coat, boiled shirt, & cravat—as if he were preparing for a joust at the General Court. He carries a silver salver replete with milk, corn mush, medicine bottles & sprays & a contraption that coughs up steam. It's clear that Father means to torture me with what he calls his regimen. It's milk & mush in the morning, with a dose of steam that could dizzify. But I am the martyr, Pa-pa's saint & good little girl. Ma-ma must be in the house somewhere. I listen to the song of her slippers, that soft staccato of hers on hard wood. But she does not appear.

"Father," I ask in a whisper, between sucks of steam, "won't your practice suffer if you spend too much time pampering me?"

"I have my clerks. And I wouldn't call it pamperin'. Young ladies have been known to die of the croup."

"But I'm Dolly. Not a wilted thing."

Father hadn't called me *Dolly* in years. I was Dolly when I climbed upon his lap at five or six, Dolly in his rye field, Dolly when I was ill with a much earlier croup. "*Where's my little doll?*" he would say. "*Where's Dolly?*"

He did not amuse himself with Sister & Brother in similar fashion. He had but *one* Dolly. Yet I could not coax it out of him while I lay in bed. In truth, Father held a grudge against me. He wanted to educate his daughters, but he still believed that it was a waste of money & a waste of time. Daughters could not become medical doctors or ministers, could not study law. We were meant to marry, but even that troubled his mind. He paid no heed at all to our future, neither Lavinia's nor my own. We were female creatures to him, mostly useless, though he adored us & would have us bred into proper young ladies. But we did not enter his dreams; only Austin did I am sure. Austin would safeguard the Dickinson name, would capture a wife & a career, procreate, & produce yet another generation of Dickinsons, while Lavinia & I would be pirated away from Amherst by a *husband*, would cleave to him, & lose our Dickinson stature. And so I was some spotted thing that Pa-pa squinted at, but still he stayed home with me.

"Father, shouldn't you take your constitutional to the Post Office?"

"What for? I won't find a letter from you."

"Good gracious. I could write one from my pillow, address it to myself, and have Sister deliver it to the Post Office. Would that do the trick?"

"No. It's not the same as having you write from Holyoke."

"Father, why not?"

"Because I couldn't hear the hunger in your lines."

"You are imagining things," I said.

But I began to blush, & it wasn't from that surcharge of steam. He must have sensed my loneliness & realized that even a letter to Austin or Lavinia was a letter to him. My life, it seems, was one long letter to Edward Dickinson, Esquire. It didn't matter much whose name or address was on the envelope. I was serenading Father with my tiny Tambourine.

After he finishes with his regimen, Father returns to his law office. And I wait for the Invisible Mistress of the house, Emily Norcross Dickinson, my Ma-ma! We are the two Emilies, Pa-pa's best little girls. Ma-ma has bouts of "Neuralgia" that cripple the nerves in her face. And she comes to me with the left side of her face half frozen. Her mouth curls, & she can hardly speak. I have a wish, cruel as it may be, to invite her into my sickbed & have her suck up some steam. But I'm the adoring daughter nonetheless.

"Mother, your skin is positively pale."

She does not have my aurora of red hair. Ma-ma's hair is streaked with gray. Her shoulders are broader than mine, but she slumps in her housedress, filled with fatigue.

I clutch her hand—it feels cold. Her eyes begin to drift.

"Mummy, if you help me into my robe, I will go down to the pantry and make us a scrumptious vanilla pudding. Father need never know."

But she doesn't have the will or the Imagination to conspire. She sits with me on the bed & braids my hair, singing to herself like a child. It was Mother who taught me the art of baking bread. Whatever witchcraft I have in the pantry comes from her.

"Emily," she says, "you are the pale one . . . When you are feeling better, dearest, we will fatten you up like a goose."

A girl without conscience, I cannot help but play at that picture of a fattened goose.

"And then Father will wring my neck, and all the Dickinsons save one will feed on Sister Emily."

"Heaven forbid!" she cries. But I've cured her "Neuralgia" for a moment, and her face begins to unfreeze.

I hold her in my arms and declare, "Mother, it was a jest. I am not a goose at all."

The damage is done. She gets up with a haunted look, caresses my cheek, & trundles out of the room. I curse my own wickedness. I can be Shakespeare with Ma-ma, put on the metal corselet of a prince, weave my words around her, but with Father I am always benumbed.

I push aside Pa-pa's little steam engine, get into my gown, & climb down the stairs in my slippers. I am all giddy with my sudden freedom. I find Mother in the kitchen, reading a recipe. There is a delight on her face I seldom see. Perhaps the clarity of measuring cups soothes her. She looks up in wonder, her mind still caught in a world of ingredients.

"Dearest," she says, in a voice as calm as can be, "what are you doing out of bed?"

"Conspiring to cook an angel cake with Emily Norcross Dickinson."

Unlike the Patriarch, Mother knows how to laugh. She roars with a great rumble up from her belly. There's a mischief in Ma-ma, a wantonness that must have reminded her of my birth, when she brought the paper hanger into the house against Father's command. Does she see the same yellow tulips on the wall in a background of twill? The two Emilies are sisters all of a sudden, with the same stubborn streak. And for a moment we're free of Pa-pa & all mankind.

## 9.

IT'S A MONTH OF DOSINGS AND HOT DRINKS, WITH PA-PA'S physician taking my pulse & peering into my mouth until I began to examine my own speckled tongue in the mirror. Brother would visit with his College cronies, all of them *so* superior to the little nun in bed.

"Austin, should we borrow the girl and hoist her up the flagpole on College Hill?"

I smile my most malicious smile, & even Brother is embarrassed by such remarks. He whispers in my ear. "We will have our revenge. Promise."

Lord, I was becoming the local menagerie. When there wasn't Austin & Amherst College, or Little Sister & her friends, there were the old ladies of the town, who had to glare at the spotted girl with her steam contraption. They must have wearied me *and* my cough, since the coughing stopped, & Father ran out of excuses to keep me as his prisoner.

And one morning in April I'm swept out of bed, & with the whole family traipsing behind him like little ducks, Father puts me on the stage outside the Amherst Hotel. Mother & Little Sister are crying. Austin clutches my hand. He is wearing a silk cravat, and I feel *soiled* beside his handsomeness. But it is Father who carries me onto the stage, though I could have climbed the single step on my own. But I will always be his little invalid, the daughter who had to return from that dame school on account of the croup. Father has given me his own leather satchel, stuffed with gingerbread, angel cake, biscuits, chestnuts, jam, and pie.

"Emily," he says, "you must come back to us without all the foolishness and frumpery of Holyoke dames."

And realizing that there will soon be a good distance between us, I can afford to be bold.

"If you think the dames are such frumps, Father, send me to Austin's school. You could get me in. I'll wear whiskers and join a secret society. Brother will guard our little game."

Father does not laugh. He would be shocked to see me in whiskers, walking on College Hill. His own father helped found the College, ruined himself in the process, & died a broken man. Squire Sam lost the Dickinson Homestead, the first brick house in Amherst, where Brother, Little Sister, & I were born. Father did not abandon the dream of Squire Sam. He rescued the College's finances & became its treasurer. But he never delivered money he did not have. He is, after all, the earl of Amherst—College & town.

Father fights with Democrats all the time. The Democrats would like to form a dictatorship of "fat" farmers, Irish Catholics, & other citified people, while the Whigs are made up of merchants, ministers, bankers, & country lawyers like Pa-pa—"White Heads" who do not labor with their hands. Our Post Master is a Democrat for some reason, & Father finagled to have him removed, but failed, since the Democrats have a certain power in this corner of the Commonwealth. Father does not take kindly to failing. He cannot control the wind, else he would have a tornado tear the roof off the Post Office & hurl the Post Master into the woods. Short of that, he will only satisfy himself when he can repurchase his own father's house.

Even were I a general & a Democrat with my own troops, I still wouldn't go to war against Pa-pa. He has Revolvers in his eyes & could make poor Emily lose her sight. I ruffle his leather satchel with its fundament of cake & pie.

"Father, I will guard these delicacies with my life."

The stage rocks once & takes off from its roost in front of the hotel. I am the lone passenger this morning. We fly from the village with the coachman up front in his tall seat & the baggage boy riding the rear. The wheels seem fragile as we gather speed & I wonder if they will slip from their axles, but we do not crash into a ditch.

The town disappears into a clutch of dots, & suddenly we are overwhelmed by woods. The trees are a maze of rough & surly bark slashed with hints of green. *"It's the slippery season,"* Father loves to say, talking like a farmer in possession of his rye field. But he is even less of a farmer than I am, since I have my own garden that Little Sister tends while I am away. I am a connoisseur of bees, a matriarch of caterpillars, a purveyor of strawberries—but there are nonesuch during the Slippery Season.

LIKE A YOUNG QUEEN IN HER COACH, I ARRIVE AT SOUTH Hadley as the school's single topic. I am the girl who came *up* from Amherst, even though I went down. But such is Holyoke's peculiar geography that it is always *north* of somewhere else. The entire school waits on the piazza, looking at me as if I were rent from another time & place, & not good old Emily of the fourth floor. But soon this strange welcome is over with, & I fall back into the rhythm of silent study.

Rumors are afloat, how Miss Rebecca had to save me from a "liaison" with the Handyman and a trip to Hell. I shudder at the prospect of meeting Missy again. I avoid her and her yellow gloves like the plague. I never had an enemy until I arrived at Holyoke.

I have another room-mate now. Cousin Lavinia, it seems, does not want to slide into Heathenism with a no-hoper such as myself who may have consorted with Satan. She would rather sleep on the third floor, near a dependable bride of Christ. I am pained to be abandoned by my own cousin, a Norcross no less, & Mother's favorite niece. But Emily, the little warrior, would rather die than woo her back. Still, my current room-mate, Florence Stone, is foolish & fickle as the wind, & I can hardly get a word out of her.

"Florence," I ask, "where is our Handyman? Is he well enough to leave his shack?"

She looks at me as if I'd just escaped the asylum.

"*Tom*," I insist. "Lord, you can't possibly miss him. He has the blondest hair in the world."

"I do not know of Tom," she says. "Our Handyman has hair as black as midnight."

"Impossible," I say. "Ill as he was, Tom would not have painted his hair black in a mad fit."

But Holyoke must have raised up magicians & rid itself of Tom during my sojourn south. And in his place was a demon with black hair, Richard Midnight—oh, his surname must have been something else, but I called him Midnight. And he was as different from Tom as night to day. He leered at the girls behind Miss Rebecca's back. I imagined him groping under our pinafores, dreaming of our flesh, fondling us, though I was not privy to what was inside his head.

Richard Midnight was much more about than Tom ever was. He dined with us, sitting at a separate table, but he was endless in his gaze. And when his eyes happened upon me, with my weak chin & dull red hair, I shivered in my seat, because it was as if a shooting star, terribler than I could have imagined, had ripped right into my heart.

Midnight must have heard the rumor about me & Tom & assumed I was part of his personal territory. Lord, I would have loved being pierced by the red arrow of Tom's Tattoo, but not by the gaze of this vulgar man. And I had a suspicion that he would bring harm to myself or another scholar.

# 10.

I TREAD UP TO THE FOURTH FLOOR & FIND A NOTE STUCK to my wardrobe. I recognize Zilpah Marsh's scratchy hand. "*Meet me in the Ironing Room,*" she writes, without offering her initials or her name. I have no business in the basement. My ironing is already done. And so I have to risk a black mark for Zilpah's sake.

I ventured down into that half-lit subterranean world where we dine & do our washing & ironing. There was no one but Zilpah in the ironing room. She was leaning over her board with an iron that must have had all the heat of Hell. That's how loud it hissed. She was working on a pillowcase, & it positively sizzled with each slap of the iron. I hadn't seen Zilpah in a month & I wasn't certain if she was friend or foe. Perhaps she's a little of both.

Zilpah blinks at me. "Jesus, how did you get so thin?"

And before I can answer, she says, "A girl would have to be a fool to fall in love with that brother of yours." Her mustache seems very definite & dark in the somber light of the ironing room. "How many sweethearts does he have?"

I'm loathe to answer her, but there's a demon in Zilpah down in the ironing room.

"You did not even give me a proper introduction," Zilpah says. "He rushed right past me in the parlor. I could have been a piece of dirt."

"I had the croup," I argue like a counselor at law in my own defense, "and Austin was returning me to head-quarters."

"He still could have looked. I had on my prettiest dress. I ironed it until my arm near fell off. But who needs to bother with him? I have a paramour now, and you'll never guess who."

It had to be Richard Midnight. There were no other males in the neighborhood. I feel sorry for Zilpah, that she would give herself to such a snake. That vile man was Mistress Lyon's protégé, according to Zilpah. Mistress had not found him at any orphans' cove in the Northampton Insane Asylum. He was her own distant, distant cousin, a boy who had no head for school & had become a butcher's apprentice. She'd plucked him from a slaughterhouse in Springfield & had him delivered to Holyoke, vile as he was.

"Sister," I say, "Richard Midnight is certainly the Devil."

And Zilpah smiles a smile that is a mite too clever for me. "Oh, I wouldn't bother with that ruffian. His breath is foul. It tastes of puke."

I am most suspicious. "Then who is your man?"

"Tom," says she.

I'm wounded through and through, as if shattered by a pistol shot, but I recover quick enough after I reckon it is a lie.

"Zilpah Marsh, I do not care one jot that you are our class monitor. It's evil to slander Tom. Miss Lyon had him tossed to the wolves, shipped him to the ends of the earth I suppose."

"Gracious," she says. "I visit him ev'ry day."

"How can that possibly be?"

"It's no miracle, Miss Em'ly. Tom the Handyman has the same ol' address—he still resides in his shack."

"Then is it legerdemain?" I ask. "Where does the *other* Handyman sleep?"

"In the church. Miss Lyon rented a room with the cash in her pocket."

I don't believe a syllable, & I wonder if Zilpah herself is in league with the Devil.

"What is Tom doing in the shack if he's no longer the Handyman?"

"Resting," Zilpah says, "recov'ring from that terrible Flue."

It's past the Flue season, and I tell her so, but it doesn't bother her one bit.

"Hell on high water! It's Nature that rules. He near died, Tom did."

I have to pinch my leg, or I might fall wounded again.

"Tom's not strong enough for too much lovin'," says she. "I can only kiss him once or twice a day. But that one kiss is much better than a whole meal."

I want to flee the ironing room & drown myself somewhere, but Zilpah grabs my arm. "Sissy, don't you want to see Tom? He keeps asking for you. He says, 'Zilpah, where's that kind girl with the ratty red hair?' "

⟶

IT'S HARD FOR ME TO IMAGINE ZILPAH WITH TOM, OR THAT MY Tom would ever say I had ratty hair. He was the gentlest of burglars. Perhaps he pined for me, & seized upon Zilpah as second best. But I couldn't wish evil upon her head, even if she took away my Tom. And I can't stop thinking of the baby deer he rescued from the snow.

We sneak out the rear basement door of Holyoke Hall, Zilpah & I, and walk in the April mud to Tom's shack. Zilpah knocks once with her fat fist.

"Tom, I brought you Miss Em'ly. May I come in?"

I hear some gruff reply from within the shack that does not have an ounce of Tom's gentleness, but I am caught in my own excitement to see him, even if he is Zilpah's paramour.

It's very dark inside. But I can catch the outline of a man on Tom's cot. He reaches over & lights the whale-oil lamp while my heart pounds, & I cannot even register my disappointment when I discover Richard Midnight's brutal black hair. The top half of him is positively naked. And the hair on his chest is just as black, & tangled up like a strange forest. I doubt that all men have such a complication of hair as Richard Midnight.

I am trapped between him & Zilpah, who blocks the door.

"Look what the cat dragged in," says Midnight in a thick voice, full of drowsiness & phlegm. "Ain't it the gal that poor Tom smooched? Didn't she live with him in this shack?"

"Darling," says Zilpah, with a purring sound that's close to song—she must have been delirious with her own sense of victory. "I couldn't care if you beat her to death. It's the last time she'll ever humiliate another soul—introducin' me to her brother as if I was a country cow."

"Oh, I wouldn't do much damage," says Midnight, patting the rough cloth of his cot & leering with his usual leer. "Come, sit beside me."

I cannot take my eyes off that tangle of hair on his chest. The perspiration that came off Midnight was like the pungent perfume of a laboring ox.

"I'd rather you did beat me to death," I tell him.

"What? And have Auntie Lyon grieve for you and send me to prison? I won't even lay a finger on ya. I'll just watch you undress, one article at a time. That's as much pleasure as I could ever take from a skinny thing like you."

I stand there in some no-man's-land between disappointment & sadness that I have to look at this creature instead of Tom.

"Well," he says, "I'm a-waitin'. *Undress.*"

But I wouldn't disrobe for Richard Midnight. I might have done so for Tom had he implored me in his own sweet voice, & I would have felt no shame.

"Sis, I'm not waitin' one second more."

I squeeze my eyes shut as he jumps off his cot in his smelly winter pants. He starts to touch my dress. He pokes a finger in my bodice—it feels like a big hot carbuncle. I'm about to scream with the horror of it, & then I hear a scuffle next to the door.

Zilpah begins to whine. "It was just a joke, Missy. I swear to God."

Miss Rebecca has pushed her way through the door with her yellow gloves. She must have smelled Richard Midnight's rankness all the way from Seminary Hall, or else she followed us to the shack, knowing that Zilpah was up to her usual tricks.

Richard Midnight stands as frozen as a deer in a forest upon first encountering humankind—that's what happened when Missy's gaze first fell upon him. But Zilpah pulls her attention away from Midnight.

"Don't you dare hurt my Richard," she sings with false defiance. "Rebecca, I will never, never let you kiss me again."

I watch the whirl of one yellow glove in that wanton light, never having seen so much mystery attached to a slap in the face. Zilpah recoils & sinks to the earthen floor of the shack. And while she sobs softly, Miss Rebecca returns to Richard Midnight.

"Vacate," she rasps, "before I pull the teeth out of your head."

And Richard Midnight spits at her like a snake. "I'll tell Auntie Lyon that you threatened me . . . and that you've been having an unnatural romance with one of her monitors."

"Vacate, I said."

I am under Missy's spell, waiting for that yellow glove to leap again. But Richard Midnight slithers around her in his smelly pants & flees the shack as fast as rotten legs can carry a man. She does not bother with Zilpah, but leaves her sobbing on the floor.

And I wonder when it's my turn. It's time for Rebecca to attack. I'm more dangerous to Missy than Zilpah Marsh or Richard Midnight. I have my father's language and law court, and the breeding of a Dickinson. I wouldn't be startled to learn that Missy was an orphan, like my Tom.

"Come," she says, reaching out to me with a yellow glove. I grip the glove, feel its cool leather skin, feel my fingers in hers. I'm all a-tremble, not from any fear, but from the surety of Miss Rebecca's hand.

# 11.

NO ONE COULD TELL ME WHAT HAD HAPPENED TO TOM. PER-
haps no one knew. He vanished from his shed while I was under
Father's regimen, swallowing corn mush and steam. Tom went to
sea, I opine, heartbroken after he spent a few precious moments
with Miss Em'ly, realizing with his weakened lungs that our love
could never be.

I have to dream that Tom felt *something*, that he took comfort
in my amber eyes, that he adored my tiny, birdlike hands, both of
which he could have captured in one of his paws. And he might
have captured them had he not been so ill. But I have to live in
the land of conjecture concerning Tom. Not so with Richard Midnight & our monitor. Midnight was cast out of Holyoke with barely
the shirt upon his back, even if he was Mary Lyon's distant cousin.
I would have plucked out both his eyes with much pleasure had
Mistress asked me to do so. But contrary creature that I am, I
might have pitied him then & led blind Richard about with his
paw clasped in both my hands.

I also pitied Zilpah Marsh. She had to go before the duchesses
& dowagers of the Female Prayer Circle, who had transmogrified

themselves into a review board upon this rare occasion. The duchesses were quite harsh with Zilpah, since they were the ones who had purchased her tuition at Mt Holyoke & had sponsored her as a scholarship student. Mistress tried to intervene in our monitor's behalf. But the duchesses remained without mercy for this stable hand's daughter who vanished from our little mountain.

"Dear Mary," said their leader, a certain Mrs. Belcher of Belchertown, "sexual congress with a handyman upon seminary grounds? If we countenance that, we might as well call the school Mt Seraglio." I was not privy to such conversation, but at least two of our Seniors swore they overheard Mrs. Belcher in Mary Lyon's sitting room. And even if they exaggerated a little, it could not have been far from the truth.

Zilpah Marsh was locked out of our grace. She was stripped of all her rights. She could not stand with other Seniors at the school's Anniversary, could not graduate with a Certificate, but had to return to Amherst posthaste. Yet our principal did try to protect her. Mary Lyon was not quite so cruel as the Female Prayer Circle. Rather than expel Zilpah Marsh & leave a devastating lifelong black mark, she erased Zilpah from our rolls, thus giving the impression that Zilpah Marsh & Mt Holyoke never existed within the same hemisphere.

Would that it had happened to me and not the stable hand's daughter. Even at seventeen I was not the sentimental sort who cried into her handkerchief about the woes of humankind. But I could not feel guiltless in regard to Zilpah Marsh. To get my own way & have her pilot me to Tom's shack, I had lied & led her on, inducing Zilpah to believe she might have a chance with my brother when she had none. And the moment Austin "spurned" that girl with one brutal glance, she must have plotted her revenge on me.

I missed her, if truth be known. There seemed to be some hollow at school—some implacable hole—where Zilpah had been. I had no one else to rouse me of a morning and lead me to the bake room. My bread & puddings suffered, and I suffered too. Even with her harshness, she had been my one compatriot. And thus I endured my last months at Holyoke as an idle daydream. I wrote to Austin & Little Sister, begging them to unearth the whereabouts of Zilpah Marsh. My dear Lavinia played detective, but could not uncover a single clue. Finally, at my behest, Austin visited the secret society where Zilpah's mother worked as a housemaid, even though Brother had no moral right to be on the society's grounds, since he had pledged himself to another such society.

"*My Dearest Emily,*" Austin wrote the very day of his encounter with Mrs. Marsh. "*You cannot imagine how that poor woman bruised my heart. Shall I describe her? She is a tiny thing, all scrunched over, with hands that resemble a lobster's red claws. She claimed that her one and only daughter was a wicked, wicked girl who had run off with a reprobate employee & relative of Miss Mary Lyon's & asked me did I know a lawyer, since she considered suing Miss Lyon for damages. The seminary in which she had put all her hope had ripped apart her daughter's reputation, said Mrs. Marsh. Sister, I think it is time you came home.*"

And I did come home, a no-hoper who had nightmares for a month. In my dreams I wasn't assaulted by Richard Midnight or Zilpah Marsh. I wasn't asked to disrobe like some harem-girl in a seraglio imagined by Mrs. Belcher of Belchertown. I was caressed by a pair of yellow gloves. But these gloves did not belong to Miss Rebecca Winslow. They belonged to Tom. I could not see his face, only a patch of blond hair. And gentle though Tom be, his diabolical leather scorched my skin. I was tantalized nonetheless. That was the worst part of my torment. I wanted Tom to touch me, & the moment he did, I screamed as I had never screamed before.

*Ben Newton*

He was Father's law student, Ben Newton of Worcester, nine years older than Emily, but he didn't huff at her and show off his brilliance, like Father's other clerks, who had fat hands and chalk on their collars. Ben had beautiful long fingers, like Chopin, and a persistent, nagging cough. It worried her, because he seemed so frail. He'd arrived at Father's office while she was still at Holyoke, and they didn't become friends until she returned to Amherst in August '48. He would often come to dinner, accompanying Father home from work at noon, carrying a mountain of briefs. But legal matters were never discussed at the dinner table, and it distressed Emily that Father had turned poor Newton into a camel that had to carry briefs.

He had an angular face with enormous brown eyes that hid some of his shyness. She wasn't frightened to show him her own scribbling. She didn't know what else to call it. And she wasn't ashamed to confess that poetry mattered to her more than the pumping of her heart.

Ben Newton didn't laugh or make light of this urgency she had kept locked inside for so long. He gave her books to read, and talked of Ralph Emerson, the man of Concord, who had toured the capitals of Europe and met Chopin and Dickens and Lord Tennyson.

Her head reeled at the mention of such firmaments. She was Father's little mouse who had been nowhere, seen nothing and no one. She would have traded all the copper in her hair, lived the rest of her life as a brunette, to breathe in Chopin and his lovely hands for five minutes. And when she told this to Ben Newton, he said, "Miss Emily, I believe that Ralph Emerson would call you the priestess of Pan!"

She was stunned, but she couldn't show her consternation. She ruffled her nose and behaved like a typical Amherst belle. "Why, Benjamin Newton, what could you possibly mean?"

But now he did laugh and immediately had a coughing fit, and she wanted to take this tall shivering man into her arms. She brought him a glass of sherry and he recovered, but he kept a handkerchief near his mouth.

"I wasn't being spiteful, Miss Emily. I meant to say that I can feel you take on the limbs of a poet."

"You mustn't flatter me, Ben. I'm a country girl, and you a Worcester man. You ought to take pity."

"I'm the one ought to be pitied. It's Mr. Emerson who writes that the priestess of Pan has to shun father, mother, sister, brother, and friends the moment that her genius calls."

She might have fainted, fell to the floor, if she hadn't been so concerned with Ben Newton's cough. How could she have shunned Father, Mother, Austin, and Little Sister, even if she ever did become the priestess of Pan? She was a country girl with note paper in her pocket and a mechanical pencil that worked only when it wanted and might make her fingers bleed on account of the splinters in its blue glass. And one afternoon Ben saw the blood and wrapped her writing hand in a wad of cotton, as if she had been wounded in war.

"That's a mighty poor mechanical pencil, ma'am, if it makes you a casualty every time you use it."

"It's a king's pencil," she had to explain. "Father found it for me in Boston. And I would not dream of betraying him by using an inferior pencil with inferior lead."

*Ben cut through her vanity by applying a bandage to her king's pencil. That's how he became her Tutor, and he might have been her Tutor for life if he hadn't gone back to Worcester. But she had him to herself for a whole year while he slaved at Father's office.*

*Ben Newton worried about her immortal soul, while she worried about his cough. She looked for signs of blood in his rumpled handkerchief, but found none. She meant to seduce him in church, sit next to him, and brush against his hand. But he wouldn't go to church with Emily, wouldn't sit in the Dickinson pew. Ben was a Unitarian. He didn't believe in hellfire, and he didn't have any truck with the Devil. Ben's Lord God wouldn't have frowned upon a priestess of Pan, and would have set aside a room in His domain for an apprentice poet.*

*Emily no longer knew what to think. She would have liked to have the Lord at her side while she wielded her mechanical pencil. And her Tutor said that Lord Jesus wasn't the Son of God, but a man with a gift for poetry who could heal the sick and the lame with words alone. Emily wouldn't contradict her Tutor, but she didn't believe that words could heal; they were dipped in hellfire. And she did believe in the Devil. But she had no one to sail with into the wind, to pull against her own ballast, without Ben. She wished that Father would take him into his law firm, not as a fledgling, but as a full partner. But Ben had no strong desire to remain in Amherst. And Emily imagined that he had a sweetheart waiting for him in Worcester, though he did not seem to carry her silhouette in his pocket.*

*So she beguiled him as long as she could. Yet what did she have to offer? A short stop at a female seminary where Ralph Emerson would have been the same as the Devil? A mask of freckles on her face? How could she ever hope to compete with a Worcester girl? She would have to devour the best parts of him like a bear in the forest, but she wasn't the devouring kind, not with her Tutor.*

*They would walk in the burying-ground behind Father's house on West Street, where the Dickinsons had moved when Emily was nine or ten. Grandpa Samuel had nearly bankrupted Father, who lost the family Mansion and whose only dream was to buy it back. But Emily didn't have the same wish. She liked the phantoms in the graveyard, feared them too, and the sound of the wind against the tall stones often soothed her on winter nights, rocked inside her head.*

*But there was little wind in the burying-ground that afternoon when her Tutor announced that he was returning to Worcester. It was like the unwinding of a marriage that never was, the dissolution of whatever small indemnity she had with Ben while he was still in bondage to Father's firm. She wouldn't cry in a graveyard. But her Tutor didn't even hold her hand. She could see the mask of death he wore, the pale mouth and bloodless eyes, and she felt like an evil witch who could only fall upon pictures of decay.*

*"Miss Emily," he said in the softest voice, "I would be grievously disappointed if I did not live long enough to see you become a poet."*

*And she chided him out of her own despair. "Why, Mr. Ben, you are a bit selfish. I'm already the priestess of Pan. Ain't that good enough?"*

*He laughed once, and in some paroxysm of feeling he kissed her hand. That was his goodbye. And she could have survived on that kiss for months if her king's pencil hadn't broken a day after her meeting in the graveyard. The blue glass split in half. It was the very worst omen she could imagine, as if that kind Lord of the Unitarians had deserted Emily and her desire to write.*

# PART TWO

## *Carlo and Currer Bell*

## 12.

"I FELT IT A MISFORTUNE THAT I WAS SO LITTLE, SO PALE, and had features so irregular and so marked." So said Jane Eyre, who was as plain and little as a certain Emily Dickinson. I wondered if she had a scalp as red as mine. No matter. There was a controversy that raged around the book. Was its author, Currer Bell, a woman or a man? Not a soul could say. The reading club at Austin's fraternity had sponsored a debate on that subject up on College Hill. The debate happened to fall in the middle of Valentine Week, during the height of winter festivities, but the parlor at Johnson Chapel was still packed with Austin's own brothers from Alpha Delta Phi, a few select Seniors from some other secret society, a couple of Tutors, two or three of Amherst's most stunning belles, and plain little Emily, who might never have been invited to this elite and wicked soiree had she not been related to Austin *and* the Squire, who, as College treasurer, was chief of the Charity Fund that helped some of the Seniors pay their bills.

*Jane Eyre* had hit Amherst by storm just as the first snow fell. Our ministers preached against the book, called its female narrator a slattern and a witch. The Amherst Sewing Circle claimed to have destroyed every single copy it could find, but its members could still recite half of Jane's soliloquies by heart. No one seemed immune to the book save Father himself, who despised Madame de Staël and every other female novelist in creation. And, in order not to offend him, I hid my copy under the piano cover. It was safe there, since Mother rarely reads and Vinnie was away at the Ipswich Female Academy, Father having decided to keep her as far from Mt Holyoke as he could. And even if Mother had found the book perchance, she couldn't have read a line in her afflicted state. She had another of her Neuralgia attacks, and could do little more than lie on the lounge. She couldn't even go on one of her "rambles," and deliver winterberry pies to the poor of the town. With Mother indisposed and a decent cook hard to hire, I was grand marshal of the kitchen—Lord, someone had to feed Father, and Austin, when he wasn't with his fraternity brothers.

But Currer Bell's admirer had done all her chores on this winter night and could sit with Alpha Delta Phi in Johnson Chapel. The debate was run by George Gould, who was attached to Amherst's monthly magazine, *The Indicator*. He was the proper person to rule over us, since he was near seven feet tall and towered over everyone at Johnson Chapel. Gould was Brother's best friend, and I will not lie: he was one of my suitors. I had seven all told, seven in one season, but it was nothing to swagger about—a prettier girl might have had a dozen or two had she been blessed with the same conditions: the closest proximity as could be to Alpha Delta Phi and the treasurer of Amherst College. But my giant suitor had played a trick on me.

I'd written him a mock Valentine, full of the wildest language, inviting him to a "tryst" that was more like a duel, suggesting swords, a pen, or a plough. And Gould published my "gewgaw" in *The Indicator*, advertising the author as an anonymous female who was as much of a witch as Jane Eyre. But half of Amherst knew that the witch in question was Squire Dickinson's daughter. Father got wind of it soon enough, and I had my own little dressing-down. He'd praised Austin's college compositions, considered publishing them in a book, likened Brother's Prose to Shakespeare. And goodness, there was little left for me. He must have feared I would become another Madame de Staël. He did not want an *Authoress* in the family. I'd never seen his face so raw and red. I worried he might have an attack of apoplexy. Lavinia was away in Ipswich, and Mother was fast asleep, or the two of them might have felt the house shake in rhythm to Father's wrath.

*"Emily, did you conspire in having that 'epistle' of yours published?"*

I was not so innocent a party. Gould had not injured me. I realized that my talented, tall nincompoop would run with Valentine in hand to Henry Shipley, Austin's rival at Phi Upsilon and editor-in-chief of *The Indicator*, and that Shipley would indeed publish it as the "gewgaw" of the month. Shipley was a poisonous fellow, a provocateur who'd print *anything* that could bring attention to himself and his magazine. He was also an unenviable slurper of rum who drank so much Domingo in the morning he had to crawl up and down College Hill. Gould had to rescue him from one rum resort or another. And so I whispered right into the eye of Father's hurricane, frightened as I was.

*"I did most certainly conspire."*

*"And what will the trustees think of my elder daughter?"* he'd asked on that occasion. *"You might just as well advertise all our linen on college grounds."*

And there I was, like Jane herself, hovering between "absolute submission and determined revolt."

*"Father, I assure you, I will never show our linen again."*

I longed to ask him what kind of linen Austin's compositions revealed, but I would not make sport of my own brother.

And now I am at Johnson Chapel, surrounded by Seniors. There is an aura of panic on College Hill. Burglars have seized our town. They broke into the President's mansion and took off with vases, paintings, and a priceless clock. Students and professors have formed their own vigilance committees and rush around with lanterns, but it's not a burglar who surprises us. Shipley enters with the odor of rum upon him, his eyes shot with blood, his cravat covered in filth. A seat is found for him, and my erstwhile suitor rises on his long legs to begin the debate. I notice how large Gould's ears are, how thin his face, and what a great big beak he has, like a peregrine.

"Seniors and fair maidens, the topic tonight is Currer Bell. Once and for all, is the mysterious author of *Jane Eyre* a maiden or a man?"

"A man," shouts Shipley from his seat. "Currer Bell is most decidedly a man. I'll wager my own teeth on that. The book has real style, and such style is a sure stamp of male authorship."

The members of Alpha Delta Phi and Phi Upsilon all agree. So do the Amherst maidens.

"What does Miss Emily Dickinson think?" asks my tall suitor.

I was terrified to utter a sound in front of College Seniors, who, at Austin's urge, had invited me on sleigh rides, to Senior levees at the President's house, and to candy pulls and sugaring parties in the woods; several of them had served almost as my Tutors. Their mastery of books was far greater than mine. And what could a former nun of Holyoke tell them about *Jane Eyre*?

But I could not disappoint Brother, who loved to boast about his little literary sister.

"No simple Authoress," I say with a certain air, "could ever have endowed Jane with so beguiling a voice."

The Seniors clap their hands and shout "Bravo!" while the belles of Amherst look at me askew, wishing *they* had said what I said, but their fathers had not permitted them to read the book, I opine, so they had little opinion of their own.

And then a voice roars out from the rear of the room. It belongs to Brainard Rowe, a Tutor visiting us from Yale. Unlike our Seniors, he wears a wide-brimmed velvet hat and a long winter cape rather than an overcoat. I had seen him on College Hill several times, but he had never joined our sleigh rides or our sugaring parties. Shipley had corrupted him, I was told, since he frequented our rum resorts. But he wasn't gawky, with bulging eyes, like Gould. He was short, dark, with a barrel chest, like Mr. Edward Rochester, master of Thornfield Hall, he who wanted to marry Jane while he had a wild wife imprisoned in the attic.

"I disagree with Miss Dickinson and the entire Senior class," says Brainard Rowe. "The book would be an utter sham had it been written by a member of our own privileged sex, and Jane a mere paradigm of goodness and virtue without her own sharp tongue."

"Brainard," says Mr. Shipley, "I cannot concur. Are you arguing that no man could possibly possess half of Jane's spirit while he plays at being a woman in his own glass?"

"*Yes,*" says Amherst's visiting Tutor. "The book is not apery. It thrills us and tortures us because the voice of Currer Bell is new. We have not found its like in any earlier woman's novel. She dares to become the Satan of her own sex."

"That's close to blasphemy," says Gould, who hopes to become a minister, like so many of our Seniors. "You wound us, dear Brainard, saying that none of us—no male—could have written *Jane Eyre.* Jane may wear a sharp tongue, but she also has a female modesty. She spurns Rochester and will not become his mistress."

"Would that she had," says Brainard Rowe. "She'd have spared Rochester and herself a lot of misery. He wouldn't have ended up a wreck of a man, blind, with one arm."

"You toy with us," says Shipley with a most bitter smile.

"Perhaps," says the Tutor. "But Jane's not acquiescing to become Rochester's mistress has nothing to do with female modesty."

"Then what is it?" asks a member of Phi Upsilon.

"Sympathy," says Brainard Rowe.

"With whom?"

"The first Mrs. Rochester."

"How can that be?" asks Gould. "She's described as a dark and crouching monkey, a fiend."

"Ah, but does not our own society acquiesce to the notion of wild women in the attic? Do we not consider *all* females half mad?"

"Now that is going too far," says another Senior.

"Much too far," say the Amherst belles, but I am trembling. Brainard Rowe was like a visitor not from Connecticut, but from Mars, who could look at males and females with his own peculiar slant.

The reading club disperses as most of the Seniors march out of Johnson Chapel. They've turned their backs on the visiting Tutor. Austin and Gould are much more civilized. They'd invited Brainard Rowe to the reading club of Alpha Delta Phi and would not leave without him. He discovers my Newfoundland sitting with that ferocious loyalty of his near the door of Johnson Chapel.

"Who's that?"

"Carlo, my dog."

Brainard laughs as I knew he would. Rochester had a Newfoundland like mine, a huge blur of black and white hair, but his name was Pilot. Carlo was a pointer in *Jane Eyre*; he belonged to that monkish minister, St. John Rivers, who rescued Jane from starvation and wanted her to accompany him to India as his missionary wife in a loveless marriage.

And Brainard addresses me in a language that went way beyond Brother and Gould.

"Miss Emily Eyre," says he. "Why didn't you name your dog Pilot, after Rochester's faithful Newfoundland?"

"Because Rivers is much closer to my own temperament, Sir, willing to sacrifice himself to some abstract religion that could be about God or the Devil disguised as art."

"Are you a sacrificer too?"

"Much more so than St. John Rivers."

And thus we tramp down College Hill in the snow, with Gould

clutching a lantern and Carlo as our leader, as he always is. He's taller than his mistress, with his head and tail held high. I had never asked for a dog, could not have imagined owning one. But with Vinnie at school and Mother at the fag end of some private tether, the Squire did not want me to be all alone in the house when he was away on business. And so he found me Carlo as my companion. It was lonely without Lavinia, but Carlo rules me now. I fly with him across the village in wind or snow as Carlo chases whatever rodents are around. Amherst and College Hill have both been besieged by housebreakers, but who would dare disturb me while Carlo prowls?

And so we return to West Street, with its burial ground, its black-smith, and its white manor-houses, but neither Austin, nor Gould, nor Brainard Rowe went inside with me. They abandon Miss Emily Eyre and race to a rum resort near the College. And I recollect what Jane herself had said—that men would shove us into a box where we make puddings and knit stockings, while I long to taste Domingo in a rum resort, with Carlo at my side.

# 13.

WHAT CAN I REVEAL ABOUT MR. GEORGE HENRY GOULD? HE wanted to make me his missionary wife. He'd cart me to another town (or continent) where he would deliver his sermons, with much fire I suppose, and I would have to feed him pudding and raise up a family of little Goulds. But I found it hard to fit myself into George Henry's picture of matrimonial bliss. I wasn't a Gould and could never be one. I was a Dickinson who communed with Carlo, talked to him night and day. But even the grandest belle in Amherst was considered an old maid at twenty, and I was only nine or ten months from that perilous age.

The future reverend wore me down with his persistence. I have a difficult time looking up into his eyes, since I'm no higher than his navel. He keeps asking if he might talk to Father about his intentions. And finally I tell myself: let Father decide.

Gould arrives in frock coat and silk cravat, looking like a minister or a baron with one frayed cuff. Mother is asleep on the lounge, and Father escorts Gould into the library. Father's face is as stern as Rochester's, and I wonder if I had invited poor Gould to his own suicide. I expect to hear sparks slap against the door—I heard nothing but the constant tick of Father's clock, like a dead man's toll. I did not want Father to annihilate Gould, just to scare him off from marrying me. But the world was much larger than Emily Dickinson's dreams. Laughter broke through the door, not Gould's, but the laugh of a lion.

Then Father strode out of the library with my suitor. Mr. Gould was smiling from ear to ear, like one of Lavinia's well-fed cats. Had Father sold me to him for silver? I panic until I recall that Gould had no silver. He didn't even have a sou. Then what kind of unholy bargain could he have struck with my father? Gould's long, spindly face swoops down and he pecks me on my brow, just like a man might kiss his intended bride. I can feel my own cheeks tremble, as if a case of Neuralgia were coming on.

"Miss Emily," he asks, "will I see you at the next candy pull?"

I fake a smile. "I hope you will, Mr. Gould." But I am burning with venom against Pa-pa. He waits until Gould leaves and then returns to the library.

"Emily," he sings like a man satisfied with himself, "where's my supper?"

"There is none. I'm much too busy. I have to prepare my trousseau."

"What the dickens are you talking about?"

"Well, didn't you marry me off? Am I not destined to be Mrs. Emily Elizabeth Gould, lately of Hindustan and Illinois?"

And I have a dose of Father's new artillery—that lion's roar of his. "There will be no brides or bridesmaids. I cannot believe you are in love with Mr. Gould."

The poison is mounting deep within my well. "And what if I were?"

"He's a pauper. The boy cannot pay his bills."

"And if I fell in love with another just like Gould?"

I have pulled his sudden joy right out from under him. He is Rochester again, with a frozen face.

"Then I would sit you down with your intended and convince you not to marry until his circumstances improved."

"And if his circumstances should remain bleak?"

Suddenly my voice is a notch or two above my usual whisper in Father's house. I baffle him with this strange battering ram, she who seldom spoke more than a sentence to him in a single day.

"Emily, must I be quizzed like a counselor-at-law?"

"But you are a counselor-at-law. What did you do with my Mr. Gould?"

"What I always do. I negotiated."

"My marriage?" I ask.

"Not at all. A new loan. He could not meet his bills even with what he got from the Charity Fund."

"And that is why he pecked me on the forehead? Because you made him fat with silver?"

"No," says Father, startled by my ferocity. "I gave your Gould a reprieve. I told him to ask for your hand again in six months. But it was a sinister move, I admit. You will have other suitors in six months."

"And none fine enough for you."

"*Dolly,*" he says, hoping to vanquish me by appealing to my pet name. "I haven't enough force in me to prevent you from marrying the man you love. Now will you feed me, for God's sake?"

I have prepared his supper, of course. There was no one else to do it. Father could not seem to hire a dependable household drudge. All our former maids took to drink and would tipple in the midst of serving a meal, and Father would find his soup in his lap. The more he raged, the faster these women ran from West Street, and Father's reputation fell—he was considered a curmudgeon in the little Irish warrens behind the hat factory, where most of the women hail from. No one in Belchertown or Amherst seemed inclined to work for "Master Edward," as he was called. He was a hard master, and hardest on his own horse. I might happen upon

him at the barn, beating Horse Henry for having the boldness to
steer him into a snowbank or cause his best pantaloons to be covered in slush. But Horse Henry isn't at the table. I am with Pa-pa. I
serve him a casserole from the sideboard, cut him two thick slices
of my rye and Indian bread. Mother is still on the lounge. Neuralgia has left her without an appetite.

Suppers on West Street are usually simple affairs, but Father is
ravenous tonight. Mother comes to the table with her sewing basket in the middle of the meal. She darns Father's winter stockings
as if she were in a dream. I'm in too much of a tempest to taste
a morsel. I haven't relinquished all the poison in my well. The
venom courses through my veins.

I serve Pa-pa his pudding. I have to mouth "Lord Jesus" over
and over to prevent myself from pouring a dollop upon his crown
of unruly red hair.

"What are you muttering?"

"Nothing, Father."

He is Bluebeard with red side-whiskers, serving up daughters
instead of wives. I will never leave this castle. He will decline whatever suitor I bring to West Street. Father might let Lavinia escape,
but not me. It's not my Indian bread *per se*. He could find another
baker. But Father seems to count on the little storms I create. Perhaps he imagines my face in his own mirror—the hobgoblin with
red hair whom he cannot live without. Such an imp can shatter his
isolation. I am his Dolly, sentenced to serve him puddings for the
rest of his natural life and most of mine.

I would not marry Mr. Gould even if he could wrench me away
from this castle. But I cannot get that Tutor from Mars out of my
mind. I do not believe that Father could ever bribe Mr. Brainard Rowe, who must have a thousand and ten sweethearts in New
Haven and would have small use for some modest belle from
Amherst with a squirrel's mouth.

# 14.

BROTHER REPORTS BACK TO HEAD-QUARTERS LIKE A SERGEANT major. He's recommended the housekeeper from his rival fraternity, Phi Upsilon, who is sick of having her Seniors revel in rum resorts and return with their coats soiled and with a sulking nastiness about them. It is Zilpah's mother, Mrs. Marsh, and she can provide a list of references as long as a scholar's scroll. President Hitchcock has appropriated her himself for certain Senior levees.

I do not utter a word. I haven't forgotten my halcyon days and nights at Holyoke, when Zilpah Marsh tried to mutilate me in the Handyman's shack behind Holyoke Hall. But I would not hold a daughter's sins against Mrs. Marsh. Ma-ma cannot aid in the interview. She is too ill. And so Father interviews the housekeeper on his own while I am out with Carlo, who has made himself master of the town. We have become an infamous couple, Carlo and I, as we sail into the snow, most of me hidden behind the dog's great black coat. Carlo can sniff out suspicious characters within one glance of a particular street.

He should have sniffed closer to home. I was suspicious the second Father told me that the housekeeper he had hired had gone to that nun's school in the hills, as he likes to call Holyoke, and had used my name as a reference.

"Father, how many housekeepers within your knowledge ever attended a female seminary?"

"Should I hold that against her?" he asks with all the acumen of the town's foremost lawyer.

"How old does she happen to be?"

"Hard to tell. Her face is worn with worry marks."

"And does she have a faint mustache?"

"No," says the Squire. "Not that I can remember."

I still should have told father to *unhire* her, but I did not. There was the lingering guilt that I had played the serpent with Zilpah, enticing her, rattling Austin in front of her eyes.

—✺—

"ZILPAH MARSH, YOU MAY HAVE FOOLED MY FATHER, BUT I have seen your sinister side. You will be out the door at the first sign of any contretemps. And if you are co-habiting with Richard Midnight, as his mistress or his wife, you will not be long in Father's employ."

I barely have the breath to complete so large a soliloquy. Father is not so wrong about Zilpah. She is wizened with worry marks.

"I left that maniac," says she. "And sorry I am, Miss Em'ly, that he was ever born."

"And why are you impersonating your mother?"

"Because who would hire me?"

"But you have an education. You could be a scrivener, work in a lawyer's office. You could teach school."

"I was thrown out of Holyoke with not one word of commendation. Mistress Lyon might have written a kind word, but Mistress is gone."

She expired the year after I left Holyoke, having failed to convert every single scholar into a bride of Christ. And Miss Rebecca withdrew with her yellow gloves behind the walls of another female seminary.

"Zilpah Marsh, I am not a demon, nor am I a tattletale. I will not ruin your chances here."

"You won't be sorry, Mistress."

She wanted to kiss my hands, but I could not bear to reign over her. Whatever defect she might have had, it was not in the matter of intellect. Zilpah Marsh is my equal, whether she works for us or not. That doesn't mean I am not wary. I watch her all the time. Thus she curtails my outings with Carlo, but I have to be on my guard. I can feel a tremor of violence in her, but I do not warn Pa-pa. I will be the policeman of the house. Yet she is kind to Mother—perhaps too kind—and cares for her while Mother has her attacks of Neuralgia. She has even assumed the burden of Mother's knitting, and now it is Zilpah Marsh who darns Father's winter stockings, Zilpah who bastes the chicken, Zilpah who pumps the water and lights the stoves.

Father is enchanted with her and boasts to his law clerks that he has a housekeeper who went to Holyoke. It worries me that Zilpah might become the siren of West Street. But how can I fault a housekeeper for her refined Prose? I am the wicked one. I am already plotting how to rid myself of her, hoping that Father might recommend her to some law office, even his own. But the Squire seems content to keep his housekeeper under lock and key.

And there was one last hurdle: Austin. Would she shiver in his presence, swoon when she served him a rack of lamb? But she was as calm as a sea captain around Brother, did not fawn over him, and Austin would never have recognized her as the monitor with a mustache from Holyoke Hall. She says not a word to him, nodding her head at any of his wants and calling him the young master of the house.

Zilpah could have lived with us, but I did not invite her to do so. She arrived just after dawn and went home late, but I had no idea where exactly her home was. I assumed she lived with her mother somewhere behind the hat factory. Zilpah did not tipple, did not drink, like our earlier housekeepers, and I had no cause to be alarmed about anything she did away from West Street. I was no longer a policeman beyond our door.

And then one morning she startles me. I catch her in the kitchen wearing yellow gloves. The sight of that shiny leather wakes unwanted memories.

"Zilpah, did Rebecca Winslow give you her gloves?"

"Yes, Mistress. Missy mailed them to me."

"I'd rather you not wear them in this house."

"But they are most practical, Mistress, when I have to light the stoves or climb under the sink. And I was hoping that Missy's gloves would not prejudice you against me."

I could not counter her arguments, and I did not want to be willful about the gloves. And so I had to swallow the memory of that assassin-poet who first wore them. But Zilpah's presence reminded me of an earlier housekeeper whom I adored: Evelyn O'Hare. She was practically my nurse, though she could neither read nor write. It was before we moved to West Street. I was six when Evelyn arrived. I loved her and became her schoolmistress while she did her chores and minded me and Lavinia. Whatever I learned at school I taught to Evelyn. She would brush my hair for hours, confide in me, talk of the "young lads"—carpenters or handymen—she intended to marry.

She smoked a pipe when Mother and the Patriarch weren't around. The burning tobacco smelled like a foreign flower, sweet *and* tart. Evelyn talked of her trousseau and all the treasure she would accumulate from her many husbands. Father had found her in an orphanage, said she was the best servant he ever had. She would bake him pies and stand silent at his shoulder until he drew her into a conversation. The Patriarch liked to discuss law with Evelyn, said she had "an undiluted mind."

But when Father went off to serve in the State House and lived in Boston for months at a time, Evelyn seemed to suffer as much as we did. She began muttering to herself and neglecting her chores. Mother found her in the kitchen one afternoon with a knife in her hand. The town marshal had to carry Evelyn out in a horse blanket. And she was carted off to the Lunatic Hospital at Worcester. Mother's relatives called her deranged. But Evelyn's "derangement" grew out of sadness and grief. She worshiped Father and couldn't survive the winter without him.

And, if truth be told, a little of my fondness for Evelyn leaked onto Zilpah Marsh. Zilpah wasn't an orphan, but she might as well have been. She wouldn't have been made invisible by the matriarchs at Mt Holyoke, removed from the rolls, and tossed into limbo, if she had ever had a father like mine. And so I was considerate of her, in spite of those yellow gloves.

## 15.

WE ARE IN THE MIDST OF THE MATING SEASON. VALENTINES continue to fly like missiles, and every belle seems to have a horde of beaus—every belle save one, since my tall suitor no longer seems to count once he bartered my love away to lighten his College bills, and my other suitors, nameless upon my lips, do not have the worth of one lemon cake. I considered writing a Valentine to that Tutor from Mars, Brainard Rowe, but I had no idea where to send it. Mars did not have a Post Office, according to my recollections. And I felt extremely barren, though the words ran amuck inside my head.

"*Sir,*" I compose like some hapless truant, "*I have neither the wit nor the charm to persuade you, but should you have the urge to meet, I will meet you anywhere.*" And I sign my missile, *Currer Bell.*

Of course it travels to no other place but the circuits and lanterns of my brain. And stillborn love notes provide small satisfaction. But I do not mope or lie on the lounge with a pretended case of Acute Neuralgia. Nor do I absent myself from the usual round of winter partying. And when Gould invites me to the candy pull, I come along with Carlo. It takes a feat of engineering to cart a Newfoundland *and* six Seniors on a one-horse sleigh, but Austin is our driver, and Father has permitted him to lure Horse Henry out of the barn for such a special occasion. And little Currer Bell doesn't count, being part flesh and part fantasy.

Sitting with Austin now, I recollect the rides we had together as children, and the times we would talk for hours, our faces in candlelight, turning us into creatures with a sinister glow. Brother was the first to have a Lexicon, and we perused his book under the fickle tyranny of a candle that obscured one word and lit another. And what a random list we had to explore. *Exaltation—Estate—Dirk—Doom—Diadem—Petal—Paragraph.* Brother had a deeper Imagination than a little girl without a Lexicon. He could splinter each word into a hundred parts, or create a stringed jewel, such as *Diadems of Dirks and Doom,* or *A Petal of Estates and Paragraphs.* But such poetry has now fled from his face. He has inherited a portion of Mother's Neuralgia and steers our sleigh with a frozen cheek.

I ride up front with Carlo, and miraculously the sleigh does not crash into a tree or tip over as we climb the hills. But Brother rules the roads and paths like Genghis Khan, and we nearly bump into a sugar-house, which could not have survived the strain of a horse, a dog, and so many Seniors. But our runners swerve at the very last moment, and the sugar-house is saved.

It is a primitive shed where the sap from nearby trees is collected and boiled down in a gigantic kettle to give us our supply of syrup and maple sugar. The sugar boys who stir the pot with ladles tall as a man do not wear shirts inside the shed. I can thank the Lord that they do not have a forest of black hair on their chests, like Richard Midnight, that renegade from Mt Holyoke. And these shirtless boys don't leer at me. They warm themselves in the hissing heat of the vapors that rise off the kettle. But their torsos have turned brown during the whole process of sugaring-off until they look like creatures made of mountain tar. I am caught in their spell.

The sugar boys are shy among College Seniors. College Hill is a

sacred place for these sons of farmers who have had little school-
ing and can hardly spell their names. But they feed us the sweet
liquid from the ladle that hardens into candy in a second and will
not permit us to pay them. They seem to take pleasure in having us
regard their brown torsos. Their muscles ripple under that strange
sticky tar, and they have a quiet beauty that I can find nowhere but
inside a sugar-house.

Our little idyll is interrupted. Henry Shipley, that wanton editor of *The Indicator* who published my Valentine, barrels into the
sugar-house with a group of Seniors from Phi Upsilon, mischief in
their red eyes. They must have come from the nearest rum resort,
since the aroma of Domingo is unmysteriously on their lips. They
challenge the farmers' sons, claim they have captured the sugar-
house for Phi Upsilon, and are now in complete charge of the
kettle.

Austin has to step into Shipley's way.

"Your rudeness is insufferable," he says. His frozen cheek has
begun to twitch.

"And you, Sir," says Shipley, "are trespassing upon the territories
of Phi Upsilon. This is *our* sugar-house."

I am concerned about Brother and the sugar boys, since Shipley has brought half of Phi Upsilon, and it seems like open warfare
between the two societies. But another man enters the sugar-house
in cape and floppy velvet hat, a scarf wrapped around his throat.
It is my Tutor from Mars, and he must have been to the same rum
resort with Phi Upsilon. He bows to me and smiles.

"Hello, Currer Bell. Forgive this intrusion. Mr. Shipley was about
to leave."

"I will not leave," says Shipley. "And no Alphas can make me do
so."

"Pity," says the Tutor. "Would you rather find yourself stuck in
Carlo's jaws?"

"Who's Carlo?" Shipley asks, his eyes like sinister red needles.

"The Newfoundland that Austin's sister is restraining as hard she can. You are an imbecile among imbeciles. Do you think that dog would allow you to attack a member of the family?"

Shipley is polite as a schoolboy all of a sudden.

"Brother Brainard, I apologize to one and all . . . I never even noticed a dog."

The Tutor had done well to come when he did. As much as Carlo was devoted to my every whim, he would have destroyed Phi Upsilon if *that* fraternity had dared lay a finger on Austin.

Shipley withdrew with his band of Seniors, and I was hoping that our Savior in the scarf would remain with us, but he did not. He had courage enough to scratch Carlo's head. No lesser personage would have attempted to do so. And then he absconds with his dastardly brothers on the Phi Upsilon sleigh, while Austin clutches his frozen cheek.

Dare I understand Brother's dilemma? I'm no prophetess. I'm not even Currer Bell. But I grew up with Austin, sat beside him at supper, breathed his very breath. The answer's in his Lexicon. Austin couldn't recover from his own enchantment, his *Diadem of Dirks*. Father has groomed him to be a master of legal documents, a prince of the courts, while Brother has a softer side that rebels against the law. I should have had the whiskers, I want to tell him, and he should have become an enchantress of Petals and Paragraphs. I'd have argued Father's cases in a lawyer's black shirt, while he wandered amid the butterflies in a crown of red hair.

We are one creature, Brother and I, but both of us inhabit the wrong half. I have to depend on suitors and their silly Valentines, when I'd love to wear a hawk's wings and pursue my own prey, while Brother has to invest all his power to conjure up an ideal wife. Meanwhile he drives Horse Henry away from the sugarhouse, while I'm the one who dreams of Dirks.

# 16.

DESPERATE AS I WAS, I WENT ON AS MANY EXCURSIONS AS I could with Carlo, but I never seemed to encounter Brainard Rowe on whatever route or trail we took. I might have asked Brother's help in finding Brainard, but it would have lessened Austin in the eyes of his fraternity brothers, since said Tutor was in the Phi Upsilon camp. And so I had to conspire on my own.

But I haven't lost the Dickinson edge. I practice my honeyed talk on the housekeeper.

"Zilpah, where might one find a rum resort?"

I cannot fool her so readily. "Mistress, why in God's name would you ever want to know?"

"Speak. Have you ever been to one?"

"They are not enamored of females," says she. "They wouldn't let you in without an escort."

"But have you been to one?"

"Yes, Mistress. Once, with a very bad man."

"Richard Midnight?"

"Yes, Mistress, before I found religion and returned to the Lord."

"And where was it? *Tell!*"

"On the far side of the Commons, at the very edge of Merchants Row."

"And what is it called?" I ask in my usual whisper, like some disinterested detective.

"Tardy Tavern. But it isn't a tavern. It's a noxious hole in the wall. And a decent young lady like yourself ought not go there, never in her life."

～

I WOULDN'T LISTEN TO ZILPAH MARSH. I STROLL ALONG THE Commons with Carlo at five of an afternoon, suspicious of pitfalls in the swampy ground. But the swamp is frozen in February, and I sail above solid snow. Commencement is held on the Commons and our October Cattle Show, when Mother rises out of her torpor to act as a judge for one or two of the prizes. The Commons is also where our militia holds maneuvers and our children launch their kites. But no one, not President Hitchcock nor the Merchants Association, has ever dreamed of draining the swamp. It's malodorous in summer, slippery in autumn, and treacherous in winter, since there are always soft spots even in the solidest snow, and local legend has it that one mad dowager drowned in the winter swamp centuries ago.

But I do not intend to drown in a sloping field of ice. And Carlo can test the firmness of the ground with his magnificent paws. It's the rum resort that worries me, not the variables of our village green. My heart pounds the moment I arrive at Tardy Tavern. It is a hole in the wall, with nothing to announce itself but a card in its filthy window. And its entrance, barely visible, was in an alley at the southern edge of Merchants Row.

I could not bring Carlo inside—he would have terrorized the place. And so I park him in the alley as my sentinel and pull on the bell. Nothing happens. I pull again, and a gruesome man with

a seam on the side of his face opens the door. He must have been
the rum resort's very own guardian. He's clutching a baker's battledore and might have crowned me with it had he not discovered
Carlo at my feet.

"Missy, this is a private club. It's not open to strangers."

"I am not a stranger," I have to insist.

"That's welcome news. But friend or foe, you are a woman
accompanied by a dog and not by one of our regular patrons."

"But I have an escort other than my dog."

"And who is that?" he asks, leaning his damaged, diabolical
head into the alley and sniffing the cold air.

"Brainard Rowe."

He vanished, but I knew I had the right key to get into this
cave. I was not left in the lurch for very long. That gruesome
man reappeared and led me into the rum resort, which was no
larger than our kitchen on West Street and had several long
tables, around which was a scattering of Seniors who resembled
scarecrows in the crooked light that came off the rum resort's
lone lantern. They must have been the college's "lost souls," the
flotsam of Phi Upsilon, Seniors who would never graduate, having ruined themselves on rum.

I thought to depart from this wretched place, but the guardian
held me with his mean little eyes and a flick of his battledore.

"Where's the hurry, Miss? You're a guest of the establishment."

I was so paralyzed, I couldn't even whisper a word to Carlo outside the door, and then Brainard Rowe leapt into that corrupted
light with a beaker of rum and two whiskey glasses. He was still
wearing cape and scarf.

"Currer Bell, did you know that rum is the preferred drink of
our bravest generals? Benedict Arnold would never go into battle
without a beaker of rum."

"Mr. Rochester," I say, "that is not much of a recommendation,
since your Benedict Arnold was the villainest man in America.

That is what my father holds, and he does not usually express himself on the subject of villains."

My Rochester laughs. "I would not dream to contradict the Squire. He is lord and master of my intended."

My eyes rove upon his darker ones. He has not even pumped me with Domingo yet, and he is up to his tricks. But I will not allow him to astonish Currer Bell.

"Goodness," I pronounce, with the plainest mask I can muster. "Who would have guessed that you cared so much?"

"Well," says he, "did not little Gould ask for your hand? Confound it! Must I be last in line?"

"Gould is not so little in my estimation, *Mr.* Rochester. He does stand at least a head above us all. He is the orator of his class, and he will make a most promising preacher. And still my father refused his request—or I should say stalled him for six months."

"But the Squire will not stall me."

"And why is that?" I ask, with a slight tremor that I manage to hide.

"Because he will hurl me out of the house . . . here, have a drink."

Both of us laugh like conspirators, but in truth my heart is a little sore. I could have married Brainard Rowe I now confess, would have run away with him, lived in China or Timbuktu, had he but asked me in earnest, and not over a beaker of rum. Perhaps I am nothing but a naughty, fickle girl, but why does little Gould annoy me, and my Rochester does not?

He pours that caramel liquor into a glass, and I taste Domingo for the first time. Lord, I am not giddy in the least.

"A toast," he says, knocking his glass into mine and producing the solidest sound I have ever heard. "To Arnold, may he rot in Hell. And to Master Edward Dickinson, may he look with a little mercy upon my desire to steal his daughter away from him."

My tongue begins to thicken after a second sip. "Rochester, you toy with me. One must not make light of marriage proposals with an old maid."

His tongue is not as thick as mine. "An old maid with the Devil's wit about her? You toy with me, I fear. I would paint your eyelids with rum and relish every lick were I a less cautious man."

I have never had such gymnastics performed upon my face, but I would not have prevented Brainard from doing so. Yet he does not move an inch closer to me from across the table, and I have to watch that silent nibbling of rum by the lost Seniors of Phi Upsilon.

"Brainard," I whisper, "can nothing be done to aid such poor souls?"

"Ah," he says, "they displeasure you. We could march upstairs to the gaming room. It is much livelier in tone. But it is the domain of Alpha Delta Phi. We might stumble upon your brother, and need I give you the scenario? He will call me a bounder for bringing you here and feel obliged to defend your honor."

"But you did not bring me. I came of my own volition."

"Austin will think the worst of me for that. And he will suggest swords, a pen, or a plough."

I redden, and it is not from Domingo. "Sir, you mock my Valentine that was so ruthlessly published in the college magazine by your drinking companion, Mr. Shipley."

He smiles, and I redden all the more. "I am serious, Sir, and I can see that you are not. Hence I—"

He has the gall to lean over and kiss me in the middle of my articulation, and it was no polite peck; he burgled my mouth while gnawing at my face, and I burgled back. I must have startled him, because he stopped. I'd been pecked at by one or two of my beaux, but never had I experienced anything close to a burglar's kiss. My mouth had been sucked raw and quivered with the taste of rum and molasses.

"Lord," I say the second my breath returns, because this burglar has stolen the wind right out of me. "Do you think that dreadful man with the seam on his face will spy on us? I told him you were my escort, or he would not have let me in."

"Old Breckenbridge? He is my protector. No harm will come to you from Breck."

"Then let me have some more Domingo, for God's sake."

We emptied the beaker and Breck brought us another; he did not seem so menacing now and forlorn with his damaged face. He too had once been a member of Phi Upsilon, but hard as I tried, I could not imagine him as a Senior at Amherst. Rum had ruined him, according to Rochester, had aged him without mercy, and that seam the result of a drunken brawl on College Hill.

"I cannot believe you, Sir. That man has the air of a troglodyte."

"You might at least call me Brainard or Tutor Rowe. We have the same rum upon our lips."

"A burglar's rum," say I, my poor head swimming in Domingo all of a sudden. "And I will call you Burglar Brainard or Bandit Brainard, and whatever strikes my fancy, but I still do not believe in that brutal scholar of yours."

And when Breckenbridge arrives with still another beaker of rum, my rambunctious Tutor begins to query him in the rowdy manner of a drunken man of privilege.

"Breck, will you honor us and perform for this young lady?"

"Shall I sing or dance, my lord?" asks this educated guardian of Tardy Tavern.

"No, you numbskull. Disclose to me who your favorite poets are."

"Lord Byron, my lord, and Mr. John Keats."

"And what is your opinion of *Jane Eyre*?" Brainard seems in a bother when the guardian purses his lips. "Be quick on your feet, man. I do not want a measured response, and neither does Miss Dickinson."

"I am at a loss for words. I cannot adumbrate with your facility, my lord. But I would mention that Jane's journey is the journey of our time."

"How so?" asks my Tutor, his lips the color of caramel.

"That women might not be deaf and dumb, but have their own grammar and music, the prerequisites of a proper voice."

"The grammar of Currer Bell?"

"Precisely, my lord."

"And would I astonish you, Breck, if I were to reveal that this young lady before you *is* Currer Bell?"

I am at a loss. Suddenly the gruesome stamp on the side of Breck's face wasn't sinister at all, and I can imagine him as a scholar who lost his footing and landed in a rum house.

"Brainard, you must stop this inquisition," I say, with tears in my eyes like great drops of molasses. "I have never met a crueler man."

"He is not cruel, milady. It is the manner of Tutors such as himself. He must behave like a predator, to rip the knowledge out of us . . . might I kiss your hand, milady?"

Lord, I have no idea what to do. But I would not insult this poor wretch of a man. I hold out my hand, and he peruses it as some great thinker would.

"It is exceedingly small, my lord, like a bird's hand."

"Birds do not have hands," says Brainard with much derision. "They have wings and claws."

"But might I correct you, my lord. I did see a bird once with hands . . . in a book devoted to mythological monsters."

"Monsters do not count," says my Tutor, dismissing Breckenbridge with a wave of his own hand. And I seethe where I sit. I would not marry Brainard, or go with him to Timbuktu, not in a million years.

"How dare you misuse that man! You are awfuller than Mr. Shipley. I will not remain another minute with you."

He laughs with his dark, undamaged eyes, reaches out and swoops me into his arms like the predator he is and seats me upon his lap. I am sick with anger and a crazy, indescribable joy, but no less curious about him.

"Brainard, why did that poor soul address you as 'my lord'?"

"Ah, but I am the ninth or tenth lord once removed of some paltry estate in Devonshire. It brings no income, and I have none. But if I were to return to a country where I was not even born, I could reign over a manor-house that resides in ruin."

"Then you are lord of nothing but air and a few burnt bricks. I like you better now. But you must promise to reform yourself and be kind to Breck."

But he does not have the chance. Breckenbridge returns with a look of great despair.

"My lord, the brother of this young lady has just entered the establishment and is looking to skin you alive. There will be carnage between Phi Upsilon and Alpha Delta Phi unless you leave with Miss Dickinson under cover of your cape."

I wanted to sit for a century. I could feel Brainard's manliness against my flanks, like some curious harpoon that swelled and did not sting. But the harpoon went away the moment Breckenbridge sounded his alarm, and I felt nothing but a quiver, as if manliness itself could jellify.

It was all a mystery, but I have no time to reflect. Brainard lifts me off his lap and carries me like a parcel under the manifest folds of his cape.

———

I SHOULD HAVE REALIZED THAT ZILPAH MARSH HAD TOLD ON me. Perhaps it wasn't her fault. I could not conceive of a fellow nun from Holyoke as a traitor. Father must have worried when he returned from his office and could not find his supper on the table *or* his Emily. And so he summoned Austin from College Hill and the two of them interrogated Zilpah until she confessed that I had gone to the rum resort at the end of Merchants Row.

Brother isn't blind. He had to notice how I'd looked at Brainard in the sugar-house and sensed that his wild sister was involved in some misadventure.

At least that is what I intuit while I travel under the cape. Carlo can barely recognize his mistress. But he does not seem overly alarmed.

"Brainard, you must put me down and flee. I do not want to be the cause of your dismemberment. I can stroll the Commons on my own. Carlo will protect me."

Brainard does put me down, but he will not flee.

"I will escort you home," he says. "How could I be any less gallant to Currer Bell?"

"But I am not Currer Bell at this hour, with Austin and his fraternity brothers on the warpath. I am the little runaway of West Street."

He clutches his chin. "Miss Emily, have you ever been in love with a man?"

Why does he have to counter with so difficult a question? Pondering hard, I practically disappear inside a snowbank.

"I had my own Tutor once, Ben Newton—my father's former clerk. I did love him, I think. He told me that the most secret friend I could have was my Lexicon. And he said he hoped to survive until I became a poet. He suffers from consumption, you see. He moved away from Amherst."

"Why didn't he steal you from the Squire?" Brainard asks, walking nonchalantly in the snow, as if we did not have a whole fraternity fast upon our tracks.

"He might have," I say, "had he not been ill. I cried for weeks after he went to Worcester."

"Did you ever sit on his lap?"

"No, my lord. There was always a Lexicon between us. But I

might have sat on someone else's lap if I'd ever had the chance."

Brainard's pace diminishes. I've caught him unawares. Alpha Delta Phi is gaining on us, but it means little to him, wrapped up as he is in a rival he had never even considered.

"And whose lap might that be?" he asks, without picking up his pace.

"The Handyman's at Holyoke."

It is dark and we have no lantern to light our way, but I can still catch a wrinkle under his mouth in the faint glimmer off the snow. Brainard is baffled. He does not know what to say or what to do. A Handyman is outside his ken, does not fit within the range of beaux for Currer Bell. He broods, and I have the glee of a glutinous child. Who would ever have believed that I could make my Domingo, the rum drinker, jealous? Finally he speaks, while I hear the footsteps of Alpha Delta Phi in the snow, and the voice of my late fiancé, Mr. Gould, resounds like a rifle shot in the icy cold. "We're gaining on him, boys."

But it is Brainard's voice that appeals to me.

"Was he a self-taught poet, your Handyman? Did he scratch poems on his sleeve with his own sweat and blood?"

"Tom the Handyman could neither read nor write. But he had the blondest hair in history. And if Mistress Lyon hadn't kept me from him, I would have sat on Tom's lap every day of the week."

This last sentence lands like a blow. My Domingo falters, lost in a miasma of words. I feel some pity for him as a lover must, since I am the cause of his pain. But I would not have mentioned Tom, would not have retrieved him from my box of memories, had Brainard not been so arrogant as to ask if I'd ever loved a man.

His questioning has cost him dearly—he has an air of ruin about him, like his own lost estate. And now Alpha Delta Phi has fallen upon Brainard, with Brother and little Gould in the lead, clutching a lantern. Austin does not even look at his wild sister.

His own face is filled with savagery, as if my Domingo were the housebreaker of College Hill who stole the President's clock.

It is Carlo who is confused. He would not leap upon Austin and his fraternity brothers unless my own life were at risk. Yet I would not have Alpha Delta Phi manhandle Domingo. I step in front of him.

I can hear his hot breath. "You must stand aside, Miss Emily."

"But I will not have them hurt you on my account. I will explain to Austin that—"

I can feel him tremble. It is not out of fear, but humiliation. "*Please.*"

I step aside, ashamed of myself. I've brought my Domingo misery.

"Sir," says little Gould, like a big-eared tower in the snow, "you have damaged the honor of Alpha Delta Phi, played most foul with Brother Austin, met with his sister in secret, introduced her to rum in a resort where no fraternity man would ever bring a respectable young lady."

"But dear George," I say to Mr. Gould.

Domingo touches my shoulder with his trembling hand. "You must be quiet, Currer Bell."

"Sir," says little Gould, "you will kneel right now and apologize to Brother Austin."

But Domingo stands defiant in the blaze of snow that feeds off the lantern light.

"Austin Dickinson, it was never my intention to wound you. But I will not kneel to you and your brothers, and I will drink rum wherever I please and with whoever pleases me."

Little Gould does not have the chance to leap upon Domingo with his lantern, as a long wooden ladle interrupts the space between the two men. Breckenbridge has arrived with his battledore.

"Breck," groans little Gould, "this is not your battle. It is a fraternity matter. You must yield ground."

"Will I now?" says Mr. Breckenbridge, shoving the battledore into little Gould's chest with a light flick that sends him tumbling into the snow.

Domingo will not depart until he rubs the edge of my shawl. Then he bows to Alpha Delta Phi and trudges back to Merchants Row with Mr. Breckenbridge. And I am left alone with Brother and his lantern boys, who have robbed me of my sudden suitor.

# 17.

I DREADED RETURNING HOME. I KNEW WHAT LAY IN STORE
for me at head-quarters—Father's wrath. I had struck on my own,
defiant of him, found a fiancé at a rum resort. But couldn't he let
me wear whiskers once in a while and behave like a man, with a
man's right to plunder? I had captured Domingo, hauled him in.
How could I make Father understand that I was a warrior, not a
meek little mouse?

I couldn't approach the Patriarch.

Father would not speak to his prodigal daughter for two days,
though I prepared his favorite dish—roasted fowl and lentils—
and sat mending his slippers, while Mother looked at me as if I
were some wicked creature who had just come back from Sodom
and Gomorrah. And Brother was worst of all. He sulked in my
presence, as if I had defiled him and his fraternity forever.

My first communiqué from Father was a note sent through his
emissary, Zilpah Marsh. I was not to leave head-quarters unac-
companied, even to have a stroll with my dog—Father considered
Carlo as one more accomplice and spy. My only authorized companions were Mother, Brother, Father, or Zilpah, whom he had

taken into his trust. I was forbidden under any circumstance to see "that Yale boy," as Father described Brainard, though it must have been difficult. Father himself had gone to Yale, and at great sacrifice; he'd had to drop out of Yale twice because his own father, Squire Sam, was adrift in bankruptcy.

He could have had Brainard plucked from College Hill posthaste and sent back in ignominy to Yale, but he was reluctant to soil his Alma Mater, nor did he want the trustees of Amherst involved in his own family affairs. So without any formal charge he had President Hitchcock limit Brainard's time as visiting Tutor to one more week.

It was cowardly of Father and most unfair. He never confronted Brainard, or asked me what had happened at the rum resort. He had President Hitchcock deliver a sermon on the evils of rum, and then seized the opportunity to have every rum resort in the township of Amherst closed. This the Squire accomplished in a matter of days, without a single ordinance—that was a good summary of his power. He was indeed the earl of Amherst.

What was it that riled him so? My new bravura? By ridding himself of Brainard, he thought to hold on to me. My Domingo threatened him in a way that a fraternity boy like Gould never could. Gould had to depend on Pa-pa's purse. But Brainard was closer to Father's own footing—a lord with a manor-house, even if such house could bring in no rent. If Brainard himself had been more rentable, would it have made a difference? Not in the least.

Father had the ultimate weapon to tame Miss Emily Dickinson. In such a state of "emergency"—said emergency being myself—he had Lavinia whisked out of Ipswich for a week to look after her wild sister. Lavinia was my closest friend and confidante, and I was much lonelier since she'd gone away for the year. Austin was preoccupied with his own "Seniorship," and I could not confide in him, could not bare my soul about girlish matters. He had hoped I would fall in love with his fraternity mate, little Gould, and instead I had "eloped" to a rum resort with his rival, Brainard Rowe of Phi Upsilon. But the irony of it all was that he had once been fond of my Domingo, had considered him the very best of visiting Tutors, had even studied Goethe's *Faust* with him, had memorized most of Mephistopheles' lines. Didn't the Devil himself wear the clothes of a wandering scholar? And now my Domingo has become that scholar!

⌒

BROTHER IS LOST TO ME FOR THE MOMENT, BUT I DO HAVE Lavinia, who arrives near the end of Valentine season on the afternoon coach. Her traveling dress is light green, and with her braided hair in a brownish snood, she looks like the Queen of the Commonwealth as she steps down from the stage. Lavinia is so much lovelier than I am, with the darkness of romance around her eyes, and I have an instantaneous bout of panic that I cannot control. What if my Domingo should feast upon Lavinia and transfer his affection from the plain sister to the lovelier one? Lavinia is a flirt, and I am not. She would feel much more comfortable sitting on my Domingo's lap.

I do not whisper a word as we march with Mother and Father from the depot in front of Amherst House hotel to the "wilderness" of West Street. But Father must have fed Lavinia a fat tale about my Domingo in the letters he sent to Ipswich. She is mostly silent during the light supper *I* have prepared, since Mother's Neuralgia still keeps her out of the kitchen. But the second we are upstairs in the retreat of our own room, Lavinia smothers me with a kiss and says, "Sister dear, I command you. Don't leave out a syllable! Who is this prodigious rake of a man?"

I bat my eyelashes like Bathsheba, the collector of kings. "Vinnie, I haven't the faintest idea of what you mean."

Lavinia laughs and wraps me in her shawl. "Emily, I will imprison you, as God is my witness, until you tell."

"Brainard Rowe," I hurl at Little Sister. "He's visiting us from Yale."

"My cats could have told me that," says Lavinia, who has her own small empire of cats, cats I have to feed while she's away. "Did he kiss you until your mouth bled?"

"More than bled."

She squeezes her eyes shut and explores the inside of her cheeks with her tongue, like a lizard in search of something. "And did you trap him with your hair, curl it around his head?"

"Lord, I'm not like you, Lavinia. My hair isn't long enough. But I didn't have the chance to trap him. He swept me out of my seat and sat me upon his lap."

"He did not! And what did it feel like?"

"Vesuvius—that's the sort of eruption I had right under me."

Lavinia claps her hands and squeezes her eyes tighter than before. "What happened next?"

"We had to leave that rum resort like a pair of outlaws . . . with Brother crazy enough to kill me and my poor Domingo."

She ruffles her forehead. "Domingo?"

"That's what I call him on account of the rum. He's an impoverished lord, with a castle in Devon that does not pay him a cent. He reminds me of Rochester."

There's a twitch in her forehead again. She has not read *Jane Eyre.* Currer Bell is utterly unknown at Lavinia's Female Academy, which is in the midst of a Revival, and Little Sister has succumbed to it. She has entered Lord Jesus' house, has become a bride of Christ. That is why Father lured her out of Ipswich, hoping she would protect me from my Domingo's unchristian ways. But he does not comprehend Lavinia. Finding God hasn't made her less of a flirt.

—❦—

ON THE VERY SAME NIGHT THAT LAVINIA IS BACK AT HEAD-
quarters, sleeping beside me under our comforter and quilt, I
have a troubling dream: Sister and I are lying under the ground,
in separate beds that are no more or less luxurious than our
graves, with a wall of earth between us. We cannot converse; try
as we may, our voices will not carry across that thickness of wall.
I am wearing my finest merino and a breastpin, as if I were at
a Senior levee, but there is nothing to celebrate while I am all
alone in my grave.

I begin to claw at that earthen barrier between Sister and myself.
My entire hand is deep inside the wall, but I cannot take any measure. Is that hand involved in an act of penetration, or is the earth
swallowing one more piece of myself?

I call out to Sister, but either she doesn't hear me or chooses not
to answer. I cannot seem to wipe the dirt from my face with the one
hand I have that is not inside the wall . . .

I wake near Lavinia, with the crust of sleep in her eyes. Neither
of us is entombed, though one of my arms is pinned under her
pillow, and I have to pull it free and try not to arouse her. I wash
the crust from my own face, descend to the kitchen in my slippers, shawl, and morning shirt, and stand like a little lord with my
baker's shovel as I watch the dough of Father's bread rise in the
oven. But I cannot shake off the patina of my dream. All morning
I seem to live underground. I am silent through breakfast, and my
mind wanders as Father reads from his Bible and asks the Lord to
bless our meal.

I am still under the same curious cloud as I wash the dishes in
our sink-room with its own little side door that I sometimes use to
escape unwanted company. I hear a rapping on the door, which is
most unusual, since none of my suitors has ever been to this side
of the house.

Then I hear my Domingo's voice. "Currer Bell," he says with a throaty whisper, "come out and play."

I am no magician, but I can tell from the tremor in his voice that he's been drinking rum, and it is not even noon. I open the door. My heart leaps through the walls of my chest and then leaps back, since there's no real place for a girl's heart to go.

He has a bruise on his cheek that I long to kiss, and there's a bit of blood on his mouth—suddenly I'm as awake as a warrior. Miss Emily is no longer underground. I calculate, wonder if Alpha Delta Phi has been hounding my Domingo, chasing him across the hills. The rim of his floppy velvet hat is filled with snow. His scarf and cape are filthy. But no one has been chasing him, he insists. He had just finished his morning constitutional at his cave on Merchants Row.

I interrupt him. "Brainard, that is a bald lie. The College has closed all the rum resorts."

"Then I am blind and delusional, since I had a beaker of rum not half an hour ago. College men are forbidden in the cave, but its walls are as sturdy as ever."

"Then I am still perplexed. Is not a Tutor from Yale still a College man?"

"Indeed," says this Tutor with snow in his hat, a soiled cape, and a swollen blue mark on his cheek. "But President Hitchcock has stripped me of all my credentials, and I am nothing but a civilian on College grounds."

"Then why are you all rumpled and bruised?"

"I fell in the snow . . . too much rum. I might not have fallen had I not lost my bearings. I was looking for Currer Bell's abode. Damn you, woman, come out and play. There is so little time for us. I'm being drummed out of Amherst like a lad with the plague."

He bows and that bruised cheek of his seems to land in my face.

"Will the Squire's daughter do Brainard the honor of walking with him in the woods? He does not bite or suck the blood out of Amherst belles, even in the nadir of his disgrace."

I begin to cry and cannot control this sobbing of mine, a schoolgirl's performance, the parody of a fit, but the truth is that I am trapped inside head-quarters, Father's prisoner of war. I had promised the commander-in-chief that I would not leave the confines of West Street without a military escort.

"My lord," I tell Domingo, "I am not permitted to play."

"Then I will kidnap you, Currer Bell."

"Sir," I say, with a smile that masks a portion of my tears, "I should have to resist."

He wipes a stray tear from my cheek with his hand—that touch is torture, a torture of delight.

"Can a sinner such as myself overcome a maiden's will?" says he with a smile of his own.

*Yes*, I long to shout, but his maiden is curiously silent. Would that he had fed me chloroform or some other potent drops and carried me away to the seraglio he kept at Yale. I'd turn into an ogre and swallow whatever wives or mistresses were about. I'd capture him under my hellish strands of hair and make certain that no one but Emily ever sat upon his lap. I'd have Vesuvius all to myself.

But my desires fade as I hear footsteps in the pantry that connects with the sink-room. It must be the housekeeper, Zilpah Marsh, who has become my father's spy of late.

"My darling," I shout with a shiver, "you must go at once, before Father's head-quarters descends upon you and devours us both."

"Ah," he says as a lover *must*, "then we will share our own ruined eternity."

It is not Father's spy who is in the pantry but Sister, who has come to warn me that Austin and his fraternity brothers are wandering about. Yet Lavinia troubles me as much as Zilpah Marsh.

"Is this your Domingo?" she asks, always the flirt. Shame on her! She should not give my secrets away.

Brainard laughs, and I do not like the electric ruminations in his eye. Is he planning to sweep Sister into his seraglio?

"Brainard," I say with a dollop of bitterness, "I must introduce you to my sister Lavinia. She is at the Female Academy in Ipswich, but Father has brought her home for a week to watch over me."

Sister smiles. "Emily, we do not have the time for such ample introductions. Alpha is at our heels."

But my Domingo plays the courtier and kisses Lavinia's hand. "Delighted," he says. "I was never told of your existence. But indulge me a little. Tell me, why am I Domingo?"

"Because you are her own plantation and sugar-house," she says, while I ready to strangle her. "But you must depart, Mr. Domingo. I would not want to have your death on my hands."

"Sister exaggerates, as always," I insist. "Austin is no murderer."

"But Alpha Delta Phi doth have a murderous look," Sister says, like some Shakespearean, and I am not in the mood for her antics.

My cheeks are frozen with a chill of the North. How can Brainard feel the agony under my Arctic cover? He does not know the Dickinsons.

"Brainard, I cannot accompany you into the woods, not while I reside in my father's house and have promised him never to look upon your face."

"But you are looking at me now, and you have not turned to stone. Lavinia is my witness."

"There are worse things than stone," I say. I long to comfort him, to feel the outline of his face, but I cannot while Sister hovers over us and my Domingo is in danger of being captured. I do not mind that Father will court-martial me, and Sister too, as my accomplice. But what hurts is that I will have lied and as a liar be forced to watch that dread look of disappointment upon Father's face. This I cannot bear.

The sudden whoop and shout of fraternity men pulls me out of my reverie—Austin's brothers have the smell of Brainard's blood in their nostrils, like a pack of wild dogs.

"What is my name?" he whispers in my ear so that Lavinia cannot listen.

"Domingo," I whisper back, and like some obstinate child who has gone against her father's wish, I fondle my lover's cheek with the blade of my hand. He twirls that scarf of his once around his neck, with the boldness of a toreador, and runs off into the woods.

# 18.

MY POOR DOMINGO DID NOT ESCAPE THE WRATH OF ALPHA
Delta Phi. The fraternity men found him in the woods, tore his
scarf to shreds, and escorted him to the stage depot. Their former Tutor was not even allowed to pack. They went into his rooms
while he was held at the depot, rummaged through his belongings
like burglars, seized for themselves whatever took their fancy, and
delivered the rest in a pair of pillowcases to their captive in front
of the Amherst House hotel.

And when the coach appeared, they tossed him inside with the
pillowcases. That was the end of Brainard's history at Amherst
College, and the start of my mourning period. But how could I
mourn? I would not wear black, since that color could cast a dark
spell over Brainard's life. And I could not deposit a letter to him
at the Post Office, as the Post Master despised my father for being
a Whig. He saw Pa-pa as an aristocrat.

Father was the village dictator, according to him, and he would
not have protected the dictator's daughter—no, he'd inform the
entire town of my telltale letter and it would finish up in Father's
pocket and never get to Yale.

So I had to become a secret agent. I posted Brainard's letters to Lavinia, who had returned to Ipswich now that my Domingo was no longer a threat to Amherst and any of its daughters. Despite her new religious zeal, Lavinia would never tattle on me. But there were obstacles to my secret agenting, since Father liked to collect our family mail. I had to appear at the Post Office before he did, but my scheming bore little fruit. There were no letters from my Domingo tucked inside Sister's envelopes, nothing at all.

I plotted voyages to New Haven inside my head, but knew I would not venture far from Amherst. No longer restricted to head-quarters, I could wander freely with Carlo, but I had no taste or appetite for adventure. I did not even travel as far as the hat fac-tory to watch the female workers parade in their leather aprons. I did not romp with Carlo on College Hill. But I went like some broken arrow to that rum resort at the edge of Merchants Row. My Domingo had been telling the truth. Tardy Tavern is not closed, but it has a guard stationed at the door to keep out college Seniors—said guard does not have a damaged face, but he is just as foreboding as Mr. Breckenbridge had ever been, though cau-tious with Carlo around.

He bows to his waist like the ignorant, mocking bully that he is and says with a lick of his tongue, "We don't allow tarts in this establishment. Best try another resort, Mamzelle."

"I will not," I answer, holding my ground. "Have the kindness to tell Breck that I'm here."

His tongue withdraws into his mouth. He doesn't know what to do with me, a plain woman in merino who looks more like a pio-neer than a prostitute.

"And who should I say is calling, Mamzelle?"

"Carlo and Currer Bell."

"Right," he says, more muddled than ever. But he leaves his post and returns with Mr. Breckenbridge, who can't seem to make up his mind whether I'm an angel or a pest, or halfway in between.

"Have you been impolite to this young lady?"

"Breck, I didn't know she was a friend of yourn. I figured she was some pumpkin who was coming here to paint her face."

"Idiot, did you ever see a pumpkin travel with a big dog? She's not looking for male company."

"Then what is she doin' at a rum house?"

"Seeking her intended who has returned to Yale, and don't you bother us."

The door guard disappears, but Mr. Breckenbridge still does not invite me inside. I start to shiver, but it's not from the cold; it's from that distance I begin to feel between Brainard and myself, terribler by the minute. And Mr. Breckenbridge seems to understand my distress.

"Would you like to share a beaker of rum, Miss Bell?"

"More than anything in the world," I say, and it's true. That beaker is as close to my Domingo as I'll ever get in a long, long while. I don't need rum to remind me of Brainard, but that taste will resurrect him a little. And wisely Mr. Breckenbridge won't permit me to park Carlo outside the tavern. My big dog would leave a significant sign, and Father might come running with the Sheriff or a slew of firemen to free his daughter from such a hellhole.

So Carlo sits under the table in that front room where Amherst's lost Seniors formerly sat night and day with their rum cups. The room has one occupant, but I cannot read his face. He could be the village drunk, or a wayfarer looking for a little peace in that curious "church" of a rum resort. Mr. Breckenbridge does not pay much heed to him, as if this man in the dark were a customer known to one and all.

The first taste of Domingo cures my shivers, and I am calm.

"Breck, have you heard from him since he was run out of Amherst by certain rascals from my brother's own secret society?"

"Miss Bell, I am a rum lord. Brainard wouldn't write to me.

But I have had word of him from an acquaintance of his at New Haven."

My heart beats with a sudden fervor. "Did he mention me?"

"Yes, he did. But I am reluctant to intrude upon his privacy. Mention you he did, but I am not certain it was for your own ears."

He must have seen the terror in my face, even in that feeble glow.

"It was nothing unkind, Miss. I give you my guarantee."

"But Breck," I whine in my whispery way, "you leave me without hope. You must tell me more."

"He said, if I might quote his remarks to a third party, that he missed Currer Bell, but was not Rochester and would never be."

I pitch my head forward the better to catch the sound of Mr. Breckenbridge's voice.

"I am lost," I say, but really I am not. My Domingo wouldn't play the blind man for me, wouldn't return to Amherst, or wait for Currer Bell.

Mr. Breckenbridge has to hold my glass while I devour more Domingo. He is called away from the front room on urgent business, and I sit there alone in the near darkness. But I am not alone. That man with a seam on the side of his face has left me with a perfect stranger.

# 19.

I CANNOT RECALL HOW LONG I SAT THERE. IT MIGHT HAVE been an hour. But now I understood the lost Seniors of Phi Upsilon, and how they had no more ambition than to sit in a rum room within reach of College Hill; learning could not fire up their souls, and thus they abandoned their caps and gowns and sat with the constant taste of molasses in their mouths. They did not want a future of delivering sermons or arguing legalities. They did not want a future at all. They wanted Domingo, and so I drank in their ghostly presence until a voice shot out of the dark.

"How are ya, Sis?"

Not even Domingo can stop my shivering now. I do not have to probe his face to be absolutely certain that Richard Midnight, lately of the Handyman's shed in Holyoke, is my interlocutor. He lights a cigar, and I can catch his dark demean in the burning coals that resemble a ruthless eye. His chest isn't bare at Tardy Tavern. It's encased in a black leather jacket that a pirate might don while he pillaged and ruined people's lives. I have no wish to engage him in banter or ask where he had gone after Miss Rebecca had forced him to vacate the shack. Lord, I am a better detective than even I had imagined. Richard Midnight had not vanished into some forlorn wilderness. He'd come to Amherst with his lady love. That's what I was willing to wager.

It couldn't be fortune alone that had landed him in the same place as Zilpah at the same time, or that the current rash of burglaries had started after Midnight was thrown out of Holyoke. *He* was the housebreaker who was haunting our village, who struck with such blind authority, pilfering from the finest houses at just the right intervals to preserve a picture of randomness. There was nothing random about his accomplice, Zilpah Marsh, and her yellow gloves. She now had a prodigious mask: she was housekeeper and maid to the village's very own earl.

It was pointless to ask Richard Midnight about his next robbery. He'd lie until he went blue.

"You're a touch untalkative for a lonesome girl," says he.

"I have nothing much to say, Mr. Midnight."

"That's remarkable, considering that I once kissed your cheek."

"You never did."

He laughs in the dark like some jackal poised to attack.

"I should warn you, Mr. Midnight, I have my dog Carlo with me, right under the table. And if you make one rude gesture or remark, I will consign him to rip out your lungs."

I have not foiled him in the least with my mention of Carlo. He only laughs the louder. "I'll bet you would, Sis. I'll bet you would. I was being hospitable, is all. I mean, I might be inclined to give your regards to ol' Brainard when I'm next in New Haven."

If Midnight was trying to stun, then he succeeded in doing so. His laughter turns into a terrible guffaw. And I can feel the same meanness that he had in Tom's shed.

"I never got to see your bony little bottom, Sis."

"Told you to be civil," I growl at him.

"I'm as civil as can be. But I do have an appetite for ya, Sis."

I'd rather be fondled by a tarantula. But that foolish man leaps out of the dark and lunges at me with amorous intent. I have to drink in his foul breath before Carlo bites into that fancy leather jacket, holds it in his jaws until half of Midnight's arm disappears, then releases him, and sends Midnight flying across the room with a bump of his skull. Carlo isn't a mean dog. He was protecting his mistress. And he wouldn't have chewed off Midnight's arm or leg unless I told him to.

I lean over Midnight and feed him a lick of water while he trembles and covers his head with his hands. I ought to rejoice in Midnight's collapse, but I can't. He starts to whine.

"Take that monster away. I swear on the Bible. I'll be good."

I don't have to shove Carlo under the table. My dog disappears without a sign from me. Carlo would rather have nothing more to do with Richard Midnight.

"Where did you ever meet Brainard?" I ask, curious about my Domingo.

Midnight's quiet for a moment, but without Carlo's whiskers in his face he regains a little of his pluck.

"Right here, in this rummy house. I had many a beaker with him. He talked about ya."

"Brainard wouldn't mention me to the likes of you."

"Wouldn't he now?" Midnight says with a sneer. Zilpah must have leaked my fondness for rum resorts. "Ah, permit me to recollect. There was something about an altercation at a sugaring party. And about having a beaker with you in this prime establishment. He described you down to a tit—your rat's red hair, eyes the color of rotting corn, your stick of a body, with the white thighs of a nun. And I says to myself, 'Richard, ain't that our Sis from the Female Academy?' "

I cannot bear to listen any longer, and I run out the room with

Carlo, while Richard Midnight's triumphant snort beats upon my back.

⤳

IT'S THE COLD WIND THAT DRIVES THE SOUND OF RICHARD Midnight from my brain. My composure seems to come back as I move along the Commons with Carlo, and once I reach our doorstep I wear a smile. I do not interrogate Zilpah like some captain of artillery with a hostile in the house. I watch her tend the stove in her yellow gloves. And when it is time for her to leave, I bid her goodbye, brooding under my own mask.

"Mistress, will ya be needing me early tomorrow?"

She has insinuated herself into Father's affections and has begun baking his bread.

"No," I answer. "I will tend to the Squire."

She takes a lantern with her since it is well after dark, and hence it is simple enough for me to follow her without a lantern of my own that might lend some suspicion of light. I dare not bring Carlo with me, as he lopes like a lion in the snow. And so it is Zilpah herself who is my beacon as she plunges into the fields south of the cemetery and east of the livery stable. There is not another light on the horizon except for the houses on Main Street, with their harsh and eerie shimmer that rises off the snow.

She crosses Main Street, and with her lantern she winds down the road, past the hat factory that looks like an abandoned fort at night, and into that dark dead-end of Rooming-house Row, where the transients live with workers at the hat factory. She enters one of the rooming houses, with its crippled porch and crippled gate, and the lantern light disappears with her, as not one of the buildings in this blind alley is lit.

Lord, I have landed in a maze. And for a moment I wish I had a third of Lavinia's newly-found religious zeal. Somehow I'd rather trust the Devil in this dark morass at Amherst's eastern edge. But even the Devil has abandoned me. I've lost my bearings and do not have the means to walk out of this maze. And I wonder if I will have to spend the night curled up against a crippled porch.

And then Satan himself provides me with a miracle. I catch a whole cluster of swinging lanterns from within the heart of the maze. And I hear the favorite rigmarole of Brother's fraternity, a nonsense song about Greek urns and the supernatural powers of Alpha Delta Phi, and I realize that the village's only brothel must be hidden in the same cul-de-sac.

I do not have to cry for help. The lanterns' conflicting light finally falls upon the old maid of Amherst.

"Gawd," says one of the fraternity men, "I do believe we have found that missing harlot. Sister, speak your name, or forever be silent."

"I am the ghost of Currer Bell," I cry as loud as I can in my tiny voice.

The brothers are taken aback. They did not expect to stumble upon so literate a voice in this blind warren. They shine their lights upon me with much more precision.

"Brother Austin," says the same fraternity man, "is she your sister or is she not?"

And Brother himself descends from the shadows while pulling up his pants and lurching from lantern to lantern like a drunken college boy. He is too muddled to have much anger on his face.

"Emily, what are you doing in this godforsaken corner?"

"The same as you, I imagine. Looking for adventure."

"And what sort of adventure could you possibly find in Rooming-house Row?" asks my late intended, little Gould, his enormous ears suddenly materializing in front of my eyes.

"I am not much traveled, Mr. Gould, being a member of the female sex who is not permitted to venture far without a male. But I had an irresistible urge to see where the maids and housekeepers of our finest families live."

"Without a lantern? And in the dark?"

"I did not worry, Mr. Gould, once I realized that Brother's fraternity was chasing harlots on the very same streets. Harum-scarum,
I knew I would run into Alpha Delta Phi."

Little Gould disappears into the darkness again, while Austin
puts his arm around me. It's as much affection as I've gotten from
him ever since that Tutor from Mars complicated his life and mine.
Alpha Delta Phi escorts me back to West Street, singing their rigmarole as they stumble along, their lanterns swinging wildly, and
under all that furor I can hear Austin's heartbeat as he clutches me
close.

But I ain't comforted much. I might have done better without
Austin and his Alphas. I could have slept on Zilpah's porch and
waited for the sun to rise. I would have learned something about
that robbers' roost of hers. But what if the robbers had swept me
inside and I never saw Pa-pa and Carlo again? They wouldn't have
bothered ransoming an old maid. And suppose their leader, Richard Midnight, tried to peck at me with his filthy mouth while Zilpah guffawed with delight and savored her own triumph? She'd
have Pa-pa all to herself. She'd inherit my pencils and writing
paper, and Pa-pa would consider it a miracle to have a housekeeper who could scratch an occasional Verse. Lord, it was too
much to bear.

## 20.

I WAIT LIKE A CROUCHING LIONESS FOR THE NEXT RASH OF robberies in our village, but there is none. Not even the most isolated farmhouse has been touched. The burglars of Roominghouse Row must have been asleep or preparing to pounce. But I promise myself not to allow them a convenient place to perch. I realize quickly enough that *our* head-quarters on West Street has become their new pilothouse, with Zilpah as an impeccable pilot. She is employed by Father, after all, and has his strictest confidence. Thus she can wander in her winter shawl as housekeeper to the earl, and select her targets without the least suspicion falling on her head.

But she hadn't counted on a female detective whose primer is nothing more than her own pernicious mind. I cannot calculate the scene of any crime that has not yet been committed. But I can scout the particular haunt of these housebreakers. And so I return under the scrutiny of daylight to the dead-end streets behind the hat factory, bringing Carlo along as my companion, hoping he will frighten the larger rats who have to reside in such a filthy warren. But my Carlo did not crush any rats with his regal front paw. There was not a rat to be found in the whole rookery, nor was there the filth I had imagined.

The housebreakers' little cul-de-sac is not unkempt. I discover many a flower bed behind the crippled gates, with roosters surveying the lawns and children playing on porches sturdy enough to hold them. I even discover a chaise parked between two houses.

Lord, it is no less a landscape than West Street. And if ever I have to flee from Father and live incognito for a little while, I might consider this cul-de-sac, except that the housebreakers themselves would unmask me, since they have Zilpah Marsh.

And just when I thought my reconnoitering had led me to very little, I notice a very blond man sally forth from Zilpah's own rooming house with a wheelbarrow that holds a large ornate clock, the very same one or a facsimile of such that I have seen many a time during the Senior levees in President Hitchcock's parlor. But that clock does not interest me half as much as the very blond man.

It's *my* Tom, dressed like the finest gentleman in a frock coat, his shoes made of Spanish leather, I'm sure, his cravat as profound as the blue of his eyes. He wheels his barrow toward me without the least alarm, though there is enough evidence within its metal walls to put Tom into the penitentiary.

What hurts me most is that Tom looks directly into my acorn-colored eyes and does not have the faintest idea who I am. Perhaps my own past with Tom is part fairy tale, and he a player in a dream of mine; I long to pinch myself and prove that I had nursed Tom one morning a couple of Valentine seasons ago, while he was ill in his shed.

I start to shiver at that lack of recognition in his face, and Lord help me, I must have swooned. I wake up in the wheelbarrow, nesting above the clock, with a blanket over me and Tom's frock coat. In my delirium I shout, "Where's Carlo?" For I am all alone in this cul-de-sac of housebreakers and handymen who are the fodder and foodstuff of dreams. But Tom reappears with a pitcher of water and a measuring cup. I adored Tom once in his handyman's smock with soot all over him, but now his fine clothes feel foreign to me. And I'm mostly bitter. Tom's wearing one of Pa-pa's paisley scarves. That little housekeeper must have filched it from Pa-pa's drawer.

"Where's Carlo?" I have to ask again.

He pours the liquid and holds the cup while I drink. "Carlo," I shout between sips. "My companion."

"Ah, your dog," says Tom like a savant. "He was hungry and I fed him."

"But Carlo would never abandon me, not for all the chicken bones in China."

The Handyman laughs, his blondness overwhelming in the sunlight. I feel certain to swoon again until I notice Carlo galloping toward us in one great leap. He licks Tom's hand *before* he licks my face. I fancy he has found a master to replace his mistress and will move into this cul-de-sac with Tom.

"I thank you for the refreshment, Sir. Your liquid has revived me. But I must go."

"Sit awhile," he says. "What is your name, Miss?"

I dare not say Dickinson, because if my Tom is indeed Zilpah's accomplice and paramour, I would not have him know I am Squire Dickinson's daughter.

"I'm Currer Bell, visiting from England with my faithful dog. My dear uncle, Widower Rochester, is waiting, and I rather he not worry."

I rise up off that ornate clock as if it were a coffin and signal to Carlo with one eye, but my faithful companion seems in small hurry to leave Tom the Handyman.

"Miss, you have yet to ask me my name."

"Sorry, Sir, I am soft in the head. What is it?"

"Tom Harkins."

And suddenly I am filled with remorse. Even with all my aristocratic upbringing, I had let Zilpah Marsh trick me into believing that a ward of Massachusetts like Tom might not own a surname. He was fixed forever as Tom the Handyman in my Holyoke hauteur.

He catches me looking at the clock. I couldn't care less what he stole. He could have waylaid every last stick of furniture in the President's mansion as long as he recognized me. It ain't asking too much from a suitor, and then I have to recall that Tom Harkins never *suitored* me.

But it's the clock that's started cooking in his brain, the President's clock.

"That old clock mean anything to you, Miss Currer Bell?"

"Oh, the clock's a curiosity," I say. "We have one just like it in Widower Rochester's manor-house."

"Then it's recognizable," says he, "and you might be able to describe it to a third party."

His blue eyes turn a little mean. And if truth be told, I love his suspicion. Let him rattle my bones. It would prove that he's taken an interest in me.

"It's imbedded in my mind, Mr. Tom Harkins. I couldn't disremember a single detail."

I close my eyes, waiting for my beloved burglar to strike. But Tom don't trespass upon my person. He whispers in my ear.

"Miss Currer Bell, I might be inclined to let ya go if you promise not to mention that clock to anyone, alive or dead."

*Alive or dead.* That was a delicate touch. I suppose he'll smother me now with a silk scarf.

"But I hardly know anyone in Massachusetts, Mr. Tom, alive or dead. And Widower Rochester is blind."

I open my eyes, and there's a smile on his beautiful face. Perhaps he sensed that I was a burglar too, a member of his trade, and that I would do him no harm. Or perhaps he saw through my disguise. Either way I wasn't worthy enough to reckon with.

He bows to me in his frock coat, as if I were no more than an illusion with red hair.

"Please give my regards to the Widower, Miss Currer Bell."

Tom removes himself with his wheelbarrow and Pa-pa's paisley scarf, and leaves me all alone with Carlo in that cul-de-sac. I'm riven with gloom, as if a monster held me in its sway. I was nothing more than the possible witness to a stolen clock. How could I ever survive if I was *so* invisible to Tom? I had an urge to jump down Pa-pa's well.

The last time I felt this dark was when I was thirteen and Cousin Sophia died of brain fever. I was allowed to visit with her during her final agony. I took off my shoes and tiptoed into the sick-room, where I looked at her pale eyes and chalk-white skin. Cousin Sophia wasn't delirious. She recognized me, I think. And she muttered, *Lord, I wish I could live inside a well.* I wanted to hold her hand, but the doctor wouldn't let me stay.

The month Sophia died I was so forlorn that I couldn't go back to school. Pa-pa sent me to Boston to soften my grief. People thought it brave for a schoolgirl to travel on her own. I didn't feel brave. I lived with an aunt on Poplar Street, and on the way back from Boston I stopped at Worcester, where I stayed with one of my uncles and visited the Lunatic Hospital at Pa-pa's request. But I didn't need his encouragement. I was dying to see our old housekeeper, Evelyn O'Hare, who had been locked away.

I trembled as I approached the hospital's portico on Asylum Street. It wasn't out of fear for myself, but out of anxiousness for Evelyn's condition. But she wasn't even a patient at the hospital. Evelyn, I would learn from the hospital's keepers, had been cured of her "violent melancholy" and lived on the grounds as a maid. The warden spent an hour searching for Evelyn. It near destroyed me just to look at her. She'd been a maiden when she worked for Pa-pa, full of her own wishes to find a man. And now she didn't have a tooth in her head. I hugged her anyway, and we cried like two sisters who had been lost on the road and found each other after five years. She said I looked like a fine little lady.

I kept touching her face, but she wouldn't touch mine.

"*Warden's watching us,*" she whispered in my ear. I couldn't even have some cake with her in the refectory. She wasn't allowed to dine with guests.

The warden kept signaling her to get to work. Suddenly there was a smile on her face, and she was the same stubborn girl I remembered. She hugged me and kissed my hair. "*Bless you, Little Mistress.*"

And that was all. I lost Evelyn the moment I was blessed. She fled from me and the warden. I wrote to Evelyn for a month and sent her little gifts. She didn't answer my letters, and the gifts came back with a stamp on my original wrapper: ADDRESSEE UNKNOWN.

⌒

I RETURN HOME WITH CARLO FROM TOM'S CUL-DE-SAC, HIS housebreaker's hotel. It's my mute Confederate who drags me along. I have no remorse, and not much sassafras in my bones. But that makes me even more of a danger to that gang of burglars on Rooming-house Row. I'm the town's tiny marshal, seeking her revenge. Richard Midnight could not belong to the same little gang, or he would not have revealed himself inside the rum resort. He must have had a falling out with Zilpah before she came to work at our head-quarters. Had he hid his identity in the dark, I would never have construed of Zilpah Marsh as a housebreaker.

I confront her in the kitchen while Mother is asleep and Father is away on business. I am carved of ice.

"Zilpah, you will remove your yellow gloves and leave them on the table," I whisper without a false note.

"Mistress, I am tired. You must repeat yourself."

"Remove your yellow gloves."

She unties the elaborate wrist straps and dangles the thick

leather fingers for a moment to demonstrate her mastery over me; then, and only then, does she put the gloves on the table.

"I will give you ten minutes to pack."

She manages to smile, but it has little force, as there is already a pout upon her lips. "I will tell the master that you have been rude to me. And I am not the one who will be punished."

"Zilpah, if you have any sense of preservation, you will run as far from Amherst as you can, or spend your days in the women's farm at Springfield."

But she's a seminarian, even if she has been erased from the seminary's books. Zilpah's no less intimate with Shakespeare or John Milton than I am. She might be a stable hand's daughter, but she can bend language to her will. Had she been born a Dickinson, I would have had no sway with her. She also wouldn't have become a housekeeper, but housekeeper she is. And I have begun to frighten her a little. She tests me with a couple of tears.

"You are a cruel mistress. What have I ever done to deserve this?"

I am cruel. I want Zilpah Marsh to die. She has my Tom in her bed. Her cul-de-sac is a kingdom. I choose my words like a rapier that can scratch deep into the skin.

"I have seen the clock that Tom burgled from President Hitchcock's parlor."

I was waiting for her to gasp, but she drills at me with her eyes. The tears are gone. She hadn't expected a Holyoke scholar to be the town marshal. She reaches for her yellow gloves. She is pondering whether to strangle me or not.

"Does Squire Dickinson know about this?"

"Yes. And it is only because he is fond of you and your service to him that he begged me to give you this chance to escape. You know how weak men are, Zilpah. He did not have the heart to fire you himself."

"Where is he now?" she asks, still reaching for the yellow gloves.

"On his way here with the county sheriff."

"I don't believe you," she says.

"Then wait and find out."

"I should be mistress here," she says. "I would sit in Master Edward's lap. What makes you so special? I could suck out your life, Miss Em'ly, with one pinch of your windpipe."

I do not like that image of her in Pa-pa's lap, but poor Zilpah, she does not have my ice. I thrust out my throat as near to her as I can, like some insane turkey hungering for its own slaughter. But I have Carlo right under the table, and that whimper of his was growing into a growl.

"Zilpah Marsh, you shouldn't have stolen one of my Pa-pa's paisley scarves."

Now I've really alarmed her. "I did not," she says.

"Then how come Tom was wearing it on Rooming-house Row?"

"You're jealous of me and Tom," she says. "That's why you are doing this. You can't bear that we're together. Tom doesn't even remember who you are. I bought him the best shirt and shoes in town with money I got from the master, and I bought him that scarf, just like Master Edward wears."

She is waiting for me to slap her with one of Miss Rebecca's yellow gloves. Then she'll flaunt her own incaution and strangle Miss Em'ly. But I do nothing, nothing at all.

She disappears into the sink-room, gathers up whatever paltry articles she has, and runs out of head-quarters, cursing me and all the Dickinsons.

"It isn't fair," she says. "You have the name and the money. And I will have to toil and toil and toil."

*As Tom's pilot*, I want to hurl back at her, but I keep to the quiet. I am trembling so hard, I have to sit. I have no rapier, I now realize; whatever weapon I had was used against myself. I have scratched under my own skin, while Zilpah is unscathed. She will go off with Tom, become his accomplice with Shakespeare in her heart, pose as a housekeeper, and plunder another village. What is all my breeding worth? I might as well live in a root cellar. I am the maiden of Amherst, who tends to bulbs and plants and rises at dawn to prepare her father's bread. But I do have one small consolation—Miss Rebecca's gloves. I would never wear them. But perhaps they can serve as my talisman, and lend me the privilege of becoming a poet.

Lord, I do not feel much like a poet. The yellow gloves are meaningless without Zilpah Marsh. Suppose she herself was the talisman? Zilpah is as scratched as I am, but I didn't want to see the scars. And I am sentenced to live in a root cellar I made for myself.

I don't sing out a word at supper, but excuse myself from the table and wander upstairs like a lonely ship captain with a storm inside his head. I lie down on my pillow and wait for the storm to begin. My eyes are closed but I do not drift. I'm struck with the Lord's own lightning and Zilpah Marsh is confused in my brain with Evelyn O'Hare. Zilpah still has her teeth, and she don't require Miss Em'ly to help her study the alphabet, but she's no less a pariah, even if she has my Tom in her bed. And part of my anger against her has nothing to do with Tom. Maybe I wished that Zilpah and Evelyn were soldered into one. And somehow I blamed her for Evelyn's incarceration, as if she were my own bad angel who had come in Evelyn's stead. I start to cry as I've never cried. My root cellar ain't much more than the darkest well.

Suddenly the crying ends, and I'm inside a carriage, but it isn't Pa-pa's one-horse affair. It's an old-fashioned stagecoach, along the Boston run, before the Lord invented railroad tracks. I can't see the driver, but I'm the only one aboard this wooden beauty, and the wheels fly right under my feet. I ain't so sure about the landscape. It seems like an endless tumble of Pa-pa's own fields.

And then we ride down a hill at breakneck speed. I'm not scared. The carriage comes to a sudden halt.

A leather snake weaves right through the curtains. It's the driver's whip.

"Miss Em'ly, come upstairs."

I step out of the coach. I'm not even startled that the driver is Tom. Who else would be on the Boston run? But I'm much too small, and I can't reach up to the driver's box. Tom bends over and lets his arm slide down like an elephant's trunk. And I ride that arm right into the box.

It's higher than an attic, higher than a church. Tom has a team of twenty horses—no, twenty-six. I can see a jumble of tails and ears, rows of glistening rumps. I climb between his legs, sit upon leather that has been rubbed raw, while Tom anchors me with his thighs. The horses whinny, but once Tom cracks his whip, the rows fall into line.

I've talked enough for a lifetime. I don't have to badger Tom. The carriage makes its own weather, and we ride into the wind.

# Pa-pa & the Reverend Wadsworth

The whole of Massachusetts was ripped with anti-slavery fever that February of '55, the whole of Massachusetts except her Pa-pa. He railed against Uncle Tom's Cabin, said that its Authoress was in league with all the Literati and other such devils. And she wondered if Father's ranting had more to do with Harriet Beecher Stowe's sex than with her ideas. But Emily didn't argue with Pa-pa.

She felt like a peacock that had strayed from its pen, wearing outfits with feathers and frills and brightly colored tails. She and Little Sister had been put on display. They accompanied Father to Washington as the proud daughters of a United States Congressman from Massachusetts's Tenth District. But their pride had been shot. Poor Father was filling out his first and last term. Dickinson and the entire Whig Party had gone down to defeat. The "Black" Republicans had tainted Father until he seemed like a champion of the South. Father couldn't even carry his own town. And the people of neighboring Pelham voted against him nineteen to one. So the two daughters followed the vanquished Congressman to Washington, while he bled out his last days in office.

But they weren't treated like abandoned belles. The staff and guests at the Willard, Washington's finest hotel, which was a few doors from the

*White House, fell at their feet. Vinnie prowled the halls like some ravishing heiress, rather than a small-town girl. She walked the muddy, broken streets of the capital with her new friends, the wives and sisters of Senators and Supreme Court Justices. But Emily wouldn't venture beyond the Willard's front door, into the noisy metropolis where lives and goods were bartered with the wink of an eye. Emily was much too worried about Father to gallivant in Washington with a tail attached to her rump. And she wasn't much happier within the Willard's walls.*

*Emily would have crushed the entire hotel, with its chandeliers, its gold cages and satin settees, crushed it to the ground, if she could have had her way. The pomp of the place disturbed her; it reeked of a citified wealth, of whisperings in back rooms, of deals made amid the smoke of cigars. That was not Father's strong suit. Edward was a rough, country man who was never roundabout in his ways, who never whispered in the dark, but who spoke in the simplest manner and couldn't involve himself in the fistfights that broke out between Slavers and Anti-Slavers.*

*Father could not function in such a wild atmosphere. He did not know how to tame the demons in such men. Their demons were so different from his own. He could rescue a horse from a burning barn, save a colored orphan from being sent back to his master, have his daughters study rhetoric and religion and ask nothing more of them, but he could ask nothing for himself. Emily had never touched Father's face, and it needed touching. She clung to Father at the Willard whenever she could, sat with him over a glass of sherry, watched the sadness collect under his brows until Congress itself seemed like a plague that would flatten him.*

*She did go on one adventure with Pa-pa. While Lavinia remained at the Willard with some potential beau, Edward hired a carriage and rode with Emily along Pennsylvania Avenue. She saw mansions side by side with hovels, and it bewildered her, this marriage of penury and unimaginable wealth. The carriage stopped on G Street, at the Orphan School & Asylum, an old red-brick castle with turrets and chimney pots.*

*Edward had a stipend for one of the orphans, a boy named Ralph, whose mother had once worked for a manufacturer in his own Congressional dis-*

*trict. But Pa-pa couldn't get any farther than the vestibule with his fifty dollars in cash. Strangers weren't allowed to visit with orphans at this school, even if said stranger happened to be a Congressman.*

*Father wouldn't stir from the spot until the headmaster sent a note to the boys' dormitory, and within ten minutes Ralph arrived in a beggar's costume, with sleeves that were much too short. Emily could see the rage build in Father's eyes.*

*"Sir," he said to the headmaster, "you will put the boy in my custody for half an hour so that I may buy him a proper suit of clothes, or God is my witness, I will find a way to shut you down."*

*The boy was alert, with blue eyes. He clutched Emily's hand and called her "Marm," while Edward delivered him to a tailor shop on the far side of Mausoleum Square.*

*"Sir," he told the tailor, "there will be a bonus for you if the boy can walk out of this shop within the hour with a suit upon his back."*

*All the gloom seemed to lift from Pa-pa when he returned with Emily to the Willard Hotel. Lavinia was startled at his sudden transformation. His old vigor had come back. The girls could hardly keep up with him as he pranced across the lobby.*

*They left the capital after three weeks and traded one metropolis for another. Philadelphia might have had its own rascals, but not Congressmen who were also duelists and slaveholders. They didn't have to wander through the halls of a hotel. There was much less mud in Philadelphia; the horse-cars didn't sink into the ground. But Philadelphia had just been ravaged by its own Great Fire; there was still rubble on the sidewalks, and some of the horse-cars looked like half-burnt carcasses.*

*Edward deposited his two girls with their second cousin, Eliza Coleman, at her father's house near Chestnut Street and returned to Amherst. Emily still worried about him, but she was much less feisty in Philadelphia. She didn't have to rub up against Senators. She could sit by the window, write notes to her friend, Susie Gilbert, listen to the bells on the horse-cars, trace the outline of the trees with her finger, feel the rub of a word inside her brain.*

*And then she had a rude shock, an awakening that was like a blow to the head. It arrived from the most unexpected place—the Arch Street Presbyterian Church, where Eliza's father had his own family pew. The two sisters had gone to worship with the Colemans on their first Sunday in Philadelphia. Emily had listened to a heap of sermons half her life, had met ministers whose fame was like a lightning bolt in a particular town. But she had never come upon the likes of "Philadelphia."*

*Rev. Charles Wadsworth didn't mingle with his congregation, didn't ride out of the vestry in a splendid robe. He appeared in the pulpit from a trapdoor, like some mechanical man sprung from a palace of toys. Emily's first impulse was to mock the melodrama of his entrance and belittle the man. But she felt a chill as he glanced about the pulpit with eyes that gleamed under his spectacles. His hair was very long, like a pirate or a ship captain, and covered his ears entirely. He wore a silk cravat tight against his throat, and she couldn't be certain he was wearing gloves, or if his hands themselves had the color of clotted cream. His shoulders were narrow, and he wasn't so very tall, but his whole face shivered as he began to talk.*

*And Emily shivered in her seat. The minister's cavernous voice was like a rifle shot in her ear. He wounded whatever small comfort she had in Philadelphia with the tremors she could feel beneath his intoxicated tone. She could tell in an instant that he had all the wiles and weariness of a poet. He sang his words as if he were reciting to Emily alone. He could have been plundering her, ripping into the peacock's garb that she wore, searing her flesh.*

*His chest throbbed with thunder as he gripped the lectern with his cream-colored hands. "What is Christian chivalry?" he asked. "What has the Lord demanded that we do? Not to lose ourselves in the ritual of good deeds. Not to bask in our little charities. Not to sacrifice our own strong will and abandon ourselves to mindless giving. Then we would be Christian by habit only, a Marist reciting her beads. No, the Lord has asked one thing of us, that we not violate our inner nature. We must sally forth, with the plumes and banners of a proud heart. We are adventurers who will inscribe ourselves on the hardest stone, with the tap of the telegraph to guide us, the whistle and smoke of the steam engine."*

*He challenged his own church to raise itself up as a Christian army.*

*"If you be a bricklayer, then lay your bricks with music in your soul. If you be a doctor or nurse, then heal with your whole heart. If you be a poet, then delve not into mysteries and dreams, with cobwebs over your eyes, nor pity us with wild plaints, but investigate a squirrel's flight and the path of a torpedo. The Lord's perfection can be found in the meekest animal and the mightiest machine. And we must rejoice in this world of ours. Heaven must not take us away from the here and the now. God revels in the work we do."*

*There was silence in the assembly hall, the silence that seizes after a rock-slide or an avalanche. And then that magician of a minister disappeared just as he had appeared, through his damnable trapdoor. She would have married him in a minute were he not a married man, with a menagerie of little children, she imagined. Her throat was parched after Rev. Wadsworth's vanishing act. Her cheeks were flushed. She had a tingling in her own narrow chest. And the minister had not noticed her, wasn't even aware that Emily was alive. She could not paint herself like Amherst's own Cleopatra. She would still have had her freckles and raucous red hair.*

*She stopped exploring Philadelphia after her visit to the Arch Street Church. There were still ruins on Chestnut Street from the Great Fire. She saw the husks of burnt buildings, roofs eaten away, leprous walls with red marks on them. And she felt like such a ruin—a ruin with red hair. But she prayed to her good angel that she might not recover from the Reverend Wadsworth and her own wreckage so soon.*

# PART THREE

## Sister Sue and the Lost Souls

*The Homestead and the Evergreens*

*Summer, 1858*

## 21.

LORD, IT WASN'T LOVE AT FIRST SIGHT. I WAS FRIGHTENED of Susie Gilbert's smoldering looks, as if she had a hole burnt into the middle of her forehead that could set the whole town aflame. Susie was an orphan and a vagabond who maneuvered like a general. She conquered me and Brother and Pa-pa. She'd spent part of her childhood in Amherst, with her own renegade Pa-pa, who kept opening and closing taverns until the day he died. I try to imagine Susie at six. Did her brown eyes burn holes in the shop windows on Main Street? Did she weave ribbons into her hair? And would she have wanted to play with a freckle-face like me?

Susie returned to live here with an older sister when both of us were eighteen. But I didn't cross paths with her until a year later. And by then *all* the Dickinsons were becoming Susie's slaves. She was just more interesting and volatile than our Amherst mice— those silly creatures who knitted their own white vails and could see no further than a bridal gown. Susan never talked of matrimonial bliss. She swore she did not need a man. Even at nineteen she was the town philosopher, a bit of a deacon, who could talk Scripture with Pa-pa for hours. Mother was frightened of the fever in her eyes. Sue prevailed in any argument. She even had a faint mustache, like Zilpah Marsh, but it wasn't unbecoming—it went with her smoldering eyes. Brother was positively blue if she didn't erupt once or twice a month. She was our Vesuvius, who rained hot lava down upon our heads. It wasn't that she screamed or spat. Susan sulked.

Brother courted her for five whole years. He grew despondent; his fine red hair began to fall out. An army of belles ran after him vails in hand, their dowries trailing behind them like a caboose, while Brother looked at them with scorn; he would marry Sue or remain unmarried the rest of his life.

Father took long walks with Sue, went to Church with her. In his own silent way he was wooing her for Brother. We began calling her Sister Sue. It was as if we were waging war in Brother's behalf. Mother kept out of the picture, but I played the diplomat. I cast a net around Sue without her ever knowing it. I was drawing her into the family on pieces of invisible string. It worked only too well.

She got herself engaged to Austin without bothering to tell us. It made no difference to her that I lived by Susan's moods and Susan's weather, that I couldn't smile until she smiled, that I wore her own expressions, sulked when she sulked, but I wasn't much of a Vesuvius, with smoke coming out of my head. And she went off on a tryst to Boston with Brother, just to be away from Amherst's eyes. It couldn't have been much of a tryst, since Sue barely had a place in her heart for a man's affections. But suddenly I did start to smoke, and I thought my head would catch fire. I was jealous of their time together, the little secrets that grew around them, their own invisible string.

And just as suddenly, Sue relented and married Austin. I was happy for them and full of misery, as if Sue and I were no longer conspirators who could hug and kiss and declare that no man would ever claim us. I'm not sure Brother ever claimed Sue; I would learn that Susie had demanded a "chaste marriage," and Brother agreed. And it's heartless of me to say it, but I took some pleasure at the thought of ice and ashes strewn on the bridal bed. I could bathe myself in ice and ash, and live there with Austin and Sue...

We're sisters now; she reads the poems I scribble on old recipes and scraps of paper, and understands the peculiar weave of my mind, welcomes it even, like a general examining the words of a rival, sending missiles back and forth.

She's become mistress of the town, fighting the scarlatina that grows worse with every epidemic. Suddenly my Susan is every-where, succoring the ill, soothing the bereaved for the loved ones they have lost, while I can barely stir from Father's mansion, with or without my dog. And when the daughter of our stableman is stricken, Susie sends Dick flowers and feeds him soup, though the stable is but steps away from our kitchen.

"God bless Mrs. Austin," Dick says to Mother and myself. "She's the angel of Amherst, Miss Em'ly, she is."

I pray for little Harriet, who is seven, but I have not ridden to see her yet in Father's chariot. Susan has enlisted Father, who accom-panies her on missions of mercy. I have never seen the Patriarch so involved in the turmoil of our little town. I watch them from my window. He has taken to calling her "Dolly" now, not by any malicious design to hurt his own flesh and blood. After all, Dolly is what her brothers and sisters called her when she was a child. So it is natural that he would find a nickname for Sue, forgetting in the flush of his involvement with a new daughter-in-law that he has not called his own daughter Dolly in years.

And when I see them now in the chariot, Susie with a piece of black crepe pinned on her bonnet to mourn the town's dead children, and Father wearing a black armband, they look like some couple prepared to do battle with all the fatalities of scarlet fever, and Lord knows, they might win. Sometimes Father even lets her have the reins, and she's the one who leads Black Fanny, Father's mare.

It is odd that the epidemic should arrive so early in the season, during our torrid summer with its attack of lightning and lady-bugs, and not during the colder months, when scarlet fever may lurk behind a wet cough and a spotted throat. But our village has happened upon a most unfortunate season, where everything is out of kilter: barns burn, children die, carriage horses drop from exhaustion, and thunder splits our brains. Sue is the one who is bold enough to move against the prodigal force of the season, defying thunder and burning barns to save as many children as the Lord will allow her to do.

I can fancy Father and Susan wearing muslin masks to protect them from catching the scarlatina that might vanish with the red spots or worsen into a relentless fever that will scorch a child's blood and bones with the same implacability as the Sahara sun. But I do not have to fancy the vanilla ice cream that Sue whipped together with her own hands; she'll arrive at a farmhouse with Pa-pa and spill that cold elixir into the raw throat of a stricken boy.

Mother and I are helpless in the manufacture of ice cream. We have fallen into a deep malaise ever since we moved back into the Dickinson Homestead. For Ma-ma and me it was a house of ghosts, with goblins and old men who lived in the attic. It wasn't like our white mansion on West Street, where the ghosts were much more pious and played in the cemetery behind our backyard. But this white mansion wasn't Pa-pa's ancestral seat, so we returned to the Homestead, with Sue right beside us. The baroness has her own manor-house, the Evergreens, which Father helped construct to tie Brother and his bride to our village. And because Mother was ill and couldn't even preside over Father's house, Mrs. Aus-tin soon presided over Amherst itself. Her afternoons and soirees at the Evergreens eclipsed the President's own levees at the Col-lege. Ralph Emerson stayed with Brother and Sue after giving a lecture at the Church Meetinghouse. He talked about the Beautiful in Rural Life, I'm told. Lord, I would have loved to listen, but I was too gnome-like to sit beside that Sultan! Yet in another life, I would have asked him if he had an Orchard like ours, and if it had the same skeletal silence that could stun a bird.

But Sue was less of a baroness this summer while the fever raged. She canceled her afternoon teas with philosophers and poets. There were no guests at the Evergreens. I watch her from my window like some forlorn spy as she returns from her latest mission. Poor Fanny comes to a stop with little rivers of sweat on her hide. Sister Sue steps out of the carriage with Father to hold her hand. She *is* the first lady of Amherst, even with the feel of sickbeds on her clothes. We are all little street Arabs in her wake, vagabonds of a lesser nature.

She's been writing a novel and has been most secretive about it. The sky don't fall on Susie's sentences—nothing does. She hasn't shown a line to Sister Emily. Father has become the guardian of Susie's flame. He is satanically serious about her writing, whispers about publishing it himself, or sitting down with a Boston publisher in her behalf. Father salaams to Sister Sue. She calls him "Master" in front of Austin and me, but I can fancy who is the Master and who is the slave.

I can't put Pa-pa in mind of me. It is not that he is cruel or neglectful. He worships my Indian bread. But I have become one more Phantom in his household, as minuscule as Mother or Vinnie. I am the female who repairs his slippers, but it is Susie he takes into his carriage on their rides to rescue feverish, spotted children, or bury those that need burying. And it is black-eyed Susan, not his pale daughter, whose sentences he scans, though how much of Susan he has read I still cannot surmise.

It is like being stabbed in the side with a Tomahawk that I have to clutch with my own hand. I do not utter a word. I keep pretty dark about what I feel and what I think. I have no novel to offer Pa-pa, and do not have the wildest scheme of how to write one. But

I have taken my phantom flowers and sewn them into little booklets from the best paper I could buy. I had meant to leave those
flowers to sit and gather dust in my drawer. But I prettied them
up for Pa-pa—no, that is an untruth. I did not prettify. I put my
own feathers on every stamen and stem, thrust them up with whatever little force I have. I am a creature of feathers. And I stole the
idea of binding my flowers into a little book from Father himself.
He's the one who saved his college compositions by sewing them
together. And I planned to leave my flowers under Father's door
in five or six booklets that might have the aroma of a novel. But
no flowers of mine could ever charm him. He lives in a world of
Prose, except when it comes to Sue.

## 22.

IT IS A SEASON OF SMOKE AND SCARLATINA, OUR SUMMER OF '58. Three barns took fire in July alone. And our fire engine is much too feeble, though it weighs 2½ tons and has to be dragged around by horses and men. It has a steamer that often explodes and its pump can't be operated by less than sixteen souls. We had a westerly wind that was brutal, and the barns themselves were dry as sticks and stones. And Father, who was our fire marshal, had to roam around in the tall grass.

"It's amazin' weather," he opined, after he finished prowling. "The Lord had best be on our side."

But the fire alarm sounds this morning at ¼ to 10. I can sniff the smoke from my window; a black patch invades the sky like a cloud sent from the Devil. It sits across from our fields—the fire could spread along the dry grass like some startling snake and arrive at our door.

Pa-pa does not panic, or signal to me with the side of his head. I do not have to fetch Lavinia and move Ma-ma and our possessions far from that hypothetical storm. The dray horses snort and rumple their noses at the heat; Pa-pa helps unhitch them from the

engine before they go berserk by the nearness of the fire. Then
Father's little band of volunteers haul that machine into the heart
of the conflagration, a monstrous black belly of smoke in front of
Coulter's barn. What mesmerizes me for a moment is that they are
wearing yellow gloves like the ones Missy had worn and lent to Zilpah Marsh, and now lie hidden in Father's attic, like some cruel
reminder of Missy's own relentless magic.

Soon I could only see little swatches of yellow in all the blackness and hear the firemen heave and whistle under their breath
as they primed the hot pump; then the whole machine shook,
and water shot from the silver nozzle with a great swoosh. These
enchanters with their yellow gloves had solved the riddle of a westerly wind. The fire sputtered; Coulter's roof collapsed, but the
barn had been saved from the worst sort of ravage. It stood like
some creature with half a head.

Father was the first to walk out of the smoke. He had a wildness
about him that was not unattractive, as if he had shed a dozen
years in fighting that fire. His red hair was unruly under his hat.
The edges of his cloak were singed, his face mottled with bits of
ash from the burning barn.

"Refreshments, boys," he said in that hoarse voice of his. "I'll
splurge a bit. I'm buyin' drinks at the tavern."

"Aw, Squire," said one of the volunteers, an Irisher who was
a handyman at the Evergreens and took care of our own barn.
"You'll only steal it back from the insurance company and the fire-
man's fund."

Father laughed. "Indeed I will."

I had never seen him so relaxed, so full of goodwill. He had
once been a major in the town's militia, and this tiny militia of firemen must have brought back memories of drilling on the Commons with his own command. He wasn't the sort to be part of any
group, even when he went to Congress. He could not parade like
other men, could not strut. He was a *Dickinson*, who didn't think

it proper to reveal more than he had to reveal. I doubt that he missed his Congressman's seat. Yet here, after the fury of a fire, with an engine that was fickle and spat steam at firemen, scalding one or two, he found a poetry he had no place else. The volunteers serenaded him on our journey to the tavern.

> *Who's the man, oh who's the man*
> *Who gives his best, his very best*
> *To fight that monster in the fire*
> *And bring us some tranquility?*
> *Squi-re Edward, Squi-re Edward,*
> *Master of the town, of the town.*

AS MORE BARNS TOOK FIRE, THEY SEEMED IN SOME MYS-terious way to burn out that epidemic of scarlet fever. Father began to see less and less of Sister Sue. There were no more carriage rides into the hinterlands and not so many whisperings about a Boston publisher for Sue's intended novel. Father had his law practice to consider and this new epidemic of burning barns. He strolled the village, hat in hand, with the Sheriff of Northampton, our shire town. There was talk about some insidious arsonist, a disgruntled farmer or a lunatic who had escaped from the asylum. But there were no missing lunatics that Father could reckon. The Governor had appointed him a trustee of the asylum, and Father was scrupulous in search of the grounds. So he and the Sheriff had to look elsewhere to solve the riddle.

They couldn't solve a thing, since the arsonist did not leave a trace in the summer grass. Father began experimenting with watchdogs. He borrowed five mastiffs from a breeder in Belchertown, had them stationed on strategic hills, but the Amherst fire-maniac poisoned all five dogs, feeding them arsenic from his own hand without being spotted by a single soul. Father wanted to requisition Carlo, but I would have died had I found that Colossus writhing in the grass, rigor mortis about to settle in. And finally Father relinquished his demands on my dog.

That don't mean I was disrespectful. I patrolled as much of the town as I could with Carlo, but I wasn't much of a sentinel, and neither was he. His shaggy ears would perk up whenever he saw a stranger. If that stranger had no evil designs on his mistress, Carlo ceased to care. He wasn't a good citizen of Amherst, just a watchdog over one old maid.

And Sister Sue? Without any spotted children to care for, she returned to her grand salon. Lord, she couldn't have Ralph Emerson every other week. But we did have charades in the library or on the lawn, tea and pyramids of ice cream in her dining room, and sporadic musicals, where I sit at the piano and pound on the keys whatever fanciful tune comes into my head. Mrs. Austin says I'm the Chopin of Massachusetts, but my improvisations have little in common with Chopin's etudes—or with Chopin, the rage of Paris while he was still alive, in love with George Sand and her men's scarves and hats. George Sand's scarves wouldn't help me much. My flutterings are more like the lopsided growth of an untamed flower than the rise of a real melody.

At least Carlo loves my music. He crawls under the piano with a look of rapture on his face; he must think his mistress is losing her mind. Perhaps I am. But suddenly the Evergreens is more of a home than Pa-pa's estate. I have Mr. and Mrs. Austin, Carlo, and sometimes Lavinia, who is less at ease with Susie's volcanic temperature. Sister is scared to death of Mt Vesuvius, and Susie might erupt at any moment. But I don't mind a volcano next door. Carlo and I—and Austin too—have learned to shiver around her eruptions, though my dog keeps as far from Susan as he can. Yet she is as sweet and calm today as the yellow in one of my pies.

And damn me if she don't get down on her knees to coax Carlo out from under a chair and feed him a hefty slice of strawberry ice cream that she herself cut from that scrumptious pyramid on the table. And while we devour ice cream with my dog, Susan starts to recite a poem she must have scratched out this very morning, since she had not read a single line of it to me.

> *Fame is for the pirate and other trackers of blood*
> *Who shirk the notion of family and household faith*
> *But I am a pirate who never seeks the far flood*
> *And would as lief remain—*

But Susie couldn't even finish the first stanza. The doorbell rang, and I, who cannot bear foreign society or any sudden rush of intruders, ran out the room with Carlo and hid in the library. From that listening post, Carlo and I, like two Comanche, could hear the sound of merriment and the clapping of hands. Then there was the rhythmic patter of feet and a determined knock on our Comanche door.

"Emily, you will vacate the library this instant," shouts Sister Sue.

"But couldn't we escape through the pantry?" I whisper.

"You will do nothing of the kind. Would you shame me in front of our guest? He will think your father raises barbarians."

"He certainly does. Lavinia says I am cross and crusty most mornings *and* a barbarian."

"Well," says Mrs. Austin, who can counter any argument I could ever make. "I would consider it a kindness if the barbarian in this house agreed to acquaint herself with Mr. Samuel Bowles of the *Springfield Republican.*"

Sam Bowles was just about the most famous editor in the land. Father and I couldn't finish a day without reading the *Republican.* And what was a metropolitan like Bowles doing in Amherst?

"Susan," I whisper into the library door. "I can't meet Mr. Bowles. I'm not dressed for the occasion."

"Emily, will you stop wasting time? Mr. Bowles begs your acquaintance. I told him I have a sister-in-law who writes sonnets."

All the Comanche had gone out of me and my bones. "Susan, how could you? You're the poet. I'm just a girl who gathers feathers around me. It's pure camouflage."

"Emily, I will *un*feather you and your dog if you don't come out."

I surrender to Sue. I scamper into her drawing room utterly out of breath and look at Mr. Bowles a little aslant. Lord, he is the most handsome fellah I ever laid my amber eyes upon. He couldn't have been much older than myself or Sue, and with his bushy eyebrows and dark beard he seemed like an Arabian prince who fell from the sky. I was blushing so hard at the beauty of him, I had to hide my face.

"Miss Dickinson," he says in that familiar twang of a Massachusetts man. "Mrs. Austin says that you are a great admirer of Mrs. Browning and her sonnets, and that you have a picture of her on your wall."

How could I not, Sir, considering that Elizabeth Barrett was an invalid most of her life and had a morbid fear of strangers. She might have been locked up forever in her father's house had not the prince of poets, Mr. Robert Browning, fallen in love with her verse. He stole Elizabeth from her father and married her in clandestinity. But how could I speak of her *Sonnets from the Portuguese* with a perfect stranger, albeit as handsome as a sheik?

It was Susan herself who joggled me out of my silence.

"Emily dear, must our guest repeat himself? Tell Mr. Bowles about your love of Mrs. Browning."

"When I read her I can feel a furnace inside my head. I cannot seem to stop. It's as if a demon were chasing me."

"Or a lady poet's muse perhaps," said the Sheik.

I echoed him. "Perhaps. That furnace explodes, but still I can't stop. I shrink with every explosion, while the furnace fattens."

The Sheik stroked his beard with the long, crisp fingers of a piano player. "That's as fine a definition of poetry as I've ever heard. Mr. Dickinson, don't you agree?"

But Austin might just as well have been invisible. He was little more than an appendage to Susie's salon. That love of poetry has fled his face. I'd be willing to wager a dozen Lexicons that my poor lonesome brother no longer dreams of diadems and dirks. He'd gone north in his own mind after the marriage, though he lived but a house away. He couldn't seem to settle in with Sue. Her displeasure at a man's "low practices" must have insaned him a bit. He seldom visited us at the Homestead.

"I have no such furnace," Brother said, and I wished for a moment that I could rip him right out of time and lend him his old room. He'd vanished into the Evergreens with an air of bewilderment, but Mr. Bowles's visit had brought some color back into Austin's face. Bowles had come here to report on an agricultural show in Belchertown and decided to pay a visit to Susie's salon.

We drink wine and sup on cucumbers and cold meats. I can feel my heart lurch. I'm always scheming. I wonder if Mr. Bowles is a bachelor and might be interested in a maiden of twenty-seven. But I learn soon enough that he's a married man with a brood of his own. His wife, I am told, had been made somber by a stillborn child, and "Mr. Sam" was said to travel with female companions; filled with wine, I fancy myself as one such female companion. I wouldn't have to travel very far with my Sheik, but would have to stay in fashion and visit one of the bonnet rooms in Springfield until Father caught wind of his daughter's new double life— mistress and old maid. He'd martyr himself for Miss Emily, give up his delight in the pages of the *Republican*, and drive Mr. Sam from our shire with a swift kick.

But I'm the vainest of girls. One look in the mirror cures me of all my vanities. Our Mister, I realize, has scant interest in an old maid. He's absorbed in the mistress of the house. Her dark eyes and brooding look seem to touch his appetite. We sit over our wine and play whist, while my Susie and Mr. Sam steal glances at one another. I fear for my brother but don't say a word. She's smitten with Mr. Sam. But she's careful not to flirt. Susan's the pirate who never seeks the far flood, as she says in her poem.

But all that hot current is deflected when Mr. Bowles challenges Austin to a game of shuttlecock. Susan and I act as referees as our two warriors exhaust themselves wafting into the air that cork ball with its cluster of feathers; I have to hold Carlo down, or he'd chase the shuttlecock, catch it in his mouth, and both referees would have to interrupt their calls of "fair" or "foul."

Mr. Sam is a marvel with the battledore—I am dizzified. I have never seen such deftness with a weapon made of gut. He moves with all the agility of a dancer or an acrobat, while my poor brother flails at the shuttlecock and watches it fly into the ceiling, the furniture, or one of the walls. And I am forced to cry "foul, most foul." He has to relinquish the battledore to Susan, who has a steadier stroke and gives Mr. Bowles a much longer run.

Helpless, hardly a match for Susan or Mr. Bowles, I remain the referee. The sun begins to vanish from the walls. There are too many shadows, too many haunted spots, to play in the irregular light of a candle or a lamp. Brother seizes the battledore again and promptly loses the feathered ball in the dark of the ceiling. We search and search but cannot find the feathers. Brother is crestfallen, while Susan lets out a great laugh that resounds in my ears like the roar of a giant.

"Good Lord, that birdie stunted us. But dearest, you must not mope. We will find that feathered thing in the morning, won't we, Emily?"

But she don't allow me to answer. She serves some berry wine that Lavinia and I concocted in our kitchen and she salutes the wine-makers.

"Emily is a wonder, Mr. Sam. She could enter her wine at any fair or cattle show."

"It's Lavinia's hand," I whisper against the musical wind of Susan's voice. "I squashed the berries, that's all."

"It's delicious," says Mr. Bowles, while a drop of wine spills onto his beard—I would love to lick it off, considering he looks Arabian, and I have no more morals than a harem girl.

Then I can *feel* that triangular light jumping off the walls. It's Father with his lantern, come to fetch me, although there ain't a hundred yards between his house and the Evergreens. Even my dog is worried, but he don't growl.

"It was divine to meet you," I say to Mr. Bowles, putting on my feathers again, but false ones, since I couldn't let him know how attached to him I was after one afternoon and evening at the Evergreens. But that's how love is—impractical and foolish. It flares up and spreads through your loins faster than a burning barn.

I'm all aglow, but he can't decipher my deep blush in the lantern light. I shake his hand and try not to let him comprehend the electrical sparks in my skin.

"Thank you for your company, Miss Dickinson, and for the berry wine."

Carlo and I alight from the Evergreens as quickly as we can and fall into the glow of Father's lantern. My heart pounds beneath my shivering. The hand that clutches the lantern is wavering with all of Father's fury.

"*Dolly*," he says to spite me and turn me back into a child. "Do you have any wonder what the hour is? *Near midnight.*"

I say not a word. Not even feathers can help me now. I cannot plume myself against his fury. I walk behind Pa-pa.

# 23.

WE LOST SIX BARNS IN JULY, AND THE AUGUST WIND WAS LIKE hot parchment that could crackle into fire. Father would return home as morose as some veteran of a vicious war, his hands and face marked with all the black vapors off burning wood. He had to buy a dozen new handkerchiefs at Sweetser's store, since he never approached a hot barn without a handkerchief under his eyes.

The Elder seemed to have little fear. He'd lope into a barn and save half a dozen horses and cows, and sometimes he'd come out of that inferno with a piglet in his arms. There was no point in talking caution to Pa-pa. He wasn't going to have some malcontent or malicious fire-maniac destroy the village and break its morale. Father was the first one into the fire and the last one home. There wasn't a citizen in Amherst who did not step out of the Squire's path whenever he took to strolling.

And I was Mr. Dickinson's whimsical daughter who pranced about the village with a large dog. I am indulged, smiled upon, a maiden moving toward thirty who didn't even have the wherewithal to become a schoolmistress. But my voice could never arrive at the far end of a class, and what principal in his right mind would allow me to keep Carlo under the desk?

I have my garden and my observatory at the eastern edge of the house, where I keep a writing stand like some clerk and scribble whatever nonsense flies into my head while I tend to my plants. But I wouldn't leave Father to find the fire-maniac all alone. If I can't be a sentinel, I can at least be a spy. Carlo and his mistress inspect the fields behind our own barn, and as I beat the tall grass for any signs of a maniac, somebody bumps along like an enormous rodent.

"Desist," I squeak. "Reveal your face, or I'll send my dog after your throat."

He rises out of the grass, unmasks himself, removes his straw hat, and the sunlight dances off the damaged side of his face. He has been following me and my dog, and Carlo is such a magnificent hound that he never listened to Breckenbridge's footsteps. That old master of the rum resort had crept up behind us with impunity.

"I was waitin' for you, Miss."

"Mr. Breckenbridge, you could have rung at our door. It is not as if you are a perfect stranger. My dog treats you as kin."

"Well, I didn't want to come a-calling," he says. "I'm on a secret mission, sort of."

"Breck, I can't believe you're the fire-maniac. And if you are, you'd best abscond. I might not tattle on you for old time's sake."

"That's what I'm talking about. Old time's sake. A certain party is back in town, and he says, 'Do us a favor and find me Currer Bell.' "

I'm shivering, but I do not show it. "But that was long ago, Mr. Breckenbridge. There is no Currer Bell—that's Charlotte Brontë, and she's in her grave."

"That's the pith of it, Miss. This party implored me to find you.

He's waitin' in the graveyard. And he's running out of time. The sheriffs of five counties are after him."

I start to shiver from the shock. "But Brainard was a scholar," I insist.

"Well, his scholarship has taken a poor turn. Rum has ruined milord. He's a cardsharper and a bit of a scamp."

"You slander him," I say.

"Well, slander or not, Miss, you'd best hurry. Posse's approaching, and the clock's ticking faster than milord can wait."

And hurry I did. We ran across the fields, dodging butterflies as huge as gold ingots, and trying not to trample on the crickets. There wasn't a soul in the cemetery, not that I could see. But when Carlo and I rushed through the rear gate, we found milord leaning against a crooked stone.

He was as pale and worn as an old candle, but he could still trouble a spinster's heart. My Tutor from Mars taught me all about Domingo. He tasted sweet. His mind was quick as a dirk. And he moved with a sudden poetry. I'm not worried about what Susan calls "a man's requirements." I only wish that Brainard *required* me. I'd use the graveyard as a bower, and let the Devil drop me into Hell!

But Brainard has a saturnine look, and I have to be bolder than my Domingo.

"Darling," I shout in my pygmy voice that can't even shatter the silence of a graveyard. "I need another nom de guerre. Currer Bell is out of fashion ever since poor Charlotte Brontë couldn't prove she wasn't a man."

He laughs, but he still don't hold me in his arms. "Then what nom de guerre would you like?"

"My father used to call me Dolly. But he's been distributing that name around, and it's lost its pungent flavor."

"Then I'll call you Daisy, the flower girl."

I'll be damned if Brainard didn't tame time. I'm the belle I used to be, and the rascal has made me blush. I am the flower girl—his flower.

"But I shan't accept it, darling, if you've used that name on another."

"Ah," he says, "will you hold me to that promise?"

He's wearing a summer coat with frayed sleeves and a cravat with crooked strings. His shoes want a little polishing, but I'd take him to the shoemaker and buy him another pair with Pa-pa's money if he'd promise to marry me, and even if he don't. He intoxicates me in a way that Mr. Bowles never could. I wouldn't mind being part of his seraglio, the biggest part. But I still can't get much of a proposal out of him. Instead he drills Shakespeare into my eardrum, pretends we're Antony and Cleopatra escaping from the battle of Actium. But he must be a confidence man, or how else would he know to seize the words of Cleopatra for himself and let me have the role of that love-sick general, Marc Antony, who gives up half the world and all his wealth for that conniving queen?

"*Forgive my fearful sails!*" my Domingo says. "*I little thought you would have follow'd.*"

"*Egypt, thou knew'st too well,*" I whisper. "*My heart was to thy rudder tied by strings . . .*"

And both of us luxuriate in the village yard with words that have a lover's lightning—lightning that can shake the world, invert what is for what ought to be.

"Daisy, how many boys have asked for your hand while I've been gone from Amherst?"

"Not a one," I say, removing Antony's armor and painting myself as Cleopatra with all her guile. "But if truth be known, I would have kissed my Philadelphia if he'd given me half the chance."

"Phil-a-*del*-phi-a?" Domingo says, toying with that word upon his tongue.

"That's what I call him—not to his face. I met him but once."

"Another handyman, I suppose, who can neither read nor write."

"You insult me, darling. He's a minister—a married man. The Reverend Wadsworth. And the sermon he delivered could have made a rhinoceros weep—it turned me to ice. It was as if he disrobed while he talked and I could see terrible puckers of pain upon his skin. I suspect that half the womenfolk inside the church wanted to comfort Mr. Wadsworth, hold him in their arms. The Reverend Wadsworth is a minister much in demand, as you might imagine."

"What was a country girl doing in Philadelphia?"

"Visitin' with Lavinia," I say. "She's the prettier one, who really looks like Cleopatra. The two of us went to Washington to see the sights while Father was still in Congress, and we stopped off in Philadelphia to see Eliza, our second cousin."

"And did she fall in love with this minister who bleeds so lightly under his skin?"

"No. Eliza thought him dragonish. She was frightened of the fire he breathes upon his flock—I am the culprit, dear Domingo, your Daisy."

He picks up my tiny freckled hand and peruses it. "Is that the hand that kings have trembled to kiss?"

"*Yes,*" I warble like the asp that poisoned Cleopatra—longing to poison my Domingo, not to destroy him, mind, but make him my prisoner, hold him in my box of Phantoms, but then I remember that Phantoms can't play.

I whisper now. "Darling, your unsightly friend from the rum resort, Mr. Breckenbridge, has slandered you. He says you're a cardsharp."

"But I am, Daisy, I am. I've been haunting the railroad cars on your father's line and fleecing whatever customers I can."

"It's not Father's line," I manage to say, camouflaging the shock I'm in. Father had brought a branch line to our village, the Amherst and Belchertown Railroad, but he wasn't its president or principal owner. He was proud of that line, though it was near to bankruptcy and had to be financed all over again.

"Your father's line or not, the railroad detectives are after me—my picture is up at the Post Office, even if they haven't tied my name to it yet."

"Lord," I moan like someone seized by Satan, "how did you get from tutorin' to stealing at cards?"

"They're not so far apart. Both take a kind of persuasion. Besides, I'm good at it, and Yale relieved me of my services years ago."

"But I could go to Father. He might be able to help."

"And do what? Ask me to become his handyman?"

He laughs at Emily the naïf, sheltered as she is like a nun, and then he touches my cheek.

"Daisy, I came here for one thing. I wanted to have a look at you before I go West, I wanted to squeeze you until you begged for mercy."

"I wouldn't beg," I say. "I'd ask for more."

It was no lie. Sitting on Brainard's lap in a rum resort was just about the most salient event of my life. I ought be ashamed to admit it, but I'm not.

And then Satan did seize me up and sing in my voice. "Darling, take me with you, take me to your West, where I can rip off my petticoats and pan for gold."

Suddenly my Domingo stops leaning on his stone. I've aroused him from that little game in the graveyard—and it's no more Antony and Cleopatra, but a misbegotten Tutor and an old maid.

"Daisy," he says, "I'll have to pay a price for one last look at you. But if I steal you from Amherst—"

"Darling, I'm the one who's stealing you."

"But the result is the same. Your Father and his railroad men will have my head."

"Then I'll call you John the Baptist, and parade around with that head of yours in my pocket."

But I'm troubled by my own *conceit*, and I start to cry. "Flee, you hear—go on without me."

And it's then, and only then, while I'm as confused and weak as a frog in a pond of crocodiles, that this cardsharper takes me in his arms and sucks at my face. I might have swooned after a kiss like that if he hadn't kissed me once before in the rum resort, and it was the recollection of such a kiss that saved my sanity and kept me on my feet.

"Daisy," he says, while I'm still recuperating, "meet me at the Amherst depot in five hours."

"Won't the railroad detectives be waiting for you?"

"Yes, but I'll make myself scarce until my Daisy arrives, and she'll be my salvation—they see their sharper as a lone wolf, and they won't expect to find him with a girl in a summer bonnet."

"I have to warn you, Brainard, I won't be carrying much coin under my bonnet—I'm not an heiress."

He laughed and swooped down to kiss me again, but I might not have survived it and gotten to the railroad depot in time. And so I pulled away from him as gently as I could, but could still hear him call.

—*Daisy, remember. Don't be late.*

# 24.

MY ROMANCE HAD NOTHING TO DO WITH SEASONS OR practical considerations. I likened myself to Mrs. Browning. Not with her beauty, of course, but with her desire to escape an overbearing father and be with the man she loved. Brainard Rowe wasn't Mr. Browning, and couldn't afford to take me to Italy. But Daisy don't need the Florentine. I'd wear a vail and bite back whatever dust the West can bring.

I was in misery over my dog. I couldn't hide Carlo in a carpetbag—he's much too grandiose. And the conductors would be mighty suspicious if I tried to board the train with him. They'd brand me as Mr. Dickinson's daughter. We'd never even get past the terminus at Montague. The railroad detectives would handcuff Brainard and escort me home with my hound. They'd keep my name and Carlo's from the *Republican*, out of respect for Father and his relationship to the line.

And so I am a penitent while I pack. Carlo can sense the doom that's hanging over him. He even manages to get the hair out of his eyes.

It's a miracle that Brainard reappeared while Father and

Mother are in Monson visiting her people. I wouldn't have had the nerve to steal myself away had Father been around. I walk down from my room with my carpetbag and my dog while Vinnie is dusting the stairs. She's quick to read that mad determination in my eye.

"Emily, where in damnation are you going?"

"Little Sister, can't you tell? I'm eloping."

She drops her duster, removes her apron, and tries to keep calm.

"And who's the lucky fellah?"

"Domingo—remember him? That Tutor from Yale."

"But he vanished from the face of the earth," Sister says, seeing if she can catch her breath *and* her bearings.

"I thought you liked him, Lavinia."

"I did. But what is his current occupation?"

"Cardsharp," I say.

She's silent for a second, her eyes gathering up intelligence.

"You can't be serious. I will not listen."

"But listen you will. Father will not come one more time with his lantern and drive me out of the Evergreens like household cattle, not while I love a man."

Sister started to cry. "Will you become a cardsharp's wife?"

"A cardsharp's mistress, I imagine. Brainard has not promised to marry me."

Lavinia's face went all white. "Then he is a worm, the vilest sort of seducer. He took advantage of your kindness with his sugary talk and convinced you to run away with him."

"Little Sister, I'm the one who had to sugar him . . . I will need some hard cash."

Lavinia is the one who kept the accounts, since Mother could not be trusted with the simplest sum, and I walked around in a daze, with holes in my pockets. But Lavinia could add and subtract like a bank cashier, bargain with the grinder who came to our door to sharpen Mother's knives, and argue with Mr. Sweetser over the cost of an item on our monthly bill; she kept a purse on a string near her waist, and it was usually fat with three-dollar gold pieces that she dispensed like the Lord's own bookkeeper.

She must have seen the ravaged look on my freckled face and took some pity. She couldn't abandon her deranged sister to the wolves. So Lavinia meted out nine three-dollar pieces into the palm of my hand. I barely had the strength to carry them. A neo-phyte as I was in matters of money, I never realized the *heft* of a three-dollar coin. I had no purse of my own. And all the pieces did not fit into my pocket.

I reached out to kiss Lavinia, but she was gone, dusting stairs in some far corner, I suppose. It was odd that she did not offer a part-ing hug, since she might not see me for a century. I had to depend on Little Sister's good nature, that she would feed and befriend Carlo, who had no friends other than his mistress.

Hair was no hindrance, and I realized for the first time that Carlo only saw what he wanted to see. That dog had a preternatu-ral intuition. He couldn't take his eyes off my carpetbag. And he must have sensed that it wasn't his cradle. I was going away and hadn't provided a proper wagon for him. It was a wound to his dignity.

"*Darling*, I'd take you if I could."

～

HERE I AM, GOING TO MEET MY LOVE AT THE AMHERST AND Belchertown depot, and I can't stop crying. The sun bakes on my back, and my brains begin to boil under my bonnet. I don't snif-fle once over Pa-pa, who will recover from my exile, my flight into Egypt. Mother hardly exists, and I've long ago put her into my box of Phantoms. I wish I could have said my farewells to Austin and Sue, but if I had confided in them, they'd have held me pris-oner in the Evergreens until Father arrived with his lantern—Lord knows, I need a brutal break. Nothing short of that will ever land me in Egypt.

I march down Main Street, past Father's meadow with its stacks of hay like little mountains of red in the sunlight, past the hat factory, past Rooming-house Row and the "graveyard" it has become ever since the railroad cut through its territories and built a depot. It's a mystery to me where most of the factory workers and the Irish maids now live. I wouldn't be startled to learn that some invisible no-man's-land near the depot had swallowed them up. But I haven't found it yet, at least not during my late travels with Carlo.

The depot is little more than a wooden hut with a narrow wooden walk and a barn at one end to house and repair broken trains. The tracks that lie between the barn and the hut look like irregular rows of rusty rails that are overrun with grass. A person would have to suffer from blindness or something close to consider the Amherst and Belchertown a thriving enterprise. I'm not sure where the railroad's capital went. But it didn't go into building a depot and laying tracks.

People start to collect on that wooden walk for the afternoon run to Springfield and beyond. I begin to fancy that some of them are railroad detectives, though I haven't the intuition to tease out which ones. There are no immediate neighbors of mine, but I am such a recluse that I wouldn't have recognized even a half-familiar face. I can still see Carlo with his brown eyes on my carpetbag, and I wouldn't want strangers to watch me cry.

But forlorn as I am, I can feel that flutter in my heart. And I sing to myself, *Domingo, Domingo, he's a takin' me to Egypt.*

I could sing until the crickets formed a chorus and chirped back at me and I'd never find Domingo.

He don't show. I fancy he's hiding somewhere, but fancying can't get me far. And finally I do see a familiar face. I don't need a wandering gypsy teller to read my fortune. Lavinia wasn't hiding somewhere in the house when I exited without my dog. She ran to the Evergreens for Sue. And with her dark eyes and fierce features, Susie looks like *she* has been to Egypt, and now I'll never get there.

"You can't persuade me," I hiss like a serpent. But my venom is small.

She smiles under her bonnet. "Will you make a spectacle of yourself right on the floorboards of your father's depot?"

"It don't matter," I insist. "I'm the extravagant daughter who never dusts the stairs and who sails around with a big dog."

"Emily, I will not leave this station until you march home with your portmanteau."

"Why?" I ask, pretending to have Cleopatra's swagger in matters of love and war. "Are you frightened of a little scandal? Ralph Emerson will boycott your salon and Mr. Sam Bowles will never leave his hat again on your settee."

"Emily Elizabeth Dickinson, you are hurtful *and* imbecilic."

"But those are useful ingredients in a war."

She laughs the bitterest laugh I have ever heard. Her mouth is blue from all the bitterness. "War against whom, my dear?"

"The Evergreens and the Homestead."

"Perhaps I have neglected you during the scarlet-fever outbreak. I did not have time to answer *all* your notes."

"But you had the time to show Father pages of your novel."

My venom seems to bite. The hardness and calculation are gone. And she lapses into her old habit of a shivering lower lip.

"There is no such novel, you silly creature. I am not one of the Brontë sisters and never will be. I have no Jane Eyres or Rochesters in my narrow constitution. I only talked to Squire Dickinson about the *idea* of starting a novel, and he had the graciousness to listen. Would you really run away with a ne'er-do-well, a gambler who robs people of their bread and butter?"

"I would."

"And break your father's heart?"

"He don't have a heart to break."

That lower lip stops trembling. Sister Sue might have commenced strangling me had she been in less public a place.

"The Squire loves you to distraction. He thinks of nothing but his family and its welfare."

"Then why don't he let me marry a man?"

"Good Lord, how many suitors have you and your sister spurned?"

"At least a hundred," I lie. "And likely a hundred more. But it's too late for Pa-pa to appear with his lantern. I'm leaving . . . with Brainard Rowe. I love him, Susie. And I want to trade in love, just like Cleopatra. I'll never have another chance. Didn't we both swear that we'd never abandon wonder? Well, Brainard is my own pale storm. And I ain't giving him up."

But Susie mocks my battle cry. "Sister, you could stand here forever and he still wouldn't come."

"Did you meet with my man?" I ask like the meekest squirrel.

"I certainly did. I found him skulking behind a barn near the depot. And I warned him that if he did not disappear and promise never to plague you again, I would make sure he was delivered to the penitentiary."

"And I will wager with my life that he cursed every railroad detective in Massachusetts and laughed in your face."

Suddenly I'm not so sure. Susan hands me an envelope with some scratchings on it in that oily butcher's crayon she carries around in case she has a fit of inspiration. I peruse the envelope.

### Daisy—Domingo!

I loved him for the terseness of that note. He didn't palaver with an oily crayon, didn't scribble ten thousand excuses. He wrote just enough to make certain I'd realize the note was authentic. I could sense the despair in that long dash between Daisy and Domingo, as if it were a frozen sea.

I shut my eyes and pretend I'm on the train with my man. His shoes still want polishing. I don't care. I nestle my tawny scalp in his summer coat, right under the crooked strings of his cravat. I cannot hear the murmur of his heart. Our seats are made of a rough rattan that's like a nest of thorns. It don't bother me. I'm an heiress with five gold pieces in her pocket and another four inside her ruche. But it ain't wealth that interests this heiress. It's the light that pours through the mucked-up windows on Father's train. It's as slanted as a melody of mine. The light is laden with dust and tiny bugs that swirl like an army in retreat. And it's peculiar, because all that busyness of bugs seems to lend the light a golden hue.

It's the same shower of light that accompanied the Savior when He visited Amherst during one of the Awakenings. I was a child of six or seven. Every face was filled with the gravity of God. Sensible women fainted in the street. Men wandered into the fields and muttered to themselves like lunatics after seeing the Lord. But I was different. I squeezed my eyes, certain that the Savior would come. And the Savior did come, shrouded in that golden light. He stood near the gate of our Mansion on West Street, his beard as red as Pa-pa's side-whiskers, while I wondered if the Lord was a Dickinson! I rushed into that shower of light, feeling the Lord's glow on my eyelids.

I don't have to rush right now. The Lord's golden light was taking me and my man West. And I'll worry when we get there!

## 25.

FATHER WAS PALE, PALER THAN HE'S EVER BEEN. THERE WAS dust on his coat. One of his boots was unbuckled. I'd never seen him in such disarray. Even his cravat hung like a pair of mousy strings. I wondered what plague he'd passed through, what storm of grasshoppers.

It wasn't a plague. He's just back from a visit to the insane asylum at Northampton as its newest trustee. Took him an hour to wash up. And out of nowhere, after reading from the Bible at breakfast, with Ma-ma's hands still enclosed like a cathedral, he said, "Can you guess the lost soul I met at the lunatic hospital?"

"Father," Vinnie said, playing up to him, "I have not the least little clue."

"Our former housekeeper, who went to that nun's school with Emily."

I was jumping with rage, but did not show it. Time couldn't heal Pa-pa on the lesson of Holyoke. He still believed I had gone to a witch's coven in South Hadley, where the Tutors practiced black magic and wrecked us for life.

"Father," I said, "you cannot mean Zilpah Marsh."

"None but her. She could recite John Milton while tinkering with the stove, and what good did it do her? That little bit of education poisoned her mind. I found her raving like the dickens in a padded cell. But the moment I questioned her, she was as lucid as a clock. She kept crying and asking you to forgive her. And I promised the poor creature that I would bring you to Northampton."

Pa-pa's talk had helped cure my ills. He took my mind off Domingo, and made me dream of Zilpah—and Tom. Of the Handyman I'd not had a word in eight years. And not of Zilpah either, though she spent months on and off in our village, in that robbers' den of Rooming-house Row. I pitied Zilpah, in spite of my abiding interest in Tom. I didn't want to reveal that interest to Pa-pa, but I was curious about the hired girl I had driven from Pa-pa's door. And so I put on my Plumage, with its attendant Tomahawk tongue.

"Pa-pa," I said, "what on earth happened to Zilpah? Do tell."

And Father, who had a lawyer's genius for straight lines, told us all the facts, as he had perceived them. Bear in mind that he knew nothing of Tom, or of Zilpah's life as a burglar's mate. She could not endure the shame of being dismissed from the Master's service, she said, and she disappeared from Amherst for six years. Setting up burglaries with Tom in other towns, I imagine, and living high off the hog on their lucre. But she returned to Amherst suddenly a year or two ago. Perhaps Tom had abandoned her, or was in jail, or hiding out somewhere. Zilpah Marsh was back in that roost behind the hat factory, living with her mother on a shrunken dead end, with ghosts as her neighbor and the factory's whistle in her ears. It was a bothersome noise from my windows—it must have been deafening from Rooming-house Row.

Her mother took ill and died, and Zilpah wasn't even left with a hair ball. She had no uncles or aunts, not one older brother, as I did. And this is where the story turns strange. She lived for a while in our root cellar, she confessed to Pa-pa. But I never saw her. She also lived in our barn, eating whatever swill she could find, and sharing hay with our horse. But why didn't she knock at our door? Father asked her that very question.

"*I was afraid of Mistress,*" she told Pa-pa. "*Miss Em'ly thought evil of me, and I could not face her, Master. So I hid.*"

Father's words tore at me as he gave voice to what Zilpah had said. I should have been gentler, Lord. I don't believe she would have harmed Pa-pa or Ma-ma, even with her pilfering and her plunder of other houses, but she might have wanted to harm me. I knew her history. Father did not. And should I have turned a blind eye while she and Tom raped the town? But I am not so fine a moralist. I might have protected my classmate and let her plunder a little more had she not been attached to Tom. I was raw with jealous rage. I had to get rid of her, or carry a Tomahawk inside my brain and become as mad as Rochester's wife.

She could not find employment. The clothes she wore had turned to rags. She thought of becoming a prostitute. But how could she lie down with drunken factory louts when she had had a first-class education? And the louts would probably not have had her. There was another reason, I surmised. She was still in love with Tom and would not have permitted other men to paw her. This troubled me, and I'm not sure why. I wasn't bitter about Zilpah's love for Tom; my bitterness revolved around his love for her. We were sisters of a sort, obsessed with the same burglar.

It wasn't hunger that hurt Zilpah the most. She could have lived forever on a diet of roots. It was having no one to converse with. She'd recite Shakespeare to her mother, a mere housemaid at the College. But after the woman died, Zilpah did not utter another sound. And this was what had insaned her, the deathly silence.

Zilpah had no one but herself to entertain her. "*I missed you, Master,*" she told Pa-pa, "*missed you and our talks about literature. And I missed Miss Em'ly too, because her words had just the right sting. She was smart as a bumblebee, and I didn't mind the pain. The sound of her stinger gave me an awful lot of pleasure."*

I was mortally ashamed, but I did not reveal it to Pa-pa or Lavinia. I listened as if I had a hair ball stuck in my throat.

Zilpah had to weave around our handymen and female servants, or she couldn't have remained on our property without being discovered. And once she had nearly been discovered.

"*By whom?*" Father had asked.

"*By Miss Em'ly. I was eating an apple in the orchard, enjoying every bite, and Mistress walked right up to me, looked me in the eye. But she must have been versifying, because I was no more visible to her than a tree."*

I did not recall such an encounter, but it might have happened. I often walk "blindly" in the Orchard, with diadems or dirks inside my head. But I had shocked her, and the thought of being exposed as some horrible vagrant, and disappointing Pa-pa, sent her into a spin. She had to run. She took the road to Northampton. She had stopped counting the days or the nights. Her existence fell into the blackest hole. She could not recall when or where she slept. A constable found her eating mud and dirt under a bridge outside Northampton and had her delivered to the insane asylum. She whimpered and whipped her head back and forth, but did not say a word. The guards had to force food into her mouth, and she would bite them whenever she had the chance. They could not bathe Zilpah or remove her rags. They had no idea who she was until Pa-pa stumbled upon her cell while making his rounds of the asylum.

She pretended not to know him. Father hid his stricken face inside his handkerchief. But she could feel his body stir, and she approached him in all her filth.

"*Zilpah Marsh,*" he said, "*would you break my heart?*"

And she spoke for the first time in six months. "*Master, you must not look at me. I have not washed. And you mustn't cry. I will not be able to bear it."*

His equilibrium shattered, Father shouted at the guards to open the cell door. A nurse scrubbed Zilpah while she stood behind a blanket, so that Father wouldn't have to compromise her modesty, and he fed her with his own hands. She trembled at his touch, kissed his hands, and Father had her removed from that cell and placed in the women's ward, where she could see other faces. Zilpah wouldn't stop crying until Pa-pa promised to bring me to the asylum.

~~~

I COULD HAVE GONE BY STAGE, BUT FATHER INSISTED ON driving me in his chariot. It must have been a burden for him. He had court appearances—he was defending a deacon who may have manhandled his wife—and continued to get cattle and horses out of burning barns. The fire-maniac was no less elusive in the final days of August. We'd lost livestock, but Father was grateful that we hadn't lost any humans yet. The village's fire alarms had roused families fast enough to flee a conflagration.

"It's only a question of time before some little girl is trapped in a fire," he said, while he clucked at Black Fanny. The reins were taut, and Father's cheeks were rippling. Black Fanny was as tense as he was. In all my life, I had never met a horse who could mimic Pa-pa's moods.

I wasn't thinking of the maniac. I kept seeing Zilpah grovel under a bridge with dirt in her mouth.

"Father," I said, "doesn't Zilpah remind you of Evelyn O'Hare?"

Pa-pa looked at me without taking his eyes off Black Fanny.

"Who's this Evelyn O'Hare?"

"You know, that other housekeeper, the one who started wearing a knife in the kitchen, when I was a child. Father, you couldn't have forgotten. You visited her at the old Lunatic Hospital in Worcester."

"I can't recall," he said. I could see that the memory was fatal for him, that he chose to forget. And I quickly changed the topic.

"Father, aren't you glad the scarlet fever has abated some?"

"But that fever has never come so early before. It's Nature's trick—to lull us into believin' it won't be back."

I didn't want to ask him about the deacon and the deacon's wife, since it would only start an argument. I failed to understand how he could defend a churchman who had nearly strangled his wife and starved her to death—but the law don't pay attention to such niceties, I'd have to surmise. And it was the deacon who was paying Pa-pa, not the deacon's wife.

But I didn't have to keep dark on the subject of Sue. And while Black Fanny sneezed and plodded through the dust, I started on Sue's salon.

"Isn't Susie divine?" I said. "Making the Evergreens into a magnet —with Mr. Emerson and Mr. Bowles."

I must have captured him with that remark. It was the first time Pa-pa took his eyes off the road. "But do you think your brother is happy with her?"

"He loves her. We all do."

"But sometimes I think he's afraid of his wife."

Who in his right mind wouldn't have been afraid? Not a person alive, even Pa-pa, could stand up to one of Sue's siroccos. But she was clever enough to work her hottest and coldest winds around him. Brother and I bore the brunt, yet we don't consider ourselves casualties. There is a certain pleasure in living around a storm.

Call it coincidence, but Father and I ran into our own sirocco on the ride to Northampton. Dust and wind prevailed. I had never witnessed such perpendicular times. Trees bent in the wind, and branches near poked into our eyes. Father had to leap from the carriage and blind the horse with an old rag, or else Fanny might have plunged off the road. He calmed her, walking beside his mare, with his sturdy fire marshal's cape slung around his head.

# 26.

WE ARRIVED LATE IN NORTHAMPTON, CREPT RIGHT OUT OF
that dust storm with Fanny half insane. Father sang to her a full
twenty minutes—a nonsense song—or we would have had to park
Fanny inside the asylum and leave her there to rot. What thrilled
me so wasn't simply Father's devotion to his horse, but the sheer
pleasure that went into his song.

> *Fan-ny, Fan-ny, Fan-ny Poo*
> *She's all black and she's all blue*
> *She's my darling dearest queen*
> *Who can't be found, can't be seen.*

Pa-pa did talk Poetry, but only with his horse. The rest of the
world was pure Prose, including his court cases, his fire truck, and
his family—and the lunatic hospital at Northampton.

I had not seen it until now. It was a marvel in my own backwoods-
man's mind. It must have been modeled after the royal palace at
Versailles, or some other chateau that escaped my familiarity. It
had a front lawn ten times as large as the Amherst Commons, but
without a swamp or a frog pond. It had cupolas and spires that

rose above its many roofs like great silvered teeth. It had a freshwater pond as fragile as glass and a winding road a little like a maze
that any child might conquer in a minute. Forgive me, but I fancied this asylum as a huge dollhouse.

Yet Pa-pa wasn't the master of these dolls. He'd come to soothe,
just as he'd soothed Evelyn O'Hare at the hospital in Worcester.
Yet he couldn't seem to make up his mind about us womenfolk.
He took care of us, but in his own heart he must have felt that we
were crippled creatures—mermaids who couldn't swim. Daughters don't matter much. I was a cripple to him, in spite of all my
Plumage. But I did have a special place at this asylum.

Since Pa-pa was a trustee, I was given the status of a local princess who could enter any room without the need of a magic wand.
But in spite of my sudden royalty, I had not come for a grand tour
of this dollhouse.

"I would like to see a certain Zilpah Marsh," I announced to
the hospital's warden, in my own new manner of a whispering
princess.

"Miss Dickinson, it will not be pretty. I can promise you that."

The warden was a peculiarity, both a giant and a gnome—
hence a small man who seemed huge, or perhaps it was the irreg-
ularity of a head that protruded like a dome and sat on weak,
inferior legs. He had his own strange suit of armor to protect
him from all the folly and the whims of an asylum, with padding
on his thighs and chest and a helmet that would have looked correct on a conquistador. Jeremiah Adams he was, a Harvard man
who had fallen from grace and sat out his exile in Northampton.
He'd been a churchman once, but I would swear that Warden
Jeremiah had gone over to the Devil's domain. And that was why
I felt a singular bond with him.

He led me through a labyrinth of rooms and delivered me himself to a great hall where the hardest cases were kept—it must have
been the largest dormitory in creation, so vast that it was impossi-

ble to gaze at from end to end. It would have been far too kind to call it a human sea. The men I saw chained to their beds had the shrewd, silent eyes of animals. Not one jot of recognition passed from them to me.

An image of our Orchard crept into my brain. Pa-pa's Orchard frightened me sometimes. It was like a solitary Eden after God had fled, after the fall of the first man. And one afternoon in the Orchard I saw a little troupe of wild, hungry bears. They had the very eyes of these chained men, shrewd beyond my own capacity to comprehend, and of a meanness I had never encountered before. The hungry bears had no intent to harm me, nor did they acknowledge my right to be in *their* Orchard. They rooted with a clumsiness that did not have a touch of grace. Relentless hunger must have dimmed their minds. They found no food. They did not seem to know where to look. I had a terrible urge to feed the bears out of my own hand, but I never did. Perhaps they were not as luckless as these luckless men. They did not live in a dormitory, did not have to endure such a terrible sea.

Never mind the foul aromas; the sick-room at Mt Holyoke had smelled far worse—still, I could not help but feel that Jeremiah was keeping his own sort of stable, that I was visiting a menagerie where chained men had lost all sense of measure and survived without the least curiosity.

"Warden, where are the women?"

"Wait," he said. "Miss Dickinson, if such creatures were trapped in a fire and could not escape, would you mourn them?"

"Yes, I would."

"But they have no more sensibility than a milk cow."

"I am fond of cows," I said. "Where is Zilpah Marsh?"

We walked what felt like a mile because of all those faces that had so little need to search. And then we arrived at the women's sector, which did not have the least mark of separation from the men's menagerie. But it was still like stepping through a wall of glass. The women's zone was shoddier and filthier, and the patients here even more primitive in their passions. They did not have the shrewd eyes of the deranged dormitory men. Their eyes were much more savage . . . and strangely serene, as if they dwelled within a maelstrom of conflicting emotion.

I felt attached to these piteous women by some powerful cord or string. They were not absent, like the men, in some far field. We could have been sisters in the same irregular sewing circle, where needles were sharp as knives, and we were all at risk of being punctured by some devil of a man. They moaned aloud and hurled cries at walls that could not answer. Jeremiah's assistants, who also wore helmets and quilted armor, struck women who tried to lunge at me despite their shackles. They meant no harm; they wanted to welcome me into their sisterhood, or so I imagined.

But still Jeremiah's assistants struck, and struck again with their clubs.

"Warden, Sir," I whispered, "you must not have your men strike these poor souls."

"But they are feral, Miss Dickinson, and could be dangerous. Can't you see the madness in their eyes?"

I would not listen to his musings. I myself was sickened by what I saw. I could only stop his men from swinging if I stepped in the path of their clubs—and I did.

Jeremiah panicked. "Miss Dickinson, you could harm yourself. *Please.* Your father will remove me from my post."

A fly was buzzing in my ear. And that's when I discovered her. She too was shackled to her bed. Her hair had been shorn, and she had a scalp of tiny tufts, as if her own head had become a wild country. And her mustache had been allowed to grow—for a minute I thought she was a man.

Her eyes were riveted on me, but I felt no alarm.

"Mistress," she said by way of hello, "I'm parched."

It mattered little now that Zilpah had once presided over a nest of burglars. She near broke my heart.

"Jeremiah Adams, you will bring this classmate of mine some water, else I will flog the whole lot of you."

My voice startled me—frightened me, in fact—since I had roared like a lion. Jeremiah let me have his own flask of fresh water, and I fed her water from the flask's silver cup. The chains were tight, and Zilpah could hardly maneuver her head. I had to hold her chin with one hand, tilt the cup, and pour water into her mouth.

She didn't moan like the other shackled women. She smacked her lips after she drank.

"Miss Emily, that was delicious."

And such was Father's authority at the lunatic hospital that I told the warden to unshackle her. He looked at me as if I too belonged in the women's sector.

"That's a stark impossibility, Miss Dickinson. I will not go against the interests of my own institution no matter what sway your father has."

He must have thought he was on stage, performing some trifle at the local athenaeum, where he himself was the star. But he was not the star today—Zilpah was, even in her shackles.

"Sir, you will unshackle Mistress Marsh post haste, or I will bring you and your duplicitous men up before my father's board."

"On what complaint?" he asked.

All the women, in spite of their incapacity, pricked up their ears.

"Manhandling your own patients with those pernicious clubs of yours."

"That's preposterous," he said, "a wholesale lie."

But he motioned to his men, had them use their clubs as mallets to knock asunder the iron pegs of Zilpah's shackles until her arms and legs were free. She lay there frozen, unable to grasp that the guards themselves had liberated her.

"Rise, you wretch," said the warden. "You have a benefactress now."

"I didn't ask," she said. But she did stand up and pirouette once on her shaky legs, while the other women stared in disbelief.

"And where will you take your new charge, Miss Dickinson? To have some tea in the tearoom, behind a curtain?"

"You will not curtain her," I said. "You have an excellent lawn. I propose to sample it. We will have our constitutional on the grass, Miss Marsh and I."

"In front of our guests, with children and members of the clergy about?"

The warden groaned, but he and his assistants led us through a packet of rear rooms that must have served as living quarters for some of these men. I discovered a blackened collar and long underpants strewn over a chair, empty bottles of ale, tattered stockings, a crooked line of boots—all with the odor of a chicken barn.

We left this bachelors' retreat and landed at a side entrance of the sanitarium. Jeremiah tried to steer us away from the front lawn, but I would have none of his tricks. I strutted with Zilpah on the hospital's grounds, with its oval pond of rippled glass. The warden had covered her in a cape and given her a hat to hide her haphazard hair, so that she wouldn't astonish visitors or the faculty. But Zilpah behaved like a duchess, bowing to women on the front lawn and flirting with the men, who did not seem to mind her mustache. But it was only pretended pluck. She began to shiver and moan midway through our walk.

"Mistress, I'm so ashamed of how I look . . . couldn't we stand behind the pond, away from people?"

"Zilpah Marsh, I will not hide one of my classmates."

"And you won't let the warden's men tickle me with their clubs?"

"No one will tickle you, I promise."

She tugged at the brim of her borrowed hat.

"Mustn't treat me like a grand lady, Mistress, or the little ladies on my ward will be jealous, and they'll bite my titties off the first chance they get."

"Then I'll have you transferred to another institution. My father has the power to do so."

She laughed. "I always liked the Master. I could get around him, but not you, Miss Em'ly—you were my iron mistress."

And then she did cry and insist she would cry forever unless I forgave her.

"Zilpah, I'm not a constable or a priest. I—Lord, I forgive you."

That seemed to satisfy her, and she muttered something.

"Repeat yourself," I said. "I cannot hear."

"Then listen harder. I can tell ya who your maniac is."

I began to doubt Zilpah for the first time in her new abode.

"What would you know about the Amherst fire-maniac? You've been locked away in Northampton."

I did not want her revelations—I feared them. But I could not remove the lightning in my mind as I pictured Tom the Handyman, *my* Tom, burning barns.

"Have you seen your old accomplice, Tom?" I asked, trying to fend her off with my own infernal logic. I was hoping to launch her into some tale where she would forget the maniac. But she grew indignant.

"I may have been a housekeeper, Miss Em'ly, but I started as a scholar, same as you, and scholars learn to listen. I read the *Republican*—after every wretch in the asylum reads it and the pages come to me torn. There are mentions of the Master as town fire marshal. I prayed he wouldn't get burnt in a barn. And I asked all my visitors about him."

"I'm not your first visitor?" I asked like a petulant child.

"No, Mistress, you are not. My Ma-ma's friends come on the morning coach whenever they can—maids and such, housekeepers at the college. And they heard about this boy at Mr. Sweetser's general store who hated the town. Seniors from Alpha Delta Phi had made fun of him, thrown him in the frog pond as a prank, and he got surly with customers at the store until Sweetser had to fire him. And so he took his revenge on the farmers he thought had slighted him at Sweetser's. Some of the maids saw him skulking around under the railroad tracks."

"But why didn't they tell my father or the Sheriff?"

"They're maids, Miss Em'ly, feared of sheriffs and squires."

"And so they let the barns burn and kept their own little private peace."

"Ain't I tellin' ya now?"

"But you could have told my father when you saw him and saved a barn or two."

Zilpah looked at me as if I were the number one lunatic of our Commonwealth.

"He's the Master," she said. "I wouldn't have dared—besides, the boy is gone. Did as much destruction as he cared to do."

"But why are you so sure?"

"The maids swore on the Bible that he abandoned his perch under the tracks."

"And you believe them?"

"Yes, I do. They ain't liars and hypocrites like some people I know. You tried to steal my Tom. You tracked him down with your devil-dog. And he didn't even remember you. Miss Em'ly, I'd call that a lasting impression."

She started to laugh and writhe like a woman in the midst of pleasuring a man—at least that is what I fancied she was doing. Her motions grew fiercer and fiercer, and she spat at me and Jeremiah, who was beside himself.

"She'll ruin my reputation," he said, wringing his hands. "I never should have listened to you. I'll throw her in the attic. She can dine on spiders and rat tails."

"You'll do no such thing," I said, but I could not keep her from writhing on the lawn.

A crowd began to collect. Children wet their fingers and pointed at Zilpah, as if they themselves had manufactured her out of the summer wind. Their mothers could not drive them away from the spectacle. Zilpah spat at mothers and children alike. "Rat turds and spider tails," she howled. Then she stood in place and called to me. "Mistress, did you see my Tom?"

"Answer her," Jeremiah hissed in my ear. "I implore you. It will calm her down."

But I could not answer. I feared the tale she had to tell.

"Tom didn't know I was carrying his child. I locked myself inside a corselet, and wore one of his long shirts at night. He couldn't rob houses and worry about a sweetheart who was vomiting into a paper sack. I didn't want to slow him down. I left him, left him flat, figuring I would catch up with him later when I wasn't such a hindrance. But I never did find him again."

"What happened to the baby?" I asked, with a fist squeezing my heart.

"I kilt it with a knitting needle while it was roosting in my belly. I kilt it dead, and when it washed out of me, it didn't even have Tom's blue eyes. I wasn't sorry."

She started to writhe again—it wasn't the rhythm of a woman pleasuring a man. She was reliving that descent into the dark, giving birth to her own butchered baby. The writhing stopped, and she lunged at the children, tried to rip at them with her own bruised fingernails. Jeremiah's men rushed at her in their quilted suits and knocked her to the ground.

"Moses," the warden whispered, "do you have the mask?"

His men blocked my avenue to Zilpah; they leaned over and stifled her in a leather mask that enclosed her mouth and left her half blind. She kicked and fought, and they beat her with their clubs.

"Miss Dickinson," the warden said, "you must not interfere."

But interfere I did. I tore into his quilted men with my own feeble fists. They swatted me away as they would a fly. I was no longer a local princess. I was nothing to them. They were beholden to Jeremiah, not the daughter of a backwoods squire. I fell upon the grass, bewildered by an array of trees with brutal red veins in their bark, as if the trunks could bleed a brilliant red.

The battle was lost. Jeremiah's quilted men were dragging her along the grass as I struggled to my knees. And that's when I saw Pa-pa in that miraculous stride of his, like Oliver Cromwell, loping across the lawn. He had his gold-crowned walking stick, but he did not have to wield it as a weapon. One look at the anger in his eyes had stopped the quilted men in their tracks. Jeremiah tried to remove the mask, but she gripped it with all her life and disallowed him to do so.

"Squire," he said, "your own daughter is a witness. We gave Miss Marsh her liberty. We let her have access to the lawn. And how does she repay us? She spat at children and nearly clawed them to death. We had to restrain her."

"Warden," Father said, his eyebrows bristling, "I see no other casualties but Miss Marsh herself."

It was then that my classmate proved her worth; she *was* the duchess of Northampton, despite her debilities. She ignored Jeremiah, ignored his men, ignored me, and took Pa-pa's arm, as if she had never been beaten and was not wearing a leather mask.

"Master," she said, "how nice of you to call on me."

And she strolled with Pa-pa, who was astute enough not to mention the mask. I could not read her expression, or catch more than a hint of her eyes, but I like to think that she took some pride in walking with Pa-pa. Not one child pointed to her now. Women curtsied, and men bowed. She could have been his daughter, a

devil, or his bride. Perhaps she was all three. I'd never seen Pa-pa
with so gallant a stride. His knees had their own melody on this
lunatics' lawn. We walked behind him and the duchess, as part of
Pa-pa's train. I bit back my own jealousy. I couldn't stop thinking
of Zilpah's butchered child, and the life's blood leaking down her
legs.

And I wasn't an inchworm closer to comprehending Pa-pa's
mystery. He fed us, loved us, would have devoured half the world
for his family, but he never looked at Ma-ma, Austin, Lavinia, or
me the way he admired Zilpah in her leather mask. It wasn't longing, no, and it wasn't pity. I'd swear on my Lexicon that Zilpah
had unshackled him while he was on this lawn. She was another
mermaid who couldn't swim, a female creature, but perhaps it was
her lower station that allowed him to reveal a certain tenderness.
He didn't have to be lawyer or squire or congressman with a stable hand's girl. He could be what he always was, a backwoods boy
without a mask of grandeur.

Zilpah walked without having to say another word, arm in arm
with Pa-pa, whose redheaded daughter fell far behind.

*Emily had her own secret service. She couldn't write directly to Rev. Wadsworth, have her letters delivered to the post office. It would have brought scandal right to the Squire—his old maid of a daughter scribbling "love letters" to a married man. So she folded each letter to Rev. Wadsworth into a letter to one of her confidantes, who lived in Springfield. And the minister's rare letters to her would arrive from the same confidante. Thus Emily had established a private post office.*

*She had asked him to be her pastor, to counsel her from afar. His letters were formal but not unfriendly, though the minister couldn't even spell her name. "My Dear Miss Dickenson," he wrote, as if she were the son or daughter of Mr. Charles Dickens. He talked about the "affliction" that had befallen her, without realizing that he was her affliction. But it was her fault. How could she tell the minister of the Arch Street Church that she had fallen in love with him like a madwoman during the length of one sermon that he had delivered five years ago? And it was not the words themselves that had moved her, but the way he delivered them, as if he had a typhoon in his chest.*

*The Reverend Wadsworth was a Witch. She had always believed that men made the best witches, and he was the prime example, with his cream-colored hands and volcanic eyes that could reduce her to ashes. She had called him "My Philadelphia" in her little notebook, but she couldn't even hint at love in her letters. And so like the feeblest of female witches, she went at him with little tricks. She deplored her own dishonesty. But she couldn't let go of her affliction.*

*His mother had just died, and the minister wore black for an entire year, but that didn't keep him from lecturing in New England. He spoke of stealing a visit on one of his tours, but Emily didn't believe it. Her heart palpitated nonetheless. She was in constant readiness, like a live torpedo. She ordered a new housedress, and wouldn't have Lavinia measured for it in her place; Emily saw the seamstress herself. She had become as volcanic as Sue. She could erupt at any minute. Lavinia had never seen her sister so full of conflicting moods. She would chatter and then shut up. She would laugh at some silliness and then start to cry.*

*"It's her monthlies," Lavinia said. "My poor sister is driven by the moon."*

*Perhaps she was. But Emily was in despair. "Philadelphia" would never arrive at her father's door. And then she heard the bell pull. And she panicked. She who never answered the door ran downstairs with tiny incautious hops, her heart in its own deep crisis.*

*And there he was, all dressed in black, as if he were mourning Emily's own reckless love without even knowing it. He'd aged in five years. His mouth was pursed. His hair had gray patches and no longer covered his ears. But his eyes held the same fury for her. He was an adorable Witch.*

*She introduced him to Father, Mother, and Vinnie as her minister from Philadelphia, who had stopped at Amherst to give her spiritual guidance. It wasn't so much of a lie. Father and Mother took it as a sign that their rebel daughter was returning to the Lord. But she bridled all through dinner, imagined black smoke escaping from the top of her head. She wanted Rev. Wadsworth all to herself.*

*He could not stay very long, but he did have time to walk with Emily in the Dickinson meadow. She would have gone back to the Lord, prayed through eternity, if she could just hold his hand. He stooped. There were marks of sorrow on his face.*

*"I should like to know of your affliction," he said.*

*Suddenly all her sauce had some back.*

*"What about your own affliction, Sir?"*

*She'd startled him, and he stood in the April grass.*

*"My dear mother passed but six months ago."*

*"Reverend, it runs much deeper than that."*

*A smile appeared on his pinched lips. "You are most clever, Miss Dickinson."*

*She did not spar with him. She made no quip.*

*"I am prone to melancholy," he said. "I had it as a boy. It was like a fever that riddled my youth. I adopted another name — Sedley. I wrote verses. But Sedley was no more authentic than Charles Wadsworth."*

*She had to intervene. "Sir, you are twice as authentic as any man I have ever met."*

*"Dear child, you must let me speak. I thought to drown myself in Sedley, to bully him and thus shake off my melancholic moods. But soon I hated him, just as I hated myself. I have no merit. I sing for my supper, whether poet or preacher."*

*"But your songs have seized my heart. And I have been smitten by no other sermons, Reverend."*

*"Because you sensed the flutter behind my mask, the song beneath the song — and hollowness can sometimes move half the world, my dear Miss Dickinson."*

*She longed to disappear with him in her father's meadow and never, never come out. And she could no longer play the minister's little disciple. She had to declare her love.*

*"You slander yourself. The hollowness you talk of is a numbing pain. I drink it every morning. It is my daily dose."*

*"But I cannot help you."*

*"You already have," she said. "You exist, my dear sweet minister. That is enough."*

She fell silent after that. They walked out of her father's meadow, out of the wet grass. Her face was flushed. Her heart pounded. He touched her hand as he took leave of her. She had been mistaken about his hands. They were not the color of cream. His hands were red and rough as claws.

They astonished her for a moment, and he could read the alarm in her eyes.

Quietly he put on his gloves.

"Forgive me. I did not mean to shock . . . You have witnessed the scars of my youth. I was born rich. My father was the lord of Litchfield, the owner of a mill. But he died suddenly, and how could a boy of sixteen pay off his father's debts? I was trundled off to a charity school for would-be ministers, a manual labor camp that was little better than a jailhouse. I had to wash the dishes for a hundred scamps like myself, in scalding water. And the results of my labor are these monstrous hands."

"They are not monstrous," she said, but they were, and she hungered to hold his hands, to soothe him and herself. But he wouldn't part with his gloves.

"Adieu, my dear Miss Dickinson."

And he was gone before she could whisper his name.

# PART FOUR

## The Vampyre of Cambridgeport

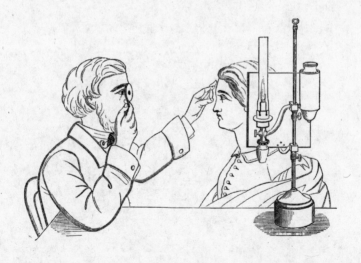

*86 Austin Street*

*Cambridgeport, July 1864*

# 27.

THE UNION DEAD WERE POSTED ON THE DOORS OF EVERY church and public building. And the bells tolled every day for the dead sons of Boston, Cambridge, and Watertown; the horse-cars stopped while the bells tolled and would not pick up passengers. Members of the Civilian Guard patrolled the streets looking for deserters. The Guard were a sorry lot. Some had been invalided out of the War, and some were the same bounty hunters who had skulked through Amherst trying to capture fugitive slaves. They had mean little eyes, most of them, and I couldn't imagine that army deserters would have been as mean, no matter how desperate they were.

There were military performances, soldiers marching through the metropolis, but they were ill equipped; half of them didn't have rifles or boots, and their officers had rag-tale uniforms that a convict might wear. I saluted them nonetheless. I mourned our lost sons and lost Rebel sons, who couldn't have been less brave than ours. But it wasn't only the dying that had put me in a somber mood. I mourned Mr. Wadsworth, who had deserted his congregation in '62 and fled to San Francisco, via the Isthmus of

Panama—it might as well have been the end of the world. Perhaps it was unconscionable to mourn a live man amid all the carnage, but my Philadelphia began to feel dead. That don't mean I had to sulk.

I was perchance a blind Kangaroo left to play in the dark, and like a Kangaroo I kicked whoever I could and boxed the ears of friend and foe with my front paws. Of course I had few foes in the boardinghouse where I lived with my little Norcross cousins, Fanny and Loo, and punched and kicked only in my Imagination, which bloomed like truculent dandelions in that wilderness I was forced to inhabit. Praise the Lord that it did not snow in July—it was the glare coming off the snow that quickened the ruin of my eyes. The headaches began last winter, like needles housed at the back of my head. The pain crippled me, and when the attack was fierce, I could not sleep no matter what the anodyne.

I understood what madness meant. Like Zilpah Marsh, who rotted away in Northampton, with memories of Tom and her own dead baby, I had little connection to humankind. That's when I became a Kangaroo, kicking with my hind legs, but the danger I did was to myself. I would have leapt from my window, but the Altitude was much too low, and I'd have ended up as Lavinia's pawn; she would have had to feed me while my bones mended and my eyes didn't mend at all.

And so I moved to Cambridgeport in April to be near that magician and his eye machine, Dr. Henry Willard Williams, the noted Boston ophthalmologist who could cure Kangaroos. Without prolonged treatment, he predicted, the headaches would worsen and my eyes would become so sensitive to light that I would have to turn wherever I lived into a cave. Thus I agreed to become his patient and his prisoner not out of my own alarm, but to appease Ma-ma, Pa-pa, and Lavinia, who were worrying themselves sick over me. What hurt the most was that I couldn't take Carlo to Cambridgeport. I wouldn't have sentenced him

to the same Jail as mine. At fourteen, Carlo was now an old fellah, and he don't like to travel. He wasn't a metropolitan dog.
He couldn't have thrived in a metropolis of houses rather than
meadows and barns.

I missed all my flowers and plants. I wouldn't get to see the gen-
tians grow and prosper in my garden. And I quaked whenever
Vinnie had to go on one of her little trips. Who would water my
plants? I realized that should I ever leave this Siberia alive, I would
find a desert of parched earth inside my observatory.

Ever since the *Republican* revealed that George Eliot was in fact
Miss Mary Anne Evans of London, England, an Authoress who
lived in sin with a married man, I began to think of George Eliot
as a fellow Kangaroo. She could not go out to dinner parties for
fear that she would be shunned; she had even been spat upon by
figures of the very best society. People mocked her long face and
lantern jaw and made fun of her attire—said she was entirely old-
fashioned. I wondered if she had freckles like a certain Miss Emily,
exiled in Cambridgeport for the duration. I kept a picture of her
on my wall, together with the Brontës and Mrs. Browning. I luxu-
riated in her *plainness*. I dreamt of us as soldiers—battlers I should
say. And in my dreams we were as powerful as any man and sometimes wore a beard.

Tolling once or twice a day, the church bells ruined my rever-
ies. Some of Cambridge's sons had been slaughtered in a wooded
place in Virginia they call the Wilderness. I imagine myself as
Sergeant Emily of the Massachusetts First, wandering among the
wounded and the dead with my bayonet, feeding water to men of
both sides, since the Confederate gray was obscured by dirt and
blood. Father and Sue were most kind with Southern boys at the
College who couldn't get back through the lines after hostilities
began and had to sit out the War in our Yankee village. Father
went with them to church, bridled whenever someone hissed,
and Susie borrowed my own recipes to bake these boys Indian

bread and lemon pie with the smoothest yellow Amherst had ever seen.

And thus I spend my days in the dark between trips to the magic ophthalmologist who hopes to fix my eyes. I cannot ride into Boston all alone like some desperado. My favorite cousins, Fanny and Louisa Norcross, serve as my chaperones. They're no taller than I am in their summer capes. They don't have my freckles, but they could still be my tiny sisters; the three of us have such mousy chins.

Fanny and Loo accompany me on the horse-car that can be hailed down on Centre Street and has to sit there until the half-blind girl in her dark spectacles hops aboard. The horse-car tracks lead right into Boston over a series of bumps, and we cross the Charles on a wooden bridge with noxious fumes right under our noses from the marshes and mud flats and other foul effluvia, the river itself as brown as a perpetual mudslide.

"Loolie," I say, "the frog pond in our Commons has better coloration than that."

"Pay it no mind, Aunt Emily," my little cousins chirp, even though I am not their aunt and never was.

I lean back and watch the spires of Boston through my dark lenses that guard me against the sunlight.

THE DOCTOR'S SANDSTONE MANSION WITH ITS MANSARD roofs is on a street that did not exist the last time I was in to Boston, thirteen years ago. Lavinia and I had come to see Austin, who was teaching the sons and daughters of immigrants at a school in the North End, where the Irish lived in boardinghouses and abandoned factories that was a monstrous version of our own Rooming-house Row. I visited the school, which was plagued with black dust and closed down right after Austin left. The whole North End was an empire of black wind and dust at water's edge.

I warned Brother that he would become a monster of the North End if he stayed too long. I pitied the children at Austin's school, with their savage, rooting eyes that must have protected them against the squalor, but I did not want to sacrifice my own brother to their desperate needs.

I didn't like the North End, no, and the Back Bay, where the doctor's office was, had been a series of tidewater flats. And here it was, many years later, transformed into its own particular paradise.

The doctor is a very tall man. He is gentle with his Kangaroo, wiping her eyes after each droplet of belladonna. His mansion on Arlington Street looks out upon Boston's Public Garden, which has the grandeur of our college grounds without the swampland of Amherst's little Commons.

I am dizzified by his ophthalmoscope, which he himself helped to design. It has its own lantern with a lick of flame, and a long tube that goes up and down while the lantern sways. He holds a lens close to my eye, looks through a disc with a tiny hole in the middle, and tells me there is no deterioration that he can find with his diabolic machine.

"But when can I start reading again, Dr. Williams, and scratch a few words on a page?"

"Not for a while," he says. "Miss Dickinson, you must give up writing and reading altogether."

I feel as doomed as a dead soldier lying in the Wilderness. I'd rather have oblivion than be a prisoner without my Pen. I cannot soothe the constant noise inside my Brain, like a fluttering of feathers that grows fierce until I can scratch the syllables that each feather suggests—see them, touch them, my own fine feathers. Emily's Brain will burst with all the bustle of her Plumage. But she does not rebel.

She watches the flutter of her physician's hands, the finesse of his fingers as he manipulates that silver disc with its own subtle eye—it's almost as if he can pull a strange, silent hum out of the lantern attached to his machine, as if he has a music that is profounder than mine.

I listen to such music, and while I sit in *his* little backless chair the noise inside my Brain subsides.

# 28.

IT'S TANTALIZING TO THINK I AM STUCK ON A STREET THAT bears my brother's name, as if Austin shared the Calvary of his sister, that blind Kangaroo at 86 Austin Street. But he is embroiled in marriage and I seldom hear from him. I have a nephew now, little Ned, a blondish boy, born three summers ago to Brother and Sister Sue. Father seems delighted to be a Grandpa-pa, and he rides Ned around in a red wagon or sits him on his new mare, who is prim as a preacher with little Ned on her back.

I am dazzled by this boy, and he's charmed the Devil out of me with brooding eyes that seem ready to erupt. I call myself Uncle Emily, because I will need all the advantages of a male to deal with him. But Sue was remote with young Ned around, and there were fewer games of shuttlecock, fewer salons. She had been frightened to death before her delivery. It took her months to recover, months to find a proper name for the boy, and Austin seemed utterly outside whatever sphere she was in. But that didn't bring him any nearer to our own little orbit.

No one could court Sue, no one could find her key. Even Father, whom she admired, could not crawl under her mysterious cloak. I

did not try. Neither luck nor intuition can interpret a Volcano. But
Cambridgeport was my amulet—I learned that I could court Sue
from afar. I risked my eyes writing to her. I did not talk of the mosquitoes that flew in from the marshlands, half as big as bats. I did
not mention the ophthalmoscope and its magic lamp, or the rides
into Boston on the horse-car that bumped and slid along its rails.
I said nothing of our landlords, Mrs. Bangs and her Daughter, who
wore silk at breakfast as if they were dressing for a ball. I talked
only of Sue and how much I missed her. All my feathers bristled as
I came out of my dark Jail, like the little soldier ready for war.

<hr />

I DID NOT SIT ON THE VERANDAH WITH THE OTHER FEMALES
of the boardinghouse. The sun would have bitten my eyes and
made them swell. We had our own theatricals in our room. Fan
and Loo picked *Antony and Cleopatra*; I was Enobarbus, Antony's
aide-de-camp who understood the queen of Egypt a sight better
than his master. I preferred to play a man; as Cleopatra I couldn't
have worn a beard.

"*Would I had never seen her!*" Antony moans after her own fleet
has fled from battle.

And I, his loyal soldier, insist: "*O, sir, you had then left unseen a
wonderful piece of work.*"

Only as Enobarbus can I read the full force of her passion: "*We
cannot call her winds and waters sighs and tears; they are greater storms
and tempests than almanacs can report.*"

Cleopatra's storms were so unlike Sue's; they were meant to trap
a man, not to drive him away. Yet Sue alone would have been a
match for Antony's Egypt, would have seen all the flaws in Cleopatra's glass. Perhaps I misjudge Sister Sue, and she has a passion
hidden somewhere beneath the volcanic ash, a passion for Mr.
Samuel Bowles or some other guest who wandered into her drawing room and played shuttlecock with her.

I am much bolder at night when the mosquitoes are a little more merciful in their attacks, and I can walk the streets without fear of any damage from the sun. I am still in disguise, under dark glasses to protect me from errant lamps. My Norcross cousins are agitated about my wish to walk alone. A kind of anarchy reigned during the night, with a Civilian Guard that caroused and stole more than it protected people, and a police force that had been denuded by Mr. Lincoln's Department of War and could not control malcontents.

"Aunt Emily, there are rascals and ruffians in a city where strange men can prowl."

I smile under my dark glasses. "Loolie, you and Fan have made a metropolitan of me. Besides, even the worst rascals wouldn't take advantage of a blind girl. They might lose status among their friends."

"But someone could mistake you for a trollop, a woman of the night."

"Dear cousins," I laugh, "I would be most flattered."

And I launch myself, venture from 86 Austin Street without the least map, wishing I could conjure Carlo with my own magic lamp. Then we would have strolled to river's edge, and I would have whistled in the dark and waited while he ran after muskrats and other rodents in the marsh. But without my dog to guide me and help me explore, I stick to half-lit streets that cannot hurt my eyes.

It is hard to express the exhilaration of fleeing my cell, that curtained-off room with its mosquito net where I have to hide during the day like the blindest bat . . . or a Vampyre, though I haven't the littlest desire to feed on anyone's blood. I wish I had the wherewithal to wander about like a warrior, but I have neither gun nor beard. I am the Queen of Cavalry out on a stroll.

On a torrid night in July, I find myself on Magazine Street, not far from the water. I pay no mind to the mosquitoes, but the marshlands have a rampant odor, and I clutch a handkerchief to my nose. I happen upon an almshouse, or what looks like one.

Even with the disadvantage of dark glasses I can tease out the words OVERSEERS OF THE POOR etched into a signboard above the front gate. But I discern no beggars or other lost souls entering or leaving the almshouse. I hear the sudden clop of a horse upon the cobblestones, then the shrill laugh of a woman as several creatures, dressed in silk, alight from a carriage that has stopped near the gate. And the Queen of Cavalry wonders to herself if the cream of Cambridge have descended upon the almshouse to assist in certain charities. But where are the beggars in piebald put in place to welcome them?

My eyes have begun to bother me, and I totter across the street to a little square. I have never felt such vertigo before. I can find nowhere to rest—my eyes are seared with fire and seem to jump out of my skull. That is the last thing I can recall . . . until I catch myself afloat in a blinding white fog.

There is a buzzing in my ear. Men are all about. I sniff the curious perfume of their skin. I can see nothing but their elegant rags. They are wearing gloves from which their fingers protrude like perverse flowers. They mumble to one another—about me.

"Drag her into the river and drown her. These ladies and gents wouldn't notice. She's not part of the same crowd. She don't have their glamour. She ain't a high hat, ain't hoi polloi, I'll wager on that. But we could strip her, sell the little darling's clothes and all her hair—red's a costly color, red will fetch us a price."

They pull on my scalp, and I can see a pair of scissors shine in the dark like the mouth of a primordial bird. I scream as that shiny bird bites at my hair. I had never been attacked in so rude a manner. Lord, I should have listened to Fan and Loo.

But suddenly an apparition appeared and drove off those wretched men with their scissors and sour perfume. He uttered not a word. I was lying on the ground, and my champion must have bundled up his own jacket and cratered it under my head—thus I had some part of him as my pillow. He did not taste of *their* sour rot. He must have watched me squirm.

"Lie still," he said.

"But where am I, Sir? I believe I am lost."

"You fainted outside the Athenaeum, Sis."

"But I was standing in front of the almshouse, and people arrived in carriages . . . help me, Sir. I am confused."

I could hear him laugh. But it wasn't unkind. His voice sounded foreign *and* familiar. He purred at me like a piece of silk and spun his little tale about the poorhouse. The poor had been trampled upon and removed, he said, not to Shady Hill with all the Harvard Professors, but to the very edges of the town, near Tannery Row, with the stink of leather that could give a man seizures.

"So," I said, "the Cambridge Athenaeum is a salon for the hoi polloi, according to your confederates, who wanted to drown me and steal my hair."

"They were puffing out their chests, Miss. They're showy people. But they knew I wouldn't let 'em touch a hair on your head."

I was still quite weak and had to depend upon my champion. "And what is your profession, Sir?"

"Pickpocket, and you've cut into my receipts. I couldn't get near the hoi polloi, what with a young lady swooning in front of my eyes."

"I'm not so young," I said, wanting to devil him a little, though I couldn't read one detail of his face under my dark glasses.

"Well, I would make you my mouse if I wasn't so busy picking people's pockets."

"You shouldn't confess your crimes to a stranger—and suppose I did not want to be your mouse?"

"I found ya," he said. "And that gives me certain privileges."

I didn't quite understand a pickpocket's etiquette. What privileges could he have possibly had? We were strangers, as I said. I hadn't even given him my calling card.

Finally my debonair pickpocket helped me to my feet. I was staggered by his strength and the softness of his touch. He did not have the refinement of my Philadelphia, or a voice that thundered down at you from a pulpit. He could not sear my flesh, but he did have his own quiet power.

"Sir, would you consider marrying me? I am tiny, that is true. But I can cook and mend your socks."

I heard the lilt of his laugh again. I could tell that I had pleased him. "Never," he said. "Marriage is not a mouse."

He took my hand, not to claim his territory, but to lead me along as you would a blind girl or a child.

"Sir, you must educate me. Why would the hoi polloi seize this almshouse for themselves and keep a sign that proclaims 'Overseers of the Poor'?"

"That's their persnicketiness. They're snobs. They want to have their Cambridge culture, their high teas and fandangos with that poorhouse sign staring 'em in the face. That's why I don't have much mercy when we pick their pockets, Sis. We're the Shady Hill Gang. But we had to move from Shady Hill. The sheriff's men started climbing down our backs. And now we're wayfarers without a fixed domicile. I like that better. Out of sight, out of mind. But where do ya live, my little mouse?"

I told him without any qualms: *86 Austin Street*. I wasn't fearful in the least that he would rush through Mrs. Bangs', battering her boarders while he picked their pockets. He would have been as courtly to my little cousins as he was to me. I believed in him, though I could not see more than the bare outlines of his face.

"Your name?" he asked, with a slight tug of my hand. "For future reference."

"Daisy. Daisy the Kangaroo," I said, using my nom de guerre. ". . . and you must tell me yours. I can't keep calling you 'Sir.' Where I come from, such formality would be a mark of rudeness."

It wasn't a mark of rudeness at all. And believe it or not, I was growing preternaturally fond of this rascal and lord of the Shady Hill Gang.

"Couldn't tell you my name, could I, Sis? The sheriff's men might interview ya, and I would have to swim in the same brine with all the other pickles. No, anonymity is best under the circumstances, even if you are my mouse."

I was the one with proper Plumage, and I hadn't expected a pickpocket, cavalier as he was, to smother me in his own abundance of feathers.

"But I have to call you something, Sir."

"Then I leave it up to you, Sis. Invent a name for me."

Even with all my loquaciousness, I could not. I was stunned into silence. Fancy feathers had failed me. I had never been called upon to name a man on such short notice.

He laughed again, and the sound rippled into the night like a switch of melody.

"Cat caught your tongue, my pretty little mouse?"

"You're a flatterer as well as a pickpocket," I said, but I could feel myself expand into a giantess. The old maid was gone. None of my suitors had ever called me a pretty little mouse.

"Sir, I shall call you Enobarbus. Not even the sheriff's men will ever unravel that name."

"I'm not so sure. Wasn't he some Roman soldier with a gaudy tongue?"

Enobarbus did have a gaudy tongue. And he celebrated Cleopatra with it. But what library had my rascal entered that he could pick at Shakespeare with his nimble hands? I'll never mock metropolitans again. Lord, I had come to this metropolis as a prisoner with failing eyes and had found enchantment across the street from an almshouse dressed in false feathers.

I would have gone into the Athenaeum with my new admirer—the pickpocket and his mouse. But the hoi polloi would have heaped abuse upon our heads and sent for the police. I'd have started my own sirocco, stronger than Sue's. Father would have to come to Cambridgeport to plead my case. He'd never prevail. I'd be sentenced to six months in the women's farm as a pickpocket's moll. Who would marry me now!

But I had one consolation. I didn't have to share Enobarbus the Pickpocket with any other mouse—at least not for the duration, that is, tonight. We walked hand in hand in that hot, mosquito-ridden air, while he swatted at the mosquitoes with his one free fist.

"It's the filth in the marsh. It breeds those monsters, the largest in all of Massachusetts. I've watched a swarm of 'em eat a man alive."

"But why didn't you help him the way you helped me?"

Enobarbus stopped for a moment, and I lost the rhythm of his stride, since my feet were infantine compared to his.

"He was a deputy's man. I owed him nothing but his death. He wasn't a mouse of mine."

His stride picked up again, and I was able to patter a half-step behind him. The mosquitoes could bite until eternity was here and gone. I did not want this night to end, my night with Enobarbus. All the men I loved had escaped from me—Brainard Rowe, my Tutor from Mars; Mr. Bowles, with his Arabian beard; Tom the Handyman, who had burgled one mansion too many; and my Philadelphia, Mr. Wadsworth, who was hiding somewhere between the Isthmus of Panama and my heart. But dark glasses had given me a boldness I'd never had with sighted eyes. I prowled like a pickpocket and had been rewarded with treasure. The streets themselves vanished as Enobarbus tugged at my hand. I had want of nothing—not the scratch of my Pen upon the page, nor that mix of pleasure and pain whenever I got too close to Sue's volcanic ash.

Enobarbus had rescued me from ruffians who would have robbed me of my hair. It was the madness of war that had made men so desperate. But I couldn't have met Enobarbus had it not been for them and their scissors.

He accompanied me to 86 Austin Street. I wished the entire boardinghouse could see my beau. But not a lamp was lit. The whole of Mrs. Bangs's entourage had repaired to bed, even Fanny and Loo, who must have started to snore while waiting for me.

"Enobarbus," I said, as bold as can be, "will I ever see you again?"

I still could not read his face in that dark blur.

"That depends," he said. "We'll be working Blue Hill tomorrow. We have to cross the river a couple of times a day to keep the deputies guessing. But I'll do my best to be there whenever you swoon."

And he went off into that wilderness of mosquitoes, with all their viciousness! I could hear them snarl in their tinny voices as they fed upon my Enobarbus. They were the true Vampyres, not this little mouse.

# 29.

I HAD MUCH TALLER FEET IN THE MORNING. THE GIANTESS slept and slept. I was the talk of 86 Austin Street. Mrs. Bangs dared not ask where I had been. And Big Daughter—Louise was her name—would offer not an instant of reproach while she buttered her toast at breakfast. But their Irish maid, Margaret Tripper, wasn't so genteel. She harrumphed in the midst of serving Mrs. Bangs's best pickled beef.

"Some's are decent, and some's are not. That is my stark opinion. If I had me way, I'd bolt the door at the stroke of midnight, tho' bless her little heart, I'm sure Miss Emily had her reasons."

"She had none," said I in a throaty voice that was the mark of my new size. I would not have been startled to learn I had sprouted manly hairs and moles during the night.

"It's her red crown," said Mrs. Tripper. "It makes her saucy. Satan himself has a red beard."

"And so would I were I a man."

She stood bewildered at my remark; her eyes wandered as if she meant to massacre me. But she was kind in spite of her truculence, and when she snorted into her apron, I began my retreat.

"O, Trip"—that's what we called her—"I was lost, and it took me hours to find my way again."

"But there are evil men about, Miss Emily, adventurers who might hook themselves onto a young marriageable lady like yourself."

The word *marriageable* made me blush. I was the one who proposed to Enobarbus the Pickpocket, since he was much too busy plying his trade even to have me as his mouse.

"Trip," I said, sinking fast from my stature as a giant. "Did you ever hear of the Shady Hill Mob?"

"Murderers they are," answered Margaret with a shriek. She commenced to shake. "The likes of them haven't been seen in Cambridgeport for years. God forbid those Shady Hillers should ever come back! Their chieftain was hanged by the neck and buried at the back of Mount Auburn Cemetery where madmen, murderers, and paupers are put without a marker."

I'd been to Mount Auburn on an earlier trip to Boston—Lord, I was fifteen at the time, staying with my mother's people. I rode the railroad car right to that City of the Dead, stood in a swirl of tulips and honeysuckle, but I never found one unmarked grave.

"What was that chieftain's name?" I couldn't help but ask.

"Byron Thrall, unless you're calling me a liar."

Mrs. Bangs had to intervene. "Trip, there will be no more talk of cutthroats at my table."

"Sorry, Ma'am," Margaret said; she bowed and begged our pardon, vanished into the sink-room and shut the door.

I could not eat another mouthful of pickled beef. My appetite had fled with Byron Thrall. I fancied that Cambridgeport itself was a Haunted House and that my Enobarbus walked amongst the population like a resourceful ghost who could linger between the Quick and the Dead.

I HAD SMALL USE FOR THIS DAY WORLD. I HAD TO SUFFER THE horse-car rides to my Physician. Boston meant nothing to me. That miserable horse labored among the tracks and delivered me and my little cousins to Dr. Williams's sandstone house and his magic eye machine. The light he shone into my eye was like a pin upon my retina that felt far worse than a scratch. I would have screamed had Fan and Loo not been there to watch my agony and consternation. My Physician did not mean to harm me. But he could not help unless he pricked my eye.

"Miss Dickinson, you have disobeyed me."

My guilt was enormous, but dear God, I could not recollect what I had done wrong.

"You have been reading and writing," said he. "Your eyes are inflamed."

"Sir, I promise you. I have read no more than a mouse."

"And even that is too much of a strain," he said, though he managed to smile at my diction. "Good Lord, shall I put you under arrest?"

I had rheumatic iritis. Salient Sarah, Father's new mare, suffers from the same disease. But horses are blessed with having a fancier name for it—moon blindness. The glare of the moon gives Sarah the most crippling headaches. Father has to steer her out of the sun and keep her in the stable when the moon is ripe. But sometimes Sarah will stall in the middle of the road and utter a baleful cry. Father is loath to whip her when she is so despondent. A horse with moon blindness is worth nil, Father's friends have told him, but he will never part with his mare.

And I have Sarah's moon blindness, a fickle irritation of the iris that comes and goes as God (or the Devil) wills. But my Physician is a Goliath in his field—no one can compete with Dr. Williams and his ophthalmoscope, neither in the North nor in the South that once was. And poor Sarah has no such Goliath. Even if Father serenaded the moon and kept it from shining for six months, Sarah's sickness would devour her and lead to irrevocable blindness, while Williams *might* be able to save my eyes.

"Under arrest," Dr. Williams repeats in front of my Norcross cousins, whom he has allowed into his examination room, since he knows I would be as fearful as a kitten without them. Also, he loves to have an audience in his little theater. Father has chosen an ophthalmologist who thinks he is Mr. Shakespeare.

"Misses Norcross," he says, "may I have your solemn oath that you will do your very best to see that Miss Dickinson does not misbehave?"

Fanny and Loo hang on his every word with watchful eyes.

"You may, Sir. You may."

"Good. Then I will relinquish her to your own command."

He ought not have lent my cousins such a powerful proposition. It was like having a pair of stern little soldiers beside you. I had my own impish power to make them smile, but I still could not peruse any of the letters from Sister Sue in my pocket during the ride back across the Charles. I had to wear my dark glasses under the bright, baking roof of the horse-car, shun the river and its sheen, which could have made me as blind as Salient Sarah.

## 30.

LIKE A HALF-BLIND MAIDEN IN MOSQUITO LAND I DREAMT OF
a trousseau, yet I was nothing but a pickpocket's appendage, otherwise known as a mouse. But a mouse could still wear her Plumage, and I decided to write a letter to my betrothed.

*My Dearest Enobarbus,*

*I think of you all the time. The housekeeper at 86 Austin says you are
a dead man, Byron Thrall, and that the Shady Hillers are no more. And
what evidence do I have that you are still alive? You came from the shadows to rescue me and returned to the shadows. Perhaps you are only a
vapor that rises out of the burying-ground at night. But your little mouse
don't mind.*

*Tell me, dearest, how to find you? Must I visit the burying-ground
and shiver like a boy while I wait and blow my bugle to keep the other
vapors from pestering me? Or are you made of solid stuff, scratchier than
a ghost? Moon blind like my father's horse, I could not really see your
face. But you did clasp my hand, and yours was as material as a hand
could be.*

*Dearest, shall we have another assignation on Magazine Street? Must*

*I swoon again before you can find me? And how will I ever get this mis-*
*sive to you? Send it flying into the wind, against a barrier of mosquitoes?*
*Pin it to a gate at the burial ground? Instruct me, and I will follow your*
*tiniest wish.*

*Yr affectionate friend,*
*Daisy the Kangaroo*

I realized there was a contradiction in being both a mouse and
a kangaroo. But my Enobarbus could cancel such contradictions.
And while I pondered, Margaret Tripper kept biting into my ear
like a pernicious mosquito.

"There is no Shady Hill Mob. Byron Thrall is dead."

"But I did meet the Shady Hillers, I swear."

And she told me I had met a malignant mob of army deserters
who loved to wear the mantle of Massachusetts's last great gang.
These deserters had a price on their head. They were unfortunate
men who ran from the smoke and blood of war. And the Shady
Hill Gang was a masterful disguise.

"Our Civilian Guard, even with shooters in their belts, run at
the first mention of Shady Hill," she said. "Miss Emily, a rotten,
stinking deserter picked you up off the ground. It's lucky he didn't
scalp you. That's how them deserters earn their living. They sell
women's hair to the factories, because silk and such are scarce in
wartime."

"I will not believe you, Trip."

"Then one afternoon you'll be looking at a hat made from your
own hair—if you survive your own scalping. But I will not pronounce another word, not in the presence of Miss Frances and
Miss Louisa. They are much too tender to hear such things."

But Fanny and Loo were enthralled; Margaret might just as well
have told them a tale about Ali Baba and the Forty Thieves. My
little cousins caressed their own scalps, as they imagined the silk
of their hair sitting in the window of a milliner's shop on Centre

Street. But they would have given their lives to protect *my* scalp.

We went to the Ice Cream saloon next to Haymarket Square, the terminus of the horse-car railroad line. Ice cream had become the rage of Boston and Cambridgeport—no neighborhood could live without a proper saloon. Boston had its own ice cream factory that could supply any town or hamlet within a hundred miles. And the saloon at Haymarket Square was more like a palace, or the grand salon at the Willard Hotel in Washington. It had chandeliers and potted plants, elephantine tables and plush velvet chairs, and it was filled with the hoi polloi I had met on Magazine Street—men in high hats and women in the finest bonnets and bustles. The children that accompanied them were not children at all, but little ladies and lords without a pinch of curiosity in their eyes. The Ice Cream saloon had become their mansion and meeting ground. They did not look once at the terminus outside their window, at the horse-cars arriving and departing, or at the horses themselves, who reminded me of Salient Sarah; these overburdened railroad horses had Sarah's stubborn dignity. They brooded with their own sense of outrage as the stable hands poked at them and removed their bridles.

I was much more interested in horses than in the hoi polloi. I kept wishing that Enobarbus would appear, drive the hoi polloi out of the saloon with a cudgel, and then sit with his mouse and *my* Norcross cousins. And we'd all revel in ice cream, seal our friendship with sweet chocolate or whatever flavor we could imagine— the Lord's vanilla or Satan's caramel—as we scooped up mouthfuls of the magical cream with the longest spoons in Massachusetts. But my man never showed, and I entertained Fan and Loo with tales of Father's moon-blind horse.

I had to twist and turn and tell lies to free myself from their clutches after sundown. I sent them off to some sewing circle or to the theatrical club on Pearl Street, with the promise that I would wear a whistle—it was meant to summon the Cambridge Guard.

But I had seldom seen such civilian soldiers in my horse-car rides and in my nighttime strolls. And so I sallied forth from Mrs. Bangs's the moment my little cousins left for Pearl Street. I had Loolie's whistle dangling from my neck. But it seemed like some worthless appendage for a kicking Kangaroo.

I had my reservations, since I was traveling under a full moon. But I shielded my eyes against the glare that crept through my dark glasses. And while on Valentine Street, I could catch glimmers of light leap off the tin roofs and hear a strange, prolonged groan, as if some giant had fallen out of a tree. Said *giant* was nothing but a surly mob—men grasping torches that stung my eyes, while pistols with long noses bobbed out of their pants.

I shivered at the first sight of them. They looked terribler than any mob I had ever seen, with chaos and a bitter wind in their wake. They might have knocked me over had I not leapt behind a fence.

"Girlie, git off the street," one of them rasped. "It's not so safe, what with deserters and devils running around." And when I didn't answer him, he said, "Have ya seen our Tom?"

That name rippled through me like some premonition. I grew taut as a crazy string and managed to whisper, "Who's Tom?"

My interlocutor laughed at me. He wore a belted factory-man's blouse and a pair of Colts whose handles looked like pearl ears.

"Every boy and kitten in Cambridgeport has heard of him . . . just as they ought to have heard of me."

He bowed in a most pretentious way. "Josiah, Captain of the Cambridge Guard, at your service."

"Who is Tom?" I asked again, no longer whispering. Suddenly I felt as morose as Zilpah in her Northampton institution, moroser even. At least Zilpah had a dormitory of other women to comfort her, or she could wait for Pa-pa's next appearance on the lawn. Zilpah had her chains to rattle, and I had nothing at all.

*"Who is Tom?"*

"Chief of all them devils," said my paladin with the twin Colts. "They pretends that Byron Thrall—bless that man—has come home to roost from Mount Auburn's. But Byron never bought and sold women's hair, Byron never ran off from his regiment, Byron never pissed upon our flag. And he ain't no lily-livered deserter, like Tom."

And this captain of the Cambridge Guard disappeared into his own hot swirl of dust. I was more disturbed by him than any rascal who might deprive me of my scalp. I no longer knew where to twist and turn. I had lost my footing after the captain had mentioned Tom. It wasn't moon blindness that crippled Daisy the Kangaroo. Daisy was also deaf! So excited was she by some new stranger on Magazine Street, fancying him as an exotic apparition, that she had not listened to the strains of his voice. Or perhaps her fickleness, her blinded heart, had stopped her from recognizing a pickpocket who sold women's hair as the burglar of Rooming-house Row and the handyman who had once lived in a shed.

What if I were wrong and had wished Tom the Handyman into a sack of deserter's clothes I could not see? My Tom had his very own mouse, Zilpah Marsh—not Miss Emily Dickinson. I cursed my own curiosity, lent me by the Devil. I'd as lief drown in one of Cambridgeport's canals than go on speculating. And if I didn't stop thinking of Tom I'd insane myself.

The mosquitoes were already tormenting me. I couldn't move without marching into a whole skirt of them. I must have been near the river. The rot of marshland burned in my nose. And then that first signal of moon blindness struck—the feel of a terrifying stitch at the back of my head. And I plunged into total darkness, as if I'd fallen into Father's well, but it was like a hollow without an end. I spun within its walls, faster and faster, and woke with a stifled scream on the front steps of 86 Austin, wrapped inside the shelter of an old horse blanket.

# 31.

LORD, I DID NOT KNOW WHO I AM OR EVER WAS. I DREAMT of the Ice Cream saloon, of enriching myself on Satan's caramel, of wearing my horse blanket among the hoi polloi. But I could not dream forever. I was giddy and sad at the boardinghouse, and wouldn't part with that blanket, though it was fat with dead mosquitoes and live fleas. Mrs. Bangs had convulsions over my filthy blanket.

"I will write your father, Miss Emily, I most certainly will. The Misses Norcross are as gentle as can be. But I will not abide boarders who roam through the night without a male escort, and who arrive on my doorstep in a trance, draped in a blanket that no decent woman would ever wear."

But she backed down the second she saw I would not budge. Pa-pa paid her a king's ransom for my upkeep. He was stingy with his time, stingy with his words and his affection, but he sent me into Boston like an heiress. My treatment with Dr. Williams would have bankrupted most country lawyers, but not Pa-pa. He was willful with his daughters, and denied us nothing except himself. That was Pa-pa's paradox. And he wasn't so different from my pickpocket, who brought me out of the wilderness of a dark street without a kiss or word of affection that I was conscious of. And I had nothing but his blanket as my one memento of him.

Daisy the Kangaroo could fight with Mrs. Bangs, but not with Margaret Tripper, whose Irish heart was fiercer than mine. I permitted her to scrub my blanket and pick out the fleas, and then I wore it everywhere, except to my Physician's office, since his seriousness stunned me and made me feel like a little child at church. But not even my awe of him kept me from wearing it on the horsecar. Fanny and Loo liked to pretend that my blanket was invisible and never once referred to it. I was their cracked older cousin, who scribbled words on wrinkled envelopes and ancient recipes and party invitations whenever they visited us in Amherst. It wasn't out of some prissy desire or need. Lines came like lightning and left like lightning, and I had to write each one down with my pencil stub or lose it forever.

But the lightning rarely came while I was imprisoned in the boardinghouse. It wasn't my Physician who punished me by taking away my Pen—the punishment was deep inside my loins, as if some rigor mortis had settled in away from Amherst and Father, Sister, Brother, and Sue. I could feel a few crackles coming back as I wandered in the mosquito-swollen streets at night, my blanket drawing them in like a mosquito-eater. Enobarbus the Pickpocket couldn't have been my Tom—Tom could barely spell his name, and would never have been on familiar terms with Antony or Enobarbus, and the "Egypt" both of them adored. His blazing blond hair and blue eyes had not equipped him for the brutal escutcheon of words. He was deft of hand, and his music came from his lithe motion, not his Lexicon.

And so I sought out this stranger with a certain sadness. I wanted to keep the false fancy inside my head that the pickpocket of Magazine Street could still be my Tom, transformed by witchcraft into a shaper of sentences. I searched the haze of darkening streets, with Loolie's whistle under my blanket, a whistle I would never blow. God help us all if I should ever need Captain Josiah and his mob to protect me. Josiah would always catch me at the tail end of his little tornado.

"Kitten, skedaddle, else a body might think you're a lookout for Tom and his outlaw army."

But he never had time to continue that topic of conversation. He always leapt back inside his tornado, and I searched in vain. The pickpockets had a route I could not readily decode, and I would return to 86 Austin, my scalp and hands tingling with mosquito bites.

I realized that night marches wouldn't do. I'd have to risk daylight, and the malignant attack of sun upon my eyes. Fanny and Loo were hysterical; stalwarts of my Physician, they kept watch over me like the stern little soldiers they'd become.

"Auntie Em, you will blind yourself," they said.

Fanny and Loo had that baffled look of children who had strayed outside their own measure; they dressed alike, had the same ribbons and curls, the same agitated fingers and eyes. I'd come to Cambridgeport to be in the care of my little cousins; they mended my clothes and looked after me, but they'd never before rubbed up against my willful nature. I'd attended to their wants whenever they visited Amherst, sat with them, played with them, let them water my plants while I scribbled out the lightning inside my head. But now they had a chance to "meet" Austin's wild sister, the kicking Kangaroo, and it agitated them.

"Loolie, you must not be so concerned. I will be back in an hour, I promise."

My little cousins resorted to the only weapon they had—Margaret Tripper, who tried to block my path to the front door.

"Miss Emily, you ought to be ashamed of yourself."

"I am, but if you don't get out of my way, I will rip the eyes from your head and roast your heart and liver on the nearest fire I can find."

I was putting on my Plumage, that's all, but poor Margaret had never seen me at work.

"That's not the language of a lady," she said. And stunned as she was, I flew right past her. I wouldn't don my dark glasses—if I did find Enobarbus, I wanted to see the true color of his hair. But I had picked the brightest of mornings, and the sun burnt down upon my bonnet like an Egyptian plague. I couldn't shield my eyes with the edge of that blanket I wore like a grenadier's cape; I would have accomplished very little with a swatch of wool cutting off my command of the street.

And so I twisted into the sunlight. I did not even have to roam very far. The Shady Hillers must have felt safe in the sun. I caught a glimpse of my darling apparition as I wandered up and down Magazine Street with its printing shops and converted poorhouse. He seemed to float on wind and air. Lord, he shook the life out of me. I could not mistake the *syllables* of his blond hair. And for the first time in this metropolis my lightning struck like an earl. The sounds came to me.

*That blond Assassin in the sunlight*

And the lightning struck a second time. I knew now where my Tom had gotten his gift of words. That *other* mouse, better known as Zilpah Marsh, had taught him to read and write. She's the one who had fed Mr. Shakespeare to him before she'd gone berserk, or at least was locked away in the asylum with that memory of her own butchered child.

He stood outside the Chestnut Tavern near Green Street with a tankard of ale that flashed against the sun and seized my eyes with a fortune of sharp, merciless pinpricks. But I did not falter. He raised his tankard as his blue eyes lit upon me.

"Hello, Daisy."

I was glad I had given him my nom de guerre. He could have connected Emily Dickinson to Amherst and the mistress who had helped ruin Zilpah Marsh. He might have stood with the Devil and sought revenge against the Dickinsons, murdered Pa-pa, Vinnie, and God knows who for having dismissed his mouse and sent her hurtling into the hospital. I was careful with him as careful could be. Lolling in that Sahara sun don't mean much to Daisy. Her blood had gone to ice. Daisy preened her feathers before she spoke.

"Enobarbus, I thought I was your mouse."

He smiled his Assassin's smile and I could have fainted with the beauty of it, but I did not. An accordion man was leaning with one foot against the tavern wall, and Tom the Pickpocket, my Tom, tossed him a silver dollar.

"Johnny, I intend to dance with that little mouse."

There were no invitations. Tom, or whoever he was, picked Daisy off the ground, held me so tight I could have been stapled to him. The accordion man tapped with his toe and started to play, and that melody was like nothing I had ever listened to—halfway between the polka and a Virginia reel for solitary couples, since no one else was allowed to dance. Tom whirled me around Magazine Street with him, and I had little breath to spare. With another man I might have been terrified. But I had only one wish—to be stapled forever to Tom.

Vertigo meant nothing now. I didn't mind the dizziness. And then the dancing stopped. Tom loosened his grip, and I slid to the ground.

"I have to scram," he said, like a sudden rip in the air.

"Without your mouse?"

"We're quittin' Cambridgeport. The town has hired too many damn civilian soldiers. There are more of 'em than cats. And a mouse like you would draw attention—particularly with your red hair."

"But that's your business, selling hair. Why didn't you just steal my scalp?"

"I couldn't," he said. "You remind me of somebody."

I was readying to fall into his arms. "Mr. Pickpocket, who could that somebody be?"

"I can't recollect. A girl with red hair was once kind to me. That's all I remember."

It was the nearest thing to a declaration of love. My blond Assassin could have scalped me with the blade of his hand. Daisy don't care. I was filling up with a vile phlegm. I was green with jealousy. It was Zilpah Marsh who had poured Shakespeare into his ears, strutting around as Cleopatra, while I was a lad with a freckled face. Cleopatra was round and dark and could smolder in the hot Egyptian sun, and I was as shapeless as a Dimity gown.

"Will you find me again if I should ever faint?" I asked, stroking my horse blanket.

"Daisy darling, I could spot your red hair all the way from Roxbury and Blue Hill."

I wanted to blurt out that I was the ruddy angel who had wiped his brow and fed him in his shack at Holyoke, but I didn't dare. He'd been ill at the time, in a dark haze, and could remember nothing but my reddish look—else I would have been scalped!

I could hear the church bells tolling with their loud, lugubrious clatter for Cambridge's war dead. The bells seemed to bother Tom. His eyes began to flutter with every peel.

"Best to say goodbye, mouse."

Would I have to spend half my life losing that blond Assassin? He finished his tankard of ale, wiped his lips with one long finger, put the tankard down, propelled his whole body with a pantherish leap of his legs, and turned the corner, onto Green Street, without looking back.

# 32.

"GREAT THUNDERING SKIES!" VINNIE SCRIBBLED FROM HEAD-quarters in her loquacious hand. "Brother will not have to die on the Battlefield." Even with the bounty it offered, Amherst couldn't meet its enlistment quota and had to draft able-bodied bachelors and married men. Brother had escaped the first draft, but this time his name had been pulled out of the lottery wheel. Father found a substitute, a handyman from Rooming-house Row, paid him a small fortune—five hundred dollars—to go to war in Broth-er's stead. An Irisher, Lawrence Steele. How could he not remind me of *my* Handyman, who liked to pose as a pickpocket? The five hundred dollars had ransomed Lawrence's life and took his five children out of poverty. There was even a rumor, so said Vinnie, that Lawrence Steele had several missing toes. But the War Depart-ment wouldn't have accepted a crippled soldier.

I didn't know whether to clap my hands or cry. I was delighted for Brother, and so were my little cousins. I would have worried myself to death if he had to wear the Union blue, but I couldn't stop thinking of Lawrence, the mutilated man, who might leave five orphans in his wake. I was a scandalous girl. I wished that Lawrence would desert the War and run to Canada with his family and Pa-pa's five hundred dollars.

I couldn't fall asleep. I kept hearing bugles in my brain. At first I thought I had gone to Heaven, not as my reward—but as my perdition, the punishment of being without that blond Assassin who had crept inside my bones. I was convinced that the Lord's own buglers were mocking me, that their refrain was part of a pernicious song about a half-blind old maid who had fallen in love with an army deserter. But then the buglers broke through my sleep. Fanny and Loo were sitting on my bed, their nightgowns awry, with a look of perdition on their faces, terribler than I'd ever seen.

"Auntie, Auntie, it's the end of the world."

I hugged them hard as I could.

"My dears, it don't make sense. God's trumpeters wouldn't come down to Austin Street with their night music."

But I trembled as I spoke. I knew nothing about this particular band of bugler angels and trumpeters. And then Margaret Tripper burst into our room. She wasn't wearing a nightgown, but was dressed all in Dimity, as if she had a winter uniform that could protect us from any peril.

"Shush," she said. "We aren't in danger. It's the Civilian Guard. They're on the march, rounding up vagrants and deserters and storing them inside the old almshouse. I'd dump 'em in the Charles, that's my opinion."

The Provost Marshal, it seems, had declared war on Boston's bounty jumpers and army deserters who posed as pickpockets, and had unleashed the Civilian Guard to round them up. But this Civilian Guard was a band of lawless men with the license to plunder at will. They were the dregs of Boston and Cambridge who were too old to be drafted—they did their own military training in the streets and attacked whoever displeased them.

"Why so many buglers?" Fanny asked, her eyes as agitated as ever.

"It's their way of signalin' to one another from afar. Each squad has its own bugler."

I wore whatever mask I could, made a fist to stop my fingers from trembling. "Trip, did they find Byron Thrall?"

"I told ya. Byron Thrall is dead."

"But their new leader. Tom the Pickpocket."

Margaret perused me with a touch of contempt. "They're all pickpockets when they ain't selling women's hair. I have never heard mention of this Tom."

And she was through with us. I pined to rush over to the alms-house in my horse blanket, but I'd only have heaped suspicion upon Tom and myself. And Mrs. Bangs and Big Daughter would have come charging after me, with Margaret holding down the skirts of her two boardinghouse queens. I'd have to lie low, wait until all the bugling ended, and Captain Josiah's infernal men vanished inside the almshouse with their sour breath and bitter wind. I did not cherish having to meet Captain Josiah and his twin Colts again, a robber with the Provost Marshal's writ in his pocket.

~

I PLAYED HEARTS WITH BIG DAUGHTER. I HAD HOURS AND hours to kill until it grew dark. I practiced being a Vampyre, since I'd have to suck the life's blood out of Josiah and his men if I wanted to free Tom from the old almshouse. But even a Vampyre could run out of breath.

Finally the gloaming crept onto Austin Street, house by house, and I did not have to watch the shadows on my wall, or fight my way to the front door. Mrs. Bangs and Margaret Tripper were strangely passive, strangely glum. And my little cousins couldn't have stopped me on their own. Perhaps Mrs. Bangs and Big Daughter didn't believe I was suicidal enough to go out on a mission, into a night menaced by mosquitoes, deserters, and all their debris.

I was alarmed, if truth be told. Under my dark glasses I saw battered men lying in the gutters; they begged for water and I had none to give. I wondered what Witchcraft was at work. The ground of Magazine, Valentine, and Green had gone to rubble. The little territory near 86 Austin was now a battlefield mummified. I nearly stepped into a crater. Mosquitoes swarmed above the groaning men, streaked with blood.

The Ice Cream saloon at Haymarket Square could offer no more solace to the citizens of Cambridgeport. Its windows had been shattered, its potted plants strewn on the sidewalk. The Civilian Guard had taken over the saloon as its head-quarters. I saw men milling about inside the windows, with ice cream on their faces like vanilla masks. Horses wandered in the streets in their broken bridles. The horse-cars had been overturned, and the terminus half-destroyed, as if visited by some wanton wind. That wind had been manufactured by men with vanilla faces.

Not a soul impeded my path. But I couldn't find any of the hoi polloi and their carriages outside the almshouse—or Cambridge Athenaeum. It was as dead and dark as pitch. Not a lantern, not a light. And then a light flashed in front of me, and seemed to sear my eyes. I hid under my horse blanket like a loon, and when I looked up again, I discovered a lantern in my face and a voice behind its glare.

"Confess, you harlot. You're a lookout for the Shady Hillers. You live with Tom."

It was that darn captain of the civilian soldiers. How could he have been so shrewd and imbecilic at the same time? I would have scalped my own little fortune of rat's hair to remain as Tom's mouse. But a girl afflicted with moon blindness couldn't have run from town to town with a renegade.

"Kitten, I am holding you under the wartime powers that have been invested in me. You can call yourself my prisoner. There's no use pretending. I ain't blind."

What wartime powers? He had the Provost Marshal's writ to mask his plundering.

"Where's Tom?" I pleaded.

His laughter sounded like crackling tin. "Then you admit you're his harlot and his mouse . . . Why are you wearing spectacles that cover your eyes with black? Are ya Satan's helpmate?"

"Where's Tom?"

I had to listen to that same sound of tin. "Tom's where he belongs. In the stockades. He'll sit there and starve to death. And if he survives until the Rebellion's over with, the judge advocate will see to it that he's hanged. I captured Tom—took ten of us to beat him into the ground. I never met such a nefarious creature, stealing women's hair. You have to be his accomplice, else he would have scalped ya."

Josiah looked me up and down, and it was shameful as far as I could tell with my glasses on. That rascal could have been appraising the flesh of a cow.

"I'll set ya free, kitten, if you follow me into the poorhouse and let a man love you to death. But give Josiah a kiss first. I have to sample your wares and see if you're worth it."

"I'd rather kiss a bullfrog," I said, though I was shivering under my horse blanket.

"Mouse, you're gonna kiss me sure as Hell."

I wasn't his mouse and I never would be. But I was still shivering while he tore the blanket from my shoulders. I could smell his sour guts. He grabbed me with his fat fingers when some Phantom leapt through the wall of mosquitoes with a swiftness that could stun a girl and gave Josiah a kick that sent him flying. I let my heart churn its own fancy. I didn't even wait until that shadow materialized into a man. I was convinced Tom had come from the stockades for his mouse. I reached out to caress him. I looked again in my moon blindness—wasn't my blond Assassin. It was Pa-pa.

He knew how to disappoint a girl. But I wasn't disappointed

all that much. Hadn't Pa-pa rescued Zilpah Marsh on the lawn at
that lunatic hospital? And now he was rescuing me. But he wasn't
soft and gentle, as he had been with Zilpah. The rage in his eye
was enough of a rebuke. I wasn't even worth the littlest hello. I
couldn't tell him I was a mouse waiting for her pickpocket. Here I
was on Magazine Street, with Pa-pa standing over Captain Josiah,
who was all agog. That rascal tried to regain his dignity. He dusted
off his pants and said, "Sir, you are interferin' with a legal arrest. I
am an agent of the law, deputized by the assistant provost marshal
of Massachusetts."

Pa-pa kicked him again, not as he would have done to Carlo,
but to some cowardly dog. I had never seen so much vehemence
in him, so much noise. He was a a quiet man, slow to anger, except
when it came to his horse. I'd watched him whip Sarah for the littlest reason. He made allowances for her moon blindness, and
nothing else. But Captain Josiah must have insaned Pa-pa.

"Shut your mouth before I smash you into little pieces. I'm
Major Edward Dickinson of the Amherst militia," he said. Pa-pa
hadn't drilled on our Commons for half a century, but he still had
the right to call himself a major, I would reckon.

Josiah saluted Pa-pa and pointed to me.

"She's a spitfire," Josiah said. "She was dancing with a deserter,
and she's his mouse."

"She's my daughter, Miss Emily Dickinson of Amherst."

The captain's eyes rolled around in his head. He was lost in
a maelstrom, and wasn't certain what to do other than humble
himself. He drifted off with his lantern, while I expected Pa-pa
to pounce on me, to ask what an old maid with an irritated iris,
who could not live near the light, was doing in a deserter's arms.
I wasn't without my weapons. Hadn't Father found a substitute
for Austin, rescued him from the draft? And if Pa-pa pounced, I'd
whisper in his ear that Austin might have become a deserter too if
he'd had half the chance.

But Major Dickinson didn't even interrogate his errant daughter.

"Mrs. Bangs wrote me that you were wandering about at night . . ."

"She shouldn't have," I whispered like the little girl I became in Pa-pa's presence.

"Emily, we were like stranded children without you," he said. "Mother can hardly bear it. Lavinia mopes. Austin swears he cannot amuse himself without his wild sister. And Carlo pines near your bed."

"Father, if you mention my dog, I will surely cry."

"I do my best. I hike with him in the fields. But he has one master—you. Vinnie has to feed him filet mignon out of her own hand, while that dog is as big as a church, bigger even. He'll reach our chimney one day, and I'll have to cut a hole in the roof for his head."

Pa-pa had me laughing and crying. He hadn't palavered so much in years. His long silences were mythical. He and Mother had their own rooms. And they had to meet on the stairs to see how the other was doing.

I should have kept my own counsel, but I couldn't. I had a cruel streak.

"Pa-pa," I said, "how is Lawrence Steele?"

He looked at me askance, his auburn eyebrows twitching once or twice. "Who the Devil is Lawrence Steele?"

"Austin's substitute," I said, "the handyman with five children and three missing toes who took Brother's place."

Pa-pa's eyebrows were hopping again. I was the only Dickinson who could crawl under his skin.

"Austin's a family man. I didn't want him goin' to war." Pa-pa's voice began to quaver. "I kept dreaming of him in a ditch . . . I'm not Steele's angel, but I did what I could. I'm looking after his children and his wife."

I was at the last lottery, before Brother's name was selected in the draft. The enrollment board met in a room on Main Street, near Pa-pa's office. Amherst had collected a bounty tax to encourage enlistment, but it still had to depend on a lottery wheel. Frederickson, a farmer who had been blinded by a lightning bolt, spun the wheel—the board insisted on a blind man, so that there wouldn't be any politics associated with the draft. But even a blind man had to guard his own impartiality. Frederickson closed his eyes, and I remember all the pulsations under his eyelids, as if a storm were collecting there. He pulled the names out of the wheel and handed them to Squire Edward, who was acting commissioner of the board. Father perused the names and intoned them one by one. He could not reveal the least emotion. I wanted to shout hallelujah when Brother's name wasn't called, but Pa-pa would have been mortified. The blind farmer did have a smile on his lips. Pa-pa let him work in our meadow as a hired hand, and he must have been glad that Brother had not been drafted. He accompanied us home to head-quarters, where we all had a glass of sherry. Some of the sherry spilled on his shirt. I can still see the spots, like the imprint of a tiger's paw . . .

Captain Josiah must have cleared the way for us. We weren't stopped by any of his ruffians with their Colts. We walked amid the debris. Pa-pa took my hand. And I wondered if bugles had sounded throughout Boston, if the Provost Marshal was trying to sweep away all deserters and bounty jumpers. The Union could have been another Vampyre, hungry for the blood of new men.

〜

I COULD HEAR A LONE BUGLE SING IN THE DISTANCE. WAS IT sounding for Pa-pa and me? Or Lawrence Steele and Tom? And I wondered if Pa-pa would have paid a king's ransom for his daughter had she been going away to war—the little sergeant of Poetry. Had I beguiled Pa-pa with my Verse, he might have paid that ransom for Tom. But I wasn't much of a soldier. I did not seek fame or send my Verses to periodicals, though a few were published anonymously in *Drum Beat*, a near defunct Brooklyn journal trying to raise money for wounded war veterans. Susie must have sent them under cover with some of her own Verses. And the *Springfield Musket* had asked us to contribute one or two "gems." But I declined, worrying that Pa-pa would trace the Verses back to me, and wishing that he would. I had even concocted a nom de guerre—Daisy the Kangaroo. Somehow it was easier to scribble when I thought of myself as Daisy rather than Miss Dickinson.

It tore at me that Father did not know one damn thing about *my* Treasure. A couple of years ago I gathered up the courage to leave one small booklet of Verses under his door. Lord, I wasn't looking for praise, but the privilege of having a tiny anthill of my own. Months later I found that booklet shoved back under my door like a misused missile. And never a sound from Pa-pa, never a syllable. I couldn't become a sergeant in any war. It wouldn't even have pleasured Pa-pa had he known that half my songs were to him.

Daisy festered, and Pa-pa must have seen the smoke pouring out of my brain. He gathered me in his arms. And he began to sing out some lines in that dry baritone of his.

> My Dolly deals her pretty words like blades . . .
> And stuns her poor Pa-pa by degrees.

The smoke inside me began to settle. I had my king's ransom. I was purring like a mouse. Pa-pa had memorized some of my Plumage. He was serenading me with my very own sounds.

"Why couldn't you tell me that you read my Verses, Pa-pa?"

"Dolly," he said, "it's taken me two years to recover. They nearly tore my head off. Ain't I tellin' you now?"

"In the middle of a battlefield," I said.

I was still purring, but my ecstasy didn't last. That lone bugle kept sounding in the distance. I felt a claw in my stomach, as if a bullet with a hundred knitting needles had suddenly invaded my loins. I didn't need a bloodhound to understand. Zilpah's own dead child had come to haunt its mother's live Mistress. I could feel its blood leaking down my legs. I couldn't tell Pa-pa, blame it on moon blindness. That barbed bullet tore at my insides. I expected to meet my own destruction on Cambridgeport's battered streets. My knees buckled. Then, as suddenly as it had started, the clawing stopped. I started to limp. Pa-pa was still holding my hand.

*Frazar Stearns*

Sue had memorized the Battle of New Bern. It wasn't from any morbid love of carnage, even if Union boys had routed the Rebels. Yet there was little to rejoice. Frazar Stearns had fallen near the feet of his commanding officer, Colonel William S. Clark of the Twenty-first Massachusetts Volunteers, his own chemistry professor at the College. Colonel Clark could not be consoled. And neither could the town. Frazar had been one of Amherst's most beloved boys. He was Austin's close friend and classmate, and son of the College's own President Stearns. The Twenty-first had captured a "six-pounder" during the battle, and this brass cannon was given to President Stearns in memory of Frazar.

Sue had gone to the president's house to see the cannon, to rub its brass with her own fingers. Emily wouldn't come along—that's how the Dickinsons were. They walked around in their own private trance. Austin said he was too dazed to eat. But having lost her mother at the age of six, Sue was closer to the rub of mourning than they would ever be. She was the youngest of seven children—the Gilberts, who were scattered across the land. She'd lost her favorite sister, Mary, who died shortly after childbirth, when Sue herself was twenty. She mourned Mary for three years, could not seem to give up the "black." She might have mourned Mary another three had Austin not pushed her into marriage.

She couldn't stop thinking of battle sites; the main site was in North Carolina, at a brickyard outside New Bern. The Rebels' right flank was holed up with its artillery in the brickyard kiln. The Twenty-first Massachusetts had to charge this kiln twice, but broke the Rebel line. The Battle of New Bern was over in one day, March 14, 1862, the day that young Frazar died.

North Carolina had once had its own fleet, the infamous Mosquito Squadron that attacked Union shipping and transported Rebel troops. But Union gunboats sank the entire fleet. And Sue loved to recite the individual names of the Union flotilla: the Philadelphia, the Louisiana, the Underwriter, the Hunchback, the Henry Brinker, the Stars and Stripes . . .

She remembered helping to nurse Frazar when he had scarlet fever during the epidemic of '58. He was braver than most, let Sue put some salve on his own red sores. She was certain that he would die, even while she applied the salve and prayed for him. But the fever broke and the redness went away. And she didn't have to preside over his deathwatch.

There were other deathwatches, but soon she couldn't attend to the sick. She began having nightmares: She was trapped in a cellar, a horrid damp place where fetid plants grew and entangled her feet. It was like a hospital room, where women lay on cots and shrieked their lungs out. The incessant sounds injured Sue's ears and gave her a terrible fright.

But Sue wouldn't give up her war work, even though she had a one-year-old baby at home, Little Ned, whom she left with a colored nurse. She traveled as often as she could to Soldiers' Rest, a retreat in Springfield for wounded veterans who had nowhere else to go. Sometimes Vinnie and the Squire would accompany her, would read to the soldiers, while Sue saw to their bandages and the balms they had to swallow. But Emily wouldn't come to Springfield. Emily was immobilized, a casualty of war. She sat in her room like a hermit and scribbled notes to Sue with the rapidity of a telegraph writer. And how could Sue express her undying devotion when she had an infant who screamed day and night and a husband who was morose half the time? She could hardly bear to be touched by him. Perhaps it was Sue's own fault. Austin was always kissing her when and where she did not want to be kissed. And if she refused him once, he would sulk for days, call himself the banished husband.

But on one of her trips to the depot, she found her sister-in-law. Emily had arrived with a tight little traveling bag and a bunch of day lilies in her hand. Sue began to shiver near the depot tracks. Was her sister-in-law going to China with another rapscallion of a Tutor? Good Lord, no! She'd accepted Sue's invitation to succor the wounded in Springfield.

What had changed her mind?

"Frazar," she quipped.

"Dearest, Frazar is dead."

"But I dreamt of him, Susie. His ghost was riding in the wind and couldn't seem to lie at rest in the burying-ground . . . until I went to Springfield."

"Did the ghost speak his intentions?"

"He didn't have to. I'm perfectly capable of reading a ghost's mind."

Sue decided to end the interrogation. Emily had come to the depot with lilies from her garden and hopped aboard the Springfield Express. The train was filled with soldiers who looked like scoundrels; their uniforms were ripped and they wore paper wrappings instead of shoes. They kept leering at Sue and Emily like wild men. Sue was the one who was immobilized now. But Emily offered them each a day lily and a coin from her purse.

"Darling, they could be impostors," Sue whispered in Emily's ear.

"Well, impostors suffer the same as we do."

She began to wonder if Frazar's ghost had possessed Emily, and was riding in some wind that Sue couldn't see. Emily rid herself of all shyness at the retreat. She was as lively as an electrical storm. She danced with a crippled soldier, read bits of Shakespeare to a little band of blind veterans, and attended to the oozing sores of another soldier like the ablest nurse.

She'd put aside the secrets of poetry and her own natural reluctance to lend a hand.

Sue was enraptured by that picture of Emily darting everywhere. "Darling, you amaze me."

And Emily pouted like a little girl. "Why, Susie, just because I never learnt to make a decent bandage, that don't mean I'm dumb as a cow."

The pair of them giggled like naughty children for a moment and went back to work.

# PART FIVE

## Queen Recluse

## 33.

I COULD HAVE HID FOREVER IN MY ROOM WITH THE SHADES
down, skulked around on Pa-pa's back porch with a bandanna
over my eyes, or buried my head in a barrel of brine. It wouldn't
have mattered. I was going blind. Wherever I went, a needle
cracked right through my skull. I had to abandon Carlo for a second time and return to Boston for treatment with my Physician,
each one terribler than the last. Our neighbors said Carlo was the
oldest Newfoundland in history—but fifteen doesn't seem that
old. Carlo will always be my Pup.

I served a six-month sentence in Cambridgeport and sneaked
home in the fall, having asked Lavinia to meet me at the station.
I didn't want a whole parade of Dickinsons to welcome the half-
blind girl with gray in her hair who was still an apprentice poet at
thirty-five. But I was forlorn when Sister took my traveling bag.

"Where's Carlo?" I asked. "Where's my dog?"

Carlo wouldn't have missed an opportunity to meet his mistress.
He would have forsaken the lemon-pie mush that Ma-ma prepares
for him while I'm away—he no longer has enough teeth in his
head to chew on something solid.

Sister was struggling what to say. "Emily, Carlo's—collapsed!"

I ran from the station with Sister right behind me clutching the bag. My head whipped with every sort of imagining. Town-folk looked at the Squire's eccentric daughter, a meteor in dark glasses, hopping along like a wingless bird.

I didn't say hello to our handyman, or look for Ma-ma in the kitchen. I called out to my Pup, but Carlo didn't come. And then I heard that *ruff-ruff* of his that wasn't much of a bark. It was the only concession to sound my mute Confederate ever made. But there was a nervous edge to that sound, as if Carlo were communicating his lament to his mistress. It broke my heart. That's all I care to say.

The sound was coming from my room. I raced up the stairs, Sister still behind me. I whimpered like a loon at the first sight of Carlo, lying down on an old blanket in an enormous bassinet near my bed, his face all grizzled, like the wounded soldiers I had met on the train from Boston.

Carlo's black tail beat against the walls of the crib with such force that I wondered when the crib would break. But my mute Confederate couldn't even sit up on his hind legs. I had to lean over while he licked my face. And like the most regal of lions who had to endure the indignity of a bassinet, he started to beller deep within his throat and wouldn't stop until I clutched his paw and recognized him as His Royal Majesty. He'd been roaming the Orchard as little as a month ago, banishing squirrels from his domain, when he toppled over like some great furry building and couldn't seem to rise again, Sister said.

Our handyman was petrified, never having seen a Newfoundland fall like that. But Father didn't panic. He summoned the horse doctor, who surveyed Carlo in the Orchard and said, "Best to shoot that fellah and put him out of his misery. The bones in his legs are brittle and can't support the bulk of him. He'll never leave this Orchard alive."

But Carlo must have sensed his own predicament and didn't want any part of that horse doctor. He rose up, like a ship battling a squall, wandered out of that Orchard with a terrible limp, went right through the Homestead's front door, climbed up the stairs, making purchase with both paws, and settled in my room.

Pa-pa didn't want me rushing home from Boston in the middle of my treatments, so he uttered not a word, and took care of Carlo, fed him and cleaned his blankets, like you would with an aging child. Carlo wouldn't let another soul near him but Pa-pa. My Pup was guarding the room for me.

And now that I was back I settled in with Carlo, who ventured out of his bassinet from time to time and crawled to my own "crib," the small cherrywood desk that imprisoned me while I scribbled my Verses under the tyranny of dark glasses. But I wasn't the only casualty of sunlight. Salient Sarah's moon blindness went from bad to worse. She couldn't walk across the barn without stumbling. It was terrifying to behold. Pa-pa put his handkerchief over Sarah's eyes, clucked at her, calmed her down, but she knew what was coming next. Sarah nuzzled Pa-pa's sleeve, bit him gently to show her regard for him. Pa-pa took out a pistol I had not noticed before. It had a long silver snout and didn't hold more than one bullet at a time. He loaded the pistol with something that looked like a shotgun shell. His hand was steady, but his left knee began to jerk. He placed the silver snout behind Sarah's ear and pulled the trigger. I heard nothing more than a clap, soft as a kiss; Sarah tumbled to the ground, as if her legs had fallen right out from under her like pieces of glass.

The clap of Father's gun hounded me and began to eat me alive. I prayed to the Lord that he wouldn't take that pistol and turn it on Carlo. But he never brought its silver snout near my dog. No, he went down on his knees with a hammer and repaired the crib when it was about to topple.

Carlo was practically born in that crib. Pa-pa had built it him-

self, since you couldn't find a bassinet that size in a general store.
It was like a barn without a roof. Even then the Pup was as tall as I
was, his eyes hidden behind all that shaggy hair. I recollect the first
time I saw that rascal. Pa-pa was carrying him in his arms, consid-
erable as Carlo was, and he wouldn't leave off licking Pa-pa's face.
But when my Confederate first laid eyes on me, he leapt out of Pa-
pa's arms and ran around in circles, as if he'd decided right then
and there that a nineteen-year-old redhead with a plain, freckled
face was the sole source of his happiness.

Lord, I've been truer to Carlo than to any man, including that
other rascal, Tom the Pickpocket. The Pup has seen me cry, throw
jealous fits, plot against Pa-pa, thunder around like Zeus himself,
and he's like a peace officer who can calm his mistress and make
her laugh. I cannot recall being lonely in his presence. I talk to
Carlo, and he don't have to talk back. His big brown eyes tell their
own prescient tale. He's met most of my suitors, long before I
turned into an irascible old maid, and he hasn't been jealous of
one. He's never asked me to play with him. Carlo doesn't consider
himself a dog, I'd imagine, and wouldn't tolerate anyone else calling him Pup. He's been my Confederate these sixteen years, and
a much better roommate than any I ever had.

And one night, a few months after I returned from Cambridgeport, there was a howling storm, and snowflakes as big as dia-
monds beat against the windows. Pa-pa's fields had a brutal white
glare. The totality of it, the immense blanket of snow that moved
in waves, frightened me and I was tempted to lie down with Carlo
in his bassinet. But I fell into a deep slumber and found myself riding on Carlo's regal back. I didn't need to have any reins or stir-
rups. I held to his collar, but I could hardly straddle the enormous
black bundle of him. Still, my Pup wouldn't let me fall. I wore my
nightgown into the wind. I wasn't cold. It was like sitting on top of
a furry furnace.

We rode above Main Street, he and I, and the houses had a sudden regularity, even in the snowstorm, as if Amherst had become a perfect winter map, with half-buried roads and a line of chimneys as mysterious as musical notes on a page.

I clung to Carlo. Riding him was like going away to live with a man and sitting on my own trousseau—the Pup, instead of spoons and pillowcases. Whoever I was marrying couldn't break into my dream.

When I woke the windows blazed with light. It seemed as if the snow had blanketed the universe. The path between the Homestead and the Evergreens had disappeared in all that drift. Brother's house had become a wall of snow wearing a chimney-hat. I said good morning to Carlo, but he never blinked once in that blaze of light. I leapt out of the covers in my nightgown and grabbed at Carlo. He wouldn't move or lick my hand. My fellah had died in his sleep, sitting on his blanket a foot from my bed.

I lay down beside Carlo in his bassinet. I must have been there five or six hours, my arm around his neck, and would have stayed another six if Pa-pa hadn't started tugging at me. He would tell people how I had all the strength of a steam engine, and that he couldn't pull me loose until I heard Ma-ma cry.

"Em," she moaned, "you cannot stay in this room forever with a dead dog."

I would have stayed, but I couldn't bear that look of horror in Ma-ma's eye.

❧

I BECAME A HERMIT WITHIN MY FATHER'S HOUSE. WHEN THE butcher boy knocked on the kitchen door, I fled—his *fairness* troubled me. He was almost as blond as my blond Assassin, and I did not want to be reminded of Tom the Handyman in the tousled hair of a butcher boy.

It wasn't only that. All encounters seemed to terrify me, as if they taxed whatever small gifts I had to natter with anyone outside my own little family. When Emily Fowler Ford, an old playmate of mine, left her card, I did not come down to greet her. Call it cruel, but I had images inside my head of a lioness who would eat Emily Fowler Ford alive. Who was this lioness? Could it have been the same lightning that arrived so suddenly and seemed to rip Verses out of my skin? I did not need Sue—Daisy had become her own Haunted House.

There was one day I dreaded most, Commencement at Amherst College. I had stopped attending Commencement exercises on our Commons a long time ago, but I couldn't desert Pa-pa, who was still Treasurer and kept up the tradition of an annual Treasurer's party at the Homestead for Seniors and the hoi polloi of Amherst.

Ma-ma played hostess whenever she was fit and did not suffer from her Neuralgia attacks, with Vinnie as her sergeant-at-arms.

I was master of the kitchen, who had to wash a barrel of raisins and supply enough black cake to glut an army of Seniors. And I couldn't hide upstairs with my door open a crack while Father prowled the front rooms and Vinnie stood behind the punch bowl.

There was also Susan, as Father's emissary from the Evergreens, with the smartest Seniors at her side, talking about Colonel Higginson's latest articles in *The Atlantic Monthly*. He was the rage of Boston, his articles read in every civilized home, including ours. The Poet, he'd cautioned, could not live without a noble mind, and Poetry itself was neither male nor female—it could be practiced by either sex. It had no hierarchy but its own excellence, bought at a bitter price, a lifelong struggle with the Calvary of the written word. It was the art of a kicking Kangaroo.

This was the Master I'd been looking for without knowing

where to look. I never even confessed to Sister Sue that I'd been bold enough to write Thomas Wentworth Higginson and send him a sample of my Verses with all the coquetry I could muster *and* several lies, saying I was a neophyte when I'd lived in the silver mines for years, waitin' for the thunder to resound and my own peculiar lightning to strike inside my skull. But I didn't say a word to Sue. I wandered from room to room like the ghost everyone thinks I've become, dressed all in white, because I will wear no other color while Carlo's soul is in Purgatory—I for one am not convinced there is much of a Heaven for dogs; they are doomed to wander somewhere, and while my Carlo was wandering, *I* will wear only white.

Of course my whiteness could be subtracted from Pa-pa's bills. I didn't have to march around in hoop skirts, like Sister Sue, and worry over the latest Boston fashion in bonnets, underskirts, or stratified stockings. I had to see the dressmaker but once in a century, and even then I did not see her—it was dear Lavinia who served as my mannequin, around whose body my wrappers and housecoats were built, since we were much the same size, and I would not suffer the dressmaker's pins or conversation and white chalk. And here I was without my corset, Treasurer Dickinson's aberrant older daughter, the Authoress of black cake, wearing a silk snood with silver tassels behind my ears, curtseying to Seniors I did not know, saluting Trustees, like some silent engine clad in white, entering and exiting all over again.

During these parties, year after year, I became the Gnome who stood at her oven the night before Commencement with her mountain of bubbling black cake. But forgive me if I forget so fast. I was never alone during these vigils. Father would descend the stairs in his slippers, a look of mischief in his eyes—Father never played, but he played now with the Gnome. Perhaps it was the calculated risk of a country lawyer, his manner of exorcizing nervous exhaustion on the eve of the Treasurer's party. But I like to think that he did not have to strut like Cromwell when he visited me in his slippers, that he had it in his mind to sample my black cake *before* the Seniors ever did. And like naughty children, Father and I stole a chunk of cake right out of the oven and took the first bite.

## 34.

MR. SAMUEL BOWLES OF *SPRINGFIELD REPUBLICAN* FAME HAS
written Brother that I am Amherst's Queen Recluse, just because
I snubbed him once and didn't cross my father's lawn to palaver
with him while he was visiting the Evergreens. If truth be told, I was
not in the mood for shuttlecocks, or to entertain Mr. Sam with my
wild piano playing—no, Lord, it's a lie! I was shamefully attracted
to his sad eyes, and that Arabian presence of his, and I did not
want to flirt with him in front of Sue, or be disloyal to my blond
Assassin, for whom I was nobody but a nom de guerre.

Mr. Bowles had had a bad attack of sciatica some years back,
when he was caught in a snowstorm between Amherst and Springfield, and had to get out of his sled to pry the runners free with
the fulcrum of his own body. This prolonged affliction left him in
a permanent state of sadness that was so attractive to a spinsterish
wildflower like me. If I had heard him rant about the *blue* of his
own life, I might have taken Mr. Bowles into my arms and joined
the harem he seemed to have from town to town, or the harem he
wished for, since he was devoted to his children and his wife.

Sue was in love with him, I could tell, but the town's leading matron wouldn't have entered into some clandestinity with Mr. Bowles. Austin and Sue had become his very best friends, but I'd have staked my own life that half his sorrow came because he loved my sister-in-law and could do little about it. That's why he went through storms and hurricanes to be near the hurricane of Sue.

And what about Brother, who had heard a hissing snake in the air, the coil of stillborn passion that was like a shadow he had to live with and swallow? And it must have eaten at his insides that Mr. Sam was his closest confidant. They could discuss everything except what was vital to them, the strange electricity in a room that held both Mr. Sam and Sue.

Austin said not one syllable about it, and Sue liked to pretend that Mr. Bowles was nothing more than her most prized "catch," considering all the celebrities who sat in her parlor. But Ralph Emerson visited Amherst once or twice, and Sue's Arabian prince would have foresworn railroad cars and traveled from Springfield on foot had that been the surest route to the Evergreens.

And when I stopped parading in Sue's parlor, or sending our handyman over with jars of winterberry wine to keep up his "spirits," he began to haunt our mansion and leave his card. I would pretend not to be at home, but my little ruse must have upset him. He stood by the stairs and shouted, "Emily, you rascal, come on down."

My heart leapt at his boldness, and I stirred from my room. I smiled as I came downstairs with the patter of my tiny feet. I was already breathless by the time I reached the bottom stair.

"Why, Mr. Sam, what more could you possibly expect from the Queen Recluse?"

I wore my full armor of feathers under my Dimity gown, and I did not have to fear the sound of my own voice.

"You are a rascal," he said, but I had made him laugh.

I served him cake and wine in our front parlor, which did not have the sweep of Susan's grand salon, with its plum leather chairs, its gilded mirrors, and lush carpets that echoed the colors and swirling rhythm of the paintings Brother had plucked out of a Manhattan gallery. Father did not have Austin's eye for detail. Our front room held the whisper of a man who read the Bible every morning.

"That's scrumptious," Mr. Bowles said of my black cake. "You should invite me more often."

"But I didn't invite you. You invited yourself, Mr. Sam."

There were already crumbs in his Arabian beard.

"Holy Moses, I had to invite myself if I ever wanted to see you. I would have whistled at your window if that would have brought ya to the Evergreens."

"I don't travel much. My father is in the habit of me."

"I'd call that an obstinate habit," he said. "It ain't much of a travel to cross your father's lawn."

I couldn't discern why Mr. Sam himself had ventured across the lawn. His Cleopatra was at the other house. Something must have dazzled him, and it wasn't my figure.

"Why, Mr. Sam," I said, with as much melody as I could muster. "You know we all travel by degrees. I turn into a snail once I depart from our porch. It might take me a dozen years to arrive at the Evergreens."

But I couldn't conquer Mr. Bowles. He took a sip of wine and said, "I'd just have to wait . . . I'm getting into the habit of you, I guess."

And for a moment the sadness fled from his soft brown eyes. They crinkled with a curious kind of pleasure as he gobbled more and more of my cake.

"Besides," he said. "I don't see a snail. You're that narrow fellah in the grass . . . one wrinkle, and you're gone."

Mr. Bowles caught my sudden shiver, and his eyes turned sad again. The two of us were unsolid creatures, *zero at the bone*, like "that narrow fellah in the grass" he had usurped from my little

treasury and published in the *Republican* without my knowledge
or my consent and with a title I had never given it: "The Snake."
That's why he had come here! It wasn't to flirt with Daisy. He was
feeling remorseful about the theft of my poem. It had appeared
anonymously on the page, but Pa-pa could recognize my very own
outline in the Verse, his daughter who slithered around with all
the quiet decoration of "a spotted shaft." And half the town figured who that Poetess was in the *Republican.* I was plagued with visitors and requests for other "versifications," as they called it. I saw
no one and did not honor a single request. But I did not have it
within me to strike at Mr. Sam.

He must have seen the Verse at Sue's; perhaps she let him read
it, and he exercised his eminent domain as publisher. Lord, he did
not mean any harm, and I understood how brittle he was, like broken glass.

"Miss Emily," he said with a formalness that must have cost him;
he was low on resources. "We do not have that stance against what
others call 'womanish,' not while I hold the rudder at the *Republican.* I was proud as a deacon to publish your snake poem."

He caught me shivering again, though I hid my consternation
as best I could.

"It is not a snake poem, Mr. Sam—Verses do not have a subject,
I should think, but a kind of shudder, as if the whole world were
born again within the flash of an eye."

"I'm lost," he said. "I cannot follow you into your terrain."

"I have no terrain," I told him. "I dance on a precipice, knowing
I will fall."

"Then I'll fall with you," he said.

"You cannot, Mr. Sam, just as my Verses cannot be written by two
heads and four hands. I wish I were some lady novelist, like Cassandra Gale, but I'm a mere old maid with a pencil dangling from her
pocket. I scribble on the sly, whenever I can. But I will not write for
publication while I live in my father's house."

Cassandra Gale was Mr. Bowles's great discovery; I'd read portions of her novel, *Passion's Corner*, in the *Republican,* and it went
on to have about as much success as the Brontë sisters. Its heroine,
Araminta Moss, was a silly girl who smoldered all the time. She was
a Volcano, just like Sue. And suddenly I had my own bit of lightnin'. Cassandra Gale couldn't appear in public because she didn't
exist outside the pages of the *Republican.*

"*You're* the rascal, Sir," I said to Mr. Sam.

He laughed. "And why is that?"

"You invented Araminta Moss. Shame on you, Mr. Sam, tricking
your readers like that."

But I was the one who blushed, not Mr. Bowles. *Passion's Corner*
was a secret love letter to Sue, so secret that not a soul could comprehend its purpose. Araminta Moss was Sue's phantom, a monster in the mirror whose passion erupted without control. And Mr.
Bowles crept outside the cover of this passion, hiding himself and
Sue, as if her Vesuvius would have devoured them both if he had
allowed it to erupt.

"Emily, will you do this narrow fellah a favor? I'm Cassandra, I
admit. I'm the culprit. But I announced a sequel to *Passion's Corner.* And I just don't have the time to write it."

Lord, I was getting angry now. Thieving my poem was unkind
enough, but I was no ghoul. I wouldn't wear Cassandra's mask.

"You can pocket a pretty piece of change," he said. "And not
one person in the universe need ever know."

My esteem for Mr. Sam was dwindling much faster than any
snail.

"But I would know," I said. "You could have asked Sue to play
Cassandra."

"She doesn't have your ice, Miss Emily. She couldn't entertain
my readers . . . and I was a little harsh. I did swindle you out of a
poem. And Lord knows, I might swindle you again."

The rascal was trying to win me over to his side. He had that terrible insouciance of the male, a shy seduction in the curls of his beard. Women followed him everywhere, but he kept haunting the Evergreens. He might plot with Sue and pluck another poem, but he wouldn't have asked me outright for one. I had to live under his manly vail. But he was hankering for something? Forgiveness? Or my own confession that I was stunned by his Arabian presence? And then he startled me. His eyes seemed to disappear inside his skull. He began to shake. He was stranded in Pa-pa's front parlor—lost, alone, as if he were still stuck in that same snowstorm between Amherst and Springfield, still trapped in his sled. I touched his beard, not to excite, but to console him. Yet it did excite me, the silk of it, that fine jungle of hair. The shaking stopped. He kissed my hand, held my birdlike fingers in his paw.

"Bless you, dear Emily. I'll never sneak into your garden, never steal from you again."

Both of us were charged up. We couldn't finish the wine and cake. I wanted to keep him here forever. But feathers didn't make me much of a sorcerer. I could only entertain with dots and discs. I was the kicking Kangaroo, not Cassandra Gale.

His sciatica must have hit hard. He left the parlor nearly bent double. I watched him cross the lawn like a huge snail with a hump on its back. But he shuddered once as he got nearer to the Evergreens and slowly his back unbent. By the time he entered Sue's domain he was as upright as an arrow. But I knew how much effort it took for him just to be Mr. Sam.

# 35.

THE YEARS SEEMED TO PASS RIGHT UNDER MY WINDOWPANE.
I'd sit at my narrow desk, stare out at the Dickinson meadow, but
most of the lightning was gone. I could only add tiny, tiny pieces to
my treasure, and none were pure gold. The lightning had erupted
around the time of war and my moon blindness. I had written
poems to Carlo, to Sue and Mr. Sam, to Pa-pa and my Philadelphia, even to poor Tom. But my hand had turned spinsterish. I was
a maiden of thirty-nine winters with a pencil in her pocket. The
pencil rarely jumped. I was looking for wonder and alarm, and it
was odd when wonder came along.

There was nothing that could tantalize me as much as the sudden appearance in our village of a circus, with its menagerie and
clowns. It did not seem to matter which circus came to town—
McGinley's or the Great North American Menagerie. The result
was the same. McGinley's would arrive before noon. A drumroll
would lure me to the window, while a streak of red passed in front
of my eyes, like a raw wound. This color mystified me. Did it come
from the red roofs of the circus wagons, or the dust and wind that
mingled with the clowns' motley uniforms? I never knew.

I could feel a beat of excitement in my own neck that held to the music of the drums, as if Emily had become an instrument that the circus could command. But I did not rouse myself from the window and follow the circus to the Commons, where huge orange tents rose and wavered in the sky with the thump of hammers. Not even McGinley's could drive me out my father's front door.

And then the circus brought with it a kind of dread. I woke to the drums and watched the morning parade, while one particular clown clung to me, and I started to shake. I recognized him, even under his rouge and curly black wig. It was my blond Assassin, or perhaps his ghost. Had Carlo still been alive, I would have rushed out with my Confederate and raced after the clown. I did not move. I was touched by terror. I tried to summon the will, but I had none.

Six days and nights the circus was in town, and six days and nights I called upon my own little powers while I sang to myself, *It's not him, it's not him.* I had hallucinated my Tom upon a circus clown, had grown as hysterical as Araminta Moss. But I pricked my ears and listened to the drumbeats, and it was Little Sister who told me that there had been a burglary in Belchertown while the tents were still pitched. A strange man had been found under the bed of a certain widow on College Street; but this strange man had gnarled fingers and a birdlike beak. He couldn't have been my Tom.

I mourned McGinley's once it left town. I had a constant tingle, waiting for the circus to reappear, and when it did, I watched from my window like a deranged falcon, but did not discover one clown who bore the least resemblance to Tom. There were no burglaries that week, no gnarled strangers who tumbled out from under a widow's bed. And I began to despair that I had missed my chance to find Tom.

The Queen Recluse did not stir. I wanted to color my face white, like Elizabeth of England, and reign from my window. A reticent ruler, I would dangle morsels of gingerbread and black cake from a string and supply my subjects, meaning Sue's second-born, Mattie, and her playmates, who stood under my window and ran off with their fealty of cake.

There were no other visitors but these . . . and my Norcross cousins, Fanny and Loo, who had succored me in Cambridgeport and would descend upon Amherst from time to time. But Pa-pa's handyman, Horace Church, had developed a most unfortunate fixation on Loolie, and would ogle her while I and my cousins were in the Orchard and he was pruning a tree. Horace Church had nothing of Tom in him. His eyes were dullish and red as a scurrying rat. His hair had the silkiness of straw. His face and fingers were coarse. He had lumps and boils at the back of his neck, not the least little blond down.

I warned him while he was up in his tree.

"Horace, my father does not pay you money to spy on us. Be gone! Get yourself down from there."

But he wouldn't leave his perch; he sat comfortably cradled in a fork of the tree. His mouth moved with a nasty pull as he spoke.

"I have my orders, Miss Im'ly. I ain't spyin'. Master Edward says the Orchard is my domain."

"Horace Church, I'll domain you with a broom if you don't disappear."

He must have sensed the rage in the Queen Recluse, because he slid down from his tree and went inside the barn to brush and comb Father's mare. I'd have fired him, but handymen were hard to find, and Pa-pa seemed to have a curious fondness for Horace.

My little cousins couldn't stay very long; they had to look after an ailing aunt. And I went back inside the hermitage of my own head. But that don't mean I didn't wear my feathers. Colonel Higginson had seen "The Snake" in Mr. Sam's *Republican*, and kept inviting me to palaver at the two literary clubs in Boston that welcomed women. But I'd have had to put on a corset and petticoats, and besides, I had a mortal fear of palavering in a public place. And so he came to Amherst, curious about the recluse. I handed Higginson two lilies from my garden and couldn't stop palavering with him. He hadn't been prepared for all my Plumage. I told him that a real Poem ripped the roof right off your head, that you couldn't recover from reading it. I'd never talked so much in an entire year.

---

LORD, I'D BECOME A POETESS IN SPITE OF MYSELF. MY couplets must have been circulating in some invisible sphere. But am I deceitful to say I wasn't part of the conspiracy?

Professors arrived at the Homestead, looking for the Poetess. I did not see them. I tore up every card save one. My hand trembled when I read that name: *Rebecca Winslow,* the late vice principal of Mt Holyoke without her yellow gloves. I had seized them from Zilpah Marsh years ago, and the gloves now lay in the attic. I did not know what to expect. Miss Rebecca had been the Poet, and I the usurper. But Dear God, she was so diminished after all these years. Her shoulders had shrunk. She wore dark glasses, the same kind I had worn in Cambridgeport to guard against the light. I wondered if she were moon blind, as I had once been.

We sat in the front parlor and fed on my black cake. Miss Rebecca swallowed three whole portions. "I'm ravenous," she said. "I haven't had my breakfast."

"Missy," I asked, "how did you ever find me?"

"It's not so difficult. I saw 'The Snake,' and I said to myself, 'That, dear heart, had to come from Emily Dickinson's Pen.' "

"But why are you so sure?" I asked, purring like one of Lavinia's cats.

I'd given her China tea, and her hand trembled over the cup.

"Because you were a sly one on the page. I read your compositions, can't you recall?"

And she had. She'd been a fierce mistress, who followed the curve of my Pen, had shredded my language, and shorn me of whatever confidence I had. And yet her rippings had been much more valuable than my other Tutors' polite remarks. She was the one who robbed me of all my pretty ornaments and gave my sentences a little of *her* heat.

"What happened to your own Verses, Missy, or would you rather not tell?"

"There's nothing to tell," she said, between bites of cake. "I lost my Pen."

I did not want to seem impolite, but I had to press her, since I was dying to know.

"And you never found it?"

"No," she said, clutching the teacup with two hands. "It fell out of whatever tiny kingdom I had."

I was the one who nearly dropped her teacup now. "Missy, I have a similar sufferance—a lost Pen that reappears from time to time. I am shorn of melody."

And Miss Rebecca laughed for the first time. "Then we are sisters in pain, cast out from the kingdom of words. You could recover. I cannot."

"But where did you land after Mt Holyoke?"

And Miss Rebecca recited her little tale of woe. She had been born into the backwoods gentry, like the Dickinsons, but her Pa-pa was a drunkard who fell from grace and left his wife and daughter in dire circumstances. Missy had to beg from her mother's people to remain in school. She was among Holyoke's first graduates. She had found God during one of the Awakenings and was all fired up to become a missionary. But Miss Lyon couldn't seem to survive without her, and Rebecca stayed on as a Tutor and vice principal.

The yellow gloves had once belonged to her Pa-pa, who wore them in his own palatial barn to wring the necks of chickens, wipe the blood from newborn foals, and wash down his favorite mare.

They were instruments of life and death, and Missy took to wearing them at Mt Holyoke. I did not ask her how many chickens she had strangled. Miss Lyon had tolerated the gloves, but the new headmistress did not and also found her harsh. And now her own Calvary began, from one female academy to the next, each one less rigorous than the last, until she was teaching farmers' daughters who snickered in class and wanted nothing to do with her Pen. And after Missy's grandfather left her a pittance, she stopped teaching.

"I live on that . . . I could not bear students without your quality."

"But you scolded me all the time."

"And you wanted scolding. But that's not the point. You weren't intractable."

"And neither was Zilpah Marsh," I said, entering a wild place where I should not have gone.

But Missy did not sputter or spill a drop of tea. "Zilpah is locked inside Northampton. Your father is a potentate there, is he not? I have seen him on the grounds—I sit with Zilpah almost every week. She's interested in your art."

"My art? Missy, I do not know what you mean."

Her teacup no longer clattered. She held it firmly in her hand. "Dearest, I think you do."

That touch of intimacy was meant to be a slap, as if she were at Holyoke, reprimanding a delinquent scholar.

"Zilpah Marsh is your ardent admirer. I read 'The Snake' to her every time I am there. She insists. She closes her eyes and relishes every word with her tongue. 'The Snake' is keeping her alive."

A shiver went through my body, like a whiplash, and I realized that Miss Rebecca was still an Assassin, even without her father's yellow gloves. But I had been fired in her crucible, formed by her, and knew how to fight back. I asked if Zilpah ever talked of Tom.

"Ah," she said, cupping her own chin. "Is that Tom the Bishop or Tom the Burglar?"

"You know the Tom I mean."

"Yes, the handyman with the mark of a foundling on his arm
. . . a deserter who ran out of the stockades and is still on the
run."

"Then Tom isn't dead. He could be hiding in a circus or somewhere else."

"Why not? He had no education. He belongs in a circus, with all
the other animals."

"Has Zilpah seen him?" I asked, like that delinquent scholar still
in Miss Rebecca's thrall.

"He wouldn't dare go back to Northampton. That's where he
was born—in the charity ward. He hasn't been on the grounds, or
*I* would have seen him. But I wouldn't have come here, Mistress,
if your father hadn't been kind to us. He told me, your father did,
that Zilpah Marsh had been his favorite housekeeper. He adored
the idea of a maid who could spell. But she was under the influ-
ence of that burglar at the time, *Mr. Tom*, and he ruined her."

"Missy," I said, "please wait here."

My head was aswim. I was nauseous, and I bristled like a porcupine. Father had adopted Zilpah Marsh, had made her my secret
sister, and Rebecca had now become my own sly aunt.

"Where are you going, child?" she said in the softest voice.

"I have a gift for you. I'll be right back."

I climbed the stairs, but not with my usual patter. I moved with
the gait of an antelope. I wanted to give Missy back her yellow
gloves, to be rid of them. I passed the cupola that Father had built
onto the house—I could have seen the roofs of a hundred orange
tents from the cupola's narrow windows. But I was not thinking
of circuses. I strode into the attic, found Missy's gloves beneath
Father's old militia uniform and a welter of dust.

I returned to the front room. Missy had removed her dark
glasses. Her eyes were watery and weak. She looked at the yellow gloves with great alarm. They couldn't restore her to her old

venue. I was the Mistress now, not her shivering seminarian. Perhaps the gloves reminded Missy of her own subterranean passion for Zilpah Marsh. She put her glasses back on.

"Mistress," she blurted out. "Do you have any stale bread?"

I stared at her. "Why?" I had a sudden image of Pa-pa feeding the birds in our backyard with stale bread crumbs while he stood in his slippers in the freezing cold.

"I'm starving," she confessed.

I did not know how to answer. I should have been alarmed when she devoured my black cake. The pittance she lived on was no pittance at all. My Plumage was gone. I started to cry.

"Missy, you must sit down and sup with us. Father will be home soon, and—"

"No," she said, "I do not want the Squire to see me here. I would rather go into the kitchen with you, Mistress. Isn't that where mendicants come knocking at the door?"

"But you are not a beggar," I insisted. "And Father will certainly help you."

She clapped her hand over my mouth, not to harm, but to silence me for a second.

"Promise you will not tell the Squire about this talk. I would die of shame. It took all my energy to appeal to you, Mistress. The two of us are bound together, are we not? You were my protégé. And please do not say another word."

She removed her hand from my mouth. We passed from the parlor through that dark, subterranean passage into the kitchen. I let her have all our stale bread. She wouldn't accept some cold chicken or Ma-ma's prize crullers, though she looked at them for a long time.

"Missy, may I have permission to speak?"

She began to crack the stale bread with whatever teeth she had left.

"If you're asking about the gloves, I gave them to Zilpah, because

I loved her near to madness, and I was hoping that the gloves would bind her to me, but the only thing that connects us, Mistress, is a madhouse . . . and the gloves don't suit Zilpah. They never did. Yours is the better fit."

Disguised again in her dark glasses, she ran out the beggars' door with her fortune of stale bread, but the glasses couldn't hide how shriveled she was and forlorn. Her back was bent like some grandma who had lost her brood. Holyoke had been half her life—she couldn't survive without her scholars. I watched Missy scramble to the side of the house, and then she disappeared. But she'd left her mark. I realized that whatever melody I had left was locked into those gloves. But I could not wear them. I went up to Father's attic and returned the gloves to that same welter of dust.

# 36.

I MOURNED MISSY AND HER SHRUNKEN SHAPE. "MISS Rebecca," I shouted at the wind, haunted by a legacy of bread crumbs that pulled me back into my past. Holyoke had fashioned me in ways I had never understood. It was my one great embarkment, a fissure eleven miles wide, between Amherst and that fortress on a hill. Pa-pa had ridiculed my schoolmarms' college, as he liked to call it, but he wasn't there. I should have become a schoolmarm. Then I might have had a few pennies of my own in my pocket. But how could I have run a class in Rhetoric or enforced Miss Rebecca's silent study? My voice couldn't echo across a classroom, and even if it did, I was much too tiny to teach.

Perhaps I was a missionary at heart, a convert who had been seized by some mysterious Awakening. I didn't have the means to help Miss Rebecca, but I could still help Zilpah Marsh. A few months after that encounter in the kitchen, I roused Pa-pa from bed so that he could catch the early train to Northampton for his rendezvous with the Trustees of the insane asylum. I put a bundle wrapped in butcher paper under his arm.

"Emily, what is that?"

"Black cake for your favorite housekeeper. And you might give Zilpah Marsh my greetings. After all, we were scholars together— a century ago."

I'd unsettled Pa-pa. His eyebrows jumped around like reddish beetles. His mouth had gone raw. He handed me back the butcher paper. And this was the hurtful tale he had hidden from us all.

Years ago, Pa-pa had asked the warden to have Zilpah removed from that horrid women's dormitory and put into her own cell, where she could paint or read and look onto the lawn without being shackled to her cot. And then he forgot about her, even on his own visits to the asylum. But Zilpah hadn't forgotten him. She kept sending messages to Pa-pa through the warden.

Finally he visited her cell. She had decorated herself for Pa-pa, wore a hint of blue on one cheek from her painter's palette. It wasn't the mark of a madwoman. She asked Pa-pa what books I had on my mantle. Father mentioned those books he could recall.

"Well, Master," she said, "I would like the same as Mistress Emily has."

He couldn't ignore Zilpah's request. Her pitiable condition disturbed Pa-pa. So he bought her a Bible and a Lexicon, a complete Shakespeare and some of Mrs. Browning. He even had the asylum give her an allowance, and she paid for things with her own little purse. She would always make a list—trinkets, paint tubes, pieces of silk, wire fasteners called paper clips.

Her greatest wish had been to be a scholar. She had wanted no other life, she said. Pa-pa asked her what purchase such a life could bring. And she said, "Bliss."

The distance between her own desires and where she was now pained Pa-pa. It was almost a year before he visited her again. Meanwhile, she'd turned Pa-pa's paper clips into jewelry, wore these fasteners on her arms and around her neck, like Cleopatra's condiments. The ingenuity of it touched Pa-pa—a necklace of paper clips.

Would she ever leave the lunatic hospital? But where could she go? She was a scholar in his mind, not a housekeeper. He made inquiries, tried to place her at the female academy in Utica, where Sue herself had been a scholar. But even with Pa-pa's persuasion, how could the headmistress there trust a woman who had been in an asylum to teach her young charges? And even had the headmistress agreed to give her a trial, it would have come to naught. The other Trustees wouldn't release her, not even into Father's care.

She languished in her room that could have been a tiny suite at the Willard Hotel, except for the cagelike door. He promenaded with her on the lawn once or twice, and still she languished. He saw her less and less. But he did visit her one last time. She did not use matted paper for her art. She painted on the walls—forest scenes with wild boars. These boars had prickly heads and powerful teeth, but their eyes were scattered and full of fright. The boars were always dark blue, with red in their eyes, but Father was too saddened by what he saw to realize that the red was written in her own blood.

And without much of a prologue, she said, "Master, you must not come to visit anymore."

"And why is that?"

"I might do ya harm—'cause you love Miss Em'ly more than you'll ever love me."

"But she's my daughter," Pa-pa said, feeling like a fool who suddenly had to defend himself before an inmate at the asylum. But he wouldn't abandon Zilpah. He had the warden hire a special guard to watch over her. Unfortunately, this guard was cruel. He clucked at Zilpah and demanded that she undress for him, Pa-pa would later find out. The guard was hoping to turn Zilpah's cell into his own private seraglio. She spat at him every time he came near, and he lost interest in Zilpah Marsh. While he was snoring she slit her throat with a piece of glass and scribbled something on the wall in the ink of her own blood, with her pinky as a Pen. No one could interpret what Zilpah had said, not even Warden Jeremiah, who was a Harvard man. But Father *knew*, and it just about broke his heart. She had scribbled "Zilpah is zero at the bone" a little before she died.

Pa-pa wouldn't allow her to be buried in the paupers' plot behind the hospital, without one calla lily, but had her carted to Amherst and put in our burying-ground. And I had never known that Zilpah was lying two fields away. After Pa-pa returned from his rendezvous with the Trustees, I wouldn't even let him finish his wine.

"Pa-pa, take me to the cemetery. I want to see the stone you put up for Zilpah."

Pa-pa rolled his eyes and pretended to be annoyed. But he wasn't annoyed.

"Child, are you gonna chase me out of my own headquarters?"

"Indeed," I said, "indeed."

I crouched like a servant girl and helped Pa-pa out of his favorite slippers and into his boots. A storm was brewing, and we put on our winter coats. I wasn't gonna be waylaid by foul weather. We wrapped our heads in woolen scarves that Ma-ma herself had knit, and we wandered across the fields. Pa-pa was in the habit of burying people. He'd buried my fellah in our Orchard out of respect for me. He'd have put up a marker with Carlo's name on it, but I didn't want the handymen pondering Carlo's grave while they picked our fruit. I knew he was lying under the Moss, and that was enough.

The wind bit into my forehead while Pa-pa opened the cemetery gate. Our own scarves were blinding us, but Pa-pa still found Zilpah's stone; it was a tiny tablet that gave her years—ZILPAH MARSH, 1830–1873—and read HOLYOKE SCHOLAR. I couldn't have chiseled anything finer into that stone.

I hadn't been this far from the Mansion in centuries. I could smell the first snow, and it was like a cool shiver in the wind that near lifted me off my feet. I wasn't scared. I read the chiseled words over and over again.

### HOLYOKE SCHOLAR

I heard Pa-pa sniffle. I wondered if he was catching a cold.

"I maligned that college of yours, Dolly. Didn't it produce a pair of my favorite scholars?"

Father had never capitulated like that before, and here he was switching sides. It worried me.

"Zilpah's in her grave, Pa-pa. And what have I ever done?"

My scarf had slipped, and Father had to wind me back into it.

"You're precious to me," he said. "Ain't that enough?"

It was dark by the time we got home, and that cool shiver had turned into a snowstorm with a beautiful blinding sheen—it blanketed the Dickinson meadow and the barren trees until I was one more creature lost in that blaze of white.

# 37.

WHAT WAS IT THAT WOULDN'T PERMIT PA-PA TO STAY AT HOME with his little brood of horses, cows, and Dickinsons? He startled us one afternoon, told us that he was returning to the state legislature, to its lower house, when he had once been a State Senator and Congressman. Pa-pa, who was so private a man, had little love of Washington or Boston rooming houses. He was now seventy-one years old, hell-bent on returning to the State House. Amherst was battling for the rights to a new railroad line, and Pa-pa had to protect the interests of the town. But it had nothing to do with railroads. Pa-pa was restless. He had to be somebody's champion again. And my foolish father got himself elected to the legislature. He was in Boston half the time, living at the Tremont, a quarter of a mile from the capitol. He had to trudge through the sleet in his topcoat and white beaver hat. Pa-pa worried all the time that one of us might disappear in a pool of ice or get squashed between two railroad cars. But he was the one who was riding the trains and wandering about in snowstorms.

He asked Brother to write him every day—Austin's letters would let him *taste* his family a little. But he don't ask Daisy to write. My letters must have feared him, made Pa-pa think of falling icicles and scarlet fever.

I moped around with Father gone, a maiden of forty-three, with my fingers beginning to gnarl. But I felt useless without slaving over his puddings and Indian bread. And whenever he returned to Amherst on the night train, I felt instantly safe, as if a wand had passed over me, even from within Pa-pa's remotest wall. I could read the weariness on his face. The winter of '74 was brutal, and lasted into the spring. And during one particular snowstorm, the birds called out their fright and collected at our kitchen door. Their cries tore at me. Mother and Vinnie were frantic. We circled the front and rear rooms like weak-willed savants, not knowing what to do. And then Father appeared in his slippers.

He borrowed my shawl and flew right into the storm. Vinnie and Mother had shut their eyes, but I watched from the window. He strode like Cromwell in that storm, Cromwell in velvet slippers, and returned from the barn with a milk pail full of grain. He opened the kitchen door, scattered the grain, and didn't have to invite a single bird into the Homestead. They hopped out of the storm and feasted on little piles of grain. Father didn't cluck like some proud hen. He hid himself, worried that his presence might embarrass the birds and interfere with the feast.

SUDDENLY THE ORCHARD THRIVED WITH PLANTS AND SNAKES that seemed to crack right through the frost, and we found ourselves in June; Pa-pa was supposed to return to the State House next morning to vote on an issue that escapes me now, and like some small-town Salome I lured him into spending the afternoon with me, sending Mother out on some fraudulent mission while Vinnie was in the midst of a nap. Father was startled to see me. I brought him wine and cake, and he began tossing crumbs to the birds.

"Emily, these are gluttons for black cake. I know. I've fed them before. They will pester us till eternity."

"So be it," I said. "A millennium of black cake in our garden."

"A millennium at the least . . . Your brother is occupied with my affairs, and while I am away, you must be the captain of this house. Mother's mind tends to scatter. Vinnie is the practical one, but she cannot lead. You can."

"Lord," I muttered, reddening all the way to the roots of my neck. "You'd think I had the possibility of bein' Goliath."

He laughed, and it was curious to hear, as if it had come out of a hidden place.

"Child, I'd be the chief imbecile of Massachusetts should I ever trust a captaincy to Goliath. He couldn't even survive a pebble cast by a boy without a beard."

"Then I'll be the same beardless boy."

He laughed again, and tired as he was, he looked like that hero who could step out of any storm with a pail of grain.

"Pa-pa, make up your mind. It's either David or Goliath. You can't have both."

"Then I won't have one or the other, but Captain Emily—"

"Whose letters you never even asked for while you're livin' at the Tremont . . . Pa-pa, a letter can't bite!"

Father held my little hand in his larger one; the grip was firm, but his face hadn't ungentled.

"You're right to scold," he said. "But you see, I cannot bear to be away from home. And Austin's letters feed my nostalgia. They're crammed with the commonplace. They're as comforting as a hot bath in a strange hotel."

"And mine are like cobwebs under your bed."

He laughed and pinched my hand, as if to single out my naughtiness.

"Worse than cobwebs, because your letters stick to the bone. I have cherished every word of yours since you were away at that nun's school . . . but I cannot savor your words without the comfort of my footstool and a cup of homemade wine."

I was beginnin' to wear Goliath again.

"Father, I could learn from Austin and write up a streak of commonplaces."

"Then I wouldn't have letters from my Emily, but some imp out of an ink bottle."

And now both of us laughed on a bench in my own garden, where the Queen Recluse had labored behind a wall of shrubs, patting the earth with her own fingers or a trowel, beyond the jurisdiction of the village's own little spies.

"Emily, I wish I had the power to slow the sun and make this afternoon not have an end."

I could see Brother coming toward us from the Evergreens, and not wanting to rob him of his own pleasure with Pa-pa, I waved to him and ran back into the house. Not even Goliath could have predicted what happened next.

I woke Pa-pa in the morning as was my wont whenever he had to catch an early train. And while he didn't step with the swagger of King Saul on his way to the depot, well, he was entitled to a little vacation from his own vigor.

I kept thinking of Pa-pa, who was like a ferocious engine on a lonely track. I pitied him and loved him as I loved no other and never can.

Next morning the sun was brutal. It seemed to rip right under the roof. There was no relief, and I wondered how Pa-pa was doing on Beacon Hill. If our village blazed, then Boston must have been a furnace. He would have to walk to the State House and stand under the rotunda in that infernal heat.

His three women were seated at the table having a light supper, brooding over Pa-pa's empty place, when Brother appeared with a dispatch in his fist, his face full of gloom. I knew it was the end of the world, but I wasn't sure why until he told us that Pa-pa was very ill. Brother and Little Sister would leave for Boston right away. The last train had already gone, so the two of them would take the Dickinson carriage. But while the horses were being dressed, another telegram arrived . . .

He'd had his breakfast at the Tremont that morning with his fellow legislators and was in a fine mood. He left the Tremont a little after eight and walked up Beacon Hill without his Panama hat— he must have forgotten it at the hotel. I imagine him standing under the portico of the State House to catch his breath, and then climbing the great marble stairs and entering the House chamber into a blinding light. He sat down to rehearse his speech about the railroad line. The chamber began to fill. His vigor returned when he began to address the House. But then a terrible flash, like a wayward streak of lightning, afflicted his eyes. And suddenly his own words failed him. He grew faint and had to sit. But he finished the speech.

He walked down the winding cobblestone lanes and returned to the Tremont, where he dined alone on corned beef hash and then retired to his room. He looked out his window at the horse-cars on Tremont Street when he experienced a sudden vertigo— the horse-cars seemed to fly up to his room. He began to pack, having decided to abandon Boston, abandon his next speech, and catch the train home. He summoned the porter, but he couldn't even finish packing. His shoehorn fell out of his hands. He lay on his bed, drifting in and out of his own dreams.

The hotel had called in a doctor, who administered morphine, but couldn't pull Father out of his spasmodic dreams. I like to believe that Pa-pa was dreaming of us, that our own shapes whirled in front of his eyes. He died toward six PM, with that doctor and other strangers scrambling in and out of the room. He shouldn't have had to die around all those strangers.

THE WHOLE TOWN WAS GARTERED IN BLACK; NOTHING STIRRED
except the black bunting—it was like a melody of merciless lines
that traveled across roofs and porches and was draped in every
window of every shop. Even the Church was quiet as a mouse. I
couldn't go down to the parlor. I was frightened to see my pale
Pa-pa in his funeral clothes. I sat in my room with the door open
a crack while Vinnie and Mother sobbed downstairs. Austin, I'm
told, had lost his ruddy complection and was as pale as Pa-pa. He
bent over and kissed Pa-pa's face.

No one had the audacity to climb up the stairs but Mr. Sam.
He'd come from Springfield for Pa-pa's funeral. All the blackness
had been bleached out of his Arabian beard. I hadn't seen Mr.
Sam in a year. He was doubled over with sciatica, and he had to
carry a cane. He had wrinkles under his brown eyes. He was as
mortally wounded as Pa-pa ever was. He didn't even ask himself in.
The Queen Recluse just opened her door to Mr. Sam.

We were a pair of old Confederates who didn't have to talk. Mr.
Sam took me in his arms. He hadn't always been polite to Pa-pa in
the *Republican,* had once even called him a relic, a dinosaur who
sat on his own private fence during the Civil War. But Pa-pa was full
of private fences, and Mr. Sam cherished him in spite of the critical remarks.

We stood there, in the shadow of my door, both of us trembling, and without saying a word he went back to the parlor. He
couldn't settle into his own skin, or decide to kidnap Sue, and so
he wandered between the Evergreens and God knows where, like
an invalid allergic to peace and war. I returned to my post and listened to the sounds in the parlor.

The Mansion was swollen with mourners, and the service itself
spilled out onto the street, as Pa-pa's friends and associates sat
on chairs spread across the lawn. The Reverend spoke, but I did
not listen—he could only praise the public man, Treasurer and
Trustee, the Squire of Amherst who was proud of his horses, but

not the Pa-pa who stepped into a storm and rescued starving birds, or watched over a mad housekeeper in her necklace of paper clips.

A cadre of the town's most prominent citizens, including a couple of College professors, carried the coffin on their shoulders across two fields to the burying-ground, where Zilpah also lay, unbeknownst to everyone but Pa-pa himself. And it comforted me to recollect that their graves were only fields away from my window. But that don't mean I didn't grieve. I nearly died of it. To think that I would never hear him paddle through the house in his slippers, or read the Bible in that raspy baritone of his. I couldn't eat. And the slumber I had was like a tiny groan in a sea of wakefulness.

I laid siege to myself and hardly ever stirred from my room. Little Sister shoved scraps of paper under my door, wanting to know if Emily was still alive. To ease her mind, I answered that I hadn't taken flight. But it wasn't entirely true. In the madness of mourning, I imagined myself as an old maid with wings—not an angel, but a bona fide bird-woman who could carry her weight into the sky and wouldn't plummet more than once or twice. Flying wasn't much of a revelation. It was as brutal as breathing air. But I had small adventure in the span of my wings. I never dreamt of Morocco or the Gulf of Mexico. My pattern was as constant as a star. I flew out my window and traveled no further north than the burying-ground. I hovered in that neighborhood with a daughter's conviction that there was no other home than where Father happened to be.

Cats! Vinnie was suspended in a demimonde of cats—pugilists, ruffians, and coquettes, they seduced her, bit her arm, caterwauled, had kittens in the shavings barrel, and she fed them, stroked their tails, slept with them, gave them all a home until the mansion was overrun with cats. She'd given up on most of mankind. Long ago she'd been in love with Joseph Lyman, a classmate of Austin's, who'd allowed her to sit on his lap, and then ran off to New Orleans and found another bride. Vinnie would consider no other man, though she'd had a dozen suitors, two dozen, who would have married the youngest daughter of Squire Dickinson, now in his grave. But she wouldn't marry. She had an invalid mother and invalid cats and a secretive sister who wouldn't even put on a shawl and stroll, as they had once done, arm in arm, while Pa-pa was still alive.

Sister was filled with intrigue. And Vinnie had become her accomplice, her messenger and post mistress. There was always some note to mail to Sister's mysterious correspondent, the Reverend Wadsworth. He'd gone far away, sailed to San Francisco, and then sailed back to Philadelphia several summers ago.

Emily called him "Master." She'd smile like one of Vinnie's mad felines *and say to the housekeeper, "Margaret dear, I have another missile for the Master." And she'd clutch the note in her hand as if it might explode any minute.*

*Then, years after all the clandestine deliveries, her Master showed up at the door. Emily was in the garden with her watering pail. And Vinnie knew it was the Master, knew it in an instant, as he clutched the bell pull. He didn't announce himself, but asked for Emily in that deep voice of his, like wind barreling out of a tunnel. She could feel the boards shake with his thunder. He had wrinkles around his lips, and he also had a slight limp. But his gaze was terrifying for such a diminished man.*

*Vinnie hopped into the garden with a puss on her shoulder and announced the visitor with the deep voice. And Emily, who'd always fled from intruders and depended on Vinnie to be her shield, rid herself of the pail and ran to Rev. Wadsworth, her Master, like a child out of breath. Vinnie tried not to listen, though Lord forgive her, she did prick up her ears.*

*She couldn't glean every word, not while Puss scratched at her, but she could catch enough of their sweet patter. Emily talked of her own surprise. She might have had the housekeeper or the handyman meet him at the station had she known about his visit. But he hadn't planned to come. He had decided in the middle of his sermon, as if in the thrall of a sudden revelation, and had gone from the pulpit to the train depot.*

*Vinnie saw Sister through the curtains, with that curious glow of someone caught in rapture. She heard Rev. Wadsworth say that he had some "affliction" and might soon be dead. And the Master's affliction was registered on Emily's face.*

*The glow was gone. Even her freckles had fled. But her pale complection wasn't a sign of weakness. Sister's voice was suddenly robust.*

*"Master, you must not go away from me."*

*"I cannot succor you," he said, in a voice that was like a cannon shot. "I cannot even succor myself. And if I came to you, Miss Dickinson, it was not to guide you in any journey toward God, but to say goodbye."*

*"And must you say goodbye to my Snow?"*

"*Your Snow,*" he said. "*I can no longer afford your Snow. I am refreshed by the music of your lines, but it fatigues a poor Philadelphia preacher. The images clash, and I find myself on a battlefield.*"

"*It was not my intention to hurt you, Master.*"

There was such lament in Sister's voice that Lavinia had to skulk away with her cats and eat some bread and butter or go insane with that sad sound in her head.

Master did not stay very long. And Emily's paleness did not vanish with him. It took a whole week for the freckles to come back. But Vinnie kept wondering about Sister's Snow. And one afternoon, while Emily was in the garden, she drifted through the mansion like a drugged woman, a puss on either shoulder. The cats were like rudders that steered her away from some dark corner and kept her from falling. She dusted the stairs, her hands gliding over the banister knobs, feeling wood that gleaned like butter, and with a stroke of raw courage, she marched into Emily's room.

She had seldom dared cross into that inner sanctum where Sister scribbled her letters, created her Snow at a cherry desk in the far corner, but Vinnie did it now.

Sister's combs were on the bureau with her toiletry set. Vinnie opened one of the drawers, thinking she would have to sift through a pile of correspondence. But she found something else. Little sewn booklets in a box, like the magic fans of a courtesan or coquette. And with these fans were scraps of paper and envelopes and fliers with poems scratched onto them in Emily's own hand.

She began to cry and laugh at this startling treasure, but was too timid to read a line. No, she wasn't timid. She was as ferocious as Saul. She couldn't say why, but she started to dance in Emily's room. She wanted to cover herself in Emily's Snow, to feel it against her skin. Perhaps she was the coquette. And old, silent "Saul" with an army of cats could grasp her sister's songs; vibrations went through her body like the shivering of the Lord. Then she shut the drawer and crept out of Emily's room.

# PART SIX

## *Jumbo*

## The Homestead, the Evergreens, and the Circus Grounds
### 1875 & Beyond

## 38.

I HAD NEITHER NIGHT NOR AFTERNOON, BUT AN AVALANCHE of dreams that shook my system, as if Daisy had been flung into a well. So it went for years, on and off, ever since Father discontinued stepping through the house in his slippers. I did not dare ransack his closets looking for clues. I never even opened his door, which had been my compass as a child, my true north. While Father lived with us, I would climb the stairs like a soldier and feel a majestic safety whenever I passed his door. But all safety has now abandoned this house.

I moan in the middle of the night. A Monster chases me, with a ruffled, unfamiliar form, yet owning my father's dark eyes. I cannot bring myself to call him *Pa-pa*. And even if I did, I'm sure he wouldn't answer to that name. So I call him *Dark Eyed Mister*, and his horrid, unnatural face begins to smile—or grin, I should confess, since he does not have a regular mouth, but a lipless hole that serves as a mouth. It puzzles the mind. Is this Monster my Pa-pa, the earl of Amherst, transmogrified by some substation between celestial and terrestrial ground? I will not believe that the Lord's anointed are hapless surgeons who have mutilated my father so. Even the direst angels would not commit such a crime.

Then it must be the Devil's work. Satan has sent me an apparition that mocks my father's form. But when the Monster utters a few syllables with his strange mouth he is most tender with me. And this is disconcerting, since I am not even allowed to hate the creature.

"*Miss Im'ly,*" says the Monster, as if he were one of Father's stablemen, "*ef it is cold, I could light a fire under yer ass.*" And laugh he does at his little profanity, with a shapeless hand to cover that hole of his.

"Who sent you, Mr. Dark Eyes?"

"*Yer father sent me. Can't ya tell?*"

And it is the affliction of my dreams that I can get no further than that—a Monster from a realm that makes no real sense, yet seems to have my father's eyes. Perhaps he is a palliative from the Devil, who has taken pity on the Dickinsons after Mother fell ill— she swooned a year to the day that Father died and woke to partial paralysis, as if she were marking that grim anniversary with her own blood. All feeling had left her Hand and Foot, and her mind could no longer seize upon what was current and what was not. Father was still alive in her Phantom thoughts, and she would chide me for going to bed before the Squire returned from his office. I did not have the heart to rob her of whatever small felicity she had left. And so Lavinia and I were counterfeiters who continued the masquerade that Father would soon be at the door in his beaver hat.

And it was amazin' how the leanest lie gathered its own flesh until both Dickinson girls believed that the Squire, or his ghost, would appear at the supper table. And Ma-ma, who had never really been able to mother us, caught as she was within Father's will, had suddenly become *our* child. I had to feed her with a spoon, and call Horace Church to carry her from her bed to the chair. But the bur-

den of it all fell upon Lavinia's back. Little Sister sat with her while
I baked or prowled through the Homestead like a burglar without
a destination. I usually ended up in the Northwest Passage, that
dark corridor at the rear of the house, where I could elude any
guest, since it had five escape routes—five mysterious doors—one
of which led right to the back stairs. I was as much of an apparition
as my Dark Eyed Mister within this corridor. Lord, I could play the
Phantom here.

But the afflictions began to mount. Father curiously had died
without a will. Hence, Brother became our new Cromwell, lord
and master of the Dickinson estate. And just as Lavinia had begged
her way into Pa-pa's purse, or I would have been "undressed" without writing tablets or ink in my bottle, she now had to humble
herself before the master and mistress of the Evergreens. Austin
was courteous and distant in his new role, but Mrs. Austin began
to ride roughshod over Lavinia. She would solicit her own first-
born, Ned, who was fourteen or fifteen at the time, dispatch him
to our kitchen as her cavalier, whereupon he would chide his spinster aunts for spending too much of Austin's money. Lavinia had
bathed him as a boy, seduced him with kites and sleds, and I had
worn a mustache for him once and posed as his Uncle Emily; now
he came to us in Sue's behalf with a look of contempt upon his lip.
He was taller than Lavinia and myself, and as father's surrogate,
hoped to bully us into submission. He had two or three hairs upon
his chin and wore a silk cravat like any young squire. I had to fight
the urge to spank this little giant.

He was clever enough to steer away from the asp's sting of my
tongue. But he went to market on Lavinia, who'd been minding
Mother day and night. Mrs. Austin must have practiced him in
brutality. He didn't even say "Aunt" or "Auntie" to my sister.

"Miss Lavinia, my mother worries that you will leave us high
and dry. You have been running up a bill at Cutler's general store
that is a mile long." He'd memorized every item; that's how Susan

taught him to attack. "A whole yard of lace and a small fortune of lacelets, two gallons of kerosene when one would suffice, and a bushel of sweet potatoes when there are only three women in the house. Surely, you could economize."

Vinnie did not say a word, she was shivering so. But I lit into Susan's courtier with his silk cravat.

"Squire Ned, if you count every needle and pin, Miss Lavinia will have to capitulate."

He turned one suspicious eye toward me. "A bushel of sweet potatoes aren't needles and pins."

"Ah," I said, "but when the handymen have to feed your father's stepper half a dozen sweet potato pies, then one bushel is hardly enough."

Brother was proud as hell of his new dappled horse, Princely Sue, and let her prance in front of the family carriage while the little squire held the reins. Ned could not answer the asp—and now I stung him on the other side.

"Dear," I said, like the most maidenly of maiden aunts. "Tell your mother that I will stop using ink, and will address all my envelopes in my own blood."

It saddened me to say that. I had to swallow some of my own feathers—it was Zilpah who wrote in blood, not I, Zilpah who scratched her own forlorn biography on a wall. But I had caught Squire Ned with this little tale of blood. He began to twitch under his collar; Susan must have told him my ink bottle was a sacred font that didn't permit the least economy. But I wouldn't press him. I adored this damn boy, smug as he was, and would have perished for him on any given day.

❦

I SHOULDN'T HAVE BEEN SO CRITICAL OF SISTER SUE; A LITTLE boy was born to Brother and Sue fourteen months after Father

died. A blond angel with blue eyes—Gilbert, whom we called
"Gib." We did not mean to spoil him, but spoil him we did; he
eclipsed his brother, Ned, and his sister, Mattie, in the wholesale
affection of the Dickinson tribe from the moment he appeared.

Lavinia and I had a cradle carved for him—it was Horace
Church, the handyman, who did the carving, the same Horace
who had leered at every female in the house and spied on us from
different trees in the Orchard. I had wanted to sack him after
Father died, but Vinnie said we should hold on to that Peeping
Tom out of homage to Pa-pa, who admired him for some obscure
reason. Perhaps they read the Bible together; Horace purported
to be a religious man. He must have had the palsy—his hands
shook all the time, but they steadied once he gripped a knife. He
was a greater genius than Michael Angelo at carving cribs. Lavinia
paid him with the very last pennies she had. That's how strapped
we were for cash under Mr. and Mrs. Austin's regime. And shrewd
bargainer as he was, Horace wanted my pocket watch thrown in.

"Miss Im'ly, ef you lend me the darn thing, I'll wire up the cradle in gold filigree. And ef not, it'll be plain and simple as a nigger
baby's bark."

And all the while he was leering at me, a spinster who was forty-
four at the time, same as Susan, with a face that often frightened
me to look at in the mirror—it had none of Cleopatra's charm.
But I wanted that cradle with gold filigree. And I had to give in.

"Horace Church, you don't deserve this watch. You're the worst
scamp I ever saw."

But he was as satisfied as the Devil to have my watch inside his
pocket. And I only realized now, reminiscing about the cradle, that
the Dark Eyed Mister of my dreams spoke with the stilted music
of Horace Church. The Monster who plagued me in the sweetest
fashion had Pa-pa's eyes and Horace's scratchy voice. Lord, it was
even more of a riddle.

The only route I had to Pa-pa was Mr. Dark Eyes. I might have
captured him without Cleopatra's wiles, but he was indifferent to
my feathers. I could have tried one of Zilpah's ruses, her panoply
of paper clips, but it wouldn't have roused the Monster. No, I had
nothing to bargain with. And no matter how hard I clucked, Mr.
Dark Eyes didn't answer my call.

## 39.

I DIDN'T THINK I'D EVER MEET THAT MONSTER WITH HIS lipless hole of a mouth either in Purgatory or Paradise, or in Satan's own Vestibule. I'd have sold myself to the highest bidder for one last glimpse of Pa-pa, even in Purgatory. And then on the night of Susan's annual birthday party, which I had stopped attending ages ago, because I could not bear the yards of silk her female guests wore like fancy hieroglyphics, I listened to the revelers across the lawn and suddenly landed in a dark well. But this dank hollow had as many cushions and pillows as my bed. And lo! the Monster was sitting upon my lap, and you could have called me naked, since my nightgown was hiked above my knees—Mr. Dark Eyes was smaller than I had imagined, practically a gnome. I was the Colossus here. And he kept whimpering in that waspish voice of his.

"Quiet, my Dark Eyed Mister, or I'll squeeze ya to death."

I had not meant to be that bold, but the words flew out of me like the cry of a trumpet, full of its own brass.

*"Miss Im'ly, I believe you ought to attend Susan's soirée."*

"Why is that? And be quick about it."

" *'Cause ya might just have some time for Ned. Ef you don't run to him,
Miss, it might be too late.*"

"Monster, who told you such a thing?"

"*Master tol' me. Who else?*"

I struggled out of my dream with an anxiousness that should
not have come from the interrogation of a gnome. I put a shawl
on over my nightgown and dashed down the stairs in my slippers,
as if I too could strut like Cromwell in my father's house. I had not
been to the Evergreens in years. It was not an embargo per se, or
a boycott. I had no malice against all its personages, including the
maids.

I slid across the narrow path of roots and rubble that sepa-
rated the Homestead and the Evergreens. The cold bit under my
shawl. I thought I heard the practiced wailing of an owl. I nearly
snagged my ankle on a treacherous root. Our gardener should
have combed this path, but it had turned wild after Pa-pa's death.
And the truth of it is that I loved the wildness and would not have
wanted it any other way.

I let my lantern dangle from its leather strap, as Father would
have done in the old days, when he crossed this path with such
magnificent strides to fetch his wandering daughter and bring her
home. Austin's green shutters glowed in the dark with a glare that
tore at my eyes until I had to look down.

I padded into the house with my sparrow's feet, past the furniture that had been piled into an alcove behind the stairs for Susan's
birthday party—she liked her guests to roam during one of her
musicales, but these guests had left behind all sorts of debris; hats
and feathered chokers lay about the floor with sheets of music that
were dusty and dog-eared. It was no surprise. Vesuvius couldn't
have had much of a birthday party without some volcanic ash.

I went upstairs to the little squire's room. I wasn't startled to
find Austin with Ned. My brother hadn't even discarded the purple pantaloons he must have worn at Sue's salon. He sat beside

Ned, his gold-tipped cane at his side, looking as dismal as a dead man. He had taught himself to play the earl, but he did not have Father's confidence, and he masked his own bewilderment with scorn.

But he was not scornful tonight. He hummed a tune while Ned tossed in his sleep, a stick wedged in his mouth to keep him from biting his own tongue. Ned wasn't aware of his seizures. He would awaken with a sore tongue, thinking he'd suffered some fitful ague in his sleep—Susan did not want to attach the stigma of epilepsy to her own son, and thus the secret was kept from him and the whole town. But Susan could not bear to sit with him at night. The attacks terrified her. She would hide under her bedclothes whenever the ceiling began to sway. It was Brother alone who held vigil, who stroked Ned's hair for hours on end. White streaks had arisen in his own red hair, and he had begun to dye it with an even fiercer red, though his scalp had a greenish look in the lantern light.

I knew about the seizures, but I'd never seen Ned with a stick in his mouth, foam on both sides of his face. Ned wasn't much of a squire now, but a boy caught in a maelstrom that left him all alone in some dark country. I pitied him and his secret seizures. He couldn't fly very far. He was grounded at the Evergreens.

Austin's face grew alert the instant he could hear my sparrow's steps. He beckoned me to sit beside him, and I kept the same silent vigil.

It was Brother who broke the silence.

"I dreamt of Father the last three nights. Lord, the only time I ever kissed him was when we carried him into the house—dead. And in my dreams, Emily, he rebukes me for not attendin' to the town. Didn't I become Treasurer of the college? Didn't I drain the swampland out of the Commons? Do you ever dream of Pa-pa?"

"Most nights," I declare with a lugubrious smile. "But he's much too clever for his own backwoods girl. He wears a monstrous shape, with a black hole for a mouth, and talks like Horace Church. But he can't disfigure his dark eyes—Austin, don't get mean if I say it. But Pa-pa disguises himself as a lover might."

Austin casts his own blue eyes at me with a certain disdain. "Father would never do that—he's too serious."

And then Ned began to knock with an unholy rhythm. Pictures fell from the wall. I thought the chandelier would plummet onto our heads. But my brother clutched that boy with all his might. He couldn't visit with his son in the same dark country. No one could. But he contained some of the fury, softened it even. And frightened as I was, I also held on to Ned. It seemed like a snake was passing through his body, right under my hands, and this snake felt unnatural. Some of it was rigid, and some of it could bend, but I held on as if my life depended on it. And after that snake fell asleep, I kissed Brother on the forehead, stroked Ned once, and went downstairs to Sue.

## 40.

SHE CONSPIRED AND BLED BITTER SMOKE, AS ERUPTING volcanoes often do. But none had been as beautiful as she, even with all her bile. I fell in love with her when I was but a Boy, nimble and full of a teasing sport. My heart thumped whenever she was near. Her olive looks were so foreign to the Dickinsons and our race of freckles and red hair. I would have gladly wooed her away from my brother had I been able to do so. Then she would not have had to worry about the barbed complications of "a man's requirements." But I did not have the courage to woo her, nor did I know how.

And so *I* was Enobarbus who loved his Cleopatra from afar and breathed in Egypt's purple smoke. Her mind was much more volatile and quick than any other woman's—or man's. She had been my shrewdest Preceptor once upon a time. Brother could not bear to look at what I wrote. Its feathers frightened him. And Little Sister, who was my fiercest ally and protected me from intruders, could not enter my House of Snow. It was all hieroglyphics to her, sounds adrift in a sea of silence. And then there were my other Preceptors, Colonel Higginson and Samuel Bowles, who saw my irregular lines as the mark of a strange enchantress, but were not half as supple as Sue. And yet I sought their acceptance, like a Circus animal that could not survive without some trainer.

I did not want to be trained, and "Marm," as servants called her, had never tried to do so with her Egyptian might. But she did not resemble much of a queen in her rumpled bedclothes. She shivered under her blankets in the royal bedchamber she condescended to share with my brother and his "low practices," by which she meant his conjugal rights and privileges.

I had to untangle the quilt she wove around herself like Cleopatra's net. I'd never seen so wide or large a bed. It could have reached the Indian Ocean—or so it seemed to this old maid.

"Is my Ned all right?" she asked, with blotches on her olive skin caught in the sway of my lantern.

"He's asleep," I said. "You shouldn't worry. Austin won't let any harm come to him."

"But when the knocking starts . . . I shrink, as if an elf lived inside me and gnawed at my picayune powers. I cannot mother Ned when he starts to bite his tongue. The Susan you know is feeble."

"As feeble as the Gulf Stream," I said, unable to stopper my own idiotic tongue.

Lord, it wasn't the first time I had seen Sue in such disrepair— she moped for months after her favorite sister died. She clutched at me now, as forlorn as Ophelia, though Ophelia could never have mustered one molecule of Susan's wrath.

"Your brother despises me, says I've turned his house into a tavern, just because I like to have a party once in a blue moon. It isn't fair. I need the noise of other people. He calls me a harridan, says I've bewitched Mr. Sam. Sometimes he will not speak to me for days without end. Mattie has to intervene—can you imagine it? My own daughter serves as ambassador of the Evergreens. She alone can make the peace—I threw a carving knife at him just last week. I cannot control my temper . . . Emily dear, I might have murdered him."

"But you did not," I said, like some judge of the highest court, though I did worry about Austin's life and limb. I got sick thinking of Sue the knife thrower. I dreamt of Austin's ear with a notch in the middle, but before I could grasp the whole bloody idea of it, Sue went galloping onto another topic, and Austin's ear fell right out of my dreams.

"I couldn't invite Mr. Sam to my birthday—he's much too ill."

I wanted to soothe my sister-in-law, but a bit of my own bile crept in.

"Lord, he can't seem to stay put. Lecturing, wandering around in his sled, writing novels under ten other names . . . half the novelists he discovers in the *Republican*'s pages turn out to be himself."

Susie seemed to stir under her bedclothes. "Sister, why do you slander Mr. Sam?"

"It isn't slander," I said. "It's God's truth."

Suddenly she wasn't prostrate and perused me like a hawk.

"You think I was in league with Mr. Sam, that I encouraged him to put you in the *Republican*. Well, I did. And it gave me real satisfaction to read your lines in Mr. Sam's pages, bold as brass, even if it gave you none. There, I've said it!"

I couldn't control myself. I was no less a Pugilist than my sister-in-law.

"But you didn't have to show him a single line. It was like robbing a grave."

And now Sue was really furious. "Pardon me, but you should have kept a trowel in your pocket if you wanted to bury your poems in the graveyard."

"Susie, I didn't say that. But I felt entombed when I saw those lines smothered in black ink, without my own meager electricity."

But all the fight had gone out of me. I couldn't burden Sue

while Ned was lying upstairs with a stick in his mouth. "Susie, shouldn't we visit Mr. Sam?"

She fell back onto her pillows. "I can't go to Springfield, ill as he is. His people will say I'm a hussy—the mother of three children, who has an infant in the cradle, and she's bent on haunting Mr. Sam. I never even held his hand, or sat with him in the dark, but I swear to you that I revile my own marriage. A slice of cake and a kiss, that's all my wedding was."

"Sister, Austin loves you."

"Do not speak to me of love, else I will run for the carving knife."

My mind wandered, and I imagined Sue running off with Mr. Sam, bent and broken with sciatica as he was. And then my Imagination deviled me, and I saw myself in Mr. Sam's sled. He was too ill to steer. I had to cluck at his six white dogs, who carried us across the ice on runners sharp as knives. But that ride couldn't last.

I heard a soft whimper in the shadows near Sue's bed. I cast about with my lantern and discovered that little darling with his blond hair, Gib, in the cradle that Horace Church had carved for him. Gib had outgrown his cradle, but Sue neglected to furnish him with a full-sized crib; it wasn't a question of guarding Austin's pocketbook. My sister-in-law could start a fire with what she spent; perhaps she wanted an eternal infant in the house, an angel of her own.

The cradle had convenient rockers that she could launch with one of her toes, and launch it she did while she was engulfed in black thoughts. She had lent me whatever scattering of courage she had when she herself was an orphan living off the crusts of an older sister, with her father's ghost as her heritage—a drunkard who had kept a tavern before he died. And if truth be told, Susan herself had become a tippler, and her fights with Brother were often drunken brawls. She had chased down Vinnie's cats with her own pointer, Sport. She posed as an empress while she "manhandled" us over money. But I still could not abandon her.

I battened her pillows with my tiny fists, untangled her bedclothes, and had her lie under the covers. Then I rocked Gib's cradle while he sucked on his lip. It was near dawn when I returned to the Homestead like some wayfarer out of the water, dreaming of white dogs and a sled.

# 41.

MR. SAM LINGERED ON FOR A YEAR, DEATHLY PALE, WITH A feeble step and a constant cough; not one sign remained of his Arabian presence. He limped when I saw him last. He still showed up at the Evergreens, but less oftener now. And he didn't have the strength or the will to appear at Austin and Sue's on his sled. All that old verve was gone. He took to his bed and no longer had the heart to climb out of it. He was dead at fifty-one, worn out from his own wanderings. But at least his family was at his side. And I couldn't help but think of Pa-pa dying all alone in a Boston hotel.

It was as if Mr. Sam's ghost still lingered, still hovered over the Evergreens. Sue went about as a widow, wearing a black vail. I didn't mourn in so public a fashion, but I missed sad Mr. Sam almost as much as she did. And it made her irascible. She had become a drunkard like her own Pa-pa. She imbibed under her black vail, even fell off the porch once. And she was mean as a rattlesnake.

Susan's piebald pointer, Sport, as if under her command, began to raid our lawn and frighten Sister's cats to death. Sister was tempted to retaliate. She planned to poison Sport by feeding him skewers of lamb laced with strychnine. But I could not take Sister's side. I myself longed to hire Assassins against that pestilence of cats. The pussies were *partout*, and filled the house with cavernous hair balls. But it was our wondrously fat dictator, Margaret Maher, the Homestead's Irish housekeeper, who arranged a truce. Sport could have the south lawn as his mandate while the pussies roamed the rear porch. Thus a battle was avoided between the two houses. But the real warfare was internecine and had little to do with our side of the family estate. Not even the blond angel who slept beside them could bring Austin and Sue together again. There were more and more of Sue's drunken carousals, more of her pulling at Mattie and Ned as her own little pawns, until Brother felt like an infidel in his own house. Sue was diabolic about trying to have me abandon my own brother and sister. She enlisted Mattie to soften me up and win me over to her side. And she planned to do it through my own weakness for Poetry.

Susan sent Mattie across the hedge to become my disciple. She was twelve or thirteen at the time, with her mother's smoldering eyes. Lord, another Volcano! I worshiped the child and would have done anything for her.

"Aunt Emily, Mother says you must instruct me how to be a Poet."

A pencil hung from her waist, and she carried a writing tablet as if it were a divine thing. I would have been overjoyed to have a disciple, yet what art could I have taught this girl, who had been schooled by a master—Susan herself!

"Mattie dear, your mother versifies as much as I ever did."

"That doesn't count. Mother has sacrificed her talent, spent it on her family, but your own melody is pure—that's what Mama says. And you must teach me."

"I wouldn't have the faintest notion. All I know how to do is sing in the dark, and I haven't done much of that ever since Pa-pa died."

I was scattered, all askew, without the sight of Pa-pa's slippers. No Monster could retrieve my Pen, even if he talked like Pa-pa. Lord, most of the lightnin' was gone, and I didn't have thunderbolts to catch or throw. Surely the best little girl in town should have recovered from Pa-pa's death. I could not. I had froze in a thousand years of ice. But Mattie was on fire. Her smoldering turned into a genuine fit. She tore the pencil from its string and brandished it like one of her mother's knives, though she wasn't really menacing me. It was part of the drama she had learned at the Evergreens, that swagger of emotion, Susan's sway.

"Then might I sit with you while you compose?"

"I never compose—the lightnin' comes, and I mark it down."

"But I've seen you at your desk in the conservatory, scribbling on scraps of paper."

"Oh, that," I tell her. "It's the recipe for a new frosting on my ice cake. You know how I love to experiment whenever I bake."

And she starts to cry, her tears as fine as crystal. "Then I will tell Mama that you have refused me as your disciple."

Even now, with slightly crooked teeth, she is beautifuler than Sue had ever been. And it's like worshiping a comet that can fly all over the place. How will I ever teach myself to contain Miss Mattie Dickinson?

"Aunt Emily, you are crueler than King Saul."

I smile to myself. *Crueler than Saul,* the king whose only song was to fight, since the Lord wouldn't whisper in his ear. Saul's kingdom was the kingdom I knew best—a land of silence where animals were stunned in midair and birds fell like bombs from the trees. This was my address after Father passed to the other side.

Without my tutelage, Mattie abandoned her pencil and decided to remain a Siren.

Half the schoolboys of Amherst flocked outside her gate, smitten by her smoldering looks. They could not comprehend the mystery of a thirteen-year-old who had become the town's latest belle.

Maggie Maher, *our* Maggie, had to chase them with a broom, while Mattie watched from a rocking chair, indifferent to the spectacle around her. Lord, I could feel that little girl's electrical charge from my window. What catastrophe awaited her suitors. She would devour them all.

# 42.

MY PENCIL HUNG ON ITS STRING AT MY SIDE LIKE A SICK snake, or a pendulum that could sometimes breathe. Not even that Monster, Mr. Dark Eyes, could make it stir. I longed for Father's footsteps, not a weasel with a wound for a mouth. And then a surrogate arrived, who wasn't a tempter, like Mr. Dark Eyes. One of Father's oldest friends, Judge Otis Phillips Lord, who ruled the Commonwealth's Supreme Court, had just become a widower. His wife, Elizabeth, had died right on my forty-seventh birthday. I should have sensed that it was an omen of some kind, but my pencil and I were fast asleep.

Judge Lord took to visiting Amherst twice a year with his niece, Miss Farley, a terrible little bulldog who watched over him and his every leap. He was only nine years younger than Pa-pa. And when he called on us with that bulldog, I ignored her as best I could, fed him black cake and berry wine; in his own vigorous face, with full jaws and fierce white hair, I'd have the sweetest recollection of Pa-pa, as if some kind of angel had lent him to us for an hour, while Judge Lord was at the Homestead.

So when the Judge came a-calling two years into his widowhood, but without his niece, I might have figured that something irregular was afoot. He could frighten the whole justice system of Massachusetts with his saber-toothed pronouncements and bullet-like stares at criminals and clerks, but he was a lamb with us on Main Street. He visited Ma-ma in her bedroom, brought her flowers from his own garden in Salem, where he lived with his niece; the Judge even played with Sister's ferocious cats, congratulating them on the mice they had captured. "Phil," as we called him, was in his sixty-ninth year. He'd grown a little deaf, but couldn't even consider retiring from the court. I had known him since I was a little girl and should confess that I had often sat upon his knee, since Phil and his wife were Father's frequent guests. He would dandle Lavinia on one knee and myself on the other while he was in the middle of a game of whist. It was great adventure as Vinnie and I flew under the chandeliers.

But we weren't flying now. And after Ma-ma began to doze, the Judge asked me to take him on a tour of the Mansion. I thought it peculiar, since he'd stayed overnight with Mrs. Lord quite often when Father was alive, and he could have walked the Homestead wearing a blindfold. But I didn't mind indulging Judge Lord, who had not looked at me once while Mother was awake, had not used that Revolver in his eyes to pierce me with a glance.

"I'm a man who doesn't like to live alone, Miss Emily."

"But I'm much too old to dandle now, and you do have a niece," I said, pitying him for that bulldog.

"She's just about invisible to me. I couldn't even tell you the color of her eyes."

And I didn't mean to trap him, but I did. "Why, Judge Lord, I find that men are not terribly observant about women's eyes. They're too worried about questions of the world, or about metaphysics and men's souls."

"I wish you'd call me Phil. That's what you called me when Mrs. Lord was alive. And your eyes are exactly the color of the sky just before a summer storm—hazel, with a strong hint of red."

I couldn't hide my own hint of red. That's how hard I was blushing. No man I can remember had discussed the nature of my eyes in half a century.

We were walking side by side in the darkness of my favorite corridor, the Northwest Passage, when he grew as flustered and shy as one of Pa-pa's mares, and suddenly I felt the squeeze of his hand. He wasn't yattering away. Both of us were silent. I did not dare move from Phil's side. I couldn't tell if he was breathing heavy or not, or if wandering through the house had tired him. His hand was firm as a steel glove. Startled as I was, I did not swoon. I took that steel glove of his and squeezed back with all my might.

THAT WAS HOW I FELL INTO ROMANCE. IF WE COULD TALK SO cavalierly of the unexpected, then wonder itself would be washed out of our race. I had not fancied Phil as my suitor, had not dreamt of him at all. Of course, it was a curious affair. How could it not be? Phil was a widower, I an old maid. He was either at the courthouse in Boston or at home in Salem. He had little time to travel, or follow his inclinations. And when he did come to Amherst now, it was always with his niece. She did not want to share the Judge and was jealous of all intrusions. And so I had to waylay Miss Farley, trap her into doing things while Phil snuck out of his hotel and stole through our gate. It delighted me to watch him romp like a Boy.

I could feel Phil's longing as we lay together, and it emboldened me to think that I could arouse the want of a man. I did not scheme like Cleopatra in my Salem's arms. If I held back, did not allow him into the Moss of my own little garden, it was not to punish or declare my modesty. I had none. It was just that my Salem was not a male witch. Whatever magic he had wasn't enough to slay me into submission.

But our ecstasy did build with all the slow craft of a snail. My

Salem could not free himself but twice a year. And so our letters flew like rockets that burst in secret. He had to hide them from that little bulldog, who had already begun to slander me, said I was a fortune hunter right in front of Vinnie—Sister had to hold back from slapping Miss Farley's puggish face out of respect for Phil. Dear God, what fortune did I have to hunt? My own small Treasure rarely left my room.

Yet I shouldn't be so coy about my Plumage. I wrapped my own feathers into the rockets I sent Phil, scratching with my pencil— *To my dear Salem from his Amherst, who awaits his words like the sweetest of wolves.* I could not allow these rockets to fall into enemy hands. Miss Farley might say I was a Siren who was trying to trap her uncle into marriage. But marriage was not on this sweet wolf's mind. I couldn't have packed up, moved my little House of Snow to Salem and abandoned Lavinia, while Mother remained an invalid. But most of all, I couldn't have abandoned my Dark Eyed Mister, who haunted whatever sleep I had.

I guarded Phil's letters and my own penciled drafts, plunged them inside my housedress, until I resembled some robust creature who was carrying a child, though I wasn't a day under fifty. I happened to meet Phil once while the Circus was in town with its pregnant elephant, Jumbo, female star of the Menagerie. I watched her waltz up Main Street, with the ground swaying under her until I thought she would provoke an earthquake.

And Phil wondered what earthquake *I* might provoke. He took to calling me Jumbo, and thus I had one more name in my Menagerie of names.

"Dearest," he said, "you would make a worn old man happy if I could start addressing you as Mrs. Emily Jumbo Lord."

I panicked at his pronouncement, as if the sweet wolf inside me suddenly wanted to be fed—fed on what? The wolf was gnawing at the very flesh of that name. *Mrs. Jumbo Lord.*

And I realized that the Circus drew me to its panorama of tents for another reason than its prima donna of an elephant. I was troubled by a particular clown, wondering if my blond Assassin was still hiding somewhere on Circus grounds under a mask of red paint. But I did not have the sass to wander over to the Commons in my shawl and find out for myself. Perhaps I was frightened of what I would find, that the clown of my dreams was a banal character who did not have half of Tom's beauty, and that I had *wished* this Circus clown into being as Tom.

My Salem kept talking marriage. Mother's illness, he said, would be no impediment.

"I will carry her on my back to Salem. Lavinia will live with us, cats and all, and your housekeeper with the truculent look. I will double her wages."

I adored my Salem's persistence, his want of me, but perhaps I was frightened that his very want would bring me woe. I was on much better terms with that old maid, Emily, than with Mrs. Jumbo Lord.

"What about your niece? She will look upon the Dickinsons as Privateers who have invaded her territory."

"Then I will teach her to love you, or else I will find her another uncle, who is more docile and less inclined to look for a wife."

He was a Judge, after all, who could beat back an entire field of plaintiffs, and though I might have been a lawyer's daughter, I was not trained in the wiles of a courtroom. But like some Egyptian Monster, I knew how to smother him in my own feathers.

Suddenly I was Cleopatra with a plain simple face. "Dearest," I cooed, "you wouldn't want your Jumbo to pine away with loneliness while you're sitting on the bench. Shouldn't we wait until you retire?"

"I will wait if you condescend to grant me a kiss."

And his eyes had a touch of naughtiness that drew me to him. All his life he'd never had a soul with whom to be a little bad. He loved me and loved my Plumage. I was his Monster—Jumbo—

whom he longed to tame. He was a man of Prose, but his words had the suppleness and the wicked pull of David's slingshot. He seldom missed his mark. He tilted toward me. I could feel the rumbling in his loins. He swallowed my mouth. I didn't suffer much. Lord, I'd left that quilted territory of an old maid.

# 43.

I COULD ROMP AROUND WITH ALL THE PLEASURES OF AN
Apache, bent on stealing love. I didn't need a Tomahawk to capture a man. I had my girlish tricks, and I had my Pen. But I couldn't
even hold on to Phil, who was plagued with apoplexy a little after I
turned fifty-one; he fell unconscious while he was in his chambers
and hovered close to death. I had to read the damn paper every
morning for crusts of news about his condition. But no bad angel
could break his will. He recovered after a few weeks and retired
from the bench.

Phil knocked on my door with wildflowers in his fist; he could
squeeze me with some of his former strength, but the fiery crackle
had gone out of his eyes. He who had been a master of his court,
a man in constant control, must have felt enfeebled after he had
fainted and lost control. His speech was now slurred. He had spittle on his tongue, but he pressed his pursuit of me. I loved him all
the more.

Wizened as he was, he continued to press for marriage and
talked of how he had the means to move our whole Menagerie to
Salem—Maggie, Mother, and all. I didn't argue. There was little

need of it. We would sit in our front room with Miss Farley, who was more a jailor than a devoted niece. She took to wiping his spittle, and I couldn't even dig my hand under that high collar of his to feel my Salem's flesh. He didn't dare call me Jumbo in her presence, and I did not call him Phil. He was Judge Lord, and I was plain Emily, discussing a marriage contract that I knew was fiction, while Miss Farley hovered over us until all the secret fervor was crushed out of Phil's face, and my own sweet wolf had gone back into the woods.

Little Sister was much more resourceful than I. She was fond of Phil, but loathed Miss Farley. So she invented every sort of excuse to lure that bulldog out of the parlor and leave us a precious minute to ourselves. But no new recipe could tempt the Little Lord Protectress, nor an invitation to discover the glorious view from Pa-pa's cupola. Vinnie had to fall back upon her surest weapon. Sister besieged Miss Farley with an Avalanche of cats. The pussies pounced onto her lap, and Miss Farley rose up with a scream and ran from the parlor, while Sister followed behind her and pretended to call off the cats.

We were alone, at last. I caught a tear in Phil's eye that glowed like a worm. Suddenly there was no more spittle.

"I have a longing for you, Em."

I could feel that sweet wolf gnaw its way back into my loins. I didn't waver. I slowly slid onto my Salem's lap, wanting him to dandle me again. I ought to have some privileges at fifty-one. My Salem started to cry.

"I don't have the words to woo you," he said. "All my songs are gone."

But I'd had a lifetime of words. And I was tiny enough to fit into Phil's silences. His skin was scratched where the razor had missed. I had never shaved a man, but I would have been a much better barber than that bulldog. His eyes had the ravaged look of someone who could not collect his own thoughts. But that only made him more attractive. My Salem was wooing me without words.

I ran the hollow of my hand along the rough patches on his skin. He moaned softly; it wasn't the sound of a man who couldn't recollect. Phil must have had his own sweet wolf.

I heard a clatter from the kitchen—I tried to break away, but Phil clapped me to him. His niece ran into the parlor, twitching like a stunned rabbit when she caught us together.

"I will close my eyes," she said, "and you will remove that adventuress from your lap."

He had the want to answer Miss Farley, but the words wouldn't come. I was proud to be an adventuress, and I would have told her so, but I couldn't interfere in the mechanics of his house in Salem.

Phil struggled to hold me, and then the struggle stopped. The tears were streaming now, and they didn't resemble worms or wet stars. I climbed off his lap. I'd rather croak than have the Little Lord Protectress see me cry. She took my Phil by the hand.

"Miss Emily, your sister is worse than you are. I have never in my life endured such an affliction—cats, cats, cats!"

I'm not certain what I would have done had Mother not been paralyzed. I might have scratched Farley's eyes out and barricaded Phil inside our doors. But the town marshal would have come and put both Dickinson daughters in Jail. It was Farley who had jurisdiction over him, not his Jumbo. A bride-to-be didn't have a whole lot of rights, particularly one who couldn't see herself in Salem as Mrs. Jumbo Lord.

Letters still flew between his town and mine. He hadn't lost his ardor on the page, no matter how apoplexy had disabled him. Our courtship seemed to prosper from afar, like some wild plant with its own irrational roots. That plant would not have survived away from Father's house, but I could not bear to tell him so. His Jumbo performed in her own Circus of little lies. I was a dreadful coward. I told Phil nothing at all.

Perhaps I deceive myself. He must have known we would never marry, and it had nothing to do with the bulldog or Ma-ma or Salem's soil. The vail I wore was my own wildflower. And a man might have been scorched had he ever dared peek under that net.

# 44.

I WASN'T BLIND TO THE ABUNDANCE AROUND ME — THE PIPES
from Pelham that sent water gurgling into our kitchen, the Ice
Cream parlor with its blood-red awning, the new Roller Skating
rink. The Queen Recluse never actually saw the rink. I had to
depend on my spies. Lavinia was frightened to prance around on
wooden wheels, but Mattie skated. So did Sue. She had special
skating skirts sewn for Mattie and herself. They practiced duets
together, took lessons from the local skating champion. No one
was a match for them in their blue skirts until Mabel Loomis Todd
came onto the rink. She could skate with one leg held high in the
air until she resembled a schooner with her own taut body as a
mast.

She wore a skirt of many layers, like a Russian ballerina, and
long white stockings that snaked above her kneecaps. Little Sister
was disturbed by Mabel's "daring show of flesh," but I doubt that I
would have been. Spectators who sat on benches surrounding the
rink couldn't take their eyes off Amherst's new ballerina. I tried
to imagine her marauding among the other skaters, marking an
infallible line as she wove around them. They must have moved

in stuttering Prose, unable to penetrate the circumference of this Poet in white stockings. I wish some angel had transported me there. I would have danced with Mabel Loomis Todd, but only in my mind.

Yes, a true rival had come to town the very year my Salem took ill. She was the ravishing young wife of the College's new astronomy instructor. Mabel had a multiplicity of talents—poet, pianist, painter of flowers—and a burning ambition to become America's own Charlotte Brontë. She was a metropolitan who had grown up in the District of Columbia, while with all her soirees and musicales and skating skirts, Mrs. Austin was still very much the country kangaroo.

At first they were fast friends. Susan had adopted Mabel, brought the astronomy instructor's wife into her own little cabal. They went on excursions together with Ned and Mattie in a hired coach. They had picnics in the mountains. Ned, twenty at the time, fell in love with Mabel, who was twenty-five, and Susan seemed to encourage this infatuation. But she hadn't expected her own husband to occupy the territories of her son—Mabel would become Austin's exclusive business. My poor brother had perhaps found a Siren worthy of himself.

He and Mabel began to meet in our parlor; it was Sister who encouraged such rendezvous. She was fiercely loyal to Brother and had also found a way to avenge Susan's rough treatment of her cats. Austin and Mabel sat on the same divan where I had once sat with my Salem. But I did not see them together in the house. Always the good conspirator, Vinnie had timed their visits to the very minute I was in the conservatory with my plants and flowers, in the kitchen with the freshwater pipes, or upstairs in my room. But I did catch a glimpse of her once, while I hid in the Northwest Passage and could not be seen. My heart thumped as I watched Mabel, who was no taller than Susan, but had a soft mouth and huge brown orbits instead of eyes. I would have loved to conquer her myself had I been a lofty soldier and not some prickly pear.

It wasn't Vinnie who bore the brunt of these rendezvous, but myself. Empress Susan had one of her royal messages delivered through the medium of our housekeeper, Maggie Maher: I was summoned to meet Sue in the Northwest Passage at 4½ the next afternoon.

❦

HER HIGHNESS WASN'T LATE. BOTH OF US STOOD IN THE strange half-darkness that was so soothing for me. My eyes had gone weak again, and I had to squint in order to determine the outline of her face; she was trembling as I had never seen her tremble. Sue was riddled with rum. I could taste the Domingo on her breath. She started to reel like a ship in choppy water. And then she capsized, toppled onto the floor, sat in the folds of her gown, her face mottled with a terrible rash that seemed to spread like poison through her skin. I was bewildered, lost. Sue couldn't seem to rouse herself. And she slapped my hand away when I tried to help.

"I wouldn't hold a witch's paw," she said. I might have been flattered if I hadn't pitied her so. Witches write Poetry, witches dance in the dark.

"You have conspired against me. You are worse than a witch."

And then Sue began to rise up like some sea monster with a mottled face. But she couldn't stand without holding the wall. And while she was struggling, I ran to the kitchen and returned with a chair. It took her more than a minute to negotiate herself into the wicker seat. But even in her wretched state she was still the Queen of Pelham, and I could have been the queen's servant.

"Dear, might I trouble you for a glass of water?"

I brought her a pitcher of well water, and both of us drank from metal cups. She patted her lips with the handkerchief in her sleeve.

"Emily, why have you welcomed this slattern into your house?"

I was the one who trembled now, defeated by so fine a riposte when I hadn't even attacked.

"I welcomed no one. I haven't met Mabel Todd. But this is also my brother's house, and he is free to come and go with his guests."

"Oh, you are as much a slattern as she."

For a moment I thought Susan had gone mad. But I smiled in the dark, a bitter smile. Sister Sue was calling me Cleopatra.

She continued. "Miss Farley said you have a craziness for men—I should have listened."

The trembling stopped as I put on my Plumage. "Listened to what?"

"I saw you once in the parlor, sitting in a man's lap."

Dear God, I wanted to slap her face, and I might have done so had the Queen of Pelham not been such a wreck in her chair. But I couldn't have her malign me and Phil.

"That was Judge Lord and his Jumbo—and he was probably sitting in *my* lap."

"Go on," she said. "Laugh at me. You're not the one who has to suffer. I married a philanderer, an uncouth man."

I could feel Susan's poison sprout on my own skin. None of us were philanderers. If Austin had strayed, it's because Sue had shuttered him, shuttered her queen's boudoir.

"Uncouth? He's the kindest brother in the world."

"So kind he calls you cracked."

"And suppose I am?" I insisted. "Suppose I am—cracked a little. You pushed Austin away from your own affections. Didn't you tell me once that your wedding was nothing more than a kiss and a soggy piece of cake?"

"I said no such thing."

She wasn't even true to our own little secrets. Perhaps all her imbibings had pickled her mind. I didn't mean to invoke a dead man but I did.

"You were in love with Sam Bowles, always in love with him."

Her eyes began to wander, and she shivered in her chair. "But I never sat upon his lap."

"Perchance you should," I said, like one of Cleopatra's snakes. I loved her and did not know how to declare this love except through little bites.

The shipwreck began to move. She stumbled out of her chair.

"Susie, I didn't . . ."

But she was already gone. And for the first time I didn't follow her after one of her explosions, didn't smooth the roughened lines of our friendship, didn't hide my Plumage, didn't play meek. Vesuvius would have to smolder all by herself.

A younger witch had replaced her in Brother's affections, a witch who wasn't so worried about "a man's requirements." I would have to reckon that Mabel Todd pretty much relished such requirements, and she clung to Austin as a Volcano never could.

I started to imagine Brother's paramour on the skating rink in her many-layered skirt. I was the only one in the audience, not Brother, not Mattie, not Sue. She was giving a command performance while I sat in my blue shawl. As she glided above the burnished wood in her long white stockings, her kneecaps could have been made of snow. And I'd have fastened myself to Mabel, remained in that rink for life, if I could have shared her two little mountains of snow.

# 45.

EVEN WHILE SHE LANGUISHED IN BED, PARTIALLY PARALYZED
and with a broken hip that never healed, Ma-ma worried about
my spinsterhood. Little Sister had her pussies and didn't have to
spear a man, while I had nothing but my gardening and a subdued
Pen. And Mother insisted on *making* a husband for me. She knew
that Judge Lord was locked up in his own apoplexy and was in no
position to court a spinster or a goose. But while she plotted in my
behalf, Ma-ma grew delirious and kept rambling on about Pa-pa,
so damn sure was she that he was still alive.

"Is Father in the barn? I don't want him to see me in such a
state. Will you help me darken my eyes, Emily dear?"

It was contagious. Ma-ma got me believing that Pa-pa would step
right out of the barn and come a-courting. She had never worn eye
paint in her life. But I wouldn't disappoint her little passion. I pretended to darken her eyes with a pencil stub. And in the middle
of my masquerade she started to cry.

"I have not been a proper mother, Emily, or you wouldn't have
run rampant . . . Oh, I saw you chase after that census man."

The census man had come a week ago, had blundered through

the house like an elephant, and when I would not converse with him, he listed me in his census book as one more female "without occupation," while Ma-ma sat with that smug little frog for half an hour and let him gorge himself on my black cake.

"Emily, you ought to have married him. He won't be back until there's another reckoning and I'm not sure when. You ought to have seized the chance."

"Forgive me, Ma-ma, but I forgot to propose."

I was sorry soon as I said it. I shouldn't have provoked Ma-ma. I promised her I would propose to the census man the instant he knocked on our door again. That calmed her. She drank lemonade and devoured beef tea and custard. Mother's appetite had come back—she ate like a horse. She'd been coughing a lot, but her cold was suddenly gone, and Mother turned tyrant. She wanted to sit in the Orchard, she said. There was a November chill in the air, and Vinnie was concerned that an escapade like that would do her in. But Mother triumphed—it was the Orchard or she would never eat another morsel.

The handymen had to carry her down the stairs. Mother could have been the Queen of England in the sedan chair they had rigged for her, handles and all. That contraption didn't waver once. We'd wrapped her in blankets and a shawl, covered her ears against the wind, and the handymen forged into the yard with Ma-ma, the new Matriarch, high above their shoulders; once they arrived in the Orchard, they set her down under an apple tree, and there she sat.

The handymen's faces had gone ripe with exhaustion, and they nipped at their own whiskey flasks after saluting Ma-ma.

"Horace," she said, "I wouldn't mind a sip."

And she drank with the handymen, pretending that Vinnie and I were as inconsequential as a broken gate. The Orchard had its own afternoon calm that was like no other noise in creation— wind and a scatter of leaves. It had always been a holy place for

Pa-pa and me, a garden that went into the woods, with its world of creatures: I imagined a coven of bears watching us behind the stone wall, their eyes on fire, both curious and uncurious about us.

"Where's Father?" she asked. "Em, is he up in the apple tree?"

The Matriarch drank too much; she fell asleep, and the handymen had to return her to her room. They were not so steady now, and I worried they would drop her; the sedan chair dipped and found its balance again, and Mother never did fall.

She had a brittle night. Her eyes were wild in the morning. Lord knows what her dreams had been like. She clutched Sister's hand.

"Vinnie," she said, "I'd like to buy a man."

"Mother, we have all the men we need."

Her eyes were raw and red. "The Lord spoke to me. I must not go to Heaven until your sister marries."

And Mother was so agitated, so delirious, that we had no choice but to deceive her and perform a ceremony on the spot to calm her down. I did not relish the idea of marrying Horace Church, even in jest. Vinnie had to provide the ring. She found one in her jewelry box, but I didn't care for the way Horace coveted it. I could do very little while Mother watched us with a terrifying interest and eagerness. Sister had to play the preacher in her housedress.

Horace grabbed the ring in his grubby fingers and snorted. And thus the wedding began.

"Miss Im'ly, wear this ring as a token of my love."

I was a-shiver with shame, but I wouldn't disappoint Ma-ma. I wore the ring and pretended to wear a vail. That seemed to satisfy her. She clapped her hands and said, "Ain't it a miracle, Em? I lived to see you as a bride."

I looked in the mirror and a freckled girl looked back—this girl didn't have to pretend; she was wearing a vail and a gown of white tulle. But Horace Church wasn't standing next to her, or the census man. It was Pa-pa in his Prince Albert coat and silk cravat. Pa-pa was perspiring, and it seemed as if he'd come strutting from the barn. *Ma-ma,* I wanted to say, *Lavinia, look!* But they couldn't see Pa-pa's apparition. And what was the girl in the mirror doin' in a bridal gown? Pa-pa already had a bride, who sat under the covers like a forgetful queen. I turned from the mirror and took her in my arms, but Ma-ma had already rambled away.

"Miss Im'ly," Horace said with a look of alarm, "your mother's passed to the other side."

Vinnie kissed her and closed her eyes. We waited until Horace Church skulked out of the room, and then we started to cry. I looked up. Father's apparition was gone, but the girl in the mirror was still wearing her vail.

# 46.

AMHERST HAD ENTERED A GOLDEN AGE WHERE DRUMMERS arrived from everywhere to sell us velocipedes that could fly. I saw these contraptions from my window with their enormous front wheels and seats that almost came up to my sill. I saw them crash into children, while their riders spilled into that relentless traffic of machines. But they weren't the town's only pests. We began to attract a new breed of housebreakers, who didn't have to pedal their way into our lives. They pounced in broad daylight, when families were in the midst of dinner, and did not leave a trace, not one clue; they could ransack a whole floor while soup was being served.

And this curious carnage always seemed to happen when some Circus was in town. Why didn't our police arrest the whole Menagerie, with its elephant cages and lion dens? It was as if the town had fallen into paralysis, or had been cast under a spell by the Circus itself. I might have become a better citizen had Father been alive. I would have gone to him, enlisted his aid in finding the burglars. We might even have descended upon the Circus together—it wasn't camped in China. It was only a few hundred giant steps away, housed on the Commons in a panoply of tents.

What burglar could have survived Father's wrath? But I dreaded that confrontation, even in my dreams. I knew the outcome. The ringleader of the band had to have been my blond Assassin, Tom, who had burgled in Amherst once before with Zilpah as his pilot; he'd metamorphosed from handyman to housebreaker, pickpocket, army deserter, and housebreaker again, while he toiled in a Circus under the guise of a clown. And what if Tom had ever hurt Pa-pa, or Pa-pa hurt Tom? I would have had to rush through Purgatory, riven with guilt and howling like a lunatic at Pa-pa's own hospital in Northampton. No, it was best by far that Pa-pa and my blond Assassin never meet.

I would suffer each time Circus season arrived—mid-May through August and September. I dreaded the drumrolls, the tinny, pathetic roar of tamed lions, the squeal of rotting wagons, and longed for these very same sounds; the nearness of my blond Assassin intoxicated me, and I wasn't even sure that Tom was a renegade clown in the Circus. But that was the disease of Miss Emily Dickinson. I had to invent what I could not ascertain—no, did not want to ascertain. I was the voluptuary who lived on the thinnest air, who survived *and* conquered through invention alone.

It seemed that the Circus would not come this summer. I waited into June and had my reward in the final week of the month, as I heard that familiar prelude of the drums. God is my witness. I was now fifty-two years old, yet my heart thumped like that of a child seeking rapture. But rapture soon turned into alarm. I shivered at the sight of Jumbo parading under my window with some fool juggler on her back. She wore red lace round her neck like a ruche; her toenails and earflaps were painted red, but she was not a proud elephant mother dancing in the sun with her newborn calf.

I saw no calf, nothing but Jumbo herself, emblazoned in magenta and completely shriveled, as if some cruel burglar had absconded with half her size and half her strength. I was so involved with my own longing, my wish to dredge up that blond Assassin from out of my dreams, it took me a full five minutes to comprehend that Jumbo had lost her calf; the elephantess under my window was in deep mourning.

⤚

THE BAND OF BURGLARS STRUCK A FEW DAYS AFTER THE TENTS were pitched. And what I feared most finally happened. The Evergreens was attacked while Austin presided over the dinner table. Not a footstep was heard. And these housebreakers did not leave their usual mark; they didn't rampage upstairs, didn't upset a single mirror. They went through Ned's room and took whatever coins were in the pocket-book he had left on his bureau. They also visited Mattie's room and took a few small trinkets that could hardly have been worth their while. Nothing else was touched.

Austin may have pondered over the mystery of it, but I did not. Vain creature that I was, the Poetess who prided herself on her Plumage had been out-feathered by a handyman. That was no robbery! It was a surreptitious, subterranean letter sent without a postage stamp—a letter from my blond Assassin.

How could I answer him! Daisy would have to deliver herself. But I still didn't have the courage to sneak into the Circus and catch Tom under a tent.

*Tomorrow*, I told myself. Were I a necromancer who could wish Carlo back into being, I would have rushed over to the Circus with him and berated that blond Assassin. But Carlo don't answer my calls. And I promised my own good angel that I would muster up whatever I needed tomorrow.

My good angel must have abandoned me—tomorrow was the fourth of July, and I was struck by it with the Devil's own tail. I shivered at night, and that Dark Eyed Monster with his wound of a mouth seemed to hover on my bed like some mammoth, tailless bird. He did not menace me, or mock my condition as a dried-up maiden, but he was agitated, as if he had come to warn me of some impending doom and could not utter a sound from that hole in his face.

I woke to the noise of warning bells and went to the window, where a brightness attacked my face, as if I had encountered some furnace-sun from another planet. Then Sister arrived out of nowhere in her nightgown and shut the curtains.

"Emily," she said, "it's just hullabaloo—the firemen are out with their trucks on the fourth of July. It ain't worth our bother."

And she rocked me in her arms, my own Little Sister, who could have attracted any man; her arms were still plump, and her figure had the fullness of a dressmaker's mannequin; she turned every suitor away except for one, Joseph Lyman, who went off to marry another. He said that my sister was nice to spoon with, but that she didn't have the brains or the accomplishment of a bride.

Lord, what did he know about Lavinia! She had cared for Father and had kept Mother alive as long as she could with her constant devotion. And now she mothered me. I could hear the crackle of burning wood, smell the smoke and hot oil, but I pretended that it was the merriment of Independence Day.

The fire raged and roared; that foreign sun seemed to rip right through the curtains and shine upon my walls—it wasn't arson, but an act of God. Barns collapsed. I did nothing until I heard an elephant sob like a frozen child on the fourth of July. I pulled the curtains apart, and there was Jumbo wandering on Main Street in her red ruche. Circus performers and firemen were trying to steer her back to the higher ground of the Commons. They clucked their tongues and stamped their feet as if my Jumbo were some ordinary cow. She remained in the hot wind and swatted at them with her trunk. And then the sobbing stopped. She stood like a lady at my window, trumpeted once, and started to ramble back toward the Commons.

Her trumpeting had restored my courage. I went down into that dying fire in my summer bonnet. I too wore a ruche at my throat; but mine wasn't red. Neighbors gaped at me; they hadn't seen the recluse in years. I curtsied and whisked past them as some waif would. I hadn't plunged into the street to chat with them about the wind.

I could see the burning tents. The fire had ruined the Menagerie. A lion shivered on the lawn. The whole Commons was thick with smoke. I hadn't expected to confront my dream clown, but there he was in his costume, a rash of red on his face. He wasn't coy or nonchalant.

"Daisy the Kangaroo," he said.

I was in mortal danger of losing my mind. The Devil was standing in front of me dressed as a clown with Tom's blue eyes and that awful smear of red paint, talking about kangaroos, and knowing that the mention of Daisy would bewilder a spinster's heart.

"Ah," he said, "where's your dark glasses? I was wondering what would bring ya to my little abode. Are you still my mouse?"

I remembered dancing with him on a dark street in Cambridgeport, during the late Rebellion, a pickpocket who was always gallant. But he didn't seem so gallant now. He grimaced under his smear of red paint, as if he meant to violate that memory. Clowns were cruel, I surmised, waltzing in a red mask while they poked fun of people. So I hid my own charity toward Tom, and that deep affection I had ever since I found him in the handyman's shack.

"Darling," I trumpeted, "I'm as constant as the North Star. But you should not have traduced my own brother."

He laughed, and the ring of it, the soft, palpitating thunder, ripped through my bowels.

"What brother is that?"

"Don't pretend," I told him. "You know who I am, and you always knew."

And the Devil didn't bother to lie. He bowed in his silly suit. But there was a sadness around his painted eyes. Perhaps he wasn't as immune to me as he liked to imagine.

"Ah, Miss Dickinson, who fed me water while I was in a damn shack. I wouldn't forget a favor. Didn't I pick you out of the gutter a hundred years ago in Cambridgeport and carry ya home like a regular swain? But if I remembered too hard I would have slit your throat. And so I made ya my mouse."

I died right there among the Circus animals. Tom was blaming me for what had happened to Zilpah Marsh, and he wasn't wrong.

"I had to let Zilpah go. She—"

"You shouldn't have taken her yellow gloves. You broke her heart. She adored your father. He didn't treat her like a common girl. He respected her book-reading. He was proud as Moses to have a maid like her."

His eyes were pierced with flecks of anger, and I meant to charm him with the small ammunition that was left to an old maid.

"Enobarbus," I said. I called him by his nickname, knowing as I did that Zilpah had introduced him to Shakespeare, not me. But he still wouldn't play.

"Daisy, Enobarbus is dead . . . I never tetched you or your Pa-pa. You were the safest heiress in Amherst."

There was no soft thunder in his voice; it sounded like terrible tin.

"I'm not an heiress," I said.

I couldn't puzzle out his features in that haze of smoke on the Commons' bumpy lawn. I couldn't tell if he was smiling or not, or just mocking me.

"Then what would ya call a girl who lives in a mansion with a fence in front of it and a wall of grass that's greener than God's eyes?"

"I'm not a girl," I had to insist. "I'll be fifty-three come December. And how the Devil would you know that God's eyes are green?"

I didn't want an answer. I was sick with love for a burglar who wouldn't even burgle his own mouse.

"Zilpah told me," he said.

"You mean your other mouse."

I couldn't help myself. I was eaten up with jealousy . . . and spite. She had enthralled my Tom with her Plumage. And here I'd thought that my feathers were so fine. But Tom had feathers of his own. And he had all the mystery, while I had none. That's what drew me to him. Lord, I'd never stopped dancing with Tom. I was still stapled to him, the way I had been on Magazine Street. I could hear the accordion man tapping with his toe to our crazy polka. But Tom broke into my melody with a brutal song.

"She wasn't my mouse," he said. "She was my little wife . . . and my college. I didn't require Senior levees and Commencement balls. I didn't have to puncture her with a fraternity pin. All I needed was to steal words from the Lexicon, with the devotion of a pickpocket. And Zilpah helped me steal."

"Darling," I whispered, struggling to hold on to what little veneer I had left. "I could have been just as big a thief."

"But it's not the same thing. You were born with words, and Zilpah had to scream and sweat to put them in her mouth. Those damn witches shouldn't have tossed her out of Holyoke like a dying dog. I had half a mind to burn their school to the ground."

A zebra walked out of the mist and went up to Tom with its nostrils all aquiver. He stroked the animal's mane, and it vanished into the mist.

"Daisy, I'm moving on," he said. "I'm leaving Circus life. And I won't be around here again. I just had to visit Amherst one last time. My valedictory. Isn't that what they call it?"

I began to sob like Jumbo the elephant; I was crying for myself, and for Zilpah too and for Tom's baby that Zilpah tore out of her womb with a knitting needle. I couldn't tell him about the baby. I couldn't. Tom took my hand, cradled it in his. And I cursed myself. He'd passed my window year after year in that silly clown's suit, and I'd held him at bay. I was an heiress, the way he'd said, a little rotten heiress without a penny in her pocket.

"Mr. Tom, don't you like me just a little?"

I could feel the static pass through him, like a strange current right under the motley he was wearing. He was no different from Daisy. He was lost in his own dark well. And that barking of his was just an orphan's badge.

"Little darlin'," he said, "I wouldn't have bothered much with Amherst if it wasn't your abode. The pickings are slim. But I'm always loyal to a mouse."

He dropped my hand and disappeared from Daisy without a kiss.

But pain quickened my blood. Tom hadn't come to Amherst to break into mansions and remember a mouse. My vanity had blinded me to his real destination. That's why he'd brought his Circus to the Commons time after time. He was in mourning, just like Jumbo.

I waited a good half hour and then walked up the road to the burying-ground. I caught Tom at the gate. He'd just come from Zilpah's grave. He wasn't wearing motley, with a mask of red paint. He'd shucked them off somewhere, and in their stead he had a long black coat that could have been a haven for his burglar's tools. He was shorn of his blond complection, that angel's look he'd once had at Holyoke. His hair had gone white at the temples. His skin was as red and blotchy as Esau's. Rough lines on both sides of his mouth gave him a jackal's grin. But his blue eyes could still stun a girl. And I loved him even more in his diminished state.

. "You shouldn't have followed me," he said.

But there was no tin to his voice. He wasn't Enobarbus, and I wasn't his mouse.

I held him in my arms, and it must have seemed strange to comfort a man twice my size. But it wasn't strange to me.

He was sobbing now. "Miss Em'ly, I hated Holyoke. Its Tutor ladies treated me like filth. But it put me near learning. I'd sneak around and listen to the girls recite. Zilpah discovered me at it. She laughed, but it wasn't to make fun. We'd meet in my shack. I didn't dare tech a Holyoke girl. But she said I could undress her if I could memorize the alphabet and a hundred words in under an hour. And I did. Then I was sick with fever, and a stunted angel with red hair visited me."

Tom took something out of his pocket—a miniature of me mounted on a silver plate. Lord, I couldn't believe it. I had never posed for Tom, not in Amherst or Holyoke or Cambridge or any other corner of Massachusetts. But there I was, with my eyes shut, right next to Tom, as if we were man and wife.

"Tom," I said, "that's the Devil's work."

"It ain't. I had a traveling photography man, a friend of mine, take the picture while you was lying on the ground next to the old poorhouse on Magazine Street—after you had fainted."

My face was so red he couldn't see my freckles ripen. That housebreaker thought enough of me to carry my miniature around.

"Tom, you might have asked my permission."

He'd wanted a memento of the little Holyoke scholar in her dark glasses. I'd startled him in Cambridgeport. "With my prettiness," he said. What other man had ever called me pretty? I must have made an impression on him in that shack, with my red hair. He told his entire gang that I had once "teched" his face in the dark. I'd have touched it again and again until the rawness was gone and his skin was as smooth as silk.

Tom reached down and kissed me—he didn't gnaw at my mouth. It was the gentlest kiss. We'd never kissed before, not even when I was his mouse. That kiss shattered the bondage of all the years between Holyoke and now. I didn't have to shut my eyes. I remembered Tom hurling that baby deer out of the snowbank. I remembered his Tattoo, how I had wanted to trace it with my own hand.

Tom was my troubled troubadour. And I was his Siren with a freckled face. He couldn't keep kissing me while the sheriff was on his trail. He dug my miniature under his shirt.

"You ain't ever coming back, are you, Tom?"

"No, my pretty."

I thought I heard the sheriff's hounds. Tom ran toward the woods. I wanted to bolt after him like a wild rabbit—his wild rabbit. But I'd startled myself with my own wild imaginings. I'd known Tom more than half my life, and didn't know him at all. The love I had for Tom was itself a wild mask. I wore it only with Tom. But it might be more truthful that the mask wore me. And in its thrall, I was not the old maid of Amherst—but Daisy with the wanton smile.

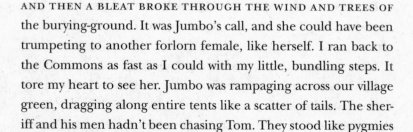

AND THEN A BLEAT BROKE THROUGH THE WIND AND TREES OF the burying-ground. It was Jumbo's call, and she could have been trumpeting to another forlorn female, like herself. I ran back to the Commons as fast as I could with my little, bundling steps. It tore my heart to see her. Jumbo was rampaging across our village green, dragging along entire tents like a scatter of tails. The sheriff and his men hadn't been chasing Tom. They stood like pygmies behind Jumbo's little earthquakes.

"Miss Em'ly," the sheriff screeched, "best to watch out. She's a roguer. No telling what she will do."

But I wouldn't move. "It's the Circus's fault," I said. "They shouldn't have had her parading in a costume after she lost her calf."

"Lord's sake," said the sheriff. "She's an elephant. She don't have the sense of a two-year-old. It's the fire that's crazied her."

When one of his dogs leapt into the air, Jumbo swatted that hound with her trunk and sent it flying across the green like a demented cannonball. She didn't want to wear a costume, and she tore away the spangles and the red ruche with her trunk. Her eyes were tiny and couldn't tell me much—two acorn-colored orbits surrounded by wrinkled flaps. But her trumpeting revealed a terrible lament. And neither the Circus nor the sheriff mattered to her. She didn't want to be without her calf. She swayed once, like some elegant dancer, toppled over, and died, while the ground swelled under her and roiled the whole green. I could feel the turbulence in my toes. It was as if the entire planet had moved with the plaintive melody of Jumbo's death.

Suddenly other stray animals appeared out of the mist—a striped zebra, acrobatic horses, a lioness and her mate—and stood around Jumbo like solitary mourners while the Circus people and the sheriff's men considered how to cart away the corpse.

# Gib & the Best Little Girl in Town

He was eight years old, and the envy of the entire village—no child had ever been so beautiful, with astonishing blue eyes and long blond hair, a silk cravat, striped pants, and boots of Moroccan leather. And no child had ever been so spoiled. Villagers couldn't stop looking at Gib; they bought him things, built him a wooden horse and a tent, and touched him all the time, hoping that some of his magic blondness might rub off on them. He would ride about on Austin's shoulders, or sit in the Dickinson carriage and wave at people.

It was Gib who held the little tribe of Dickinsons together. Sue would have gone berserk without Gib. She went everywhere with him, dressed her blond angel as a little lord.

He had more friends than any other child in the Commonwealth, and that was his undoing. During the summer he could reconnoiter with one or two of his favorites inside the tent on the Dickinson lawn, and no harm was done. But in late September, after a storm, he played on the Commons with a wild boy, fell into a mud hole, and landed in bed with typhoid fever.

Emily did not require a summons from Sue. She stepped across the lawn with Maggie Maher. She hadn't been to the Evergreens in ages, not since

*Ned had one of his epileptic attacks. She had a coughing fit on the stairs. The whole house was filled with carbolic acid, and she couldn't have climbed up to Gib without clinging to Maggie. It broke her heart to see that blond boy in bed. He was burning up; his nose bled, and Austin had to keep wiping him with a wet sponge. Sue hovered over him like some fierce mother dragon. It was Austin who was most tender, who dared touch Sue's shoulder, who comforted her as much as he could, though he himself was pale under his greenish copper scalp, like a painted mask.*

*"Open the Door," Gib said in his fever, "open the Door—they are waiting for me."*

*Then his blue eyes widened with a sudden clarity, and poor Gib expired with a purr in his throat and without the least shiver—and Emily couldn't even comfort Austin and Sue; the odor of acid in the sick-room had made her nauseous, and she had to run home from the Evergreens at 3½ in the morning. She vomited all night and stayed in bed for a month with the shivers.*

*Emily mourned to the edge of madness—with Brother, Sister, Susan, Mattie, and Ned. Susan never left the house, never rode in her carriage, while Emily never left her room.*

*Sister and Maggie lured her back into the kitchen, swearing they couldn't survive without her black cakes. And one afternoon, while Emily was washing raisins in the sink, the whole kitchen went black.*

*She didn't wake until well into the night. She was on her blanket, in her Dimity gown, and couldn't recollect how she'd gotten there. It was the first of her fainting spells. They'd come in their own season, without much warning. Sometimes her nose would bleed, sometimes not. Once her spittle was nearly black, and she saw her father's face. But she never woke up to Pa-pa's apparition, not in any form. And how could she converse with a wraith who wasn't there? Lord, she was alone.*

*But after one of her fainting spells, she was startled by a memory that beat like little feathers against her eyelids. She was eight years old again, just like Gib. And Father was in Boston with the Legislature. The State House was very cold, and Father had to wear his hat and storm-coat or freeze to death. Father put her in charge of Mother and Little Sister while he was away. Hadn't he written home how he expected her to be the best little girl in town?*

*It was terrible to be without Father. There were ice storms every day. And Amherst was a relentless river of ice. And just as she was about to curse Pa-pa and the State House, Pa-pa arrived from Boston, his collar wet with snow. The floorboards whined with each of Father's steps. It was Little Sister who leapt up and took off his white beaver hat. Emily would not have dared. It was Austin who found his slippers, while Mother fed him a glass of wine and prepared tea and scones with a neighing noise that was almost like a laugh. There seemed nothing for the best little girl to do.*

*She couldn't even slide the footstool under his feet. Austin was there first. She would have warmed Father's winter stockings with her own hands, but he would have thought her a pickaninny come to pester him while he had his wine. And so she stood like a sentinel and watched Father's raw red brows through the wineglass.*

*Father removed something from his pocket and placed it on the footstool. It was a tiny cylinder of blue glass with a piece of graphite sticking out like a lizard's tongue. Emily had glimpsed at such a marvel in a handbill. It was a mechanical pencil made in the British Isles for princes and kings, and a replica of it was sold in Boston shops. A drummer must have come into the State House with a king's mechanical pencil in his sample kit and caught Father's eye. There was no other explanation that Emily could imagine.*

*Austin couldn't have cared a whit, but Father must have known how much she would covet a king's pencil. Her shyness was gone. Emily clutched the king's pencil in her hand, felt the smoothness of the glass, and Father's eyes lit with a laughter only she could share.*

# PART SEVEN

# The Boy in the Barn

# 47.

HOW GLORIOUS IT WAS AS I LAY ABED, DELIRIOUS AT TIMES, barely able to breathe, that I should have a sudden Avalanche of suitors, as if some gentle Robber were knocking at my door. I was so pale I dared not look in the mirror. Yet that chalkish color becomes me, I think, or is it the vanity of the oldest maid in Amherst? The first of such admirers was a visiting Tutor at the College, a Tutor from Yale no less, like my poor Domingo, Brainard Rowe, who had been run out of town by Brother's fraternity.

This second Domingo, Carleton West, was insidious in his pursuit of me. He did not seem to care how often I rejected him. He redoubled his overtures like some artillery master who was closing in on his target. He sent flowers and little notes. He stood outside my window, the steadiest of swains. And each afternoon there would be another note from him, another flower, carried upstairs by Maggie Maher, who would have chased him with a broom had I signaled her to do so. His ardor began to intrigue this recluse. He was but half my age. Why should he have cared about so pallid and sickly a maiden?

It was Miss Emily's House of Snow. He had compiled a tiny

booklet of my Verses—all the lines that had escaped my bedroom bureau somehow and had appeared in the *Springfield Republican,* or in *Drum Beat* and other journals with a circulation that had vanished long ago. My admirer did not intend to publish this booklet. He had prepared it solely for my sake. How could he have guessed what my reaction to the booklet would be? Looking at those lines was like looking into a mirror that accented your skeleton and the brittleness of your bones. But I could not blame Carleton for this. He hadn't meant to bruise. And so I observed him from my window, apparitionally. His ears seemed a little too large. I did not have that mad urge to touch him, which had always been the barometer of my affection for a man. But I would not abandon this Tutor with the big ears.

I scribbled a few lines under the last of his love notes. His language was florid, I fear. But perhaps it was the price of his rapture over me.

> *Dear Mr. Carleton West, I am not in the habit of visits from strange men who bear even stranger fruit. It is a mystery how you compiled a catalogue of my Verses. You must have ranged through many an attic. And how can I hold the ardor of your pursuits against you? But I so seldom hear the sound of my own voice that it startles me at times, and should I add another voice—your own—it might overwhelm me with Awe. I will honor your request, but in my own fashion. If you agree to stand outside my door tomorrow at 10½ in the morning, I will submit to an interview. My maid, Margaret Maher, will let you into the house. But you must promise beforehand not to look at me through the door. Should you do so, Sir, I will be impelled to terminate the interview.*
>
> *Yrs,*
> *E. Dickinson*

And on the morrow Maggie did let him in. I heard this compiler of poems trudge up the stairs. My suitor was not fleet of foot, and it made me wince. Lord, I had merciless expectations of a man. With all my feebleness, I was finicky as a porcupine.

I was embalmed in my bedroom, with my door ajar. He could not see very much through this crack; hence, I had him in my thrall. I could hear him sigh and suck on his teeth.

"Miss Dickinson, couldn't I see a little slice of your face?"

"Mr. West, did you not agree to the terms of this interview?"

"But I have been waitin' so long. Your poems are my life's work."

"Then it cannot be much of a life, digging in a cemetery devoted to a spinster's ragged rhymes."

I had not meant to be so cruel, but the scratchiness of his voice upset me, like the aromatic wine bitters I was supposed to breathe to waken my nerves. The wine bitters and Carleton made my head spin and threw me into a kind of delirium. I clutched the doorknob.

"I could recite every line," he said.

"And that would sicken me, Sir."

"Couldn't you call me Carl?"

"No," I said. "Now you must entertain another topic, or I will narrow that crack in the door until even an ant could not navigate the space, and my voice, whatever is left of it, will sound as if it were floating through a fog."

"I would cherish it still," he said.

Even with my vertigo, I had an itch to crash through the door and behave like a Pugilist.

"You're a scavenger, Mr. West, who would rob me of whatever little Treasures I have."

"But I adore those Treasures, and if I weren't so impecunious, I'd ask you to consider marrying me."

I'd really have to wrestle back his big ears. He was full of confidence in his own mission—to steal what he could from the Queen Recluse.

"Are you in the habit of marrying wraiths, Mr. West? I may not even exist."

"A trifle," he said. "A mere hindrance."

And he did what he should never have done—peek through that crack in the door. All I could remember were two ears that looked like truffles and eyes that were splashed with the pink silver of a wolf, not a man. I summoned Maggie, who arrived from some secret well and carried my suitor down the stairs by the seat of his pants.

That should have been the end of Tutor West, but it wasn't. He would appear outside my window in wind and rain until I asked Maggie to feed him in the kitchen and send him back to the college with a kick. But it seems he wasn't the only one in the habit of haunting Father's house. Maggie had sighted a beggar outside our kitchen. I took scant notice because I was breathing in the bitters much of the time. But once, as if in a dream, I had wandered down to the kitchen and stood in front of my pastry board like a little girl in a trance.

Behold! I leapt back when I discovered a man rooting around in the yard. It was not my Imagination taking advantage of the wine bitters, nor was it a whimsical twist of words. This tattered gentleman groveled on the ground and ate at the roots, much as would Nellie, the Dickinson sow. The sight of him should have sent me reeling out the kitchen. But I did not look away once. I recognized my Domingo in all his dishabille. And I was overcome with a pity that lent the Queen Recluse a certain boldness, despite her weakened state.

I opened the kitchen door and went out into the February frost in nothing but my nightgown. I was not cold at all.

"Domingo," I whispered. He didn't bother to glance in my direction. Finally he did look up, and I was bolted right out of my dream, because it wasn't Brainard—it was my other Tutor, whose eyes had the color of dirt today. And I had to pity him too, even if he wasn't much of a swain.

"Tutor, I told you never to return."

"I couldn't stay away, Miss Emily. Your poems keep boiling inside my head."

He was crying like a baby. I took him by the hand.

"Why are you eatin' roots in my yard?"

"I was paying homage," he said, "hoping that the earth in your yard would bring me closer to you . . . Besides, I had hunger pains, and I have to fill my stomach with something."

I couldn't behave like a criminal. After all, his devotion had impoverished him, reduced him to rags.

"Mr. West, I can't ask you to dinner because I'm ill, but would you care for a cup of water and a slice of black cake?"

And I scolded myself, for I had none of my black cake to give— Emily the Baker was a denizen of the past. I could not measure, could not concentrate on little spoons. I had to depend on Maggie and Sister for black cakes that were no longer moist, and filled with crumpled raisins that resembled rats' eyes.

He followed me into the kitchen and fed on water and burnt black cake. I offered him a glass of wine to help him swallow the cake, and suddenly he was the suitor again.

"Only if you'll drink with me," he said.

I consented to a sip of wine and wondered how to get rid of him. It wasn't completely his fault. My poems had given him a sort of brain fever. But I couldn't have him groveling in the yard.

"Tutor, if you promise not to pester me for five years, I'll consider marrying you."

It was a desperate ploy—I didn't have five years to wager with— but it worked. He salaamed and kissed my hand. All I could see were his big ears.

"I'll be faithful to you, Miss Emily—I promise."

He went out the kitchen door as if he were in the middle of a waltz. I couldn't take much pleasure in my mean trick. And I began to miss those big ears after a while.

But he crept right into my dreams again, if pale imaginings can be called a dream: I'm back at Holyoke, and Carleton is one of my Tutors, but he's wearing a bonnet and a housedress. I can't find a single scholar—not on the stairs, or in the space-ways, or in the ironing room. Holyoke has become a Haunted House. Tutor West keeps calling to me, but I don't listen. I climb up to the attic. The door's open, and the attic is filled with old examination booklets and lit with a blue light. A man's waiting inside, dressed in a robe and red beard. He's a magistrate of sorts who sits behind my own cherrywood writing table. But his legs are much too long, and he cannot fit his knees under my table, so he has to lean back with his legs in the air, like an acrobat. All the while he leers at me and reads out my crime.

"Dickinson, I charge you with desertion of your father's memory."

I am trembling now. All my bravura is gone. "Sir, I dream of Pa-pa every night."

"Dreams are not enough. Deeds, my dear. You clung to your writing tablet and deserted him."

And suddenly my classmates appear behind this judge, but I cannot see their faces in the blue light, only the mechanism of their mouths.

"The Poetess of South Hadley and Holyoke Hall," they hiss.

The magistrate claps his hands. "Dickinson, you will remain forever in this attic."

"I will not," I scream, but the magistrate disappears, and in his place is my Tutor, reading from that little booklet he has assembled of my Verses. The sounds crackle like hellfire.

But I wake on my pillows, in my own wooden bark, without Tutor West.

# 48.

BEDRIDDEN AS I WAS, WITH BUT FEW EXCURSIONS INTO THE "wilderness" below, I could command an audience, have my own levees near my comforter and pillows. And I did command Brother to come, in a note that Maggie delivered.

*A., I require you instantly.*

He must have thought I was halfway to Heaven. He arrived utterly out of breath, his red face blue with worry, and saw his sister presiding like a female pasha upon her bed. Brother had become the Beau Brummel of Amherst. He pranced through the village in purple trousers and a Prince Albert coat, his hair tinted green, and clutching a gold-hatted cane.

"Austin, you must not abandon Sue."

"Abandon her? I got up this morning with Sue beside me, a look on her face that could freeze a man's blood. Thank God she wasn't holding a knife."

Maggie's spies at the Evergreens had told me that Sue no longer slept; she walked the stairs at night and stood outside Gib's old room. I had tried to summon Sue with another note Maggie delivered, and it came back in Sue's own scrawl.

*I'm out of the country, Dearest.*
*The Volcano you admire has lost all her lava.*
*Susie*

Suddenly I felt stranded. Sue had taken flight from the Dickinsons and did not want the female pasha to intervene.

And for a moment I fancied that my good angel had visited me in the guise of Gib; this angel had Gib's blond hair and silk cravat, and I was hoping it might restore the peace. But the angel was adamant and wouldn't sit with Sue. And I realized it was no angel at all.

The weaker I grew, the more of an appetite I had, even with the wine bitters. I was ravenous. I could have devoured half a chicken, gobbled Maggie's bone-dry black cake, as Tutor West had done. And then my dream of comestibles disappeared, and I did not even have the strength to walk from my bed to the chair beside my window.

I felt as if I had been ravaged by some foreign war, left with a piece of tin in my skull, so that my mind was like a mouth harp with missing metal teeth. And I could only play on certain registers, certain reeds. But I couldn't bring Pa-pa back with that mouth harp of mine, and I couldn't console Sue.

———

ONE MORNING IN MARCH I WOKE TO AN ODD COMMOTION. There seemed to be some palpable music coming from the rear of the house. I struggled to put on my slippers and housedress and climbed up to the cupola that Father had built long ago. It was a place for spooning, but I never did spoon in Pa-pa's house, and I seldom visited the cupola. But this morning I was glad I had made the trip. Surely I had gone to Heaven, since I saw a man—a boy, really—dance with a cow. Cows do not stand on their hind legs in the Commonwealth of Massachusetts. But this cow did. And danced with the boy-man. He wore a red neckerchief, and I wondered if he were a fugitive from some Circus, like my Tom. He danced with a grace I had seldom seen while he hummed a song and beat time with one of his boots. The cow was caught in rapture—her face was phosphorescent.

I pinched myself to decide whether I was a ghost in the midst of some Illumination, but I was still all skin and bones. I returned to my room, and when Vinnie arrived, I declared with my own enraptured smile: "Sister, I saw a miracle—some fellah dancing with a cow."

"That's no miracle," she said. "It's the boy in the barn."

"What boy is that?"

"*Our* boy," she said. "He lives in the barn, sleeps there with the cows and horses and pigs."

"Does he have a name?"

"Dennis, I think. We call him the Boy in the Barn."

"And where did he learn to dance with cows?"

"Gracious, he taught himself I would imagine."

"Are his eyes blue?" I asked like some detective.

"I think so, but I never much concerned myself with Dennis's eyes."

"Well, you must go to the barn and see whether his eyes are blue."

Little Sister saw the urgency in my own acorn-colored eyes. She scrambled to the barn, holding the pleats of her housedress, and returned with a bewildered look on her face, as if she had to appease the preposterous female pasha who posed as Emily Dickinson.

"Blue," she said. "His eyes are blue."

"Then you must bring him to me."

Little Sister did not argue. I washed up and awaited the Boy in the Barn. He must have arrived with a pair of wings. I listened for his tread on the stairs and heard no sound at all. He was carrying a cap in his hands, kneading it like a lump of dough. His hands were strong, but with fine blue veins that could have been some tributary of the Nile.

Lord, I was shy in front of him. My heart was pumping like the fiercest engine in Massachusetts. His eyes weren't as blue as my blond Assassin's, but blue enough. And his blond hair was giving me even more palpitations. I had to speak before I fainted in front of this Boy.

"My dear," I said, trying to sound like his own lost maiden aunt. "How kind of you to come."

"A pleasure," he said, his voice a musical score dipped in honey. "Miss Lavinia says you have been ill. And Maggie says I am not supposed to disturb ya. Otherwise I would have shouted hello."

"But you are my physick."

"Mum, I am not aware of such a word."

"My tonic," I said. "My rhapsody. I saw you dance with the cow, and I have begun to bloom. Aren't my cheeks a little red?"

He peered at me as if I were the cow. "Splashes of red, mum, mixed in with all the paleness—but a roaring red, if I might say so."

"Indeed, a roaring red."

This Dennis had a razor in his mind even if he hadn't conquered College Hill. His Treasures were far more natural than mine. I asked him to carry me over to my chair, and he did. He covered me in a blanket as you might a doll, swept me up in his arms with a lyrical motion that seemed to defy the air, and put me down with such a lightness, I seemed to float into my seat.

I was hungry to have him around. Dennis had work to do, but after he was gone I seized the cowbell that Vinnie had placed near my bed and rang for the Boy in the Barn.

I had spots of blood in my napkin when I coughed. I dared not show them to Lavinia. But the spots had a certain symmetry, as if they were part of some celestial puzzle. I did not believe that my blond Assassin had become the Boy in the Barn. Still, I saw Tom in his every move. And therein lay my delight. I did not have to worry that Dennis would disappear into some mysterious Circus. I shook the cowbell, and lo! Dennis was there.

He chose to live in a barn rather than a boardinghouse. He wasn't an orphan, but his father had rented him out as a beast of burden, and Dennis ran away. He didn't become a handyman at Holyoke. He felt more comfortable with cows. And sometimes, when the mood struck him while he was carrying me from the chair, Dennis would dance with me in his arms, whirl his maiden aunt gently until she thought there was no other such pleasure on earth.

I never grew dizzy in Dennis's arms. The room did not spin, and I fancied myself Emily the Dancing Cow. It was one more name, one more niche, to put in my Treasure box.

Suddenly, amid April's racket of insects and birds, I could no longer rise out of bed. My mind would wander. I lacked the force to reach my bell. I drifted into dreams and then could not rid myself of them. I'd waken to discover Austin at my side, clutching my hand.

"Dear God, do not leave us, Em."

I did not even have the strength to speak. I pitied my brother with his purple pantaloons and his hair painted green, but the tin in my skull started to reverberate and kept pulling me back to that draft during the late Rebellion and all the Union dead. Austin and Tom had both escaped battle, but Tom had to hide in a Circus, while Brother had found a substitute for five hundred dollars. And in my own selfish way I wished the five hundred had gone to Tom. I was a shameful, tempestuous girl, even as my eyes slid out from under me.

There were no more visits from the Boy in the Barn. And how could I call for him when I couldn't shake the clapper? And so I decided to visit the barn. Without wings I could not travel far. But I girded myself in my own feeble will, and moved with each palpitation of my heart. I wore my Dimity gown, like a bride who had to season herself. My slippers were made of velvet, tulle, and air. I do not remember bumping into the ground. I floated past Margaret, at work in the kitchen while Vinnie slept in a chair, her snores like a silver trumpet. I tried to touch her hand as a little goodbye, but our hands did not meet in the giddy atmosphere of Father's house.

I sneezed as I left the kitchen—a soundless sound that could not even wake a pack of field mice—and spied the barn's open door, with its slant of light softened by swirls of dust. I sneezed again.

The light of the barn shimmered like a soft wound that could still pierce skin and bone. I shed not one drop of blood while my feet were off the ground. I was the conqueror of all. I had a clarity I did not have when I was housebound, with my pencil for a shield. Centuries unfolded in front of my eyes. But Daisy was particular. She don't want to meet David *or* Goliath. What she discovered were the hills of Holyoke in that crooked light of the barn.

Carlo didn't appear, and then he did. I was delirious to see my dog. I didn't recognize him at first. He'd lost his shaggy black coat somewhere. He was all gray around the ears. Carlo wouldn't greet his mistress, wouldn't even wag his tail. And then he was gone. I could not find a single face. It was Missy's yellow gloves that held me in their thrall. They must have flown from the attic, followed me down the stairs. But I could not capture them, wed my fingers to the fingers of the gloves. They flew in the wind like flapping birds or magnificent butterflies, between myself and the barn, but I'm not an old maid anymore who deals in whispers. I was as ferocious as one of Vinnie's cats. I trapped the gloves in midair and wore them on my way to the barn.

I put on their power and their certitude. But it's not my writing

desk and my Lexicon I long for—it's my moon blindness in Cambridgeport and my horse blanket, with its fleas, when I lived on
Austin Street. I had a lot of lightnin' when I couldn't use my Pen.

I shake the gloves once and see my own Pa-pa courting *his* Emily,
Ma-ma. I'd never have imagined how beautiful they were in their
courting clothes. Mother isn't meek. She smolders at her man.
And Father, who never stumbles, is caught within her halo. *Ma-ma,*
I want to say, *why didn't you teach me a few of your tricks?* But I must
be moving too fast. The halo is gone. And Pa-pa's the backwoods
lawyer I remember with a blizzard between his eyes. And then the
territory shifts.

I see Zilpah Marsh in front of a mirror. She has freckles and my
red hair. A man is grooming her, and it could be Tom, but he's
hidden from me. She tilts her head back and lets him brush her
hair. I start to cry, because I can feel the bristles of Tom's brush
while I'm afloat. And it's like putting honey on top of a toothache
to realize that I wouldn't have needed much certitude if Tom had
ever combed my hair.

Suddenly I have flashes of Austin and Sue on my ride between
house and barn, but it's Sue before her marriage. Austin is a young
swain again with a burst of red hair, his own mark of manliness.
And I long to shout, *Do not marry, my dears. It will all come to bitterness and strife.* But even with the advantage of yellow gloves, I ain't
much of a Sibyl. Where else did Brother and Susie have to go?

And then Pa-pa reappears without a single shake of my gloves.
He isn't in his courting clothes. He's wearing a nightshirt, and he's
all alone. Perhaps he's been with the fire brigade, because his nose
and ears are covered in ashes. He puts on his silk cravat, and Pa-pa
starts to dance. He holds his arms out, embracing a partner who
isn't there. I long to dance with him, but I'm flyin' far too fast.

I'm all a-shiver now. I haven't heard any angels sing from within
the barn. I wonder if the Devil is stationed inside the door with
some insidious song to send me howling. But Daisy will match his

own meter. And the shivering stops. I am wearing a bridal gown with my slippers and yellow gloves, though I'm not certain whose bride I am.

And thus I travel in my Dimity and tulle, but that barn could be Peru. I seem nearer and nearer, but never near enough. My bridal gown could be in tatters before I arrive.

## Illustrations and Permissions

Frontispiece      Courtesy of the Jones Library Inc., Amherst, Massachusetts

p. 15      Mount Holyoke College/Library

p. 73      Courtesy of the Jones Library Inc., Amherst, Massachusetts

p. 141      Historic Northampton, Northampton, Massachusetts

p. 193      By permission of the Houghton Library, Harvard University

p. 239      By permission of the Houghton Library, Harvard University

p. 279      Courtesy of the Jones Library Inc., Amherst, Massachusetts

p. 333      By permission of the Amherst History Museum, Amherst, Massachusetts